Praise for the novels of

# ROBIN D. OWENS

"RITA® Award-winner Owens offers a world strongly imbued with a sense of magic in this contemporary fantasy series launch.... Romance and fantasy fans will enjoy Jenni's preparation to enter a new world of compromise between the Folk, humans and technology."
—*Publishers Weekly,* starred review, on *Enchanted No More*

"A multi-faceted, fast-paced gem of a book."
—*The Best Reviews* on *Guardian of Honor*

"This book will enchant readers who enjoy strong heroines."
—*RT Book Reviews* on *Sorceress of Faith*

"Fans of Anne McCaffrey and Mercedes Lackey will appreciate the novel's honorable protagonists and their lively animal companions."
—*Publishers Weekly* on *Protector of the Flight*

"Strong characterization combined with deadly danger make this story vibrate with emotional resonance. Stay tuned as events accelerate toward the final battle."
—*RT Book Reviews* on *Keepers of the Flame*

"A glorious end to the series."
—*Wild on Books* on *Echoes in the Dark*

**Also available from**
**ROBIN D. OWENS**
**and Harlequin LUNA**

THE SUMMONING SERIES

*Guardian of Honor*
*Sorceress of Faith*
*Protector of the Flight*
*Keepers of the Flame*
*Echoes in the Dark*

and the digital prequel

*Song of Marwey*

MYSTIC CIRCLE

*Enchanted Once More*
*Enchanted Again*

# ROBIN D. OWENS

# *Enchanted Ever After*

Recycling programs for this product may not exist in your area.

ENCHANTED EVER AFTER

ISBN-13: 978-0-373-80347-7



This edition published by arrangement with Harlequin Books S.A.

For questions and comments about the quality of this book, please contact us at CustomerService@Harlequin.com.



www.Harlequin.com

**Printed in U.S.A.**

To Kaia and Jane and Rose,

Thank you.

# Enchanted Ever After

*Mid-September, Denver, Colorado*

LIFE WAS NOT A GAME. IF LIFE WERE A GAME, KIRI Palger would ace it…or reach level sixty-five with massive amounts of gold, arms and armor, not to mention a fabulous wardrobe.

But real life had no do-overs. She couldn't go back two years and *not* take the energy and soul draining computer support job with a national company in downtown Denver. *Big* mistake. Especially when she trudged home at seven-thirty on a Friday evening too exhausted to enjoy the thought of the weekend.

Though buying this house in Mystic Circle had definitely been the right thing to do.

Her hands were full of keys and key card and she was punching in the security code when her phone rang. She swore and went in, laid the keys and workbag on the rickety console table next to the door.

The phone was not in its proper pocket, but had migrated to mix with stuff at the bottom of her tote. She found her cell after the call had gone to message. Her best friend Shannon had called—all right, her *only* good friend, someone she talked to a couple of times a week. Kiri could always count on Shannon, and her friend could always give her a lift.

"Hey, Kiri, it's Shannon. Sucky that you had to work late at the sucky job and can't play Fairies and Dragons with me tonight. I know how much you want that new job so remember you *promised* me you'd go to your block party tomorrow and meet Jenni Weavers. *Don't* duck out of it! And, no, I can't make it, Averill has a family thing. Tell us all the deets Sunday brunch. Smooches!"

Kiri's smile faded. She always liked backup when entering a new social situation. She squared her shoulders. Much as she might want to, she wouldn't skip the party. It was important on two levels—really interacting with her neighbors and meeting Jenni Weavers, Kiri's heroine.

Her gaze went to her computer set up in the bump of the side bay window. She'd stay out of the game, Fairies and Dragons, tonight—sometimes the game beckoned more than reality. And once you began spending more time in the game than anywhere else, you were in trouble. Not in control.

She sighed. Her living room was bare—she had a lot of house and not much of anything else, like furniture.

But quiet and peaceful. Her shoulders relaxed more than just from the release of the bag's weight.

A soft golden sunset slanted through the window. The smack of an early autumn had already swatted summer evenings gone for the year, but there was still enough light to walk around the cul-de-sac, Mystic Circle, to wind down from work. Get the kinks out. She was at the age, twenty-six, where she considered how wide her ass would spread if she stayed in a chair all day long every day.

And she'd check on the fabulous koi in the center park's pond.

She'd recently moved from concrete and asphalt near Capitol Hill and the beautiful fish captivated her. With a smile, she slipped back out into the cool evening.

Hers was the first house of the cul-de-sac, Mystic Circle number one, located on the southeastern corner. The craftsman bungalow was the smallest home and slightly more than she could afford. But, if she could land that new job, maybe... She wanted to love her work. To live her job, not do it.

Like much of Denver, the homes in Mystic Circle were a variety of styles, each house different. She'd passed the small house named "Fanciful," the Spanish-influence two-story with orange-tiled roof; the redbrick four-square with the many window-paned porch and neared the top of the Circle and the Castle. She walked quickly, the day dying faster than she'd anticipated with thick gray clouds blocking the sun.

A movement caught her eye and she glanced toward the round center park.

The first thing she noticed about the pale man with the pale hair was that he was tall. The next was that he had pointed ears...like a Vulcan...or an elf...and a certain shimmer like a famous vampire.

Halloween was a month and a half away.

He stepped from the shadows of the tall pine, almost as if he'd come from the pond, but there was no splashing.

"Kiri Palger?"

How did he know her name? She hadn't seen him before, and though she hadn't met all her neighbors, she knew them by sight.

Kiri scanned the area. No one was around. Mystic Circle

was safe, but… He didn't live here and he'd been lurking in the dark shadows of the park. She backed up to the far edge of the sidewalk. No help from the Castle residents—the owners were never home.

"I was told to approach you tomorrow, but since you're here tonight…" He shrugged elegant shoulders under a thick capelike coat.

Not overly broad shoulders, a runner's body. And not threatening, but she'd moved from a rather dangerous neighborhood and was wary.

Should she yell? The houses were old and nearly soundproof. There were lights in several of the homes, and if she zoomed… But the guy had a runner's musculature. She didn't think she could beat him.

"Pardon me." He dipped a hand in his pants pocket. When he brought it out—something funny about his hand, too, like he might have more joints than the norm or more flexible bones—he held out a card. "I'm with Eight Corp. Human resources."

He put an odd spin on "human." Had some sort of soft, lilting accent she couldn't place.

"Eight Corp," she murmured. The parent company of the game Fairies and Dragons, where she'd applied for the job she yearned for, to create new stories for the game.

He turned his body so he looked at the two-story redbrick Denver square where Jenni Weavers lived. "Jindesfarne Mistweaver Emberdrake will vouch for me."

Again the unfamiliar accent.

Jindesfarne Mistweaver Emberdrake? Kiri slid her glance to the house he'd indicated. Jenni Weavers's house. Did he really know Jenni? Kiri had never heard the "Jindesfarne" bit.

Day had gone, darkness was falling. She wanted that perfect job badly, that career. She wanted to love her work.

But his hands were in his pockets now and the card seemed

to be floating in midair. He puffed a breath and it drifted toward her.

She blinked and blinked again and the evening was just dark enough that she wasn't sure she saw what she'd seen. She hadn't been in the game; this shouldn't be a game, but reality…but…

One too many too weird items. Kiri whirled and trotted home, her feet slapping concrete, her breathing ragged. She hopped up the stairs to the porch. Sticking the key and key card in the slots, she swept through the door of her home, slammed the door. She stood sucking in breaths in the entryway on smoothly finished honey-colored wood floor. Walls safe around her.

He hadn't tried to stop her. Might even still be where she left him. She wasn't going to look.

Instead, she yanked on the cord that drew the thick burgundy curtains over the front window and hustled past the bay window bump with her home office setup and into the tiny bedroom. Safe.

The man had been too fascinating—compelling—and he was so not her type, urbane and with the runner's body. She liked men burlier. Overtly muscular. No, this man wasn't what she wanted. Really.

He said he was from Eight Corp. The company that was looking for a story developer and writer for Fairies and Dragons. Everything she'd ever wanted. She sniffed, realized her nostrils were straining to get the last whiff of the guy's scent. A fragrance she couldn't pin down, just like all the rest of him. Sweetly musky? With a faint sharp tang? His skin had seemed to shimmer. That couldn't be good.

Would she really see him tomorrow?

Lathyr Tricurrent watched Kiri Palger hurry back into her home. She seemed odd even for a human, the waves of her personal field resonating in ways that he recognized—Kiri had a potential for magic.

It was that potential vibrating around her, bending the light into tiny rainbows enveloping her, that had drawn him out.

He'd underestimated the charm of this place and of Kiri herself.

In the spring, more magic had graced the world and much had changed for the Lightfolk. Lathyr was one of those who had begun to experience new powers. And the Meld—merging magic and human technology—had rapidly increased.

Some humans could actually *become* Lightfolk, transform into magical elemental beings.

Lathyr was one of those who could sense such potential in certain humans—his new talent. He'd been unsure whether to be pleased with this or not.

He was not quite a full Merfolk; there was the slightest trace of elf in his background, enough to give him a point to his ears.

And the highest Lightfolk did not value anyone who wasn't pure Lightfolk—or purely of one element. He'd been abandoned by his mother, no family claimed him, he had no home. He'd mostly lived on sufferance as a servant at the royal palaces or a guest of lower nobles, forced to be a drifter, and he hated it.

He could never reach the highest status, or even be awarded a tiny estate by the eight who controlled all the true domiciles under the ocean. He wanted a home of his own, not a rough cave.

He wouldn't have had a chance at that home before the infusion of magic that had given him his new power.

But a notion was edging into his mind that the stratified lines of rank and status were cracking…becoming as fluid and as new as the Meld. Great change brought new opportunities.

In the spring, a halfling—half-human and half-Lightfolk—

had become a Princess of the Lightfolk, a Fire Princess. Unprecedented.

He glanced toward the abode of Princess Jindesfarne Mistweaver Emberdrake. He didn't need to see the light in her office window to know she was home. The waves of magic—human and Lightfolk and from the Treeman who was her husband—blended and flowed to him, like the taste of rich chocolate on the air. She'd summoned him because she thought the human residents of Mystic Circle could become magical. She was right.

People with such potential—as well as other Lightfolk—had migrated to the cul-de-sac because of Jindesfarne's powers.

Evil magical ones, Darkfolk, could not live in Mystic Circle, and Lightfolk magic even kept wicked humans from the neighborhood. Too bad Kiri Palger didn't know that—yet.

Princess Jindesfarne—Jenni Weavers Emberdrake—had been right. Lathyr should have waited until the next day to approach Kiri Palger. But Mystic Circle's cul-de-sac threw all his talents, not only his new ones, off. He'd never been in a place so rich with magic where all four elements were balanced. When balanced, magic was so much easier to do, to experience.

Balanced magic made living heady, and he'd felt the rush when he'd coalesced from a cloud to the pond in the park a few minutes before. The richness of the place and Kiri had made him act impulsively, speak when he should have stayed silent.

Now Lathyr could feel the minor earth elementals who were attached to two of the households—brownies—running through the tunnels they'd carved under his feet.

Even as he thought of them, one of the brownies popped out of the ground before Lathyr.

"You have any chocolate?" the small man with wrinkled face and large triangular ears asked.

Lathyr frowned. "You should be able to smell that I don't." He'd heard the brownies in this area were out of control in their demand for the rare sweet.

The brownieman sniffed lustily. "I smell drying merskin. You go back to your pond. There's nothing for you here, now." The less-than-a-meter-high being glanced at Kiri Palger's shut door.

Lathyr set his teeth, let his lower lip curl.

"When you come back tomorrow, bring us chocolate." The little earth elemental frowned, looked up at a sky full of dark clouds and shivered. "Darkfolk are very aware of Denver, now. Glad I am here, safe." He vanished with a discourteous pop.

And Lathyr had to face facts.

He'd liked the looks of Kiri Palger, had wanted to impress her and show her real magic. He'd floated his card to her. That had not gone well.

He'd failed at first contact with the human in a project that might bring him the chance his birth had denied him. A chance to provide outstanding service and be rewarded with an ocean home, some small ocean valley with an acceptable current. The stability of not having to move every few months. He aspired to more than a cave in the ocean or a house on land. He wanted a real home, a place where he could—perhaps—start a family or at least secure his future.

With this project, with Kiri Palger, he could get it. Gaining the notice of a high noble like Princess Mistweaver Emberdrake was the first step.

That was worth any cost.

THE MYSTIC CIRCLE NEIGHBORHOOD PARTY WAS the first since Kiri had moved in a month before. The residents she'd met seemed like a friendly bunch—most of them extroverted. Unfortunately, she wasn't.

So the party was a big deal to her. Not only would she have to come out of her shell and be personable with her neighbors, but she wanted to impress Jenni Weavers.

Jenni Weavers was the project director of the online multiplayer game, Fairies and Dragons, that Kiri wanted to write for. Kiri had her application in to Eight Corp for the job. A new area of the game called Pegasus Valley had been announced and Kiri'd written a couple of story arcs for it.

She wanted the writing job—and a career like Jenni had—so badly Kiri could taste it.... Sweet joy like melty caramel.

As soon as she'd heard that Fairies and Dragons' main location had changed to Denver, she'd begun watching the website for job opportunities. Then she'd discovered Jenni Weavers actually lived in Denver, had for years.

Kiri had done a tiny smidge of discreet snooping and found out Jenni lived here in Mystic Circle. Though Kiri had spent time with her grandmother in Denver on and off all of her life and lived there the past four years, she'd never heard of the small cul-de-sac. She'd driven to it…and fallen in love. With the cul-de-sac. With the houses. And one had been for sale. A month ago she'd taken all of the savings she had left from the nest egg her parents had given her and bought the place.

She didn't regret it. Now maybe she could land her perfect job, too.

But she hadn't actually met Jenni yet, and Jenni would be one of the people hiring.

That meant good clothes. For any other block party, Kiri would've gone in jeans and layered tanks, the top with a sparkly design. For Jenni Weavers, it meant pressed beige linen pants and white, man-style shirt with tiny beige pinstripes and cuffs. Kiri was glad she'd gotten only a temporary tatt of the Fairies and Dragons logo and it had worn off a long time ago. That would have been over-the-top fan-girl.

Her pants were a little loose—power walking around the Circle and down to the small business district had its benefits, as long as she didn't stop at the gelato shop.

She slipped on her lucky silver bracelet and hurried to the kitchen to pick up the huge pan of still-warm brownies she'd made for the potluck.

As soon as she exited her house, she could hear the cheerful noise of voices at Jenni's home. "You're going to be fine. You *like* the neighbors you've met," she reassured herself. "Amber and Rafe Davail, Jenni's guy, Aric, and the gay couple, Dan and Frank. You'll find something to talk about."

The Mystic Circle people seemed nice, really, a real community, almost a family. Since Kiri and her parents weren't close—hell, Dad was in Baja and Mom in Florida—and they'd emotionally abandoned her as a child, *and* neither had the same values as she—Kiri had the hope of joining this extended family. One more reason Mystic Circle appealed to her, she'd heard they were a tight community. Another thing she wanted to accomplish today, get further along that path to being accepted.

And if Kiri was going to work with Jenni Weavers, she'd better learn how to speak to her without stuttering.

Kiri turned and locked her door, stopped at the junction of Mystic Circle and Linden and checked for vehicles. Nothing. Crossing Mystic Circle, she skimmed the south edge of the park, taking a few seconds' time to watch the koi, sluggish this morning in the shadows. She drew in a deep breath of flowers, including a lush bank of roses—the thick and heady last scents of summer. Then she walked to Jenni Weavers's place, number eight. Kiri *was* invited; she'd be welcome.

Would the man she'd seen last night be there, or had she been in a haze of work exhaustion and created him from the shadows of the park?

Had he really said he was from Eight Corp's human resources, the company that had the job she wanted? Well, if he was at the neighborhood party, she'd see him.

She strode up the steps to Jenni's house and saw a brass plaque: Emberdrakes. Right! Right, Jenni wasn't Jenni Weavers but Jenni Weavers Emberdrake—or, maybe, like the guy the night before had said, Jindesfarne Mistweaver Emberdrake. Very cool name and Kiri had better remember it. Names were important.

Another big breath and then she went through the enclosed

porch and was at the front door. She rapped with the silver Hand of Fatima knocker.

Aric, Jenni's husband, opened the door. He was a tall man with wide shoulders who looked like he had Native American blood. Again the recollection of the guy from the night before wisped through her mind in comparison. Aric had the build she preferred, but the man she'd met earlier had certainly been interesting.

"Hello," Aric said. "It's Kiri, isn't it? Number one?"

"Yeah."

He offered a huge hand and she propped the brownie pan on her other arm and put hers in his and got a quick shake before he stepped aside and held the door wide. "Welcome. Appetizers are on the kitchen counter, salads et cetera in the dining room, and we're grilling in the back." He glanced down at her brownies and laughed. "Brownies. We all love *brownies* and chocolate, but don't often make them. Can be confusing."

"Huh?" Kiri said.

A charming smile from Aric. "Sorry, neighborhood in-joke."

"Oh." She wanted to learn all the in-jokes, wanted to be truly a part of the neighborhood.

"But we'll really appreciate your brownies," Aric said. Since he noticeably swallowed as if saliva had pooled at the thought of the taste, Kiri believed him.

"Good," she said.

"The dessert table is in the back, too."

His stride was long and fast. She got tingles when she entered the house. Evidently her nerves about the job were twitchier than she'd expected. But she wanted the position, the *career,* so much.

And now she'd lagged behind Aric and had to hurry through

the kitchen and sunroom to the backyard. That space, too, seemed to have…a little something extra. A little more of the feeling that the whole cul-de-sac had. Increased ozone, maybe.

The smell of sizzling meat teased her nostrils. She glanced over and nearly froze in place. Jenni Weavers—no, Emberdrake!—was at the grill. Kiri recognized her from web pics. The woman wore a red apron and poufy white chef's hat and wielded a long fork as if it were a weapon.

But Jenni in the flesh was more vibrant than her photo, dark red hair instead of red-brown, light brown, very sparkling, eyes.

Kiri wrenched her gaze away to sweep over the people. Almost all of the residents of Mystic Circle were there along with folks Kiri didn't recognize, a few guests, she supposed, clumped together in small groups talking. About fifteen people. The guy from last night—who would *not* have pointy ears or a shimmer to his skin that must have been some cloud-cast or rising moonlight illusion—wasn't there.

Kiri wasn't disappointed. Really.

Something bumped Kiri's knee and she joggled the pan. What? She looked around and saw an old, fat cat lying in the sun. Neither of the Davails' yellow Labs were close, they ran back and forth along the iron barred fence to the north—the Davails' place—with the occasional bark.

Tamara Thunderock walked to Kiri and swept the pan from her hands even as Kiri lost her balance again. She windmilled. "Wow," she said. "Good catch. I think my ankle twisted." She wasn't sure what had happened and offered a weak smile to the woman, who was even shorter than she. Kiri was about five feet five inches, but Tamara stood a good four inches shorter.

"Brownies," Tamara said. "You have to watch out for them."

"Yes, nearly dropped them," Kiri said.

"Your treats look fabulous."

Since Tamara was a baker, a pulse of satisfaction went through Kiri at her praise. "Thank you."

Brows raised, Tamara said, "If you want one of these, I suggest you get one right away. They'll go fast."

"That's okay," Kiri said and relaxed enough for her smile to widen. "I got enough when I cleaned up the bowl and the spoon."

There was a little moan and Kiri blinked. She wouldn't have expected that from Tamara; the woman worked with goodies all day long.

"I'll just put this on the table, why don't I?" Tamara said, not meeting Kiri's eyes. The smaller woman's gaze was fixed on a lower point. "I'll make sure the brownies are taken care of. There will be no more accidents."

"Sure." Which meant Kiri had to suck up her courage and greet her hostess and heroine, Jenni Emberdrake.

So she did, after hoping her smile was sincere and discreetly wiping her palms on the sides of her pants.

"Hi," Kiri said, offering her hand. "I'm Kiri Palger. I live in number one, the craftsman bungalow without the enclosed porch," she babbled, as if anyone in Mystic Circle wouldn't know which house was number one. Jenni appeared to be five feet nine or ten inches.

Putting down the fork, Jenni took her hand in a really warm clasp. Kiri hadn't thought her hands were so cold. Nerves.

"Pleased to meet you," Jenni said with a penetrating stare. "You *do* fit here in Mystic Circle."

"Ah. Thanks."

"And my colleagues and I at Eight Corp are interested in your background and résumé."

Kiri's relieved breath puffed out a little harder than she'd expected. She followed that with a slight smile. "Thank you again."

"We'll talk in a bit, so why don't you relax and get some food. Plenty of it here." Jenni picked up the fork again and gestured to a steak. "What kind of meat do you want?"

Kiri wanted to resolve the job thing, but that wasn't going to happen right now. Meat-wise, she longed for a fat hot dog. "I'll have one of those skinless chicken strips."

Jenni reached toward the far side of the grill for an empty plate, plopped a chicken strip on the bright red paper dish. The tender meat fell apart.

Kiri's mouth watered. "Looks great."

"Eat and enjoy. We'll talk later."

A dismissal, though said with a smile that reflected in Jenni's eyes. Maybe Kiri would pull this off after all.

She shifted tension from her shoulders. She was so nervous she probably shouldn't eat. Food might have trouble squeezing into her clenched stomach, but she could hardly dump her plate.

"Come and sit, Kiri!" called Amber Davail who lived with her husband, Rafe, in the Victorian house next door to Jenni. Amber gave a welcoming wave and Rafe smiled and lifted his fork.

So Kiri crossed to one of the picnic tables that had been set up in the shade of a box elder tree and sat.

It took a while for her to settle down, and she gave credit to Amber, a genealogist, and Rafe, part-owner of the Denver Fencing Lyceum, for helping her. The couple was easy to be with. They also didn't seem to be as…intimidating as Jenni and Aric or as intense as Tamara.

Soon Kiri had munched a mixed green salad, raw veggies, chicken and fruit and felt full enough to ignore the dessert table in the corner of the yard. She was glad there were no irresistible potatoes or French fries. She even managed to stay away from the chips and salsa and guacamole, which were a real weakness. She wanted to lose a few pounds before she started her new job.

She *would* get the job.

"Your brownies were incredible," said Rafe. He laughed lustily. Now that she'd spent more time with him, Kiri thought he was a man who appreciated every moment of life. "They didn't last at all. Some folk went straight for dessert."

"Fine with me." Kiri drank deeply of a bottle of raspberry sparkling water and glanced around the backyard, a large pretty lawn with lilac bushes edging both side fences. The space wasn't quite as lush or groomed as the Davails' own next door, but Jenni's sunroom was awesome.

"We're glad to have you join us here in the Circle," Amber said. "The man who lived in number one before you kept to himself. Didn't come to the block parties, traveled a lot and disapproved of the rest of us playing together as a team in Fairies and Dragons every Thursday night." She wrinkled her nose, then cocked a golden-brown eyebrow at her husband. "Even Rafe plays now. We've assimilated him."

Again Rafe laughed and lines crinkled at the corners of his blue eyes.

Amber poured some red wine into a glass and lifted it. A ray of sun slanted through it, and it appeared as if she held a glowing jewel. Smiling, she tilted the rim toward Jenni. "And we're close here, and want to support each other however we might."

Kiri leaned forward and low words tumbled from her. "I want that, too." She wetted her lips. "Jenni's my hero. I've applied for a job at Eight Corp. I'd love to work with her."

Rafe's and Amber's gazes zeroed in on her, one shrewd, the other considering. Kiri flushed. Did she sound like a stalker? She hoped not.

Amber dabbed some bruschetta in flavored oil. "Well, you know what you're doing in Fairies and Dragons for sure," she said.

"Thanks." Kiri grimaced. "Eight Corp said on its website that they'll be making the decision soon." She cleared her throat. "Did you see a guy walking around the Circle yesterday evening? He said he was from Eight Corp human resources. He was a little…" Fascinating. "…odd. Might have been practicing for Halloween." Or her vision had been off.

Rafe's smile was brilliant. "Kiri, we're all a little odd here in the Circle." He pointed his bread at her. "Including you, and thank God for it." His lips quirked up, then he popped the bread in his mouth.

Kiri smiled. She didn't mind being different, especially in a way that meshed well with Mystic Circle people.

"We didn't see anyone," Amber said. "But bad guys can't get in the Circle. It stops them."

"What!" Kiri'd never heard of anything like that in her life.

They nodded in unison. "True."

"Oh." Hmm. Nope, didn't believe that.

"Great party," Jenni said as she walked up, holding a glass mug of frothy beer and grinning. "Glad that you started this tradition, Amber."

"I am, too," Rafe said. "Ancient tradition." He winked at Kiri. "Seven months, a party a month."

Kiri tried to keep upbeat. "Sounds fine to me."

"We'll move the gatherings inside when the winter comes," Amber said. She and Rafe rose and cleared their cheerfully colored paper plates and plastic utensils. "Later, Kiri."

"Sure. See you later." She wondered if there really would be a later. How humiliating that she'd spilled her guts to near strangers who might repeat her words to Jenni or Aric. What if she didn't get the job? Would she still feel okay living in Mystic Circle? Hell!

Jenni slid onto the wooden bench opposite. She glanced around the backyard at the clusters of people talking and laughing. "Just great to have neighborhood get-togethers."

Then she turned her head to meet Kiri's gaze. "We've discussed you quite a lot at Eight Corp. Aric works there, too."

Here it came.

KIRI FROZE.

Something in Jenni's eyes, a downward curve of the corner of her lips made Kiri's stomach clench. She wasn't going to get the job.

The sun went behind clouds—wasn't it supposed to be sunny all day?—drying her sweat.

She was glad she was sitting down and braced herself, forced the overwhelming disappointment back down her throat. She hoped she'd kept a pleasant smile on her face.

Jenni continued, "I—we—were very impressed with your work on the prospective story arcs for Pegasus Valley…."

Kiri said it for her. "But?"

Jenni gestured with her mug of beer. "*However,* our preliminary planning took the characters and story lines in a totally different direction."

"Oh."

Jenni smiled and it hurt Kiri. "Now for the *but.* We have

a very new, very exclusive game we are developing we'd like your help on."

Kiri stared. "What?"

"You'll have to interview with Eight Corp, and take a look at the preliminary sketches and plot arcs. They need to be fleshed out. Also, there is some preliminary game testing."

What did that mean?

Jenni's husband, Aric, came up and wrapped a hand over her shoulder. "Enough business talk." He frowned. "Clouds have rolled in and I don't like the feel of the wind. Let's talk with Rafe and Amber." He inclined his head to Kiri, blinked, then said, "Ah, I mean socialize."

New game. Exclusive. Preliminary testing. Before Kiri could get even one of the questions swirling in her head to her mouth, Jenni had stood and she and Aric had moved away.

Then *he* stepped from the shadow of a tree near the front gate and Kiri's heart began to pound. He moved with casual sophistication through the gathering. She'd been wary of him the night before—all right, she'd been a little scared of the man—doubted his claims that he was an Eight Corp rep. But here he was. He still evoked a buzz of fascination along her nerves.

The man nodded to Aric, inclined his head at Jenni, lifted his hand to the Davails, but Kiri got the idea that he wasn't local.

Finally, he reached her and he made a half bow that Kiri had only seen in movies and at Ren Faires. Never had one aimed at her in real life. "Lathyr Tricurrent," he said with an accent she couldn't place. His hand dipped into his pocket and came out with another blue-green card. He held it to her. She just stared at the pasteboard.

After a few seconds, she took it and tried a tiny experiment.

She let go and it fell to the table. The card landed faceup and she saw his name and Eight Corp engraved on it in dark blue.

"I believe Jenni spoke to you about our new project." Again that fluid accent.

Somehow, as she'd watched him move to her, in that short amount of time, she'd forgotten the first dozen questions she'd wanted to ask. She took a sip of her drink. "Jenni said it was a new game."

"We are doing preliminary work and hope to market it before the winter holidays."

"Ah."

"Stage one is a prelude to the game and mostly developed." She met his eyes and couldn't seem to look away. They were deep blue, and his pupils dilated when he looked at her. He liked what he saw? That was nice and she felt heat crawl along her neck and up into her face. So stupid to stare, but she couldn't stop it.

His eyes were so pretty, blue and misty, and there seemed to be even more of a depth that sucked her down and she heard the rushing of air in her ears and the humidity of the day was pressing against her so she felt droplets on her skin and her breath was caught in her chest and reality seemed to fade and gray fog edged her vision....

Lathyr glanced aside and Kiri panted, sucking air. Her shirt was sticking to her. So not sophisticated. Could she be any more lame?

"Have some water," he said. His voice seemed to fade, then amplify in her ears. Ebb, flow.

Get a grip!

"Thanks," she managed weakly, but she couldn't seem to reach for the bottle. She looked up to see his long fingers twist off the top and set another plastic bottle of carbonated raspberry water into her curved fingers. Her hand trembled, tightened on the bottle, squirted water.

Damn! Now her cheeks were hot from embarrassment.

"Lathyr," said Jenni Weavers with a scold in her tone, walking up to them.

"My apologies," he said.

Kiri managed to get the bottle to her lips and gulp down her drink. Thankfully, she didn't choke. Her brain felt fuzzy, as if there was stuff going on around her that she didn't see. Maybe like she was stuck in a sepia dimension and everyone else was colors.

Yoga breaths—three, then another sip of water, blink and smile and *think!* She wanted to know more about the job. She *wanted* the job, the career, and to accomplish that, she had to impress the man.

Jenni had moved away, but left the guy a beer. He was running his index finger down one of the drips of condensation. His eyes met hers briefly and his pale lips curved in a smile that seemed genuine. "Sorry I disconcerted you."

Was that what he'd done? Kiri didn't know. She wiped her hand across her eyes and shook her head. "No problem." Another deep breath. "I lost track of the conversation. You were telling me about the, uh, new game?"

"The game is called Transformation and has a preliminary stage, almost a tutorial, like a few other games in the past." He gestured with his beer. "The individual is 'tested' to determine what area they begin the game in."

"I've heard of that." Vaguely...she couldn't snag the detail, though.

"Yes, we have lands of rivers and volcanoes and aeries and caverns."

"Hmm." She pummeled her memory. "And there was an old game that measured...um...qualities? Like loyalty and honor and compassion?"

"That's right." Again the smile. "Though the prelude of the game has tests which will actually determine your powers and attributes. A...player...does not choose them ahead of time as is usual in most games now."

"Interesting twist." Her water went down better this time. Her breath was steady now. Whatever stupid moment she'd had before had passed.

His eyes narrowed, the color intense, though he didn't meet her gaze. "We believe you are an excellent candidate."

Kiri blinked. "Yes?"

"To test through the prologue. Anyone who will be working on the new game will need to go through and clear that part, so you know the basis of the world building."

"That makes sense."

He leaned over the table. She looked into his eyes again, then he cut his gaze away, seemed to scan the party and flicked his glance back to meet hers. "I believe that you have great potential for this...employment. Can you start on stage one, the prologue of the game on Monday?"

Her heart thudded hard. She wanted this opportunity to break into game writing so much! She tried to look casual and swallowed another gulp of water. "I can after work is over. I'm downtown—it wouldn't take me more than a few minutes to make it to Eight Corp's offices."

Lathyr frowned, his fingers slid back and forth on the table. "I would like to offer you employment, but I can't until you finish going through the preliminary stage of the game. We would, of course, prefer you to be at your best when you work with us. Naturally the person with the highest score—who develops their character to the highest level and with a minimal amount of defeats—will be offered the position first."

He was right. She'd be better fresh instead of struggling with a new game after a tiring day of being on a computer and handling complaints.

"I overheard. We *do* need to move on this fast." Jenni sat down beside Kiri. "Do you have any vacation time coming?"

Kiri gritted her teeth. How much did she want the job? How much did she believe in herself? Enough to use her full two weeks of vacation?

Yes.

Gamble, roll the dice and hope. "I can take a full two weeks, but beginning on…Thursday?" A quick glance at their faces. Lathyr seemed attentive, but Jenni had twisted in her seat at the sound of metal sliding on metal. Rafe Davail and some of the unknowns were fighting…with swords. People from the Fencing Lyceum, then.

"You can ride with me to work on Thursday, if you don't mind getting in early and waiting while we set up," Jenni said.

Her husband was there, shaking his head, looking at Jenni, not Kiri. "No. I'll be taking you to work, Jenni."

Lathyr made an abrupt sound, maybe a curse in his own language.

"Eight Corp will send a car for you," Jenni said. "We'll pay you for your time, though I know it's not the same as having vacation days. I'll let Lathyr here close the deal, tell you more."

Another dismissal, this one distracted. "That would be good," Kiri said.

Lathyr met Princess Jindesfarne's eyes and inclined his head. The clouds and wind had only been a precursor. As Jenni moved away, he believed she'd be reporting to more powerful Lightfolk that minions of a great Dark one were flying over Mystic Circle.

He could feel the evil, see the gigantic stingray-like creatures as they circled and flickered against the sun. They couldn't land, but they cast shadows that humans could uneasily sense.

It pleased his ego that the interesting Kiri Palger remained focused on him. He stood and offered his hand. "Why don't we walk around the Circle?" This place was safe, but she was human and the others might want to use more magic that would disturb her. The park in the center of the Circle, the koi pond she liked, would be safer for her.

"You can ask me what you need to know about the project," he coaxed. Not that he'd tell her much of the truth, but he wanted to touch her and gauge her potential for transforming into one of the Lightfolk, especially here in the Circle where magic was balanced.

The more time he spent with her, the more he liked her, though he'd made a mistake in holding her gaze. She was human and susceptible to his glamour. He wasn't pure Waterfolk, but he was pure magic.

She stayed seated, looked around, then squared her shoulders, something he sensed showed determination. Gestures were different for the Merfolk underwater. If she'd been mer and in the ocean she'd have flipped a hand to send a push of water current aside, indicating power and the willingness to follow through. Both those qualities he thought she had, along with the most important two that he'd discovered humans needed to become Lightfolk—a flexible imagination and a high level of curiosity.

But as she didn't rise, he deduced something held her here. "What is it?"

She flushed, a pretty habit, also not seen much below water

where mers kept their body temperature steady and cool. The rush of blood to her skin was unexpectedly enticing. "I still haven't met all of my neighbors, or interacted with them. I want to stay here." Her fingers went to the buttoned ends of her shirtsleeves and aligned them some way that seemed right to her. "The job is really important to me, but so is my place here."

He stared at her, blinked a couple of times to keep his eyes wet. If she turned into a dwarf or a djinn, even an elf—earth, fire, air elementals—she could possibly remain here. But if she became mer, she would have to move. What waters there were in Colorado were already claimed by naiads and naiaders.

What were the odds she'd become mer? He didn't quite know. There had been less than twenty humans changed into magical Lightfolk and though he had recognized their potential, his guesses as to what they might become had been poor. So he dropped his hand and stepped away, disappointment cooling the blood in his veins.

Princess Jindesfarne, her husband, the Davails and several brownies had disappeared into unruly green brush in the corner of the yard and Lathyr sensed they were working magic. They didn't seem to care that they had humans, including Kiri, in their midst, who might witness such.

A wave of balanced power pulsed under his feet, flowed through him, pushed into the sky. Princess Jindesfarne and friends sending the great Dark one's servants away.

Sunlight became bright and hard and burning in the thin air.

Lathyr said to Kiri, "We can talk later. May we send the car for you early Thursday morning, so you and I can discuss this before the workday at seven-thirty? I will be in earlier for a meeting and we can talk after that."

"You aren't staying?" Kiri asked.

It was a warm autumn day and he hadn't soaked for over twenty-four hours. His skin was drying and he also needed to breathe water and keep his bilungs damp. He'd accomplished his first goal of getting Kiri Palger to agree to the testing game, and evil had faded.

A line had appeared between her brows as she studied him—perhaps too closely. He shook his head. "I came in to Denver just a few days ago and still have not acclimated."

Her expression cleared and she nodded. "Yes, people have trouble with the altitude." She hesitated. "You aren't living here on the block?"

"No, I am near—" what was the name of the park with the lake he was living in? "—near City Park." Higher-status mers had convinced the old naiader whose lake it was to let Lathyr have a small domicile there. On sufferance, as always.

Kiri's eyes widened. "Oh."

He raised a brow. "Oh?"

"I just, uh, thought you'd live somewhere more sophisticated. Cherry Hills or something."

"Eight Corp arranged my lodging. It is…sufficient."

Now she appeared slightly offended. He tried a smile. "I am used to living near the beach." Recently off the coast of Spain.

Kiri laughed. "Not many beaches in Denver."

"No. I miss the ocean." An admission he hadn't meant to make, and not in public.

"Only natural."

"Would you miss the mountains?" he asked.

Her smile was quick. "I suppose so. I was born here and spent time with my grandmother, and moved here four years ago, but I'd miss Mystic Circle even more."

He nodded gravely. "It is a very special place."

Rafe Davail, a human with a magical heritage, crossed to

them with a swordsman's swagger. "And Eight Corp doesn't own nearly as many of the houses of Mystic Circle as it used to. I think it's better that the homes remain in private hands."

The man meant in human hands like his own, not owned by the Lightfolk royals of Eight Corp. "We still have the Castle," Lathyr murmured.

"And Eight Corp owns the other bungalow across from Kiri," Amber Davail, Rafe's wife, who was related to a great elf, said. "Number nine."

"Really?" Kiri said. "I didn't know that."

Rafe smiled easily, but Lathyr was aware that the man was blowing spume at him for some reason. "Maybe Eight Corp will let you have number nine."

Jenni joined them again, shaking her head. "Nope, no pool."

Lathyr dipped his head. "Yes, a pool is necessary."

Kiri looked puzzled and Rafe laughed.

"I am weary. I must go," Lathyr said. "I am sorry that we didn't speak more, Kiri."

"I'll expect the car at 6:50 a.m. on Thursday morning," she said.

Lathyr smiled.

Princess Jindesfarne's husband came forward. "I'll see you out," Aric said. Lathyr sighed. The Treeman meant that he would take Lathyr home by way of tree. In this dry country it *was* faster than letting his molecules disperse into water droplets and finding a stream or cloud to take him where he needed to be. But Lathyr found traveling from tree to tree profoundly disturbing. Instead of moving as individual components, he felt solid and trees seemed to move through him. Stressful. "Thank you," he said politely but with an underwash of resignation.

Aric laughed, jerked his head toward the park, then glanced at Jenni. "Be right back."

She grinned. "Sure."

Lathyr decided everyone was enjoying themselves at his expense. He was the outsider. He rippled his fingers as a land man would shrug. Nothing new. That small bit of elven air magic in his being had always made him an outsider, ensured he had no permanent home. Most mers had their own space and were territorial. Ocean-living Merfolk preferred to live in communities—as structured as any other Lightfolk setting. He'd always been on the bottom level and so had become a reluctant drifter, always an outsider.

Then Tamara Thunderock was there, and he realized that he was wrong about the residents of Mystic Circle. Everyone here believed they were outsiders but had melded together as a family, and thought he was the *insider* with the Lightfolk. Jenni was half-human; Aric was Earth Treefolk, not other-dimensional Lightfolk; Tamara was fully magic but half-Earth and half-Air and no doubt despised by both due to their opposite natures; Rafe and Amber were human.

So he was the outsider of their Mystic Circle, but they believed him to be more accepted by the Lightfolk than any of the rest of them. Very discomfiting.

Right then he decided to ask his superior for leave to live in the Castle of Mystic Circle while he tested Kiri. The Castle had a huge pool in addition to a natural spring and a well on the grounds. He, too, would become one of the Mystic Circle community—for a while.

Always and only for a while, until he was more valued.

Since all their gazes were on him, he ran a finger along the curve and the point of his ear, let it show for an instant along with the bluish tinge to his skin that was all mer.

Demonstrating his own mixed heritage that would keep him from the highest ranks.

Rafe stopped laughing and narrowed his eyes. The human must not have noticed Lathyr's mingled water-air nature before.

Tamara said, "Or I can see you out, Lathyr."

Again they were confusing Kiri, making too much of walking him to the front door. Tamara would no doubt take Lathyr through tunnel and rock. He suppressed a shudder, worse than tree being passed through him was rock. "Thank you for your offer."

"I'll take care of him," Aric assured the small dwarf-elf woman. "Tamara, why don't you load up a plate or two for him."

She nodded and moved toward the tables, efficiently making a box of food that Lathyr would encase in a bubble to store underwater. He'd noticed they had salmon, a treat.

He realized he'd underestimated the sun and the altitude and the dryness and had to draw on a bit of his air magic to keep the pressure around him and prop him up. His blood had to pump hard through his body.

Kiri's eyes were wide—beautiful, beautiful sea-foam-green eyes. He also admired her curvaceous body. He'd let the attraction to her, as well as this magically balanced place, keep him too long.

His skin was beginning to tighten and flake. He needed to be in water now! Another foolish mistake that would cost him. The royals would hear of his errors, of course.

Aric or Princess Jindesfarne or Rafe Davail would tell them. Then Lathyr would be sent away.

And he didn't want to leave this magical place. Here was community and safety.

Outside was a begrudged sleeping spot, solitariness and the threat of a Dark one and his creatures.

The threat of evil pained less than the certainty of loneliness. For the first time, ever, Lathyr considered living permanently on land, though a prized place here in this special location would not be given to the likes of him.

Despite everything, all his mistakes, all his past experiences, the sun beating on him, he wanted to stay.

"Let's go," Aric said, clamping a large hand that felt like wood around Lathyr's biceps.

He shrugged off the hand. After another half bow to Kiri, he followed the Treeman.

He'd made more mistakes. The project wasn't beginning well. He hoped that wasn't an ill omen for the whole thing.

He didn't want Kiri Palger to die.

AFTER THE PARTY, JENNI EMBERDRAKE AND HER husband, Aric, closed up the house and sank into plump cushioned lounge chairs in the sunroom—a room her brownies had made earlier in the year. She loved the place.

Aric grunted. "Good party."

Leaning back and closing her eyes, Jenni said, "Yes. I love the neighborhood parties, but don't care too much for hosting them. I think Amber and Rafe should do it all the time."

"Our turn," Aric reminded. "Thank you, Hartha and Pred."

From the sound of his voice above her, Jenni figured he'd stood and bowed to the two brownies who lived with them.

Opening her eyes and hauling herself up, she bowed to the couple, as well. "Thank you for all your work."

Hartha shrugged little brownie shoulders. Taller than her husband, she still stood less than a meter high. Her mouth was straight and the tips of her huge triangular ears folded over in concern, and Jenni sat sideways on the chair so she'd be eye to eye.

"The party was easy," Hartha said, then crossed her arms. "We don't like that Darkfolk are flying over Mystic Circle, trying to harm our homes."

Pred said, "We don't like it at all."

Jenni sat tall, stared at the brownies. "I have it handled. They can't get in. No evil, not human and especially not Darkfolk, not even great Dark ones."

"But only here is safe," Hartha pointed out. "We are stuck here."

Aric said, "We can all take care of ourselves—you brownies and Sargas the firesprite, and we Lightfolk. Amber has defensive Air Spells from her magic. Rafe has his sword and shield."

"Kiri the human does not have anything," Pred said. "We liked Kiri." He grinned big. "She made us brownies."

"And you want her to continue to make brownies," Aric put in, coming over and sitting next to Jenni, sliding his strong arm around her waist, letting her lean on him a little. She loved that, being a couple. Loved him.

Hartha tapped her foot. "You are not listening to us. Kiri may be in danger."

"I *do* hear you. We'll figure something out," Jenni said.

Hartha gave Jenni a look, sniffed and trundled away, followed by Pred, who glanced at them over his shoulder, mouthing, *We need more chocolate.*

Jenni turned into her husband, rested against his broad chest, breathed in the Treeman scent of him, redwood needle spice.

"They're right," she said.

"I will report the Darkfolk incursion to the Eight royals, of course."

Jenni hissed, letting off some of her fire nature steam. "You know they won't do anything."

"The great Dark ones rarely leave their domains, and are unassailable there. We cannot prevail against them in their strongholds." Aric stroked her hair. "I'm sure the one who showed up today is already back on his estate."

"But they are vicious, and since they are down to a handful, they are even more rabid." She paused. "More violent. They'd like to kill us all." Frowning, she forced herself to consider the matter. "The great Dark ones are more powerful than individual royals. Than some couples, too, I think." She glanced at Aric. "Some are older than the royals, aren't they?" Jenni was half-human, new to associating with the Eight royals. Aric had served them—and with them—for years.

"That's right," he confirmed. "They're very old and powerful."

Restless, she stood to pace back and forth. "Why are they attacking, now?"

Aric winced and she caught his expression. "What have the Eight told you that they haven't told me?"

"The Meld Project is doing well. It would be tempting for them to get their hands on it…or people who know how to make magic and technology meld together."

Jenni shrugged. "I don't spend that much time on the Meld task force anymore, not with my own new concept." She grimaced, and sank down next to her husband again. "Kiri's in danger from my new idea, too. Maybe I'm wrong about starting up the project to discover humans who have potential to become Lightfolk, making it a mass market online game."

He squeezed her. "You believe in humans becoming Lightfolk."

"I really do. Despite the recent influx of magic, Lightfolk are still declining in numbers, so having humans become Lightfolk is good for both races," Jenni insisted. "Heaven knows the Lightfolk need to become less stratified." But images of what she'd witnessed haunted her. Human servants in a Lightfolk palace spontaneously triggered into attempting to become pure magic, and dying hideously. "But with the game we can find humans, lead them into acceptance, give them a choice to become magical or not."

"Your project is much better than standing by and watching, or doing nothing."

"Yes. And I'm scrambling to get the bones of the game done. At least the Fire Realm is shaping up." Her spine stiffened as resolve banished uncertainty in her heart. "If we're careful, we can..." She couldn't promise even herself that Kiri might not die.

"Minimize the risk," Aric said.

Jenni sighed, snuggled against her love. They'd survived troubles and struggles, too.

"I think mass and magic are linked," Aric said. "The humans who died trying to transform might only have had enough magic to become a small air or fire elemental, but they had human mass and..."

"Couldn't make the change." Jenni scrubbed at the tears on her face, breathed through her clogged throat. No, she wouldn't be forgetting the sight of the dying soon.

Again Aric circled her with his arm, and they rocked a little side by side, until she realized tension ran through him and became suspicious of his silence. "What's up?"

Aric turned and looked down at her, clearing his throat. "It occurred to someone—"

"Who?"

"Amber Davail, who brought the idea to me and I spoke to the King of Air about the matter—"

"What matter and why didn't you tell me?"

"I wanted the king's input first and I am trying to tell you now. So listen." She heard his large breath. "Have you considered that now some humans have spontaneously transformed into Lightfolk when the royals did rituals, that some near-Dark ones might also transform?"

"What! No, I hadn't thought of that." Jenni gasped.

"Not at all good," Aric said. "We believe evil humans might also become magical abominations—more than human criminals."

Jenni swallowed, twice. Looked around for a bottle of water. Hartha appeared and gave her a cup of hot and soothing tea, vanished again, obviously not wanting any part of the discussion.

After letting the horrible notion circle through her brain for a bit, Jenni said, "But the humans becoming Lightfolk have a poor survival rate. We can only hope that spontaneous Dark transformations have the same." She nibbled her lip. "Most Dark ones are affected by their evil and, uh, twisted physically."

Aric's brows rose as he followed her reasoning. "Then human evil might also twist and be noticeable. Abominations and monsters in truth," Aric said. "I'll add that to my report to the royals."

Jenni noticed the trickle of the fountain in the corner of the sunroom. It wasn't very loud because the more she leaned on her magic and her natural fire nature, the less she liked water. Slowly, she said, "I think Lathyr will work well with me and my new game project."

"The sniffer?" Aric bumped her shoulder, teasing.

*"Sniffer?"*

"That's what the Water King calls him. For Lathyr's ability to sniff out potential Lightfolk. The scholars believe that when we got that extra magic, some Lightfolk who are mixed elements also received a boost in their magic or an extra talent. Lathyr has a touch of elven blood."

As did her Aric, and Jenni herself.

She hesitated, doubts still creeping.

"You were right to call him to scan Mystic Circle," Aric said.

"Yes. I had a strong feeling about Kiri."

"Did anyone else have the potential?"

"Dan. He might be able to transform."

"Dan, but not Frank?" Aric matched her gaze.

"Dan is fully human, Frank has a touch of air in his ancestry. I'd rather just stick to fully human right now. We don't know how other innate magics might react."

"So we won't be recruiting Dan or telling either of them about the project."

"No. They're a couple and good together."

Aric's smile was slow. "As we are."

"Yes. Lathyr is handsome in a mer way, but not nearly as attractive as you. I don't care for pale blue and shimmery skin. Though the ears are cute." With a low chuckle she rose, sliding her hand to grasp his. "Let's go upstairs and have a private party."

"Sounds great." He paused. "How's the game making going?"

"Despite my whining yesterday, I've got a handle on it. I've decided not to make it *too* real. We'll have control."

Another grunt from Aric. "Good. Now let's concentrate on *us*."

"One last thing," Jenni purred.

"Yes?"

"What else have the royals decided about that you aren't telling me?"

He swept her up into his arms. "They're involved in another scheme."

"More important to them than me and my game, and even the Meld of tech and magic." Jenni nodded. "Thought so. What?"

"Establishing a permanent gate to another dimension."

Jenni gasped again, and her husband, her lover, showed his true talent in taking her mouth with his and making all thought drain away.

Lathyr slipped into the muddy lake, changing his form to full mer with genuine relief. Traveling through trees with Aric had dried Lathyr's skin even more. Now his legs melded together into fintail, his skin scaled and his bilungs pumped as they converted from air-out-of-water atmosphere to air-in-water, and his sex was tidily tucked away and protected. He sighed out greatly relieved bubbles as water caressed him. Cracks in his scales, even a few scrapes, stung, adding a whiff of blood to the lake. Fish would come and investigate, as would his host, a very grumpy naiader—minor water Lightfolk. And there he was.

*You are back,* the naiader sent mentally and with emotional vibrations that moved through the water. His accent was terrible, as if he'd always lived on this continent, never been oceangoing at all. Lathyr hid his pity, though the man had not hidden his disappointment at Lathyr's return to the lake.

*Indeed,* Lathyr said, swirling a little curtsy, inclining and twisting his torso, slipping his fintail to the side. *And I have requested another domicile.* He'd politely asked Aric to forward the suggestion that Lathyr be close at hand to Kiri during her testing, and Aric had agreed to pass the notion on.

The naiader's heavy nostril frills showed in pride. *Mine is the greatest lake in this city.*

*I hope to stay in the house that the Eight royals keep at Mystic Circle.*

*On land! In human form!*

*That is correct.*

Shuddering from scalp to finpoint, the naiader backswam a yard or two. Lathyr had gotten the idea that his host had not transformed into his human shape for a long time, and this seemed to confirm it.

A sizzle zapped through the lake—great and powerful magic. The Water King, Marin Greendepths, had arrived, a large and heavily muscled merman.

*Well, sniffer, I heard you don't like the ambience of this lake.* He spoke telepathically and with mer signing in the brown murk, then spurted air and laughter. Lathyr held himself courteously stiff, tips of his tail fins digging into the mud to anchor him. He didn't know why the mer king was in the middle of a continent, or whether other royals were at Eight Corp headquarters in downtown Denver, and didn't ask. The Water King had a sense of humor bordering on cruel.

Lathyr moved his head so hair would cover his face, helping mask his expression. The king's long green-blond hair streamed behind him. He had enough magic to be arrogant with it.

*I thought to make a change, my lord,* Lathyr said, keeping his head lower than the king's. Due to his elven blood, Lathyr was taller than most mer and only an inch shorter than his king and had to keep track of his posture at all times.

*This is a hole,* the king said. *Humans destroyed it as they do most things,* he sneered, lips curling.

*Yes, my lord.*

Scratching his hard-scale chest, the king said, *Landlocked. Dreadful.* He *pushed* power out in a huge underwater wave.

Lathyr swallowed a nasty air bubble with water that seized in his bilungs. He kept the pain from showing, the effort to process the air.

The King of Water smirked.

The naiader shot to the bottom of the bed, facedown, breathing dirt, then pushed backward until he was near the bank, nearly out of sight of the king.

*The King of Air requested a meeting at Eight Corp. The full Eight are here.*

Maybe the evil Dark one had sensed that. Lathyr was suddenly glad he was very low status. No reason a Dark one would be after him.

*The Meld Project, to combine magic with human technology, goes well, actually making more magic. Just a trace for now, but soon...* The king smacked his lips; the tiny scales of his body rippled. The intricate pattern of his ridged scales gleamed silver against pale green skin. *There is more magic in the world, and more magic here. I will be pleased when it cycles through the water to the reaches of the oceans.*

Lathyr kept his mouth shut.

*Our other plans progress.* The vibration of the man's thoughts and feelings carried a dark richness imbued with pleasurable secrets. Lathyr didn't believe the royal was thinking of humans becoming Lightfolk. Some other plan delighted the king.

The king rose a little in the murky water. *We have agreed Lightfolk numbers are still below optimal.* His jaw clicked shut. *Therefore the project that involves you has been approved for eight years.*

Not much time, but maybe enough for Lathyr to win a permanent estate and home. A home of his own would be a sanctuary, a place where he could be completely himself, with no one to please or impress.

The king's tail flexed with muscular power; the magic that flowed from him actually cleared the water, giving more visibility. *I am pleased that one of my subjects can contribute to this situation. That your power was augmented.*

From the corner of his eyes, Lathyr saw the naiader twitch. That one didn't believe the king's last statement, either. But at least the royal merman wasn't actively hostile.

The King flicked his fingers. *You actually wish to live on land in that Castle?* Water snorted from his nostrils. *As if a few rooms and two turrets make a castle, a palace. Not even enough rooms for my own retinue let alone my lady's or anyone else's.*

Keeping his head low, Lathyr said, *Yes.*

A massive shrug sent the water rippling. *We royals come to this wretched place as needed. We have purchased a compound closer to Eight Corp's headquarters and raised a mansion with four separate wings around a common hub. Cloudsylph has the half-breed Fire Princess balance the place as necessary, perhaps monthly.* Another shrug. *We prefer that place. The Castle in Mystic Circle will be used for guests only—it's so small.*

All the better, as far as Lathyr was concerned. He didn't know the last time that the royals had stayed at Mystic Circle or visited, but it was clear to him that the neighborhood was a treasure. If they couldn't appreciate it, too bad.

Then intensity replaced tedium in the king's vibrations. *I don't want you anywhere near the Queen of Water,* the king said.

Lathyr's nictitating membrane flickered over his eyes as he blinked in surprise. He backswam a space.

*I know you will have some contact with us eight royals, but do not come near my wife. You talk with her and you will find yourself more of a drifter than you are now, with no one offering you the hospitality of a stay space.* The king grinned and dropped the illusion that his teeth were dull and humanlike. *You may have to stay on land and in our weaker form forever.*

Lathyr remained motionless in the water. Everyone knew the King of Water was a volatile man, did not care for fools, but did not react well to aggression. *I am unaware that your queen knows of my existence.*

*She does not, and I wish to keep it that way.*

HEATING FROM THE INSIDE IN EXCITEMENT, Lathyr strove to project calm, and subservience. There was a mystery here, but one he didn't dare solve…not without powerful allies to stand behind him. *I will strive to remain beneath your lady's notice.*

*Good.* The king's nostrils showed frills as he unfolded them in a sneer at the place around them. His gaze went to the naiader cowering near the bank and he nodded with royal condescension. *We thank you for your service and will have gold nuggets brought to you.*

A squeal of delight and vibrations of awed loyalty emanated from Lathyr's host. Lathyr let himself sink into the silt of the lake, his head significantly below the king's, who pivoted with a hand twist toward Lathyr. *We will allow you to stay in the Castle at Mystic Circle, during this time you are associated with those other folk and humans.*

Lathyr ducked his head, darkening his second eyelid so the

king wouldn't see that he still watched the royal man. *My great thanks.* But knowledge trickled through him. The king understood that Mystic Circle was balanced since Jenni had lived there for a decade and a half, but preferred pure water magic around him. Lathyr believed the merman hadn't been often at Mystic Circle and experienced the difference, hadn't spent much, if any, time at the Castle, owned by the Eight for over a decade. So he didn't know the true boon he was granting.

Denver was not a place the merman would care to be—landlocked with no beaches for thousands of miles, high altitude instead of the deep ocean depths where the primary water palaces sat. The city was *very* dry. And like the king had indicated, surrounded by humans and land animals instead of ocean fish and mammals and a large society of other mers. The naiads and naiaders here would be mostly isolated.

So the king would not consider giving Lathyr leave to reside in the Castle much of a favor, if one at all, and would believe spending time human, on land, more like a trial than a pleasure.

*Just a duty, my lord king.* Lathyr attempted a casual note with an undertone of pain, of wanting to please and thus putting himself at a disadvantage for the king.

Since that aligned with the royal's own ideas, the merman nodded. *We have discussed reward for you.*

Lathyr wanted to bring up his need for his own home, a small valley in the ocean, but kept his thoughts tight, unleaking. This royal could be fickle, best to continue to hide his own needs.

Again the king looked around and his lip curled. *Some of my elder subjects, with a more scholarly bent, wish less responsibility.*

Meaning they'd rather live in a palace than run an estate. Excitement pulsed through Lathyr in a burst he couldn't control. Yes! A tiny domain, even under the royals' scrutiny, would do.

*Your reward will be commensurate with your success.*

As decided by whom? The king? The entire Eight? Lathyr did a lowly swirl.

*Someone will be by with a key to the Castle in Mystic Circle, where you can reside as long as Princess Emberdrake needs you.* That was mocking. The king would not be able to conceive of taking orders from a Fire Princess, not to mention a half-human Lightfolk. Marin Greendepths had been born of a royal line, had moved into the position of King of Water long before Lathyr's existence. The great mer paused. *You will recall ALL that I instructed today?*

A definite threat.

*Of course, my liege,* Lathyr said.

*Schllllluuurrrppp.* A column of mud and detritus swallowed the king and he vanished elsewhere.

Lathyr allowed himself a cough and swam fast out of the swirling mess. It would take days to settle. Somehow he'd make it up to the naiader who had offered him hospitality.

Lathyr would move to the Castle, a lovely idea. He had no doubt it would be a mansion fit for the Eight, luxurious, matching the palaces he'd served in as a child and now occasionally visited. That would be a pleasure, luxurious surroundings, a pool of water of his very own. Living in Mystic Circle would also be very good. Wouldn't being there help him develop and stretch his magic? He hoped so.

Far from scorning the inhabitants of Mystic Circle, he was intrigued by them. Brownies would probably run the Castle; Princess Jindesfarne was friendly and interesting and easy to work with. What he'd seen of the Treeman, Aric Paramon Emberdrake, Lathyr liked.

Kiri Palger was enticing.

But what was important was that both Aric and Jenni worked closely with the King of Air and knew the other royals. And Lathyr might find out from them the answer to a new and urgent question. What was it about the Queen of Water that might affect him, the low-status Lathyr Tricurrent?

Kiri had stayed at the neighborhood party as long as she could manage. She'd made sure to talk with all her neighbors, and thought she was being accepted by them. Progress. She'd also conversed with some of Rafe Davail's sparring buddies from the Denver Fencing Lyceum. Again thinking of her ass—and a better paycheck if she was hired on by Eight Corp—she toyed with the idea of taking fencing lessons.

Now, though, she lay in her sweats on her thin yoga mat, on her living room floor. Her feet were on the cushion of the comfy chair-and-a-half she'd found at a thrift store. New age music drifted around her, sank into her. She loved the tonal progression of this piece, even though it was supposed to balance her chakras. Maybe it did.

She was decompressing from the party.

That she didn't get the job developing Pegasus Valley wasn't as much of a disappointment as she'd imagined. No sulking there. She could be in on the launch of a new game as a writer! How cool was that? *Très, très kewl.*

She'd accomplished what she wanted—she'd met Jenni Weavers Emberdrake. The woman had impressed Kiri; she could only hope that she had done a bit of the same—and with Rafe and Amber Davail, too. She'd liked them, liked being in their company.

Her muscles relaxed. Her mind floated on the music and she noticed undertones she hadn't heard before, the slow, quiet beat that sounded heartlike, the crackle of flames.... Kiri turned her head to her empty fireplace—nope, the music was not reality.

She rolled her neck back, delighting in the easing of knotted tension and shut her eyes. Yes, as a counterpoint to the fire there was the ebb and flow of surf...and the light whistle of wind.

Nice, very nice. She'd thought she'd known the music, but had never heard this before.

And in a few breaths sleep claimed her.

Then, nightmares, glassy and bright, trapped her. She heard a dome thunder down, clamp around a twisted Mystic Circle. She was stuck in the terrible landscape. Like a game world. Or a horrible snow globe.

Though Jenni's backyard and the cul-de-sac looked the same, it had transmogrified into threat—now the clouds weren't clouds but flickering black flying monsters, overshadowing. Huge *things* that would suck her soul from her body and leave her dead. Circling, circling, ready to dive when her terror was strong enough for them to taste.

Something pushed her. Hard invisible hands. More and more came at her, tiny but strong, beings she couldn't see, couldn't elude, pushing her from Jenni's yard.... No sound from the nasty small ones...at first...then evil whistling giggles, laughing at her, knowing they could kill her...thrusting her south to the edge of the Circle...which fell away in a gigantic waterfall no one could survive. Crushed to death by water.

Her fingers dug into the earth, grabbing, trying to defeat the inevitable. Shards of rock jabbed under her nails. She screamed and screamed and nothing came from her mouth.

With a hiss, a fiery whip wrapped around her wrist. The giggles became long shrieks pitched at the very top of her hearing, spearing into her head. She'd stopped, but the fire ate through her skin and flesh searing down to the bone. Not saved…just dragged north to the Castle, five times its normal size, not brown brick but black stones, slick with dripping blood. Something waited there to feast on the rest of her.

The monsters in the sky dove.

Sharp beaks pierced her, ripped. A huge clawed birdlike foot grabbed her around the waist, puncturing internal organs. Hideous pain, then they flew *through* the Castle walls and she was dropped onto a hard stone floor inscribed with a magical pattern. A hooded figure sat on a throne above her. She *knew* she'd been captured and was trapped until torture brought forth every bit of information she had. And she didn't even know why.

Lightning stormed around her, the walls of the Castle disappeared and she floated in an electric universe that transformed from lightning to brilliant fireball stars….

Kiri's feet thunked from chair to ground and she quivered, not enough muscle control to even curl up into a ball and hide.

Whoa. Really intense scary nightmare. All from her anxieties about meeting her neighbors and fitting in and the wrenching hurt earlier of not getting the job and the excitement of being a writer on a new game and maybe a teensy fear of failure. The threat of using all her vacation time for an entire year and then washing out of the effing game prologue, having to stick with her present job with no relief.

Her breathing sounded loud and harsh, the house too quiet. Something she didn't often notice or mind, the memories of her parents' loud and ugly fights still echoed from her childhood so that a quiet house meant peace.

How long had she been out? She couldn't see the clock, her arms and legs jerked once as she tried to move, then she rolled over. The cheap wall clock from the dollar store showed that her dream couldn't have lasted more than a few minutes. Though it had seemed like infinity stretching to doom.

She rocked to her feet and passed her computer and the game with no more than a glance, almost shuddering. Even if she entered Fairies and Dragons and defeated monsters there, it might spark more dreams or nightmares that night. She didn't want to chance that.

A little scritch at the uncovered window made her jump and whirl. She thought she saw a *thing,* a little brown triangular-eared rat *thing,* peering in at her with big round eyes.

She sat down hard on the floor and noted the computer hum. It clicked and she flinched. Soothing music wafted out, the album repeating. Maybe her chakras had been overbalanced.

Rising slowly, she looked at the bay window. Nothing there, of course, no scratches on the glass, of course.

A pounding at her front door had her breath trapped in her chest and her body reflexively surging forward.

"Kiri! Kiri!" shouted her friend Shannon from beyond the door.

Kiri looked wildly around the place. Since there was only the chair and two small tables in the living room and she'd mopped and dusted that morning, the room was clean. She glanced down at her sweats. You could barely see the hot chocolate stains against the black fabric, and Shannon and Averill—Shannon's husband who was probably with her—wouldn't care.

Rushing to the door, she threw it open. "What is it? Is something wrong—" But Shannon's beatific smile stopped that sentence.

Shannon flung her arms around Kiri in a tight hug, they rocked and Shannon snuffled. "I have news. Good news!"

Kiri returned the hug. "Fabulous, come in."

With only a little geek-gawkiness, Shannon pranced in. She was a tall, skinny woman with a pale complexion that showed light freckles. Her carroty hair sprang out from her head in a thick mat and her smile made her cheeks high and round.

Kiri gestured to the big chair and unfolded a camp seat. Shannon's joy washed over her and she grinned back at her friend. "Tell all."

Settling into the chair with a quick butt wiggle, Shannon beamed. "I'm pregnant. Averill and I are having a baby."

Air whisked around in Kiri's mouth and she understood it had fallen wide open. "Wow." Her wits scrambled. "I didn't even know you guys were hoping for a baby."

Shannon flushed red. "It was an accident, but we're thrilled."

Kiri swallowed. "That's fabulous," she enthused. Meanwhile her thoughts spurted in a thousand directions, like brain synapses misfiring. Shannon was her oldest and best friend and if Kiri knew anything it was that their relationship had just changed irrevocably. Shannon would be focused on Averill and the baby, rightfully so, but Kiri felt a little cold.

Then she felt a lot cold and the open door creaked. Kiri hurried to shut it. "Wow," she said again.

"We're so happy!"

"That's absolutely great!" Kiri went over and hugged her friend. "I have milk for the coffee to celebrate!"

Shannon laughed. "Thanks. No more caffeine for me for the duration, but could I have some herbal tea?"

"You got it." Kiri went to the kitchen and filled a glass measuring cup with water. She set it in the microwave, rooted in her tea drawer and found chamomile. That was supposed to be good, right? Soothing? She shrugged. The box said it was caffeine free. She plunked a bag in a mug. "How are you feeling?"

"Fabulous." Shannon hopped up and whirled around then strode to Kiri and hugged her again. "Revved."

"Great," Kiri repeated. She couldn't scrape up different words. "I'm happy for you." That she could say with full sincerity.

"Averill and I wanted you to be the first to know."

"That's so nice. Thanks."

"And I wanted to tell you myself, so Averill is getting us drinks down at the Sensitive New Age Bean. You know how restless he is," Shannon ended fondly.

The microwave dinged. "You sure you want the tea?" Kiri asked.

"Yeah, I do. He'll probably bring me chai. He can never remember that I hate chai." Shannon tsked. Kiri poured water on the tea bag, handed the mug on a saucer to Shannon.

Shannon sank back into the chair. "We've just been to a birth center and have already gotten masses of information. They are so nice there and we met other soon-to-be parents, too." Dimples showed in Shannon's cheeks as she blew on the tea water, then sipped. Her glance slid away.

Kiri made herself smile as she took the camp seat. "Sounds awesome, though I think you have a 'but' for me?" Another "but" that would send her life in a different direction today. She glanced at the clock. It was 7:40 p.m. and getting dark, so there shouldn't be too many other strange things coming up.

Shannon said, "Our first set of parenting classes are on Friday nights, so I can't—"

"—play Fairies and Dragons with me." Again Kiri deliberately put oomph in her smile. "Do you want to change nights?" she asked lightly, sure she already knew the answer, but hoping she'd still have good connections with her best friend.

"Oh. Of course. We're working on our scheduling, but I think Tuesdays would be good."

Kiri's breath released on a "Whew," and her smile turned completely genuine.

"Gotta have some amusement, right?" Shannon said.

"Right."

Shannon patted her stomach. "And little geek here is growing up in a wired household so she-he should get used to it."

Kiri laughed, but figured there'd be plenty of missed nights due to baby and parenting stuff.

Shannon drew in a large breath. "Averill and I are going to get a new house. Our place is too small for us and a baby and I'll need something closer to work."

"So you're moving way south in the city." That hurt. They were just within walking distance.

"Yeah."

Kiri raised her brows. "Sounds like you're going to be really busy."

"Yes. A good kind of busy."

"Of course."

Shannon put the mug down on the tiny scarred table by the chair that Kiri had also bought at the thrift store, leaned forward and grasped Kiri's hands. "You're still my closest friend."

Leaning forward herself, Kiri kissed Shannon on the cheek. "For now." She swallowed her tears.

"WE'VE HAD TO BUDGET BRUNCH IN FOR TWICE a month instead of weekly," Shannon said.

"Fine. That'll be good to keep up." Kiri felt the friendship slippery in her grasp.

Shannon's slightly protuberant blue eyes gleamed with excitement. "Now tell me how it went with Jenni Weavers. Is she amazing?"

"Very. And really smart."

Shannon squeezed Kiri's hands. "And you got the job!"

"Not exactly."

"An interview for the job?" Shannon pressed.

Kiri wet her lips. "No. The story lines for Pegasus Valley weren't what they wanted."

Shannon frowned, her eyes firing, and her hands clamped down on Kiri's. "They don't deserve you, then."

*"But,"* Kiri ladened the word with meaning.

"But?" Shannon perked up, tilted her head.

"They want me to work on a brand-new game."

"Yay, Kiri!" Shannon hopped to her feet and swung around and Kiri whirled with her. "Go, Kiri!"

"Go, Shannon and baby!"

When they were both out of breath, Shannon collapsed into the chair again and slurped her tea.

"It's not completely set," Kiri said. "They have a pregame prologue that they want me to clear, see how I do in the game and, um, handle the world-building, I guess."

Shannon nodded. "You can do it."

Kiri's lips thinned. "I can. I *will*."

Shannon studied Kiri for a minute, brows dipping. "Is this new job in Denver?"

Kiri blinked in surprise. "I didn't think to ask, but Jenni Weavers Emberdrake is here and so is the corporation that runs the game. S'pose so."

"Okay, you'll let me know how it goes?"

"Of course," Kiri said, but figured Shannon soon would be more occupied with the reality of new life in her body than Kiri's triumphs in game-land. Watching Shannon find new friends, turn down a new path away from Kiri was going to be hard.

A scuffing kick came at the door. Averill with his hands full, no doubt. Kiri jumped up to let him in.

He was a tall man, as skinny as his wife, with a gorgeous caramel complexion and a thatch of thick, straight black hair. His grin was as infectious as Shannon's. "Hey, Kiri."

She stood tiptoe to kiss his lower jaw. "Hey yourself, Averill. Congratulations!" She took the tray that held three large drinks from him.

"I got you and me a mocha steamer," he informed Kiri, and sent a tender look at Shannon. "And you some herbal chai."

"Thanks," Shannon said. She still smiled, but when Averill turned to close the door she rolled her eyes at Kiri. "Kiri met Jenni Weavers and is in line for a new job."

"Most excellent. For the development of Pegasus Valley in Fairies and Dragons?" Averill grabbed a folding chair propped against a wall, put the seat down and sat, jiggling ankle across knee.

"Nope," Kiri said. His obvious happiness, combined with Shannon's, soothed Kiri. Life was change, after all, and she was pushing at her own changes as much as she could. "Brand-new game with a prologue that determines character attributes instead of choosing your own."

Averill snorted into his cup. "Huh, might cut down on those who prefer close-in fighting, melee, rushing in and striking with sword or fist." He cocked an eyebrow at his wife, who only lifted her chin and gave a little sniff. Shannon's preferred character had stinger fingertips at the end of deadly hands.

Turning back toward Kiri, he asked, "Looks like you can get out of IT and on to a career track that suits you better? More creative?" Of the pair, he was the web designer.

"Looks like," Kiri said.

He nodded. "Good for you."

Then Kiri turned the talk from Eight Corp to house hunting and babies and they spent the next half hour talking before Averill stood, then pulled Shannon to her feet. "Come on. Early to bed. Since we visited so much now, shall we cancel brunch tomorrow morning?"

"Sure," Kiri agreed.

Averill wrapped her in a strong hug. "Later."

"Bye," she said and hugged Shannon, and then all three of them rocked together. That was one of the best parts of Sunday brunch, the hugs.

"Keep in touch," Kiri said, kissing Shannon's cheek.

"I will," she said.

But when they walked out of the door, Kiri knew things would never be the same.

She plunked down in the chair and the pillow released the slight fragrance of Shannon's perfume, the scent she'd used since Kiri had bought her the first bottle as a birthday gift in college.

Kiri swallowed, beat back tears and allowed herself a three-minute sulk. No children in sight for her. Crap, not even a man. Visuals of the Mystic Circle couples rotated in a slide show before her mind's eye—Jenni and Aric, Rafe and Amber, Dan and Frank. All seemed very happy.

Why was she brooding about this, for heaven's sake? She'd decided to concentrate on her career, get to a place where she was happy there, before she started looking for a guy. Or before she expected to find the right guy looking for her.

That's what she wanted, a good, solid career, not to depend on a man to support her, like her mother. Kiri had had acceptable jobs, but now she wished to pursue her passion and get paid for it. Husband and family would come later. She thought of Lathyr, but if there was a less-likely man to have a family, she didn't know one. He'd seemed solitary, and liking it that way.

Her sulk time was over so she stood and stretched and cleaned up the cup, saucer and tea bag that Shannon had used, poured the untouched chai down the drain and tossed her own and Averill's empty cups in the trash. So much for domestic chores.

The sky held streaky clouds tinted with gold and pink sunset colors. A good walk would shake off the cobweb grims. Not too long before snow would fly and the nights would be too frigid for saunters around the Circle.

Sticking her keys and key card in her pockets, she headed out and went directly to the koi pond, since she hadn't really watched them today. A half hour of observing the fish and the sunset let her inner calm well through her. She rose to leave and saw lights on in the Castle.

Kiri's heart bumped with excitement. For the first time, the iron gate at the bottom of the stairs of the Castle was open. She angled out of the park and back onto the walk in front of Dan and Frank's house. As she jogged, twilight became night. The Castle's front door was open, too. Soft yellow light washed out around Lathyr Tricurrent's shadowy form.

And on the steps were people—Jenni and Aric, Rafe and Amber. Rustling came from the heavy plantings of bushes and Kiri thought she saw darting shadows. Cats? Didn't seem to move like cats. She shivered again.

Amber and Jenni held food dishes in their hands. Dammit, Kiri didn't have any food offering. Her cleaner-than-new brownie pan was back on the kitchen counter.

She did have boundless curiosity. She hesitated in going forward, just craned to see. She told herself that she hung back because she'd had enough of people today—and heaven knew that she'd been watching every minute of her behavior, very self-conscious earlier at the neighborhood party. But the truth was, the foursome had a friendly intimacy that she both yearned for, but thought she'd break up if she joined them. She wasn't an insider yet.

"They're opening up the Castle?" Amber Davail asked.

Jenni Emberdrake smiled at her with teeth that seemed to flash. "Lathyr Tricurrent got permission to move in." Her dark brows dipped and her chin jutted. "Eight Corp informed us that this will be strictly a guesthouse from now on."

"Oh, that's such a pity," Amber said.

Rafe Davail snorted. "Jerks."

A corner of Jenni's mouth lifted. "Yes. We'd been hoping for a permanent resident—"

"It is best that none of the…officers…of Eight Corp decide to live here," Aric said in his deep voice, curving his fingers around Jenni's shoulder. He nudged her up the steps. Amber and Rafe had already gone inside.

"Very true," Jenni said.

At the door, Lathyr seemed to glance Kiri's way, but said nothing, then Aric asked a question and Lathyr faded back, bowed to his guests and closed the door.

Wind tugged on Kiri's sweatpants like tiny hands and she shuddered. Too damn imaginative the past couple of days.

Loneliness wrapped around her like the night, echoing that vague wish for a man, a life partner. Someone sort of like Averill, in the computer industry, who wouldn't think she was wasting her life writing games as her parents and most of the other people Kiri knew believed. Not much respect from them.

She trotted faster. Like her current job of dealing with irate people and their problems was fulfilling! Maybe for some, but Kiri wanted to tell stories illustrated by graphics, let people fall into worlds and play. Entertaining people, giving them an outlet for frustration or boredom or a place away from the troubles and despair of real life was important, too. And *that* was what was fulfilling to Kiri. Why, she could even consider herself in the mental health field. Heaven knew she'd taken enough mental health breaks where she'd played Fairies and Dragons to rid herself of the insanity of working inside a structured and office-politics company.

She wondered how different Eight Corp was.

Again, she shivered. Yes, summer was truly gone and autumn would come soon and bring snow. She hurried home.

Lathyr had gritted his teeth at the knock on the door, sensing beyond it stood Princess Jindesfarne, her husband and the humans-with-magic couple. He should have expected this, but he hadn't. He had only arrived a few minutes ago.

And when he opened the door, they stood there, discussing him and the Castle, rudely. He blinked. They held food in their hands—a human custom he hadn't anticipated.

A slight wave of a more sensual feeling hit him, and he realized that Kiri stood in the shadows of the street, watching. As he had watched her the night before.

"You gonna stand there blocking the door or let us in, man?" asked Rafe Davail, the human with strong magic. Underwater, that would have ruffled the fine fins on Lathyr's arms and along his spine. In human form, the hair on the back of his nape rose a little in challenge.

It had been too long since he'd dueled in human shape to match with Davail now. And Lathyr wanted to be accepted here.

"Welcome to Mystic Circle!" Rafe's wife, Amber, said cheerfully, holding up a covered dish of salmon and rice that wafted to Lathyr's nostrils. His mouth watered, and he liked how she elbowed her husband in the side.

So he smiled and stepped back, bowing.

The mansion—the Water King was right, the house wasn't large, only four bedroom suites and eight bedrooms—was furnished like any royal palace, with the best Lightfolk and human items money could buy. But what was more important was that the balanced energy was exquisite, sliding along Lathyr's skin and slipping through his veins carried by his water nature.

He welcomed the Emberdrakes and the Davails and they toured the Castle together since none of them had been in it before.

That didn't stop Rafe Davail from being cocky…and Lathyr noted the man kept himself between Lathyr and his wife, and not altogether automatically like a fighter would. As if the human sensed some threat from Lathyr. Lips curling, Lathyr didn't reassure Rafe that only Kiri Palger interested him.

Amber Davail's magic was too developed for her to become pure Lightfolk, and too elven.

Rafe fingered some of the Lightfolk silk tapestries and slid his hand across the fine leather of the couch in the living room. The person who was least impressed seemed to be Amber Davail—a woman Lathyr gauged was more interested in people than objects.

Aric Paramon Emberdrake, Jenni's husband, had lived with the royals often enough in their palaces to recognize and accept the quality, and Jenni, as a previously sneered at half-breed, seemed the most struck.

The glass conservatory held a good-sized swimming pool set in a floor of colorful hand-painted Italian tiles. The water was turquoise and Lathyr's nose twitched at the Merfolk scents in the water. Large potted trees and flowering plants rimmed the windows.

"Fabulous," Amber enthused.

"Nice," Jenni, the quarter-air, quarter-fire Lightfolk said politely, staying at the doorway.

"Don't think I've seen a merman in mer shape," Rafe hinted.

"We have three solid shapes," Lathyr said, then turned to find the source of water he sensed in the basement.

Underground was made especially to be comfortable for Earthfolk—with warm stone floors, thick rugs and wood-paneled walls, large pillows on the floor. But down a hall, Lathyr looked through a large porthole to a room holding a seawater reservoir, a full submersion chamber for mers. He grinned and rubbed his hands. "Wonderful."

"I suppose," Jenni said doubtfully.

Instead of taking one of the bedrooms resonating with royal energy, Lathyr had chosen a small room on the first floor near the conservatory, meant for a servant. The others looked at him askance, and when Rafe opened his mouth again to comment Amber elbowed him, and no one said anything.

Lathyr was very aware of always living on sufferance.

The couples stayed only long enough for the tour and a drink afterward—Rafe, Jenni and Aric drank dwarven beer, and Amber some mead.

Amber hugged him before they left. Aric and Rafe—and Jenni to a lesser degree—remained slightly formal, not quite trusting him.

Lathyr sighed as he stood at the front door and watched the couples walk arms-around-waists back to their homes. He liked them all, even Rafe, and hoped he could earn their trust during this project. They'd make good friends.

Leaning against the wide doorjamb, he strained to see Kiri's house at the end of the street, nearly opposite the Castle. Not much was visible through the trees of the center park since like the other bungalow, it was only one story. But, there was a light from what he believed to be a back bedroom.

He'd hoped she was coming to greet and welcome him to Mystic Circle, too. She hadn't, and he'd been more disappointed than the small slight warranted.

One thing he had determined that day, he was definitely attracted to her. It had been a long time, since his adolescence, that he'd wanted to have sex with a human woman. Perhaps it was because he sensed the inherent potential in her to become Lightfolk…but he hadn't been drawn to the other women and men he'd seen transformed.

Should he phone her? He had her application, with telephone numbers, on his personal computer tablet, but he wanted her to be aware of him, wanted her to come to him. However, he'd inadvertently used glamour on her earlier that day; the Emberdrakes wouldn't forget that.

So he dragged in a breath that brought him the scent of leaves ready to turn in the autumn, losing their water flexibility and becoming dry and brittle, as well as the fragrance of the pond and the koi within, stupid and not good to eat. Considered beautiful by humans—and Kiri seemed to believe that—but compared to ocean creatures, the koi were ugly and clumsy. Most of all, the scent of balanced magic curled into his nostrils, layering on the folded frills.

He felt that balanced magic in the soles of his feet, and Jenni, as she'd trailed through the rooms, had balanced the magic in them. She'd ventured into each of the royal rooms and made the fire suite all of that element, then changed the energy of each of the others to match.

Wondrous.

But he was still landlocked, still had to live in his human form, even in this very special place. And the Castle wasn't his. He stayed here at the whim of the Eight, or the Water King.

He closed the wooden door with a thunk, walked through the entryway, then up to the top of the four-story small tower. From here he could see all of the Circle, each house with bright squares of living.

He was alone. Occasionally, he was allowed to stay in a secondary home by himself—the last perched like a carbuncle on the shelf of a deep marine trench. It had been smaller than this, and cold. But usually he was a "houseguest" of some other person or family. His own family was gone—his father, who'd been the last of his line, was dead; his mother had listened to her relatives and abandoned him soon after he was born. He shook off the memory.

Luxurious to have a home of such quality to himself. It felt good, but he wouldn't forget that he had no permanent place, no family. That was his goal, something he could win with the success of this project.

The quiet in the mansion hummed with magic to his ears, and pleased him. No intolerant naiader begrudged him here, a relief. Even as he enjoyed the peace of being by himself in a special place, he knew he'd eventually become lonely.

He wished Kiri was here to share the serenity…and make memories.

By the time Thursday morning rolled around, Kiri and her friend Shannon had spent a couple of cherished hours on the phone speculating about details of the new game, Transformation. They'd agreed that it would probably be another fantasy-world with the magic-based systems that Jenni Weavers Emberdrake was known for.

Both Kiri and Shannon had decided that having the game determine your character—strengths, weaknesses, types like magic user or long-distance shooter—sounded extremely dubious from a marketing standpoint. Good for novelty, but there'd better be an option for character creation. Kiri hoped she had the guts to give that opinion…but at the end of the trial, not now.

She hadn't slept much and got up when predawn light filtered into her bedroom, still undecided about what she would wear. In the game she was a fashionista—and perfectly proportioned. In the real world, her breasts and hips were full, she was short-waisted and short-legged and if she didn't watch it, she'd be plump.

Definitely not a business suit and stockings, even though she was meeting Lathyr in a downtown Denver high-rise, and there might be other people there to interview her, too. If she knew Jenni Weavers Emberdrake a little better, she'd have called the other woman and asked for advice, but Kiri still considered Jenni as one of the people who'd be watching her.

What mattered was the game—handling herself. Her shoulders had lifted with tension and her shoulder blades had squeezed together. Learning a new game was just like learning anything else—a new craft, a new job. There was a curve. Kiri wanted to be at the top of the curve. But she had no doubt that though she might spend most of her time in the game today, appearance mattered.

She'd already worn her beige outfit to the block party. Maybe it was time for businesslike black. She dragged out black slacks and a pale gray, thin cashmere sweater, then put the sweater back. The Eight Corp offices were probably warm and she'd probably sweat during the game—no doubt in her mind that adrenaline would spike through her a few times—and she didn't want to mess up her cashmere, no matter how comforting it might feel.

Ditch the whole professional business bit and go for what she was: computer tech and gamer. She put on a Fairies and Dragon tee, covered it with a plum-colored hoodie and wore her best cargo pants. Done. She would *not* dress up for Lathyr.

Breakfast was half an English muffin with cream cheese and coffee.

She perched on the edge of her living room chair until the

car taking her downtown beeped out in front, and her stomach gave a little squeeze.

Whatever happened, her life would never be the same....

HALF AN HOUR LATER, SHE WAS THE ONLY ONE in the elevator rising to Eight Corp's floor, although the huge lobby of the building had bustled with other people. She adjusted her hoodie and her workbag—this one a pristine bright red Fairies and Dragons carryall—over her shoulder, and did a few deep breaths as she watched the floor numbers light.

The door opened and she was met by Jenni and Lathyr. Jenni wore casual, too, but Lathyr had on a pale gray silk suit.

No one sat at the receptionist's desk—odd, because Kiri had only worked places where the receptionist had the earliest hours. With her first step, Kiri's feet literally sank into a deep green rug. She got the impression of elegant luxury before Jenni held out both her hands with a big smile. "Glad to see you again."

Once more, the woman's hands were warmer than her own. Damn nerves. "Yes. I'm excited."

"We are, too." Jenni beamed.

Lathyr offered his own hand, and Kiri shook it, ignoring how nice it felt. Firm grip, meet his eyes—gorgeous deep blue. Breathe, because the initial greeting went okay.

"A pleasure," Lathyr said.

"For me, too," Kiri said.

Jenni turned and moved around a huge freestanding wall of granite. "Let's head to the room where the game server is set up."

"Sounds fine to me," Kiri said.

"Do you want something to drink?" asked Lathyr.

Coffee would tweak her nerves even more. "Water would be great."

He peeled off and Kiri followed Jenni down the hall to an interior room. It was painted an uninspired beige and was longer than it was wide. To Kiri's surprise, an actual wooden counter polished to a gloss ran along the wall as a desk setup. Atop the counter, four huge monitors sat. The most comfortable of ergonomic chairs—smelling of new plastic and metal—were placed before the monitors. Several different types of game controllers waited on a floating platform a little lower than the desk under each monitor. All top-of-the-line electronics.

"Wow, nice setup," she said.

"Thanks." Jenni went to the last chair on the left, sat and swiveled toward Kiri.

But Kiri's stare had fixed on several sets of gloves that appeared to have filaments embedded in them, and four wraparound visors.

"As you can see," Jenni said easily, "we're experimenting a bit with virtual reality, also. Put on the visor and you'll feel as if you're really in the game. Wear the gloves and your gestures will be translated as powers. For instance, if you want to throw a fireball—"

"I'll really act as if I'm throwing a ball."

"That's right."

"Hmm." Kiri stayed where she was.

"We'd like you to wear the gloves and visor."

"This isn't monitoring my vitals, is it?"

The line between Jenni's eyes cleared. "No. Absolutely not. The gloves and the visor are simply to immerse you in a deeper gaming experience."

"Uh-huh."

"I have your water," Lathyr said from behind her.

So Kiri sidled into the room, stood near the third chair. The man offered her a large bottle of fizzy water—the same brand of raspberry that she'd chosen at the block party, and somehow she didn't think that was by chance. "Thank you."

"You are quite welcome." He did a torso incline thing, then closed the door and the room felt pretty small. Reaching out, he took a pair of large teal gloves and slipped them on, raising a brow at Kiri as he did so. He held a visor by the slim end and twirled it in his fingers.

"I, um, am pretty simple in my gaming," Kiri said. "Monitor, keyboard, mouse."

"Please," Jenni said, gesturing to the gloves and visors. She donned some red ones with gold "embroidery" of fiber optic filaments or something. Kiri narrowed her eyes, then blinked. It looked like the pattern might be almost a mathematical algorithm—or, in a different game, a spell—and the design lit up.

"I thought we were going to have another interview?" Kiri said weakly, looking at Lathyr.

"That's so stuffy," Jenni said.

It *was* stuffy.

"What's wrong?" asked Jenni.

Kiri grimaced. "The gloves and visor might interfere with my play." She swallowed. "I really don't want to screw this up." It meant too much to her.

Lathyr set the visor down and stripped off the gloves. He held out both hands. "I am a good judge of energy. I am sure I can reassure you that you belong here. Please?"

Kiri stared, cut her eyes to Jenni, questioning this new age stuff. The woman looked bland, so Kiri shrugged and put her hands in his. Yes, tingles, for sure. And the texture of his palms and his fingers was so smooth, but there was strength in those hands. Nice.

"Pregame visualization exercise," Jenni said. "Close your eyes and visualize—ah—the Fairy Dome in Fairies and Dragons."

Kiri shot her a glance. "You take the game very seriously."

"Well, of course. It's my livelihood. An attitude I expect from you."

Kiri closed her eyes, recalled the Fairy Dome, tried to bring it into focus. She'd always sucked at visualization except right before and right after she slept.

She became all too aware of Lathyr, his hands, the closeness of his body to hers, as if energy cycled between them. Scents came to her nose, a hot and spicy smell, a fresh odor reminding her of the ocean—Lathyr's aftershave? Eyes shut, she *felt* the atmosphere in the room...fancifully enough, she thought that Jenni's and Lathyr's energy clashed, did not mix well. Kiri realized her breathing matched Lathyr's, slow and deep. Her ears strained...trying to hear the hum of the computers...no, she was too used to her barely up-to-date equipment at work. Not the tiniest buzz of fans, but she was right, the room was warm and getting warmer. In fact, the tingles within her seemed to also press against her skin, as if she were immersed in fizzy water. Fun, energizing. She stifled a giggle.

Lathyr released her hands and stepped back. Her eyelids flew open and she smiled at him, only to see he'd moved and was leaning over Jenni, speaking quietly. He glanced up at her, nodded, then said, "You will do well."

When he returned to talking to Jenni, all Kiri's doubts swarmed back, despite his assurance. Jenni had indicated that it was Lathyr who had decided—or would decide—whether Kiri was a good fit, hadn't she? She wished they'd done this earlier and in a conference room or something, not where she was supposed to work.

Stiffly, Kiri walked over to the long desk, noted that the edge wasn't squared off, but rounded, lovely. Scanning the gloves—twelve pairs in various sizes and colors—she went with impulse and chose a pair of pretty pale green ones that looked to be her size. She pulled them on—they felt like the finest chamois, and again her hands tingled. The metallic silver embroidery glittered, nearly seemed to spark. Wow. She chose a visor she thought would fit, but didn't put it on. And she sat in the chair, turned on the monitor.

A rainbow-colored word appeared in flowing pastel script. *Transformation!* Frowning, tugging on the wrists of her gloves, she looked over at Lathyr and Jenni, who watched her.

"Yes?" asked Jenni. Kiri thought the woman hid a smile. Maybe that should relieve her, but it didn't much.

"I've heard there are some biofeedback games out there," Kiri said. She flexed her fingers; the gloves clung, almost massaged her hands. Felt good, but she'd definitely miss a keyboard. Obviously, she wasn't as flexible as she'd thought. Not a good thing to consider when she was on the job interview of her life. Not when she wanted to be on the cutting edge of the gaming world.

"Yes," Jenni said. "I've heard of those games, too, even tried them. But, I promise you, the gloves are not recording any information. They are for virtual reality purposes only."

"I don't see the connectivity to the computer system."

"Optical," Jenni said promptly.

Lathyr walked toward her and put his gloves on again—they weren't the same texture, more like thin silk. Jenni's were velvet. He said, "I assure you, Ms. Palger, that you are a prime candidate for this job."

All the repetition brought relief. "I *do* want the job."

Jenni's brows rose. "Let's go then." She waved and the other monitors blinked on, along with the cheerful cheep of keyboards, game pads and mice coming online.

Kiri stared. "Wow, your gloves really work."

"Like magic." Jenni laughed. "Ready?"

Kiri put her visor on, nothing odd happened. What had she expected, tentacles slipping into her brain? No, don't think that.

"Is everything…okay?" asked Lathyr.

"Fine," Kiri said, though she felt a little stupid with the gloves and visor on. She didn't think most casual gamers would want to wear the accessories unless the immersive factor was really amazing. But she sure wouldn't say that yet. Not when she was at the starting post, ready to surge forward and hit the game running.

No. That might not work with this game. Not all were fast; some that mimicked real life were deadly slow in her opinion. An alternative to real life, just trying to make it better with a choice of mate and children…no, that reminded her of Shannon, and Kiri's thoughts were too scattered!

She had to focus, to be primed.

"Ready?" Lathyr asked.

"Ready."

Light engulfed her vision. *Transformation! Brought to you by Eight Corp!* The words vanished in an explosion of yellow and Kiri dropped into the game.

She stood atop a low hill, breathing in summer air and looking down on a carpet of many-colored wildflowers. She could almost believe wind lifted her hair from her neck. She touched her hair, held it before her face. Looked exactly like her own hair. She wasn't wearing gloves, and her hands appeared to be her own, too, with the glittery tint she'd put on her nails.

She was *there*. No visor narrowed her vision.

"Wow." She reached out for the water bottle on the counter beside her in real life. Nothing happened but her arm slicing thin air. "Wow," she repeated. "This really is full immersion."

"This is the opening sequence," Lathyr said. He stood beside her, dressed as he had been in real life—European-cut suit, pale blue shirt, no tie.

He swept an arm around in an expansive gesture, and turned in place. Kiri did, too.

"As you can see, there are four realms in Transformation." His smile crinkled his eyes and Kiri thought it was the first carefree one she'd seen from him. Was he easier in a game setup, too? "Since many things in the game are complex, such as the virtual reality…hardware…" Now he waved a hand and Kiri thought she saw the outline of a sparkling glove. "We are keeping the magic portion of the game fairly simple. Each realm corresponds to an ancient element—water, air, earth, fire."

"Ah." From the hill, the realms were vivid quarters of a round pie and looked different and colorful. Excitement and just plain fun began to seep into her—why had she balked, this looked so kewl? She flexed her fingers and tiny sparkles rose from her hands in spirals. Oh, yes, cool! She did a little rock in place, a little butt shimmy, and tried another wave. Her mouth dropped open as small butterflies rose from her fingertips. Her laugh got stuck in her throat and came out a low chuckle. "I *love* these gloves!"

"Good to hear," Jenni's smug voice came, vibrating through the band of Kiri's visor over her ears.

"Examine the realms," Lathyr said. "This is the only time you will be on this hill and have this panoramic view. Your time here—our time here—is limited."

That thunked Kiri's heels back down to the ground. Had she actually been dancing? Yeah. And this wasn't just a new game to love and hate and be exasperated with and prize and master. *This* was a realm *she'd* help create and refine. Write for the enjoyment and entertainment of others. This was the job, the career she wanted.

The realms showed bright colors of cartoonish intensity—one was mostly green. Green, green hills, an equally verdant ridge with a wooden door in it. Towering mountains looking a lot like the front range of the Colorado Rockies rose behind the lush hills. "Earth Realm," Kiri gestured and more butterflies streamed from her fingers down the hill toward the Earth Realm.

"Each realm has a major race and a minor race—the Earth Realm has dwarves and brownies." A note in Lathyr's voice had her turning her head and she caught him eyeing her—her figure? her stature?—before a bland expression covered his face.

Green and brown earth was in front of her on the left when she'd arrived. To her right appeared a blue-and-green realm with a spring becoming stream, widening to a river, flowing to lake and beach and ocean. Easy to figure that out, "Water Realm?"

"Yes. Mers—mermen and merfems—are the major race who usually live in the ocean. Naiads and naiaders of ponds and lakes and streams are the minor folk. Most Waterfolk are the size of humans."

Kiri had bent down to sniff at the grass—something smelled fabulous—and how could she smell in the game? She didn't know, but the scent went to her head, spiraled through her body.

Think! She straightened slowly. "So dwarves and brownies aren't our size?"

"Dwarves are shorter and stockier than humans, perhaps the tallest is four feet tall. Brownies are even smaller."

"Uh-huh." She peered at the distant waves of the really blue ocean, beyond the sparkling white beach. Yes, too-bright colors, but in those faraway waves did she see the hint of a castle? Maybe turrets occasionally revealed to be pearlescent shell-pink?

Lathyr's hands came down on her shoulders. He'd moved behind her. Pure sensation rippled through her. She couldn't help herself from sniffing the fingers on her right shoulder, again a little salt, some sort of fresh odor, and the fragrance all around her, though more intense. "What is that smell?"

"In the game?" He chuckled. "Magic."

"Oh, of course. I still can't figure out how we can smell stuff in the game." Maybe there was scent on the visors, or they emitted fragrance in bursts like air fresheners.

Another amused laugh from Lathyr. "Magic. Now turn and look at the other two realms…our time is running out."

"Huh." But she did turn, scanned the white-blue-violet mist and the castle in the air, perched on a huge puffy white cloud with streaks of violet. "One guy explaining the realms to me? This is a lame opening, I could write better." Too late she realized she'd been offensive. "Sorry."

"I didn't write the scenario," Lathyr said coolly. "We will have a virtual guide. We were given permission for the new game no more than a fortnight ago. Ms. Emberdrake has been concentrating on the game itself."

Kiri winced. Yeah, she'd offended him, maybe Jenni, too. She swallowed. "I'm sure it's amazing." She pushed a little. "And that's why you need me. I can help." She waved again, still enjoying the butterflies. "Okay, that's the Air Realm. Castle in the clouds is a big clue."

"That's right. The denizens of the Air Realm are elves and airsprites."

She twisted from his grip to stare at him. "Elves? Really elves?"

"Yes."

She couldn't prevent a girl-squeal from emerging. "Awesome. I could be an elf?"

"In the Air Realm, yes." His voice remained cool. Ah, well.

"How big are they? Bitty like Santa's elves or big and—" sexy, no, she wouldn't say that "—hunky like Tolkien's elves in the movies?"

"They are usually taller than regular humans, but more slender," Lathyr said austerely. Kiri guessed her "hunky" irritated him as much as "sexy" might have.

"Oh. And airsprites?"

"They might be considered your elves—though I believe airsprites appear as described more often in huma—literature and art depicting fairies."

"Oh, small then?"

"Yes, they are humanoid-looking when they care to be."

"All right. You've already done a lot of work on this game."

"Yes," Jenni said in her ear again, in a slightly choked voice, like she was laughing? "Though not so much on the opening."

Kiri winced again.

"And we will have eight races, and only eight," Lathyr said.

"Oh, no humans?"

"Not at this time," Jenni said. "Thirty-second warning, Lathyr and Kiri."

"Oh." Scanning the Air Realm, Kiri didn't see any great detail. She could definitely make a contribution there, if it really was only sketched in.

She turned to the red-yellow Fire Realm. This appeared very detailed, as if it might be the best developed realm—red and sandy rock formations, desert, sand dunes of white and brown. Multicolored hot flames dancing in the air, even forming into sheets of heat waves distorting the rest of the picture. "Wow, Jenni, Fire Realm is great. You must have worked hard on it."

"Thank you!" Pleasure radiated in Jenni's voice.

"Fire Realm has djinns—" Lathyr began.

"Djinns like genies?" Kiri asked.

"Yes, djinnmen and djinnfems as the major race," Lathyr finished.

Kiri imagined herself in a turban, maybe a metallic golden one. Gold lamé with a big ruby. Tacky but wonderful. "What kind of costumes do you have?" she asked. And did djinn manifest from smoke? Did they have lamp domiciles? Did they fly? Or have flying carpets?

"Not nearly as good a range of costumes as our game Fairies and Dragons," Jenni said with regret.

"Oh." Kiri cleared her throat. "*Yet*. Not as good a wardrobe *yet*. I can help with that."

"I like your attitude," Jenni said. "And what I've seen of your costumes in our times playing together in Fairies and Dragons, you'll be a great help."

Kiri was glad she'd already deleted all hideous fashion mistakes.

"The minor folk are firesprites," Lathyr continued. "Like airsprites, they are significantly smaller than humans, perhaps as tall as eighteen inches as the maximum. Again, they tend to be less substantial than the major folk, the djinns."

"Time," Jenni said. "Logging Kiri Palger and Lathyr Tricurrent out of the opening to the prologue of *Transformation*."

KIRI BECAME AWARE OF THE MESH CHAIR UNDER her butt. Her nose missed the scent of magic, and tears nearly squeezed from her eyes at being back in the real world. Stupid! She swallowed hard, made sure her eyes were dry before she pulled off her visor. Her monitor had gone into sleep mode. She wanted to jiggle the mouse to see if she might recapture the view from the hill.

"Well, Kiri, what do you think?" Jenni was right there, staring down at her. Kiri pulled off her gloves harder than she'd anticipated because her palms were sticky. Looking up at Jenni, Kiri had to blink a bit because the woman actually looked a little red, like she'd gotten a sunburn.

Kiri rubbed her eyes, her fingers definitely smelled like her own sweat, and said the first thing that came to her mind in response to Jenni's question. "I'm starving."

"Hmm." Jenni's brows dipped. "Maybe I'd better talk to my kitchen staff."

Kitchen staff, in an office? Jenni sauntered to the door.

"No, no!" Kiri amended. "Don't worry about it."

On her way out, Jenni tossed over her shoulder. "Sounds like the virtual reality might burn some energy."

Lose weight while game playing. Oh, yeah, a win-win situation. "If that's true, the marketing possibilities are incredible," she said to Lathyr. He looked just the same. "Are you hungry?"

His smile was slow and male. His eyes didn't really linger on her. Not really. "For food? No." He sat in the last chair, his trousers still with knife creases. Kiri felt a little wrung out, glanced down to see if the slight dampness between her breasts showed. No. Good.

"I am more accustomed to the…ah, game, than you." He swiveled until he faced her and set his arm along the edge of the desk. The keyboard platform was still tucked under it.

"More accustomed to the game? You don't strike me as a gamer."

His smile frosted. "Not often in this alternate reality."

"Huh."

His gaze turned considering. "Perhaps I should say that I am more accustomed to a magical atmosphere."

Like that made sense.

Jenni walked in with a steaming omelet. "Here's a mushroom, spinach and cheese omelet for you, and an English muffin."

Kiri stared. "I love mushrooms, spinach and cheese." She always stocked all three items. Amazing that the kitchen here had something like that.

Jenni's smile was close to a smirk. She set the plate, a paper napkin and a fork down on the desk beyond Kiri's monitor. "Eat up. We'll have to, um, generally keep track of the physical energy drain with regard to the virtual reality of the game."

Scooting over to the meal, Kiri dug in, but only ate a scrumptious bite before replying. "Like I told Lathyr, losing weight while gaming is one hell of a marketing point."

"Ah, hmm." Jenni frowned as she returned to her own seat. Like Lathyr, she faced Kiri and put her arm on the desk. Unlike him, her fingers drummed on the polished wood. "Well, the hardware is very expensive. I'm not sure how widespread we'll be disseminating the game."

Kiri stopped midbite. This was her game, her career, her future. "What? It's not going to be an online massive multiplayer game like Fairies and Dragons?"

Jenni's brown eyes widened. "Yes, of course, the general software…and available in stores, too, to lead people online to *Transformation*. But the gloves and visors are currently quite proprietary intellectual property items."

"Oh."

"We may allow only some players to buy into the virtual reality aspect of the game," Lathyr said.

Discrimination. For the rich? Kiri chewed the omelet. The flavor should have stayed the same, but it hadn't. Bitterness on her own taste buds maybe. "Like who?" she asked.

Again Jenni answered smoothly. "Like those who do extremely well in the general game. This isn't the only game to have tiers of players, according to who wants to pay and who wants it free," Jenni pointed out.

"Oh," Kiri repeated. She drank some raspberry fizzy water—it went unexpectedly well with the eggs. Her taste buds had perked up. "That's all right then."

Lathyr snorted.

Jenni chuckled. "I sense a discrimination by skill level, here."

Kiri nodded. "Choice and skill. You make the choice as to

how long and involved you want to be with the game, and develop your skill."

"Meritocracy," Lathyr said.

He actually sounded dubious.

"Americans believe in that, even though it isn't true," Jenni said, her accent British. And Kiri belatedly remembered that Jenni lived in Denver, but had grown up in England.

Kiri stuffed egg in her mouth, drank and hurriedly finished her meal. "I'm so sorry for this, eating on the job."

Jenni shrugged. "Not a problem." She glanced at Lathyr. "We're easy enough on this project, and have some wiggle room."

"Thanks." Kiri stood and picked up the breakfast stuff. "Kitchen?"

"We'll take care of that," Jenni said easily. "I'll show you the bathroom to wash up."

"Thanks." And was Kiri going to be embarrassed and repeat the word all day long? She put the plate, crumpled napkin and fork on the counter and followed Jenni down a still-empty hallway with a murmur of voices sounding only behind one door.

"This is the executive area and like many executives, ours work more out of the office than in it," Jenni said, as if catching Kiri's stares.

"Um-hmm," Kiri said. She hadn't ever worked on an executive floor so didn't know what to expect.

"What do you think of the game?" Jenni asked.

Kiri didn't have to fake a smile. "I really like the concept and the taste I got of it."

"Good." Jenni waved at the women's bathroom door.

When Kiri had finished, Jenni was still in the corridor, talking on her cell. "That is correct. Later." She hung up and smiled at Kiri, stuck the cell in a pocket. "Ready for full-immersion and to start play?"

Sounded a little daunting, but Kiri nodded. "Absolutely."

Another wide smile with sparkling eyes. "Good." Jenni actually rubbed her hands. "This project is going to be a winner."

"I hope so." And Kiri hoped she was a part of it.

Soon she was back in her chair, green chamois gloves on, visor wrapping around her head.

"Initiating game," Jenni said, and Kiri heard it both aloud and as words vibrating from the visor.

To her right, Lathyr said, "I'll accompany you initially once more."

"Thanks."

Meld magic swept Lathyr up and to the pocket dimension of the game. Rock slid through him, nastily. At least the transition was fast enough that it didn't absorb his water magic. His toes—feet in shoes were not as hardy as his webbed ones—tried to dig into the earth, but he found himself standing on the stone bottom of a cave, a place just large enough for himself and Kiri.

"Wow," she said, sounding breathless. He glanced at her temples and the tracery of veins he used to mark humans' heartbeats...and had to glance down.

Her skin was brownish, what humans would think of as deeply tanned. Lathyr kept a mild look on his face. Like all Waterfolk the actual color—blue, green, gold—didn't matter. Her ears were large with fleshy lobes, her features broad, her figure sturdy with not much waist but ample breasts and hips. Lovely, heavily lashed chocolate-brown eyes with split black pupils looked up at him as she smiled at him—with pointed red teeth.

Also beautiful was her golden-brown hair, the color of light honey with hints of true metallic gold and streaks of wheat-blond—all earthy comparisons for an earth elemental.

"You're a dwarf," Lathyr said.

She literally jumped, then appeared surprised as she didn't rise in the air as much as a human would have.

Staring at her feet, she said, "A major earth elemental."

"Yes. And one that other dwarves would find beautiful." If there had been any other dwarves in this area. But no dwarves or other players were here, only in the Earth Palace, which was her goal.

"Thank you, sir." She looked at her clothing. "Hmm. A robe." She skipped forward and back a dwarf pace. "Comfortable and I can move in it. A nice, fine weave." Then she turned in place. "This really feels real."

"Yes. Your robe should have some protection spells woven into it," Lathyr said.

Kiri cleared her throat. "Jenni?"

"I'm here," Jenni's voice echoed from the walls.

"How do I know what powers and equipment and spells and qualities I have?"

"You have a belt with a pouch. The info's in there."

Shock crossed Kiri's face. "I have to stop and open a pouch and, what, read my data?"

"Welcome to real life, kid. It ain't all gesturing and chanting up earthworks," Jenni said. "And you're at beginner level."

"Huh."

"Take a look at your staff against the wall."

"Ooooh." Kiri trotted the three steps to the wall and picked up an intricately carved staff that appeared to be solid gold.

"It's light," Kiri said. "Like balsa wood."

"Gold leaf," Lathyr said.

"Real gold?"

He knew the smell of gold. "Yes."

"I suppose that's a plus," Kiri said, but a dubious note had entered her voice. She found the dark brown suede pouch, though the minute she touched it, a piece of paper popped into her hand. "Nice. But it's too dim—" The staff brightened to a steady yellow light.

"Okay. That's pretty," Kiri said, then, "I don't like the looks of this character, though. Magic user—sorceress—and magic users tend to be squishy."

"Squishy?" asked Lathyr.

"Not many hit points, easily defeated."

"Ah. May I see your paper?"

"Yes, how good are these spells?"

"That, I believe, you would have to ask Jenni. I am here to show you how to use them."

"Sorry, Kiri," Jenni said, "but that's how your innate qualities manifested you into this game—as an earth elemental, dwarfem magic user. But you also have healing powers you can use on yourself."

"That's something," Kiri said, this time absentmindedly, as she stared at the paper. "All right. My robe has a high-level defensive spell woven into it. That's good, and I can also draw a shield around me."

"A stone dust shield. That will protect you, but it will not allow you to throw offensive spells at your enemies."

"A trade-off," Kiri said. She didn't seem as concerned as Lathyr was. He knew the spells she was being given were those practiced by true dwarves. But of what use was a purely defensive shield, except to huddle behind like in a fort—or a cave? He disapproved of the notion—but much of mer magic was based on movement.

She took back the pitiful list. "I have two offensive spells here, beginning level, I imagine. One is 'stiffen enemy' and the other, 'barricade.'" Looking up at him with her beautiful eyes, she asked, "How do I cast these?"

For the first time Lathyr was glad that he'd spent a few decades in a seaport as mostly human. The town had held an unusually eclectic mix of minor Lightfolk, and he'd fought with them against sea monsters, the occasional land monster and some bloody-minded humans. At the time, he'd seen the spells often enough, and he'd learned the few that Kiri would be able to master in each realm during the short time she'd be given.

It only took three minutes for him to show her the gestures, make sure she had them memorized, before she went to the cave opening. Looking at a winding path, she touched her information sheet again. "My goal is to reach the Earth Palace and make my curtsy to the Dwarf Royals before receiving quests from them."

"That's right," Jenni said. "Though due to your limited amount of time, once you reach the palace, we will call it done in the Earth Realm, then will renew the settings so you will manifest in a different elemental realm."

Kiri's shoulders squared as she nodded. "That's right." She took a step out, and glanced back at Lathyr, who hadn't moved. "Aren't you coming?"

"I'm afraid you are on your own," he said, keenly regretting he couldn't help her. "My presence here is limited to this cave." And he was beginning to dislike the smell. The magic had gathered around Kiri and moved with her.

"Oh."

"Fare we—" The last syllable was cut off and rock jabbed at his nerves again as Meld tech-magic moved him from the "game" back to the tall building in Denver.

Lathyr vanished from Kiri's sight. She was on her own. Her

heart jumped in her chest and she wiped her palms on her robe. Her staff stood upright beside her. Magic.

She inhaled deeply. Wow. Magic had a scent in the game, like sleeping under a tree full of spring blossoms and having them drop down and cover her, fragile and pink. Wonderful, wonderful fragrance.

Against the wall she saw a brown leather pack that turned out to be full of food and journey items and medicines. Kiri picked it up by one of the straps and her brows rose. "Also light." She studied the bulging bag, shrugged and slipped it on her back.

So she left the cave and stepped into warm sunshine…which appeared to be more yellow, too. Hmm. She'd see if she liked that; it did seem more cheerful.

How closely would Jenni and Lathyr be watching her? She didn't know, but time to get on with the game. Fun and stressful all at once.

"Welcome back," Princess Jindesfarne said to Lathyr.

Lathyr shuddered as he pulled off his visor and placed it on the counter. "I do not like that construct. Real and game."

"Face it, Lathyr, you don't like games."

"I have no problem admitting that."

The princess chuckled throatily, her cinnamon-colored brows winging up. "But you do like our charge, Kiri Palger." There was a beep from the machine in front of the princess and she swirled toward it, fingers racing over the keyboard.

"Problems?" he snapped, striding to the monitor, not even taking time to remove the loathsome gloves that soaked up and channeled his magic in ways he didn't care for.

"Not really," Jindesfarne said. "I have the game set up to notify me when Kiri reaches some important goals. She's through the first rath—first magical Hill." The large screen in front of the Fire Princess lit up and showed Kiri with a staff in one hand, a long dagger attached to her hip.

"Explain the pocket dimension to me," Lathyr said.

Now Jindesfarne swung her chair to look at him. "We can form and populate it as we please," she said.

"I thought all dimensions were closed to us." He knew the more magical Lightfolk, the royals, yearned for a permanent gate to intensely magical worlds...dimensions. "How can this be?"

She gave an exaggerated shrug. "The two guardians developed it."

"Do you mean those who are older than the royals? The dwarf and the elf?"

"That's right. I don't know whether the pocket dimension is a place between Earth and the other dimensions or a variant of the dryad's 'greenspace.' Maybe it's in another world and Pavan, the elf guardian, has arranged that whoever logs into the game is transported there. The guardians have their secrets from the Eight. I asked, but Pavan just smiled and refused an answer. I *do* know that it is a real place." Her eyes fired, literally showed a tiny orange flame "Fights can be real—people can be hurt...they can bleed. Right now we don't have that option on for Kiri, but I'm hoping she will accept it."

Lathyr's gut tightened. "Because the more real the game, the more she survives and prevails, the more likely she will be prepared for a true transformation into Lightfolk, should she choose that."

Jindesfarne's smile was small, but sincere. "Exactly. Tough love."

His gaze went to the monitor. The colors seemed too vivid. "This pocket dimension idea has been used before?"

"Yes, the original 'game' was a mock-up of Fairies and Dragons, installed on Rafe Davail's machine to help him find a special shield and dagger." Jindesfarne's hands lifted from the keyboard and mouse to tap a rapid tattoo on the desk. "I haven't been able to figure out what Pavan did…does. I do know that we set up the realms with constructs of the four elemental magics the Lightfolk work with—and populated them with monsters, structured it like a true computer game. That was my part, and I could've used some help, let me tell you." Jindesfarne linked her fingers together and stretched her arms out.

A horrible buzz came from the monitor. Jenni winced and swiveled back to the screen where she'd been monitoring Kiri, tapped a key. "Oops."

"OOPS?" LATHYR STOPPED PEELING OFF THE DELIcate silk gloves. He didn't like them, but had tried all the other textures and these were the best.

Jindesfarne grimaced. "Kiri's in the healing cave. She was nearly defeated."

"By whom?"

"A rockwyrm got her."

Lathyr stilled as he saw a long, stone creature. "I have only heard stories of rockwyrms."

"When the magic faded, they died," Jindesfarne said with satisfaction. "At least from Earth. I'm sure they remain in more magically rich dimensions. And when the Meld begins to work—increasing magic—they aren't beings that we will allow to revive. Kiri did a good job turning it to stone, though she was injured in the process." Nevertheless, Jindesfarne shook her head and hissed through her teeth as they both watched Kiri's character leave the healing cave.

"She didn't manifest as a very strong dwarf," Lathyr said. Kiri used her magical staff to trudge up a green hill. "A good magic user, but weak physically."

Again Jindesfarne turned to him. "That concerns you?"

"I want her chances to survive transformation to be high."

"At least she didn't become a brownie."

"I thought that wasn't an option."

"The design team—" Jindesfarne tapped her chest with her forefinger "—wanted to include only the major Lightfolk elemental races. We were overruled by the Eight royals, who wanted a 'more realistic assessment of an individual human's capabilities.'"

Lathyr dropped the gloves, glad his magic was his own again, sat, then wheeled up to Jindesfarne. His jaw flexed with anger a couple of times before he managed to say in a calm tone, "They don't accept my assessment."

Jindesfarne slanted him an equally ironic glance. "They told me that they preferred the game technology to determine Kiri's Lightfolk status rather than your talent, and the royals are not comfortable much with technology."

"Or distrust the new talents that some of us are gaining," he snapped. Then he caught Jindesfarne's gaze with his own. "They wish the humans attempting to become Lightfolk to fail."

The Fire Princess sighed, her breath drying his skin, he was so close. "Yeah, that was my conclusion, too."

"But the game is relatively safe," Lathyr pressed.

"Relatively, at least for now. Even when we lift the restrictions, it will be relatively safe. Then Kiri could get hurt—bruises and scrapes and whatnot—but no blood or, hopefully, fatal wounds."

"Hopefully?"

"The cave really *is* a healing cave, and she is transported there when she is badly hurt or defeated. It can heal most injuries."

That didn't satisfy him. "You have human physicians on call?" Lathyr scanned the room—sent his senses beyond the walls and through the two floors the Eight commanded.

"We have a mer healer on call," the princess said.

Lathyr relaxed. "They are the best."

"You would think so," Jindesfarne said.

Lathyr gave her the bow due to a princess, flourishing hands and all. "Of course, Princess Jindesfarne."

The half-Lightfolk stared at him. After a pause, she said, "You aren't mocking me."

Appalled, Lathyr said, "Of course not, Princess Jindesfarne."

Her head tilted. "And you aren't teasing me."

"No." He bowed again, a small one and he kept his eyes on her, since she acted so strangely.

Breath puffed from her with the heat and the scent of a desert. Lathyr hopped a pace back—couldn't always tell with Firefolk whether flame would follow breath.

"You're being respectful," the djinnfem said.

"Yes, Princess."

She rubbed her temples. "Don't. We're partners in this endeavor."

If they were, he knew he was a very junior partner.

"And don't call me Princess or Jindesfarne. Call me Jenni." Her brown eyes deepened. "And why are you being so respectful?"

"You are a princess of the folk."

"I am a half-breed human and you are fully magical."

"You are a princess, the daughter of the Fire King and Queen."

"I am the adopted sister of the Fire King."

Lathyr tensed. He'd simply forgotten that a change had been made at the highest levels of the opposite element than he, though, at the time, his own new powers had hit him like a sickness and he'd suffered for a week. Yet now he'd made an unforgivable lapse, especially since he recalled Jenni had been involved in the whole situation—the battle. "Please, accept my apologies, Princess..." She scowled. "Jenni."

"Sure." Though sadness crossed her face, then she tilted her head. "But most full-blooded Lightfolk wouldn't treat a half-human like me well."

"Then you didn't know the right Lightfolk," he said.

She looked skeptical. He'd have to watch his tongue. "And things have changed. You are close to the royals, not only the Fire couple. You are high in the ranks of Eight Corp. Your husband is also high in those ranks. You are the sole elemental-balancer in the world, and have great magic."

"Hmm. I guess I really am special or something."

"Yes."

A quick knock came at the door and Jenni's husband, Prince Aric Paramon Emberdrake, opened it and said, "Jenni, you're wanted for the Meld Project."

She frowned. "I'm needed here, more. *They* promised I wouldn't be interrupted. Especially not today."

Aric smiled slowly. "The Lightfolk programmers got stuck when trying to increase better magical battery storage. They need a human-tech algorithm work-around, and you're just the person for that."

"Oh, all right." She stood and strode to the door and kissed him on the lips. Lathyr sent his glance elsewhere. Humans and djinns were less discreet in their liaisons than mers.

"Five minutes," Jenni said as she stepped from Aric's embrace.

He nodded and closed the door.

"Here, you observe." Jenni handed Lathyr a headset and waved toward her place before the computer.

He put the headset on. It smelled of cloves and fire and wood smoke.

"How do I get her out?" he asked.

Jenni beamed. "Thinking of her welfare first...I like that." She indicated a small cylindrical device that had a red button at the top. "Just push that."

It hadn't been anywhere near her hand. What if Kiri had needed to be pulled out?

Lathyr sat in Jenni's chair.

"How do I speak to her?"

Jenni tapped the mic. "Here. Say 'testing.'"

"Testing," he said.

"I hear you, Lathyr," Kiri said. She was climbing a hill.

"I have a meeting on another project, Kiri. Lathyr will be your control," Jenni said.

"Okay," Kiri replied.

Jenni held out the recall device and Lathyr took it. His palms were damper than usual, not a good sign. He pushed the platform holding the keyboard firmly under the counter.

At the top of the hill, Kiri rested, her breath soughing out. "Nice view. Hmm. Three paths." Kiri muttered to herself, something about eenies, that Lathyr didn't catch, then started down the left-hand dirt track between tall, flowering bushes.

"No offense, Lathyr," Kiri said, head down and watching her feet as the path steepened. "But I didn't get the impression that you've played a lot of games."

"How did you guess?" Jenni said drily.

That stung. "No, but I've been in plenty of fights," Lathyr said. He'd lived nearly two centuries, after all, in uncivilized places—and also in "civilized" human cities. He'd watched and felt the magic decline, moved from places near inland seas or large lakes to ports and shore villages, to a couple of stints as a servant in Water Palaces, then other, less-rich domiciles, to whomever offered to guest him.

"Oops," said Jenni. "We'll get you up to speed on Fairies and Dragons, now you're here in Mystic Circle," she ended.

"Oh. Sorry," Kiri said. The track had turned from dirt to stone stairs down.

"See you later," Jenni said. A polite smile flicked on and off her face. For the fact she had to leave rather than being in his company, Lathyr decided. She fairly vibrated with longing to stay.

"We'll be fine," Lathyr said. He'd do his utmost to protect Kiri.

Now Jenni frowned. "Don't..." She shrugged and left.

Kiri was humming as she hopped down the stairs, built to the proportions of dwarves, of course. They'd be a little too high for brownies.

On the monitor, Lathyr could see her...and the track leading straight to the dragon's den. He checked a tutorial quick list Jenni had placed on the desk. She'd called it a "cheat sheet." The color of Kiri's aura was yellow signifying a magical being under the fifth level. He looked at the big red dragon, jaws open, forked tongue out and tasting the air as if it scented dwarfem. Its color was an oily black. Highest level.

Doom for one small sorceress.

"Ah. Kiri?" Lathyr said.

"Yeah?" She was shortening and lengthening her staff, making it wand and doing magical passes, then baton and twirling, then quarterstaff and lunging.

"I suggest you return to the hilltop."

She stopped. "What?"

"I strongly suggest you return to the hilltop."

"No. Reeaally?" She pouted.

Lathyr had never considered a pouting dwarfem cute before.

"Really," he said, nodding, though she couldn't see.

Calculation came to her eyes. Her shoulders squared. "You can see more than I can."

"Yes."

"What—hmm, no, that's unfair. How bad does it look?"

"Do you want to end up in the healing cave again?"

"Awww. You know I'm not sure of these almost-physical sensations of hurt. Not to mention weariness." She turned and looked back at the hill, drooped. "I'm only three and I don't have any travel powers yet." But she started back up the stone steps.

The dragon curled up and settled into sleep. Lathyr gauged whether Kiri could ever make it by the dragon. He glanced at the cheat sheet. "Do you have invisibility to all senses?"

"No. And when can I get a travel power, and what power will it be?"

"Ah." He studied the sheet. "You should be able to see the list of potential powers on a card in your pouch."

"Oh, all right." She shrank the staff to the length and thickness of a pencil and put it behind her ear. Interesting. Reading her own sheet, she said, "Oooh. It's teleportation as far as I can see. Wow. And at level eight. Bummer. I don't suppose you'd care to tell me which trail I should take at the top of the hill."

He looked at the one to the Earth Palace, easy and with jewels and weapons and rest at the end, then the other to a door that opened on a series of tunnels, with increasing levels of tough opponents, considered who he was talking to. "Take the one straight down the hill to the Twisty Caverns."

"Fine."

Jenni and Lathyr dragged Kiri out of the game for lunch before she was ready. They had gourmet sandwiches in a large conference room looking east over the plains. Still plenty of green in the city, though there was a touch of autumn color on some trees and the ever-present dried yellow and brown shrubs and grass.

Between bites, Kiri first enthused over the game, watching from the corners of her eyes to see any indication that she was doing good…or bad. She'd only been defeated a couple of times, which, for her and a new game, was a record. But Lathyr was sober, as usual, and Jenni smiling, which also seemed standard behavior. So Kiri had no clue how she was progressing, and it would sound too needy to ask after only a couple of hours.

And though she'd planned on bringing up the opening later, she'd already had an idea about minigames in each realm, none of them lasting more than about ten minutes, max.

Jenni listened and recorded her own shorthand notes about the concept on her handheld, then sketched a couple of outlines of the minigames with Kiri. She could only comment on the Earth Realm, but she thought she had a good feel for it already.

At least she had until she was back in the game, sliding down a grassy hill…and being attacked.

She was attacked no more than a few yards from the top of the hill by a group of small creatures.

"Dust!" she yelled, casting the spell the way she'd scatter such dust. The small group of creatures froze…some in odd postures. They continued to glare at her with split-pupiled eyes, the tips of their small and furry triangular ears quivering.

Licking her lips, anxious about how long they'd stay that way before they'd renew their furious attack, she encased herself in her protection bubble, and fumbled at her belt. Just as she touched the jewel, the hologram appeared at the left edge of her vision with a pic of one of the creatures, along with notes. She'd reached the level for that spell.

"Feral prototype brownies," a tinny, mechanical voice stated in her ear. That voice needed fixing, too.

"Very minor threats to a dwarf, though when ired, can be deadly to humans and Dark minions." What were Dark minions?

"Particularly dangerous when in a group of ten or more." Kiri counted, eight. Her breath sifted out.

"Minor Earthfolk can be commanded by the major Earthfolk, dwarves. Excellent servants to all elemental folk—Lightfolk—and the occasional human."

*"Brownies,"* Kiri breathed. Of course. She pressed her lips together as she studied the group. How to command them? Could she?

Now their ears were flicking back and forth, probably a bad sign. Enough time had passed for her "Dust" spell to relax, and she folded her fingers in as if she was ready to cast the spell again. More than one flinched.

"I could use—" she didn't want a servant "—help on my journey. Of a brownie or two."

A couple sneered. Two more shook their heads. It appeared as if the dust spell wore off from the top down.

She held her staff braced, and the whole group trembled, gazes glued to the golden stick. "Not going to hurt you." They weren't worth many points anyway, much better if she got a helper. From all the legends about brownies, they could be very useful.

Then their little shoulders twitched and she took a step back. They were thin, and not as tall as she was, but there were still eight to her one. She bet she could swat a couple if they came near.

"We hate you!" One of them cried out in a shriek that nearly pierced her ears, definitely left them ringing.

"Human in dwarf disguise!" One of the larger ones—a male?—sneered.

Then the dust spell wore off. One ran, one jumped in and *bit* her on her wrist where her sleeve had fallen back and she actually *felt* something as if big-time pain hovered.

KIRI YELLED AND SWUNG, AND THE REST TOOK off…except one. It hunched over, but angled up its head and met her gaze. Big brown eyes stared into her own, the ears flattened against its round head. Planting her stick in the ground, Kiri stared at the realistic puncture wound.

"You should put some ointment on that," the brownie—browniefem, isn't that what Lathyr had called them?—said.

Frowning, Kiri answered. "I have some healing spells." She touched the jewel in her belt and the mechanical voice recited how to heal herself—gather and emanate the magic from your core to your wound, feel the earth beneath your feet and send the sense of life to your injury.

She did the best she could and it worked!

Huh.

"I like clothes," the female brownie said. "And I like warm campfires, and good foods." She stared at Kiri's pack. "I will indenture myself to you," the brownie whispered.

"It would be good to have your help," Kiri said.

The brownie smiled and showed red serrated teeth. Kiri ran her tongue over her own and found them equally sharp—she didn't know about the color. Wow.

Scuttling a little closer, the browniefem touched the pack. "Are there clothes in there?" she asked pitifully.

Kiri didn't know. "Open it up and take a…shirt…tunic, if you want," she offered.

"You are so generous!" The brownie's fingers moved so fast they blurred, even to Kiri's dwarf vision. The buckles and ties were undone, the clothes unearthed, spread, a shirt chosen and everything tidily packed back into the knapsack in a few seconds.

When Kiri stared from satchel to brownie, the woman was wearing a shirt—that had been altered!—to fit her, in a berry red. Kiri swallowed.

"Could you heal me, too?" asked the creature, holding out thin arms that seemed covered with bites. She glanced aside. "I used much of my magic this morning working for those… *feral* brownies." She spit and stamped her foot on the wet spot, ground it into the earth.

O-kay. "Sure," Kiri said, again gathering, emanating, bathing…sending green magic along the small arms, actually enveloping the whole little woman in green light.

She squealed with pleasure. "This is good! Thank you, thank you, thank you."

"'Welcome," Kiri said, and slid her pack back on. It felt the same weight…light. Clearing her throat, she said, "What's your name?"

The browniefem's eyes slitted and she replied, "You may call me 'servant.'"

"I can't do that." Kiri was horrified. But this was a magical universe, and some of those names had meaning. "I'll call you Tanna." Tan, like brown, with a female type ending.

Ducking her head and smiling, the brownie said, "Thank you. I will call you 'Mistress.'"

"Um, why not call me Mistress K—" Kiri stopped. This was a very odd and real game, enough that she should probably be discreet, too. "Mistress K," she said.

"Yes, Mistress Kay." With a jaunty step, the browniefem strode down the path and Kiri followed after, ready for more adventure.

Jenni's body tensed beside Lathyr's as they watched Kiri accept the brownie as a servant—though the image didn't match the brownies he was accustomed to. These beings' ears were shorter, their faces rounder and their whole bodies furrier. More like caricatures of true brownies.

"How's she going to treat the browniefem?" Jenni muttered. "This wasn't supposed to happen now. She should have been awarded a companion as part of making it to the Earth Palace."

"The Eight wish to determine any leadership abilities immediately," said a musical voice with the timbre of age. "So I, ah, tweaked your story limitations."

Lathyr sent his chair skidding away from the counter, leaped to his feet and bowed low, even keeping his gaze on the floor. He had never been privileged to meet *the* greatest elf in the world, the elven guardian.

"Hi, Pavan." Jenni's voice was high with a stress Lathyr didn't understand.

"Salutations, Jenni." From the dip in the elfman's tone, Lathyr deduced Pavan had bowed to the princess.

"Please, Sir Tricurrent, let us speak face-to-face. My salutations to you."

Lathyr had to deliberately raise his second eyelids that had snapped down in surprise. His "title" had been given to him a century and a half ago by a minor Prince of Air and, as far as he knew, was never accepted or recognized by any Lightfolk. He straightened slowly. "Salutations, Guardian."

Pavan was the epitome of a male elf, tall, slender but with a duelist's musculature, pale skin tone and thin face that would never be considered human, beautifully formed pointed ears, silver hair and piercing bluebell-colored eyes. He didn't appear several millennia old.

But when Lathyr stood straight, he could hardly bear the intensity of the elfman's scrutiny. This one could bedazzle and beglamour him as easily as Lathyr had Kiri, the elf's magic was so ancient and powerful.

Jenni Emberdrake stood tall, hands fisted, expression closed. "Another change. Next time you decide to mess with my work, could you possibly inform me prior to doing so?" Her accent was heavily British, with a hint of Northumberland.

The elf appeared disconcerted, as if he hadn't expected such scolding. Lathyr kept very still.

Again Pavan bowed. "Accept my apologies…Jenni. I was informed of the Eight's request late and you and Lathyr moved quickly with Ms. Palger."

Jenni gave a short nod, but her hair was standing out from her head. Her lips pursed, she seemed to breathe deeply as if she was restraining her temper, then her body relaxed. "Excuse me for snapping at you, Pavan. The Eight's manipulations still rile me, particularly with regard to those they see as lesser, and that manipulation has now shown up in my game."

"I understand," Pavan said, which was more than Lathyr did.

Laughter came from the screen. Kiri and Tanna were walking side by side with lively converse between them.

Pavan's brows dipped slightly as he studied Kiri as dwarfem. "Even as a beautiful dwarf, she exhibits American human values."

"Some Americans," Jenni said. "We aren't all alike."

"She treats the browniefem well, as you do, and as the Davails do."

"The Mystic Circle people values," Lathyr said.

Pavan nodded to him absently, eyes still on the screen. Reflexive satisfaction that he'd pleased a powerful one infused Lathyr.

"Whether or not the Eight were right to have me initiate changes in your story with regard to the leadership factor, the matter has now been raised, with the accompanying questions."

Lathyr's curiosity stirred. "Such as?"

Pavan replied, "How long will she keep the brownie? Does she want companionship on her quests?" He gestured for Jenni to sit, and Lathyr waited until both the others sat before he went back to his chair.

"She'll learn soon enough that her enemies will attack the brownie before they attack her," Pavan said lightly. "That will be a test of her mettle will it not? Will she sacrifice herself to save it? Or sacrifice it to save herself? If it falls, she will also have the chance and the choice to resurrect it from her own magic and energy, but that will weaken her dangerously."

His voice remained light, nearly mocking, but his eyes flickered with storm winds.

"Ethics, and morality," Lathyr said, both concepts that varied from culture to culture, even within the Lightfolk.

"We both know, Pavan, how the current royals have answered those questions, don't we? What they consider to be the right answer under such circumstances." Jenni's voice was tight.

A chill wind seemed to pass over Lathyr. He knew any of

the royals would sacrifice him in a heartbeat if that served their purposes, perhaps even the two powerful people in this room with him. "There is always debate with regard to the needs of the many versus the needs of the individual," he croaked. Usually bad for the individual in Lightfolk terms.

Jenni sniffed.

Pavan smiled and stood. "Watch yourself, Jenni." He inclined his head to Lathyr. "You, too, Sir Tricurrent." The guardian's voice went even lower, softer. "And both of you watch Ms. Palger." Pavan paused. "I am pleased that magic will transform humans. Many are not."

"Any word about Dark ones who might be attacking here in Denver? You know of the flyby over Mystic Circle last Saturday?"

"All have discussed that incursion." Pavan's shrug was graceful. "The remaining Dark ones usually stay in areas of world strife, to feed off the negative energy...and to cause trouble and darkness for their prey. Now they have learned of Denver and the Eight's occasional presence here, no doubt it is tempting to try and kill the Eight."

Lathyr shuddered. The Eight ruled the Lightfolk and elemental powers, danced to keep magic strong and shaped and helpful. Without them, chaos would ensue.

The guardian continued. "We believe the Dark ones have also become aware of the Meld, and perhaps other projects."

"My husband told me that evil might like the Meld. And about that other major undertaking..."

Again the elfman's brows rose.

"Since they'll need my help. Eventually."

Pavan nodded. They both glanced at Lathyr, who attempted to appear innocuous. Jenni looked as if she wanted to ask more questions of the elf, but wouldn't with Lathyr in the room. He wasn't leaving while Kiri was in the game.

Pavan cocked a pale eyebrow. "Yes, they will." He smiled and seemed to be approachable. Lathyr didn't know that he would trust that, but Jenni relaxed again. "If all goes well. The Fire King and Queen are new—" grief crossed Pavan's expression "—and we don't know their stamina or limitations or how their power will grow as they come into their royal personas. So dance rituals are written and planned that will be testing them soon." Another smile, full of affection. "You have grown well into your own rank and status, Jenni, and have caught some of the Eight off balance. They will not want to reveal the weakness of their team to you."

"Heh," Jenni said, grinning back at Pavan, who had done such a good job of soothing and distracting her that Lathyr was wary again.

Then she looked at Lathyr with approval as she stretched, fingers linked and arms up, glanced at the monitor where Kiri battled swamp monsters alone, the brownie nowhere in sight. Kiri sent the last one flying into a swamp with the thump of her wand and phased through elemental colors as the defeat had her reaching the next level.

Jenni spoke again, eyes alight with challenge. "I bet I get my team together faster than the Eight do."

"I would not take that bet," Pavan said. "Both of your teams prosper."

The Fire Princess flushed. "I'm only a member of the Meld Project."

"A very valued member. The Meld team is well guarded? We do not want them to fall into evil claws."

Jenni's delight at a challenge fell from her and she stood like a royal, chin tilted. "Yes, they are well guarded. They live in the new compound." She eyed Pavan. "You and Vikos could stay at the Castle. There's plenty of room."

Lathyr kept his face masklike, though he flinched inside. Of course he shouldn't have expected to have the place on Mystic Circle all for himself. He always had to accommodate himself to others' wishes and orders.

Pavan glanced at him and Lathyr thought the elf saw what he strove to conceal, but the guardian answered Jenni softly. "We prefer to arrive and depart as needed here in Denver, not to stay."

"Oh," Jenni said.

There weren't many who would have the power to repeatedly travel great distances in an eye-blink, but Lathyr reckoned the guardians could do so. The two checks on royal power were greater than any royal, perhaps even any royal couple, though rumor had filtered down that the Air royals and the Earth royals could command each guardian in dire straits. Lathyr wasn't sure he believed that.

"Vikos and I just visited Mystic Circle. It remains safe from all Darkfolk and human evil. Well done, there."

"I have the support of Aric, the dryads who've moved in, the brownies, the firesprite, Tamara Thunderock and the Davails."

"Formidable." Pavan's lips curved.

"Formidable enough." A chin jut from Jenni at Lathyr. "And he will help us in the future with water." Her smile was like a sunrise. "We've been missing water, and now we have him."

The possessiveness in her tone didn't threaten Lathyr so much as please him.

"It's good that you are all guarded." Pavan tilted his head. "Ah, my partner, Vikos, requests that we leave for the Air Palace." Another formal bow from the guardian, from a noble elf to a royal princess. Then Pavan vanished.

Shrieks from the monitor had Lathyr and Jenni pivoting to look.

Kiri was covered in blood and ichor.

"WELCOME BACK," JENNI SAID TO KIRI…WHO WAS glad she hadn't worn her cashmere, since she was damp on her chest and her nape as well as under her arms.

"Thanks." Kiri stood and shook her body out—very aware of unusual pangs. Not her shoulders or her neck or her elbow or the thumb of her mouse hand.

Nope, her wrists that had held and twirled her staff, her fingers that had flicked, her arms that had waved…all ached. And her legs actually felt like they'd done a lot of walking.

She also still felt the adrenaline dump from the last fight, the fury at seeing her brownie fall. Kiri was limp from the use of energy-draining power as she defeated the monsters and resurrected her Tanna.

Steadying her ragged breath, and with what she hoped was nonchalance, she pulled off her visor and gloves. Her hands had really sweated. In the fluorescent light, they appeared as if they were a full shade darker than they had been that morning. She stared and blinked. Because her skin had been darker as a dwarf? Because she'd spent all day in the sun? Couldn't be. She was just seeing things.

Then she glanced at the wall clock, nearly shocked that it was five minutes from the end of the workday.

Thoughts, concepts, comments about the game sizzled through her brain. She'd have to hurry to put them all down. She lunged toward the keyboard, called up the word processing program.

"Kiri?" Jenni asked.

"Sorry, sorry. Gotta get my ideas down now, while I still remember them. You know the toons—the characters? Their graphics need to be a little more refined. Those brownies, I dunno, they didn't look quite right…and the side mishes—missions—for jewels were fun but not very complex…and maybe the way to the Earth Palace should be shorter, especially if this is only a prologue. I dunno, I think a prologue should only be twenty minutes or so, maybe just one element or a smattering of the four…" She continued inputting her ideas as quickly as her fingers could move.

Jenni laughed behind her, and at the side of her vision, Kiri saw Lathyr's long and elegant hand place a bottle of raspberry fizzy water within her reach. At the end of several minutes of fast and furious notes, her words petered out and she saved the document. After a few seconds' hesitation, she dropped the file in the network box for anyone to access. Then she fell forward and had to brace her arms on the desk.

"Kiri?" Lathyr asked.

"Umm." No use, she had to tell the truth. "I guess the excitement got to me."

Jenni chuckled. "Intense, huh?"

Kiri lifted her head and swiveled her chair to face them.

Lathyr stood, calm and sophisticated as ever in his gray silk suit. But after watching him during the day—of course!—it seemed like he wasn't really into his clothes, as if they were just stuff he put on his body. He was expected to dress a certain way and he did, but he didn't buy into the image. She liked that.

She'd love to see him in jeans. But that would probably make him too fine to resist.

Jenni's hair looked a little wild, which cheered Kiri up. "Yeah, intense," Kiri said.

"Sounds like you've got a lot of ideas."

Kiri flushed. "Don't mean to offend..."

"You aren't," Jenni said calmly. "Transformation *is* in the developmental phase, after all."

A big sigh escaped Kiri. "Yeah." She cleared her throat, the business environment beginning to seep into her brain. "Yes."

The door opened and there stood the receptionist, who was a very short and stocky woman—under five feet and looking much as Kiri had in the game as a dwarf. Did they use employees as avatars? That was cool.

Mrs. Daurfin stared at Jenni and Lathyr and sniffed in a superior sort of way. "Cloudsylph wishes to speak to you." The woman's gaze lasered to Kiri and her mouth turned down, almost as if Kiri wasn't even worth a superior sniff. "About this project."

Jenni sprang from her chair and it went rolling to bang against the counter. "This project is important! Just as important as anything else the Eight have going."

But the woman had turned and was marching out with a heavy step that Kiri could actually hear on the thick carpet.

Lathyr stepped toward Jenni, did the half-bow thing, and offered his arm. "Cloudsylph doesn't like to be kept waiting."

"Who does?" Jenni said, then turned to Kiri. "You did an excellent job."

Kiri beamed as the warmth of Jenni's approval washed through her, and noted that Jenni tidied herself, pulling the wrinkles from her shirt before she took Lathyr's arm. She winked at Kiri, a cheeky comment on European manners.

Kiri chuckled and watched them leave. They looked like a beautiful couple, and she was glad Jenni was happily married, and only earlier that year so she was almost a newlywed. Jenni had looked even better with her husband, Aric. And then the back of Kiri's brain kicked in and she wondered who this "Cloudsylph" was. She'd looked up the Eight Corp website and everyone listed on there and there were no "Cloudsylphs."

Frowning, she glanced at the computer, wondered if it had a net connection, or whether Eight Corp was keeping the proprietary game offline. Would it be rude to check out the company online again? Maybe. Her brows dipped. As far as she could recall, Jenni only answered to the CEO of Eight Corp, the game designer was that high up. Lathyr hadn't shown up in the chart at all, but then he was in Human Resources, not Creative Development.

Still, the only person above Jenni was an Alex Akasha, whose bio read like a standard CEO of a big company. Eh, didn't matter.

Kiri stood and stretched, glanced at a small clock on the wall by the door, opposite the computers. Five-thirty. Exhaustion swamped her. She hadn't ever realized how much a day of learning a new game could take out of her. It wasn't only the game, but trying to impress Jenni...and Lathyr. If she hurried now—and she should have taken more stretching breaks, for sure—she could make it to the bus stop four long blocks away and home so she could do her evening walk around the Circle and sit awhile at the koi pond.

No one had said anything about her staying past five, and she'd put in over nine hours, so she should be able to leave. She grabbed her bag and pulled on her jacket and left the small room.

The office was as quiet now as it had been when she'd arrived a little after seven. Her mouth turned down; everyone must have come and gone while she gamed. She drew in a deep breath and her nose tingled at some sort of spicy fragrance. She found herself smiling again and her energy renewed. Great air freshener.

As she passed open offices with large windows facing downtown, she saw the day had clouded over and she grimaced. Her hoodie wasn't waterproof. She should have worn her trenchcoat, but it was shabbier.

Like everywhere else, the reception area was empty.

By the time she reached outside, a nasty wind had picked up and pressed against her as she hurried to the bus stop. Naturally, the bus was late, and she got in just as rain spattered.

"Dammit," someone grumbled. "The weatherman didn't say anything about rain today."

Kiri was making her way down the aisle that smelled of wet people and wool and dirt-turning-to-mud when thunder roared and lightning seemed to crack just ahead of them.

Slashing sheets of rain hit the wide windshield, covering it and the struggling wipers. The bus jolted and Kiri toppled sideways.

"Watch where you're going!" a heavy guy in a pristine raincoat snapped.

"Sorry."

She crammed into the corner of the last row, stared out the

gray window and saw nothing but running water beyond the condensation, even though the bus crept along. She'd traveled the route long enough to judge when they were crossing the bridge over the Platte River and then the highway. The bus made the sharp turn into a hilly neighborhood, highway below.

A crack of thunder. Lightning struck the bus!

It tipped and she was flung down, people atop her. Yelling. Screaming. The crack of glass and the smell of gas.

She struggled to get up. Struggled to help.

Lathyr was staring out at the sunlit wide plains and paying attention to the King of Air, Cloudsylph, as he relayed the doubts of the other, more conservative, royals about the game project, when he *knew* Kiri was in danger.

He jumped to his feet and the king stopped midsentence.

"Kiri Palger! Danger." Stretching his senses, he could *feel* a heavy, unnatural rain to the northwest.

Cloudsylph's expression changed from annoyance to concern. He tilted his head and his beautiful elven features hardened. "An evil, great Dark one, and monstrous shadleeches and weather magic."

"What!" Princess Jindesfarne stared at the dwarfem receptionist. "What's Kiri doing out on her own? Didn't you call a car for her?"

The woman rolled her shoulders with a movement like a landslide and pursed her lips. "I was not informed."

Cloudsylph frowned at her and she shrank back.

Aric said, "You *were* informed that Dark ones have recently become aware of us, and this building, that we might be a target—we and anyone who works here."

"Which includes Kiri Palger," Jenni snapped. Her head angled like Lathyr's and Cloudsylph's, toward the weather disturbance. She shook her head. "I dare not use the Dark one's lightning to travel."

"Air transport is not as quick as water in these circumstances," Lathyr said to the king. He disintegrated into mer mist—water, mer, cloth—and *stretched* to the farthest raindrop and *flicked.* And stood along a drop-off, being drenched. Looking up, he saw massive shadleeches—the last in the world and obedient to a Dark one. They herded the clouds, setting off and directing lightning at a bus lying on its side—a bus close to an incline that dropped to the busy interstate highway.

People were screaming, some fallen across the outside windows.

*"Stay inside!"* Lathyr yelled. "It's safer inside!" He projected his voice, but not many paid attention. Being outside the bus, against the metal during a Dark one–directed lightning strike was a sure way to be executed. He ran to slumped and singed limp bodies. A couple of people were dead. The uniformed driver was motionless.

"Kiri Palger!" he yelled. He wanted to connect mentally with her, thought they might have enough of a bond for him to speak to her telepathically, but that could scare her more.

"Here!" she called.

"Stay inside!" Through the broken windows he saw people thrashing around in the bus. Kiri was helping others get their bearings, wrapping a cloth around a man's bloody head, urging him to rest.

She was alive. Thank the great Pearl.

"Gas!" she yelled.

He blinked, not quite understanding.

"Gasoline! Petrol!"

His heart just stopped. Another lightning bolt hit the bus…

and the shadleeches, invisible to humans, began to shove it over the bank.

"Stay inside."

"You're crazy!" a woman yelled.

"Don't!" Kiri shouted.

But the woman began to crawl out the window. Lightning struck again and her body jittered, lay still.

He spotted the pool of gasoline, close to Kiri's position, showing greasy rainbows, a liquid easy for a mer to separate from rain puddles. Gasoline or shadleeches. The rocking wasn't too quick yet—maybe he had time.

Running to the petrol, he stood in it, suctioned it up through his shoes into his body. Bad, bad feeling. He flung out his arms.

Sirens sounded, loud, insistent. Humans coming—police or fire, didn't matter. He couldn't save everyone, couldn't explain. He sent the gasoline through his molecules, and through his fingers *shot* the noxious stuff toward the shadleeches—one, two, three! More lightning and they flamed, shrieked in and out of his hearing. Sizzled. Died. Crumpled into bone-and-flesh bundles half-in and half-out of this dimension.

Another bolt hit a fraction before his toes. Not enough petrol to burn, he'd taken it all inside himself. Sickness, unconsciousness threatened.

"Good job," said the King of Air, Cloudsylph, standing dry as it rained around them. His glance swept the shadowy mounds of dead shadleeches. The king stared at the bus then peeled it open with a wave of his hand. Thunder roared, reverberated, as he smacked clouds together, crushing the remaining shadleeches.

The rain stopped, automobiles with flashing bars skidded to a halt on the street and the highway below.

Kiri stood, sopping wet, on the side of a seat, staring at him and the king. Lathyr wanted to speak but the filthy effects of the petrol poisoned him.

Then the king grabbed him and they were gone, to the pool of the Castle at Mystic Circle. The balanced elements eased him slightly.

Cloudsylph shouted mentally, "Queen Greendepths to me!"

Lathyr's control gave out and he fell into the pool, knew he would separate, perhaps into too many droplets and be lost to death. His last thought was that the King of Water would be furious that his queen would be tending to Lathyr.

Water filled his lungs, his ears, his eyes and in between his molecules.

Kiri stared at the spot where Lathyr, looking gray-skinned and sick, had been. He was gone. So was the guy who'd been slightly taller than he, white-pale and with pointy ears. And who was dry.

She rubbed at her eyes, her bangs dripping water down her face. No more smell of gas. She must have overestimated that danger. Too many movies where vehicles blew up, though lightning striking gasoline couldn't be good.

No more bone-rattling thunder, no lightning and the rain seemed to be slacking off. No, it was simply gone and the clouds high and white and showing sunny undersides. That was Colorado, sudden weather.

"Kiri!"

Wiping a wet arm across her face, Kiri settled her work-bag strap across her body, and stepped down to the side of the bus that was now the floor, the width was still wider than she was tall. She was the last one in the bus, and she thought she recognized Jenni Emberdrake's voice. Kiri picked her way toward where the bus had broken open. How had that happened? Then she saw the end of the bus was hanging in air and the drop-off was a steep hill leading to I-25 southbound. Just the sight made her heart race again.

"Here, miss, grab hold," she thought a fireman said. Her ears still rang with thunder and cracking lightning and screams and sirens.

He stood on a jutting piece of metal that was now the top of the bus and had a harness on and looked safe and solid and wonderful. She leaned out and he grabbed her arms, then her torso. "Thanks!"

He nodded. "You're welcome." He set her aside and shouted, "Anyone else?"

"No, I'm it." That was pretty much all she knew. Her mind didn't seem to be working. Especially not if she'd seen Lathyr, then didn't. A horrible smell wafted in the air and she shuddered, and couldn't stop.

"Here, Kiri." That *was* Jenni Emberdrake. Kiri stumbled to her. People were huddled together under space blankets, cops were taking notes, firemen were working around the bus and one of the news trucks pulled up. A disaster area.

Kiri rubbed her head, then saw a body bag out of the corner of her eye. "No!"

But it was "yes." She'd helped but not enough. She realized the awful smell was burned person. Not something she'd ever forget.

Death surrounded her.

"LET'S GET YOU HOME," JENNI SAID.

"Shouldn't I talk to the cops?" Kiri said vaguely.

"Do you want to? Is there anything you can say that others can't?"

"No."

Jenni nodded, opened the door to a gleaming black car, and Kiri ducked inside. She didn't slide so well on the warm leather seat, though.

"We'll head for the Castle," Jenni said.

"What Castle?" Shouldn't she know? Her thoughts felt thick, dull, slow. Slower since she'd gotten into the car.

"Mystic Circle's Castle."

"Oh. Why?"

"We're gathering there. Lathyr lives there now."

Kiri wasn't about to mention that she thought she'd seen the guy and he'd disappeared. "Oh."

"Are you all right? Maybe we should get you looked at."

"No, I'm fine." Kiri wasn't sure.

And when Jenni took her hand a spark jumped between them and Kiri strove to stay conscious.

"Is she all right?" a deep voice asked from the front, Jenni's husband, Aric.

"I put her under." Jenni sighed.

Did Jenni think that? How could she believe she could slip Kiri into unconsciousness? But the effort to comment was too difficult. Jenni pushed Kiri's wet hair back from her face, drying it as she did. Felt really good. Kiri moaned.

Jenni said, "It didn't take much. We'll have a healer look at her."

Aric said, "Sounds fine. Queen Greendepths is at the Castle."

Queen Greendepths. Kiri must have fallen asleep and the bus and everything was all a game. That would be good.

She awoke as she was placed on a comfortable leather couch, and grabbed Aric's hand, scanned his serious-as-usual face, then her gaze went to her filthy fingers clutching his well-manicured ones. "It wasn't a game, was it?"

"No."

"People died."

He clenched his jaw. "Yes. We didn't anticipate—" His mouth clamped shut.

Horror invaded her. She sat straight, feeling every bruise. "You didn't have anything to do with this! Eight Corp?" How could that be?

His fingers grasped hers and his green gaze was steady. "No. We didn't."

"Oh." She shook her head. "Of course not." She looked wildly around for her bag—there it was, smeared and dirty and sad. "I need my phone." She pointed a forefinger at her tote. With an efficiency of movement Aric handed it to her.

Her calendar popped up with "Fairies and Dragons in one-point-five hours with Mystic Circle Gang." She swallowed hard. That wouldn't happen, but she had to at least sound calm when she called Shannon and Averill. She scrolled to the schedule they'd given her. They'd be out all evening at another tour of the birthing facilities. That was good, and the center was southwest, so they should completely miss any traffic problems. But she wasn't sure when they might hear of the accident. They *would* know it was a bus that she might have taken home.

Kiri coughed her tears away and wiped her face on the arm of her hoodie, sucked in a deep breath and tapped to connect to Shannon's number. Went straight to voice mail. Another blessing. "Hey, it's Kiri. First, I'm absolutely okay and home, don't worry! Yeah, there was a bus accident and I was on it, but am really fine. You have a good look at that birthing center. Don't call, 'cuz I want to soak a long time in a bath and then go straight to sleep. Love and smooches to Averill. Bye."

Jenni walked in. "Do you want to go home? We'd like you to stay here for the evening, for company and—"

"Observation?" Kiri asked.

"Yes. We promise to keep you warm and feed you and have someone look at your bumps and bruises."

Kiri looked around at the luxury, thought of the three pieces of furniture in her living room, her high-tech computer setup and the cheap futon in her bedroom.

"There's a spa tub in several of the rooms," Aric said.

"Sold," Kiri said. She rose from the couch and felt creaky and cruddy, glanced down at her clothes. Her fav Fairies and Dragons tee that she'd hate now. Tears leaked from her eyes.

"Amber will get more clothes from your house."

"Thanks. Don't want these, ever again." Kiri plucked at her hoodie. Her voice was croaky, too. Creaky, croaky and cruddy, what a mess she was.

"Come along." Jenni put her arm around Kiri and she didn't mind leaning on the taller woman. "How's Lathyr?" Kiri asked.

"He's fine," Jenni said.

"That's a lie." Somehow Kiri knew it, too much concern in Jenni's voice for a man she'd been a shade distant to every time Kiri had seen them together. "Oh, my God. Did I just say that out loud? Sorry, so sorry." She wanted to huddle but the only place was against Jenni.

"You're not thinking straight, and no wonder." Now Aric soothed. "Let's get you to a place where you can clean up. There's a tower room with a view of the Circle and your house."

His charm derailed her mind. He picked her up like a child and marched up the stairs and they entered a round room with a tub that gushed out steamy water.

Her memories went fuzzy after that. She thought she recalled looking over dark treetops to the small dark block of her house, and wept again. She barely recalled different clothes and a good, tasty, hearty dinner before she was stuck in the corner of the sofa and fell asleep again.

Lathyr thrashed to consciousness. Not in ocean! His bilungs pumped in fear.

*Easy.* The mental comment was more than a word, a command backed up by a wash of comfort. *You live. You will recover completely.*

The woman—must be a healer—swam into view. Gorgeous. Voluptuous figure, the lightest green skin he'd seen, scale pattern in stunning pale blue, beautiful face with dark green eyes. His heart stuttered.

*He's awake. You've done your duty. Let's go.*

Lathyr recognized that sneer, Marin Greendepths, King of Water. Lathyr backswam until he bumped into the wall of the tank. Tank!

Bubbles frothed from the merfem's lips in a sigh as she swam toward the porthole high in the chamber.

Saltwater tank. Chamber. Memory smashed like a tsunami. He was in the Castle, in Mystic Circle, Denver, middle of the United States, the North American continent.

Petrol! He nearly lost the frame of his tailed merform again at the remembrance of agony.

*Kiri?* he managed, even as his gaze attached to the lush and beautifully patterned tail of the merfem.

She glanced over her shoulder with a sincere smile. *She is well, also. As are the rest of the staff of Eight Corp and Mystic Circle.*

*Let's go!* demanded the Water King.

*On my way, dear. We need to talk a little,* replied the merfem, and knowledge clunked into Lathyr's brain. He'd been tended by the best Waterfolk healer, the Water Queen herself. The king's anger washed toward him in waves. He formed a defensive bubble.

The queen flipped through the porthole, and her hair wafted aside, showing the small points of her ears. Shock rippled through Lathyr. The Water Queen was part elf.

Like he was.

An inimical glare from her mate had him stilling into immobility, then the king kissed his wife deeply, looked into her eyes, smoothed his hand over her hair. *We'll talk. Later.*

The Water royals vanished and Lathyr wondered what punishment the king would think to inflict upon him. And how he could go about learning of the Water Queen's heritage.

*Looks like you made an enemy.* Jenni Weavers Emberdrake looked through the glass window, and he swam close only to see her frowning face.

*He is not pleased I met the queen,* Lathyr said, emotions mixed. Trepidation, curiosity. He did know the new Fire Princess wasn't strong enough to shield him from the Water King's displeasure. The water around Lathyr seemed too cold and he shivered. He'd have to be extremely careful in asking about the Water Queen.

*Marin allows his emotions to rule him more than is wise,* said a crisp telepathic voice, and Jenni's face at the window was replaced by the Air King's, Cloudsylph's.

Lathyr flourished his most elaborately courteous bow.

Cloudsylph's pale lips turned upward at the corners. He inclined his head toward Lathyr. *Well done, Sir Tricurrent.*

Another little jolt, that the Air King recognized and accepted Lathyr's minor title. Perhaps, perhaps, he would survive this contretemps.

*The Water King didn't want you—Lathyr—to meet his queen?* Jenni sounded curious, too.

Cloudsylph shrugged. *A minor matter.*

Lathyr didn't think so. Perhaps his feelings projected too strongly because the king's forehead showed a crease. *I will remind Marin that you did not call for the queen to heal you.*

*Lathyr is a hero!* Jenni's comment snapped with heat.

Lathyr moved back from the window.

*He saved a busload of people!*

Lathyr figured that saving humans meant little to the Lightfolk royals.

*He did well in bringing the battle to the shadleeches and destroy-*

*ing them,* Cloudsylph agreed. *I am not pleased that our building and our people and our projects have been targeted by the Darkfolk.*

Tiring of being in the tank, Lathyr did a stretching swim circling the room to test his health, then exited the tank in his legged form in time to hear Jenni reply.

"So far as we know, it's only one great Dark one."

"So far as we know," Cloudsylph agreed. "I will speak with the other royals regarding these threats—that a great Dark one is in Denver, spying on Mystic Circle and our building and targeting Eight Corp employees. I believe the great Dark ones and their minions are more dangerous than we originally thought." With a background as a warrior, the Air King would tend to think that. The royal caught sight of Lathyr and gave him a slight inclination of his torso. "As I said earlier, you did well."

Lathyr bowed again. "Thank you, Your Highness."

The king's light blue gaze went to Jenni, who'd retreated from the puddles of the water corridor to the main room. "The transformation project is third on our list of priorities, but it *is* important. There is no sign that Lightfolk fertility has suddenly increased with the advent of more magic in the world. So to keep our numbers up and the power we wield strong, we remain in favor of Princess Emberdrake's current solution to the problem of increasing the Lightfolk. I will remind Marin of this." A brief but wide smile flashed across Cloudsylph's face, and he sent Lathyr a glance before looking at Jenni again. "I believe I can convince Marin that Sir Tricurrent's status as a staff member to you, Princess Emberdrake, is punishment enough for discomfiting the Water King."

There was meaning sighing behind the Air King's words, but Lathyr couldn't grasp it yet.

He bowed. "I thank you."

Jenni snorted. Then she stared at him. "You're still looking a little puny. I'll send the brownies over with a feast—" she slid her gaze to Cloudsylph, smiled "—fit for a Water King, and then you, Lathyr, should spend the night in the pool or something." She waved grandly as if she thought that was a royal gesture.

He bowed to her, too, and didn't feel too steady on his feet.

With one last nod, the Air King disappeared.

Jenni's breath whooshed out.

"Kiri?" Lathyr asked.

"She's okay. She was a little confused, and after I put her to sleep, she might be more confused, since I blurred her memory some, for her own sake as well as ours." Now Jenni looked grim. "The television newscasters are all over the damn incident. A couple of the channels are starting investigations. I guess they think the driver of the bus should have pulled over or something, poor bastard. He's dead."

"How many more?"

"Rush hour, bad storm, so the bus was packed before it left downtown. Six."

Anger stirred inside Lathyr. He hadn't spent much time in human company for a while, but the ones he knew, he liked.

"Anyway, Kiri will probably remain confused until she is transformed." Jenni's lips flattened. "Game can get mixed up with reality, you know."

"You think she can be transformed and will choose to be," he said.

"Don't you?"

"She certainly has the greatest potential I've seen."

"She did fabulously well today." Jenni's eyes narrowed, she crossed her arms and her fingers drummed on her opposite biceps. "So Transformation is number three of a priority. You don't know why the Water King would be mad at you?"

Lathyr considered his words. Enough to give her a push in the right direction, but be discreet. "He is not pleased that I came to the attention of the Water Queen."

"Why not?"

"Because she also has a mixed nature, I believe. She has pointed ears, so she must have a tiny thread of air elemental in her bloodline. I didn't know that before tonight. I thought all of the Eight royals had to be fully one element."

"Huh," Jenni said. "Amber's the genealogist. I wonder how she'd feel about setting up a Lightfolk database. Or the old elf scholar, Etesian, might know something." Then Jenni scowled. "You're weaving on your feet. Go to bed—to the pool."

"Kiri is here." He felt her.

Jenni raised her brows. "Yes, she is. Fully human Kiri. You're still in legged-mer form. Can you change to fully human and dress yourself?"

Lathyr cringed at the thought. He didn't want human lungs or skin. He didn't want cloth coverings. The effort it would take to change and maintain the form in Denver's dry air would be great. He turned and walked away, disappointment at not seeing Kiri in every lagging step to the pool.

Kiri sat in the drawing room of the Castle, near the fire, supposedly warming up. Though she was dry, the chill of fear still permeated the marrow of her bones as she considered what might be true and what false.

Lathyr had been hurt. She was sure of that, though not the why or how. Just that he'd done something during the whole bus situation that had helped her and the others, but had hurt himself. Tears for him clogged her throat. She pummeled her memory, but she'd missed something and her recollection of details remained foggy.

Yet, she shivered as the atmosphere around her seemed to tremble. She wouldn't have thought the place would have drafts, but apparently so.

Jenni came to Kiri much later, as she dozed propped up in the soft corner of the fat leather couch.

"Kiri?"

"Yeah?" Her voice was hoarse from smoke…and screaming.

Sitting next to her, Jenni reached out and took her hands. Warm hands as always and for once Kiri just figured that Jenni's body ran naturally warm. Felt good, though. "Do you want to continue with the project?"

KIRI BLINKED. "IS SOMETHING REALLY WRONG with Lathyr? Can't he go on?" This time her voice cracked as it went high. Her insides squeezed with fear for the man.

Jenni's smile reassured. "Lathyr's a hero. And he should be fine by morning."

Clearing her throat and blinking more, sniffing hard, Kiri said, "Good, that's good." She wiggled in the soft cushions to sit up straighter, then tried a smile, but thought it went a little wonky. "It's been a long day—" She looked at the clock on the fireplace mantel, 1:00 a.m. "A long day and a night, but, yeah, I want to continue." Logic coagulated back into her brain. "I only have two workweeks. That's only two and a half days per elemental realm." She nodded. "Gotta do it."

Jenni sighed. "Good, I was hoping you'd say that, though I do have a couple more conditions." She raised a finger before Kiri could get words out in protest. "You don't take the bus to or from Eight Corp. We have a driver and he'll take us to work…or if I have to be there early, like I do tomorrow morning, the driver will take you and Lathyr to work. No more buses."

"Huh." Kiri shrugged, and movement hurt. From the unaccustomed gestures during the day of spell-casting? From the accident? From sleeping upright? "Okay, if you say so, I'll go with a driver."

"I do say so." Jenni stood and drew Kiri up, too. The woman was strong. "Now go home and get some sleep. The driver will pick you up at seven-thirty tomorrow morning, and I'll expect you in the computer room at eight."

"Sure. Good night."

"Good night, Kiri." There was a load of feeling in Jenni's tones—affection, respect…other stuff Kiri was too tired to sort out. It was going to be a short night. She opened the door and cold moonlight shone on wet stone steps and the asphalt of the street, silvered some of the soaked bushes and trees in the park. The koi would be quiet and sleeping, not that she'd be able to see them anyway.

The scent of a damp autumn night came to her, something she'd smelled for years, and it was reassuring, replacing harsher scents that had coated the insides of her nostrils, smoke and gasoline and oil and lightning-strike.

Her jacket was a little too thin for the hour and she hurried home, opened the door and fell into bed.

Shannon and Averill woke Kiri at six, pounding on her door and bringing her favorite breakfast from a local place—an egg on a waffle, complete with syrup—and it was still hot.

Seated around her card table, her friends listened to her about the accident, and asked a few questions. Shannon was pale. Averill's brown eyes were dark and intense, examining her to make sure her mental health was good or he'd haul her off to see his mother, who was a shrink—the threat they'd made when they came in.

"You didn't know anyone on the bus?" Kiri asked.

"Only you," Averill said shortly, curving his fingers around Shannon's hand. "Thanks for letting us know you were safe."

"Of course I would," Kiri said, at the same time Shannon said, "Of course, she would."

Averill sucked in a breath and his face hardened. "My family isn't close and sometimes forget to tell us things."

"You would have worried," Kiri said.

"How are *you* doing?" Shannon hesitated, then said, "I hear that the city and the bus company are offering counselors for victims."

"I'm not a victim!"

"They didn't mention you on the news," Shannon said. She gave a weak smile. "Good job."

Kiri swallowed. "To be honest, Jenni Emberdrake showed up and I got in her car and she drove me home." Well, nearly. "I didn't stay to talk with the cops." Kiri fought incipient nausea. "You think I should?"

"You have anything important to tell them?" asked Averill.

She shook her head. "I don't think so. I was in the back of the bus. Rain, lightning, the bus turned over. I helped out in the chaos as I could."

"Stupid people climbed out on the damn metal bus during a lightning storm." Averill shook his head.

"There was the smell of gas."

"Oh."

A small silence enveloped them as Kiri stared at them and they at her.

"You look okay," Shannon said doubtfully.

"I didn't see anyone hurt more than a scalp wound," Kiri said. She wasn't going to mention the smell. Not now, maybe not ever.

Shannon sighed. "Good. That's good. Are you sure you want to go to work?"

"The time is running on my vacation and Eight Corp's evaluation of me for the game—my career." She looked around her empty house. "What the hell would I do here?" There were only so many minutes she could stare at the koi pond.

"You could drive to the mountains and look at the turning aspen," Shannon offered.

Averill snorted, nudged his wife. "Hello, dying leaves? Coming winter. Depression, anyone?"

Shannon winced. "Oh. I didn't think of that."

"Best if Kiri stays busy, and with something new to distract her," Averill said.

"Um, how are you getting to work?" Shannon asked.

"Not driving." Not that she ever went the way of the bus route. She cleared her throat. "Jenni Emberdrake and Eight Corp will be having a driver take me to and from."

"Good," Averill said. He stood and came over to Kiri, pulled her up and rocked her in a hug, kissed her cheek. "We're here for you if you need us."

Shannon joined the hugfest, warming Kiri when she hadn't known she was cold. "Thanks a lot, I love you two." Since she was shorter than them both, her voice was muffled against Averill's chest.

"Okay, that's settled." Shannon stepped away, swooped up the take-out boxes and the paper plates and dumped them in the trash, quickly washed the plasticware and put it in the dish drainer. "Call us if you need us."

"I will."

"Now we've gotta get to work," Averill said, bussed a kiss on Kiri's temple. "Later." He aimed forefingers at her. "In fact, Sunday, dim sum. Be there at ten-thirty."

Kiri nodded.

They left on the swirl of a cold autumn breeze.

She sighed as the quiet formed around her again. It had been really good to see her friends. Glancing at the clock, she noticed they hadn't given her too much time to brood before the driver came.

She'd eaten a good breakfast—in her bathrobe. Now she dressed in nice jeans and a winter-weight cotton-blend shirt that should be okay with any sweat. Checking the weather on TV, she tensed when the freak rainstorm of the day before and the bus accident and casualties were mentioned, then listened only as far as "sunny weather, in the upper sixties, no rain at all, humidity thirty-four percent."

Kiri got out her computer tablet, and did some freewriting of her feelings, a technique Shannon had taught her to let go of stuff. It usually worked. When she'd drained out some of the grief and fears, she moved on to typing in more notes about the game Transformation as she waited for the car to take her to work.

She wanted to talk to Lathyr. Okay, she just wanted to *see* him, maybe touch him, make sure he was all right. So when the car pulled up to her door, she hurried out and didn't wait for the driver to come around.

The backseat was empty. No Lathyr.

"Ready?" asked the driver. He held the door for her.

She sighed, but her stomach tightened a little. "Yeah." She beamed a smile at him, tried to make it sincere. "Thanks."

"You're welcome."

She slid over on the soft, smooth leather and strapped in,

swallowed. "We aren't going by way of Fifteenth and Central, are we?"

"No, Speer all the way downtown."

"Good." Since he didn't say anything more about the accident that was still heading the news, she thought he was either a huge introvert or had been told not to discuss it, probably the latter.

Jenni and Eight Corp were very efficient, and hired very competent people.

Kiri hoped she'd be one of them.

She didn't see Lathyr until she walked past a formidably scowling Mrs. Daurfin, who only grunted in response to Kiri's "good morning," and into the long and already boring computer room.

"How are you doing this morning?" Jenni asked softly.

"Pretty good," Kiri replied.

"You are well?" Lathyr asked. He looked a little different, and not just his casual trousers with no crease and a fisherman's sweater, both black. Should she have worn black, for those who died? Grief cruised through her, again. She figured that was typical, so she nodded, still staring at him. Something about his skin tone or texture seemed off.

"I'm fine. Are you okay?"

His smile was tired. "I am well enough."

"Okay."

"Are you ready for your next session? Need breakfast?" Jenni asked, a little too heartily.

Kiri flushed. "No, I'm good."

"We've decided to give you a choice," Jenni said, swiveling back and forth in her chair. "You can continue on with your journey to the Earth Palace in the Earth Elemental Realm, or you can choose another for today."

"Air?" Kiri breathed. "I could be an elf?" The day was looking up.

Jenni and Lathyr shared a glance.

"You would prefer that as opposed to fire or water?" Jenni asked.

"Oh, yes!" Kiri set her old and battered tote down and hurried over to the desk and got her gloves. They looked like the shape of her hands—creepy, but she pulled them on, set the visor around her head.

"Here we go," Jenni said. "Countdown to the Air Realm of Transformation, three, two, one."

Winds whirled Kiri around and set her down on a rock surface. She was an elf! For the first time since the bus accident, her spirits lifted and her heart felt—unsmudged. She and Lathyr stood on a craggy cliff side, surrounded by stepped pillars that whistled different notes as the wind caught in the staggered holes.

"Amazing!" she shouted. Yes, being here, in a game she had a chance of controlling, of *creating*, soothed her. Nothing like life where there were uncontrollable things like horrific bus accidents.

One of the pillars had a mirror-shiny side and she admired herself. She was gorgeous, tall and slender, perfectly proportioned, with a fabulous thin face and long platinum hair. Not much breast or hip, but a lovely avatar. She touched the points of her ears and shuddered—they were so sensitive. Positively erotic.

As she fingered her clothing, she scowled, dark blond brows angling down. "Jenni, this stuff is like, like rhino hide or something, all gray and wrinkly."

"It's standard elf armor," Lathyr said.

"Level one armor," Jenni replied at the same time.

Kiri stared at Lathyr. Sure enough, his ears were pointed, like the first time she'd seen him—or as she'd first imagined him, and his face and body seemed slightly elongated—taller and thinner than regularly.

"Are you accompanying me?" she asked.

"No."

Her disappointment was stronger than she'd anticipated. Maybe it was the deep feeling that he *had* been at the scene of the accident, and somehow he *had* helped, at a cost to himself. She couldn't shake that notion, but didn't think either he or Jenni would speak of it.

But this was work. This was her job. And though it was a wonderful job, if she didn't ace the prologue tests she'd have to go back to the one she hated. "Look." With a sweeping motion, Lathyr gestured to the panorama in front of them—hilltops and spires connected with rope-and-wood suspension bridges. Kiri gulped. Normally she didn't have a problem with heights, but it appeared much of the Air Realm, was, in fact, walking through air.

"Elves—people of the air—don't have wings?" Everyone in Fairies and Dragons could earn wings, in fact the whole world was based on flying.

"No," Lathyr said. Another graceful gesture as he pointed to a huge cumulus cloud in the distance tinted with gold and pale pink light and violet shadows. Naturally, there was a tall and turreted castle there. A castle in the clouds.

"Let me guess, I have to get to the Air Palace and present myself to the King and Queen of Air. They're elves?"

He nodded.

She rolled her shoulders. "I've got experience now. Maybe I'll make it to the palace today. Nothing's completely new."

"I have every faith in you," Lathyr said. His smile was subdued.

"Would you like to access your companion now?" Lathyr asked.

"I get one right away?" Another delight.

"Yes, you have proven your leadership skills with your treatment of the brownie, Tanna."

He rapped with his blue-green gloves on the rockface. A whoosh of air shot from the hole just above and a white-violet tiny swirl came out and moved to hover near his shoulder. "An airsprite," Lathyr said.

"I don't get a brownie?" Kiri was outrageously disappointed; she'd really liked Tanna, and this airsprite didn't look at all humanoid.

"Airsprite," Lathyr repeated.

She didn't want an airsprite. She wanted a brownie. Apparently mixing realms at this level wasn't an option. Yet. "Great."

"Call me Airsprite!" said a high whistling voice as the little whirlwind moved in front of her nose, bringing rock dust too close. Kiri sneezed.

It laughed and stretched and the wisps gathered into a rudimentary violet-white head and limbs. Like elves, it had a thin body.

"Hey," Kiri said.

"Heyyy!" it squeaked, again in a high voice punctuated with a whistle. Kiri thought she might get tired of that fast.

"Airsprite will be your guide," Lathyr said.

"Fine," Kiri said. Sure didn't look as if it would be any help in a fight.

Lathyr took one of her limp hands and kissed the back of it, surprising her. His expression held amusement, too, but seemed to also have a little affection…maybe even a caress of attraction. Her heart gave a little bump in her chest and she turned her fingers to squeeze his, being rewarded when his smile bloomed.

"You will do well," he said, and she *felt* his confidence in her.

With a little mental push, she sent gratitude...and affection, back to him. "Thank you."

With a tip of his head he vanished.

"Off we go to the Air Palace," Airsprite squealed.

"Watch out for the banshees," Jenni said.

"Kiri, end of the workday," Jenni warned through the visor as Kiri had just stepped onto the thread-thin invisible bridge to the Air Palace.

"I'm almost there!" Kiri cried.

"All right, but Lathyr and I are needed in the small conference room to report on the project. I've set the server to disconnect you at the end of a half hour. If we aren't back by then, meet us there as soon as you get done, to the left at the end of the hall. We need to discuss things with you."

Kiri fell off the bridge. Her levitate spell failed.

She hit with a splat and watched all but one of her health points vanish.

Damn, she'd have to use the last of her flying spells to get back up, but she did nothing until she heard Jenni disconnect from the program. Maybe Jenni hadn't seen her mistake.

Yeah, right.

Sighing, Kiri began the spell preparations, keeping an eye out for the very nasty banshees. The airsprite whistled encouragement and Kiri hummed so she couldn't hear it.

Lathyr sat straight in his chair, his face expressionless. There were only the three of them in the conference room, Aric and Jenni Emberdrake, and himself. A chair had been left for Kiri.

Jenni had brought her handheld computer that ran on Meld and was logged on to the game to monitor Kiri's progress.

"How is our applicant doing?" Aric asked.

"Really well." Jenni grinned and her hair lifted and snapped with the static electricity of her optimism.

Aric glanced at Lathyr, and gestured to an object on the table that Lathyr finally recognized as some sort of monitoring device, so someone or *someones* were listening in to this report. The dwarfem receptionist, the Lightfolk Meld staff, perhaps even a royal or two.

"Exceedingly well," Lathyr said smoothly, projecting his voice to the monitor. "We are conditioning her to accept her magical potential, and hoping to discover beforetime what element she might be best suited for so that we can ensure her survival during the transformation." He reached over to the portfolio that Jenni had brought with them, glad he'd glanced at her charts, and pulled out the top one that showed Kiri's progress. "If you will note the anticipated learning curve, in green, you will see Kiri's development in the game."

Aric's eyes widened and he gave a low whistle. "Nearly twice as good as you'd wanted."

"That's right." Jenni beamed. "She's an ace student…not that I think she understands that."

"It would be good not to inform her of that," said the voice of the Air King, Cloudsylph, from the monitor.

Jenni hesitated, frowned, then replied, "As you wish."

"Earth was chosen for her as her first element?" asked the royal.

"That's what the program determined her best element might be." Jenni cleared her throat. "The game *is* weighted to steer the applicants toward an elemental form that they might be able to master."

"A dwarf or brownie, then," the Air King, Cloudsylph, said. "Or, since she seems to be a likely candidate for transformation, and she might keep her human mass, a merfem or naiad of water."

"Um, more than likely," Jenni agreed. Her gaze flicked toward Lathyr. He nodded and continued the report.

"I've been observing Kiri Palger during her games," he said. "As she is playing, her mind is being affected by the Meld and magical energy in this building, I believe that she is a strong prospect to be transformed into a true magical Lightfolk being—and, most possibly, into a major Lightfolk elemental."

After a moment, Jenni broke the silence. "So far, she's indicated that her wish is to be an elf."

Lathyr winced.

"Is that at all possible?" asked Cloudsylph, King of the Elves.

"Possible," Lathyr confirmed. "Though I feel...I believe... that her mind in that particular matter doesn't agree with her emotions or her heart...or soul."

"She doesn't have the soul of an elf?" Cloudsylph sounded almost amused.

Lathyr wasn't so stupid as to insult the elf by stating Kiri's emotions were warmer than most elves. "I don't believe so."

"Ah," Cloudsylph said. "Keep me informed."

"We will," Jenni said. "I'm transmitting my files regarding the project to you."

"Thank you," Cloudsylph said. The lights on the monitor flicked off.

Three minutes later Lathyr and Jenni were back in the computer room, watching Kiri bob and weave in her gloves and glasses, fighting banshees—and swearing. The airsprite was whistling encouragement. Kiri was at the far end of the invisible bridge to the Air Palace.

On one of the large monitors, they saw her take down several banshees.

"She is doing very well as that cross between a magic user and melee fighter," Jenni murmured. "Not as strong as a magic-less warrior."

"She likes the magic," Lathyr replied, sensing it from the woman more than seeing it on the screen.

"Indeed."

The last banshee succumbed with a shriek and Kiri ran swiftly and nimbly across the invisible thread bridge and rang the bell on the arched and pointed glass door, the main entrance to the Air Palace.

A distinguished elf answered the summons. "Welcome, Mistress Kay. The King and Queen of Air, the Sylphs of the Clouds, await you." Bells and whistles sounded and jewels clicked into a pile at Kiri's feet along with several scroll spells as Kiri gained two levels. *First Goal Achieved in the game of Transformation! Congratulations!*

She'd done it! Pride surged through Lathyr...and, he thought, affected Kiri as he noted a small bond had formed between them.

"CONGRATS," JENNI SAID.

"Thank you!" Kiri nearly sang as her hips swayed in an attractive manner. "Logging off." Her hands moved in the closing spell, then she took off her visor and smiled at Jenni, then Lathyr. Small tendrils of hair stuck to her temples with perspiration and she seemed to glow with pleasure and excitement.

As she peeled off her gloves, she whisked her lips with her tongue, squared her shoulders and said, "What did you need to talk to me about?"

Jenni raised her brows and gestured to Lathyr.

He said, "You have exceeded our expectations."

"Whew, good to hear." Kiri sat suddenly in her chair, then glanced at Jenni. "I have a couple of requests."

"Yes?" asked Jenni, taking her seat at the end of the counter as usual.

Lathyr decided he shouldn't stand and stare at the beauty in front of him and took his seat next to Kiri's empty one.

Kiri pushed back her damp hair, her face falling into serious lines. "The way we have this set up, I'll have only two days to master each elemental level."

"Two business days, that's right," Jenni said.

Kiri's body tensed and words rushed from her. "Is there any possibility that I can take the software home for the weekend… or, if I need to, come in and work at the game here?"

Lathyr stared, but understood from Jenni's posture that the question hadn't surprised her.

Jenni folded her hands. "You're that interested?"

Kiri nodded. "Oh, yes. The game is fun, but I've made some notes and I want to explore the world more." Her voice got softer and trailed off.

"We are not allowed to have nonemployees on the floor without supervision," Jenni said matter-of-factly.

Kiri's face fell.

Opening a hidden drawer in the counter, Jenni brought out a tablet computer with a tiny piece of hardware in one of the slots, and something that had Lathyr staring again. It looked like a truncated version of a human's idea of a magic wand. Jenni slid the computer down the desk, using mostly magic.

"You can take this. Only the Earth Realm of the game and a notes program are loaded on it. You can make either spoken or typed notes with regard to the world of Transformation."

"Wow." Kiri leaped toward the counter and picked up the tablet, eyes gleaming. "That's wonderful!"

Jenni lifted a finger. "You are not allowed to show the tablet to anyone. No one on Mystic Circle, and no friends of yours."

Kiri swallowed, nodded, though he saw a hint of disappointment in her eyes. "Okay."

"And the computer is connected to our servers, and the servers will be recording the games, as these have." Jenni waved to the monitors. "So be aware of that, and you must agree to have your games monitored and recorded."

"That's fair," Kiri said.

Jenni waved. "All right, we're done for the week." She smiled. "Take some time for yourself over the weekend. Don't play too hard."

"No, I won't. And…I have something else to ask." Again, anxiety flashed through Kiri's eyes.

"Yes?"

"I want you to let me know immediately if I have failed the prologue at any point."

"Beyond redemption?" Jenni asked.

Kiri nodded. "Yes. Please let me know as soon as possible if I wash out of the application process."

"Easier on you if we don't string you along," Jenni said, and nodded. "That's fair, too. All right. Done."

Lathyr stood and offered his arm to Kiri. "Would you allow me to see you home?" As soon as he made the gesture, said the words, he knew his old-fashioned human manners had betrayed him again.

But Kiri chuckled, put the tablet down on the desk only as long as it took to shrug into her jacket and pull the canvas handles of her bag over her shoulder, then slid her arm in his.

Wonderful.

Kiri got a call Sunday morning from Shannon, reminding her they were meeting for brunch at the dim sum restaurant on the west side.

Kiri was deep in the game and grumbled about it, but Shannon insisted. *They* wanted to talk about house hunting. Kiri wanted to continue exploring the game. It had her hooked, even in just the Earth Realm.

Then, of course, Shannon said she and Averill were worried, wanted to check up on Kiri after the terrible bus thing.

But the morning away from the game was just what she needed to get perspective, and Kiri felt really confident that she'd get the job—a buoyancy that reassured her friends.

They all headed out to look at a house Shannon and Averill were interested in, southwest and at least an hour from Kiri when traffic was good.

The place was a charming two-story Victorian with a pretty paint job, large yard, and within walking distance of Shannon's work and a highly rated elementary school.

Kiri made a pitch for the couple to buy one of the empty houses in Mystic Circle, said she'd talk to Rafe Davail about the two he owned, but Averill and Shannon just shook their heads, so Kiri had to let it go.

Monday, at Jenni Emberdrake's request, Kiri loaded one of the Earth Realm characters she'd developed over the weekend into the main game computer and played her. The toon was a configuration that Jenni hadn't anticipated and the woman was full of praise.

It was also great to see Tanna the brownie again.

Tuesday and Wednesday Jenni requested Kiri explore the Air Realm thoroughly. She nailed it and even led a team Jenni had provided with no losses.

Though Kiri loved being an elf, she wasn't too fond of the realm itself, or the spells, and she really, really loathed the banshees. Not to mention the airsprite.

Kiri thought she was doing fine, had the job, the career she wanted, in the bag. Though she had noted that the energy drain increased and a few odd things continued to happen, like sore muscles, a bruise on her knee when she fell down a bank. Had she fallen in the room, too?

Yes, she was sure she was doing well. Until she reached the Fire Realm on Thursday. With Jenni Emberdrake.

She made it fifteen minutes at the max before dying. Ten times. She'd even tried a couple of missions on her own after Jenni and Lathyr had been called to one of their meetings. Then Kiri'd just given up and requested—and got—permission to leave by email. She felt like she'd slunk out with her tail between her legs, her dreams smashed.

Kiri fumbled her key card and keys as she unlocked her front door, grunted as she kicked it behind her, and dropped her bag, hoping she didn't have anything in it that would break. Her mind was so fried with exhaustion that she couldn't recall what was in her tote.

All she wanted was bed, but as she shuffled toward her bedroom, passing her computer set up in the window, big red letters seemed to pop in front of her eyes, as if she still wore the visor. "It's THURSDAY." Thursday. She was scheduled to play Fairies and Dragons with Shannon for an hour, then hook Shannon in with the Mystic Circle group team.

For a minute Kiri wondered if she could log on to her online email account after turning off her monitor, her eyes throbbed so at the idea of looking at more bright light. The firespells had really done a number on her optic nerves. Squinting, she got to the mail, composed.

To: Gothicperky. Sorty cn't makee tonigght. Gam wiped me tt. Love, Kii.

With a few last lunges, she made it to bed and fell facedown onto the futon. OWIE! Whimpering, she passed out.

"Kiri, Kiri, wake up!" The voice was Shannon's. Hell, Kiri wasn't going to be late to class *again*, was she? She had to stop the last-minute wee-hours essay writing.

"Yo." She jackknifed up and moaned as every muscle in her body protested the movement, then blinked at the bright light. Bright light, dark night. Pale yellow walls. Bedroom. Her bedroom in Mystic Circle.

"Kiri." Shannon sat down onto the bed next to her. "Oh, Kiri, you look bad. How on earth did you get so sunburned?"

"Fire Realm?" Ouch, her dry lips cracked open. Damn.

"Doesn't look like virtual burns to me," Shannon said tartly.

"Seriously, Kiri, you look like shit," Averill said from the doorway. He was holding a sopping washcloth that dripped water onto Kiri's wood floor.

She held out an imperious hand for the plush terry square. "Thanks a lot. Gimme."

But Shannon intercepted the cloth and dabbed at Kiri's face. Cool, delightful, soothing water.

Kiri whimpered again, her mouth felt better. "Thanks."

"We haven't heard from you often enough," Shannon scolded. "And you misspelled your email. You don't do that. Oh, your poor eyelids, they look swollen."

From the inside out, they felt swollen, too.

"Figured you were working too hard on the game," said Averill with a grin and a wink. He tended to be a workaholic. "We brought Thai food."

"Nom," Kiri said reflexively, just as her stomach rumbled. She sniffed and, sure enough, smelled Pad Thai. Her mouth watered. "Lemme grab a shower, and you're always bringing me food, lately."

"It's the nesting mother, here." Averill walked over and kissed the top of Shannon's head.

Shannon said, "All right, you can have a shower. But I'm sitting on the toilet seat to make sure you don't fall."

"Most household accidents take place in the bathroom. We'll

be babyproofing ours to the nth degree," Averill said cheerfully. "I'll set up the card table and stuff."

After a cool shower, Kiri felt much better, but still put on her oldest, softest sweats before she sat down on a folding chair with a plateful of rice noodles and chicken with peanut sauce... including real peanuts.

Shannon still frowned at her as she ate. "What happened?"

Since Kiri had a little time to think about it, she offered a logical explanation. "I had a long lunch break and ate on the top of the building. Fell asleep. Got sunburned."

Shannon shook her head and tsked.

Averill paused with a forkful of twined noodles. "I think you should have stuck with the Fire Realm injuries, myself. More exotic."

"Yeah?"

Lips pursed, Shannon scanned her. "You weren't moving well, either. Sitting at a desk so long isn't good."

"Nope," Kiri said. Neither was getting trampled on by a few heavy, muscular djinn, but her body felt like that had happened.

"But, other than that, how's it going?" Averill grinned.

Kiri deliberately relaxed her shoulders that had tensed and risen again, and grimaced. "I don't know. I did okay for a newbie in the Earth Realm, then went back and nailed it, complete with a companion and a team." She smiled, then took the lip salve from Shannon and rubbed it on her mouth. "I think I was above average in the Air Realm." She sighed. "But I really wiped out in the Fire Realm."

"Today?" Shannon asked sympathetically.

"Yeah." Kiri wiggled her shoulders again. "I don't think I could have done much worse. I suck at being a djinnfem. Just couldn't get the hang of it at all." Hadn't mastered the movements and her spells had misfired more often than not.

"Sort of like Shannon being a squishy ranged magic user," Averill said. "And thus the reason why the game shouldn't assign characteristics. Will they let you repeat, you think, play to your strengths somehow?"

Just the idea of entering the Fire Realm again made Kiri shudder. "After ten times? I don't know."

Shannon pointed a fork at her. "You did all right as a dwarf and…what was air, elf?"

"Yes."

"Surely all of the realms must be visited by every form of magical elemental critter," Shannon said. "Maybe you can redo fire as a dwarf or elf."

Kiri let the tang of good food explode in her mouth, comforting. Just eating was helping with her attitude—when she didn't remember lying facedown on tiles and djinn running over her poor body, mashing it. "That would be good."

"What did Jenni Weavers say?" Shannon asked.

"Just looked appalled, at first," Kiri managed between mouthfuls. She didn't want to admit she'd been a little cowardly and hadn't hung around. Cowardly, yes. Human, yes. She'd have to do better, though.

"So Weavers might be better at fire than any other element," Averill said.

"I hadn't thought of that." Kiri drank the iced tea they'd ordered for her.

"And her being good at fire doesn't necessarily mean that you should be," Shannon said.

"True."

"And you still have the last element, right? And you're learning as you go—"

Averill took over, "And the last element is water, so if you sucked large at fire, maybe water will be easy-peasey and you could ace it." He grinned. He was one amazingly handsome guy with the light brown skin and dark brown eyes and black hair; Kiri had always thought so. But now Lathyr's paleness seemed to be more of her standard for men. She winced at the thought that she hadn't seen him before she left, either, but she hadn't wanted to face a man she was beginning to have feelings for with failure in her eyes.

Yes, changes were happening.

"Thanks for the support," Kiri said.

"You're still one of the best game writers I know," Averill said. "Don't give up."

"Don't give up," Shannon said at the same time as her husband, and they shared a smile.

"I was creamed," Kiri said, then, "Nope, I was fricasseed, in the Fire Realm." And she was glad she'd managed to find the humor in the situation.

The others laughed and she rose with only a few twinges of her abused body and cleared the paper plates. They'd demolished the meal. "So, thanks a lot for coming over to check on me."

She blew out a breath, sent Shannon an imploring gaze. "Jenni Emberdrake and Lathyr Tricurrent promised to let me know immediately if I washed out of the program." Kiri pressed her lips together, then sent a stare in the direction of her workbag. "I didn't hear my phone. Can you check it in my tote? And my email, too?" Pitiful that she didn't want to look herself, that she was using her friend to find out and face the music. Her pregnant friend.

"Sure." Shannon rose and went toward the door where Kiri's bag was, pulled out her phone. "There's a call here from Jenni Emberdrake." Shannon walked back with Kiri's phone.

Kiri had to drink some iced tea before she had enough spit to answer. "Go ahead and put it on speaker."

Averill reached over and linked fingers with her.

"Hey, Kiri, I guess you're exhausted, right? Probably don't want to play Fairies and Dragons tonight?" The woman sounded way too cheerful. "I know you were going to introduce your friend to us, so if you get this voice mail tonight, have her message me in the game to my DevGem handle."

"Oooh." Shannon's eyes gleamed and she pressed Kiri's phone to her breasts. She did a little prancing around. "DevGem is *Jenni Emberdrake!* And I'll be on her team." Shannon pumped her fists.

"Aren't we supposed to be checking to see if Kiri still has a shot at the new job in Transformation?" Averill asked.

Shannon grinned. "Oops. But she wouldn't offer this to me if she was going to dump Kiri, would she?"

"Jenni's a really nice person," Kiri said.

Averill slanted Kiri a glance. "Not so nice that she'd keep on an incompetent."

"No other messages," Shannon said.

Averill shoved his chair back, flexed his fingers and went to Kiri's computer, opened her email account. "What's your password?"

"Capital *R,* lower case *e-x-x-a,* same word, capital *R,* lowercase *e-d,*" Kiri said.

He glanced at her. "You got an offer for half off at Shout! restaurant and didn't let me know?"

"Grrr. Is that all?"

"All. Nothing from Jenni Emberdrake or that guy from human resources or Eight Corp." Averill shut down the program. "Your eyes still look terrible. Go back to bed."

Relief dropped from Kiri so fast and hard that if she'd been a dwarf, rock would have crashed off her body. Kiri squinted at him. "But you have news." Finally she was concentrating on someone other than her poor, pitiful, selfish self.

Shannon crossed to Averill and slipped her arm around him, then they both beamed at Kiri. "We bought the house."

"You bought the house." Kiri sat suddenly. They were really moving far across town from her. She put cheer in her voice. "The one close to your work."

"Yup," Shannon replied. "I can walk to work, and Averill is getting more work-at-home days so he can take baby to the wonderful park that's close."

"Awesome! I am *so* happy for you."

Shannon hugged her tentatively, keeping pressure off Kiri's skin, though that felt much better. "And I've got a good feeling about this career for you." With a smacking kiss on Kiri's cheek, Shannon stepped back, waved the phone before putting it on the table. "Now we gotta hustle to get back home and log on to Fairies and Dragons and hook up with the Mystic Circle team. Since you're going to be off tonight, can Averill take your slot?"

Averill rubbed his hands. "Good idea."

Kiri looked at her computer setup. "Sure." She shook her head. "Nope, I don't want to play tonight."

"Great, I mean take care of yourself." Averill gave her a soft kiss on the cheek and he and Shannon left.

Kiri cleaned up the dinner, took the trash out, then folded up the card table and stashed it in the closet.

Her bare home was pristine again, but didn't have the same feel as even a few short days ago. Change had come and more was imminent.

Shannon and Averill were moving away, and not only physically. Transformation was affecting Kiri in odd ways that she didn't want to acknowledge—like being able to feel her face pressed against hot tile in the Fire Realm, or the pounding of boots on her body.

*Couldn't be!* But amorphous fears lurked in the back of her mind.

She went to her chair-and-a-half and huddled in it. Her life was spiraling out of control again and she didn't like it.

A knock came at her door and she straightened. Almost, almost, she thought she *sensed* Lathyr there.

Just logic. Unlike many of the inhabitants of Mystic Circle, Lathyr wouldn't be at his computer and playing Fairies and Dragons.

So when she opened the door, she wasn't surprised to see him.

SHE WOULD *NOT* PLAGUE LATHYR WITH WORRY-questions about her job.

He dipped his head. "Hello, Kiri. You left while we were in a meeting and I came to see how you were doing."

She was very aware that an exceedingly empty house was behind her itchy shoulder blades, not at all like the luxurious comfort of the Castle he was living in. There was no help for it, she stepped back. "I'm doing all right. Would you like to come in?"

"Thank you." He walked in with an easy glide that reminded her of how the elves had moved.

"I don't have much." She gestured to the chair. "Please, sit. Would you like some coffee or tea or iced tea?" She shut the door to the cold night air.

"Nothing, thank you." He was staring at her, came up close and took one of her hands in his. Tingles, oh, yes, the guy attracted her. "And you have a lovely house, and whatever you do have in it is your own."

"Yeah."

"And I don't think that you are entirely well since you aren't playing Fairies and Dragons with the rest."

"Oh."

He pushed the sleeve of her sweatshirt up her arm. "What's this?"

She winced. "Just a little burn from the Fire Realm."

"You did not look like this when I left you. You didn't tell me!" He stepped close nearly brushing her body, way within her personal space. Then he set his hands on her shoulders and…somehow, somehow, Kiri *felt* her skin tissues plumping up, easing. Even her muscles felt better. Probably because she really liked Lathyr's hands on her.

On a sigh he stepped back and dropped his hands, scanned her. "Better?"

"Yes, thank you."

"We must know if the game is affecting you, Kiri."

She didn't want to think about that. "Can't be."

He angled his head, opened his mouth and she put her hand on his chest. "Please, let it be for now. I'm tender enough." Her smile was a little wobbly, got even shakier at the gentleness in his look.

Reluctantly withdrawing her hand, she took a leap of faith and broached the matter. "I didn't do well in the Fire Realm."

Lathyr inclined his head. "Not as well as in the other realms, and not as well as expected, but no one believes it is unusual for someone to have a problem in at least one of the realms."

"Oh."

He waved toward her computer setup. "Are you universally competent in Fairies and Dragons?"

She laughed and grinned. "With the right characters, yeah."

"But not with all characters."

Her brows came down. "Not all archetypes can handle everything. The heavy fighters have the best chance, but even then real good magicians can get 'em."

"And you've played Fairies and Dragons for..."

"Years."

"And Transformation for..."

"Days. You've made your point." She sighed, slid a glance at him. "You're looking better than you did at the start of the week, too." Memory of what happened last Thursday night socked her and she flinched.

Lathyr drew her arm within his. "We'll never forget what happened last week."

She wasn't quite brave enough to ask him about his role in saving people in the bus, or how he'd left so quickly.

He said, "You like to watch the koi. Let's go."

"It's dark."

He smiled. "Then we'll walk around the Circle and look at the lights on in the windows and perhaps see people hunched over their computers instead of enjoying the evening. And I will take you to the Sensitive New Age Bean for cocoa."

"Sounds good. Let me get my jacket." She got the bright quilted jacket that would focus attention away from her sweats. Lathyr took it from her and held it for her.

He opened her door, watched as she locked it and took her fingers.

And she couldn't resist any longer. "I guess if you're here and being so nice, I didn't screw up my chances for the job."

His face was serious as he looked down at her. "No."

"Not yet," she amended.

He hesitated, then nodded. "Not yet."

"And since I did so poorly in the Fire Realm, I might do really well in the Water Realm?"

His lips twitched. "Perhaps." They walked north, by the dark and empty Fanciful House. Kiri sighed and grimaced.

"What makes you sad?"

"My best friend and her husband live close." She waved toward the west a few blocks. "And they're moving away. I wish they could have bought one of the open ones in Mystic Circle."

"Rafe Davail controls the dispensation of some property, yes?"

An odd way to put it. "Yes. It's a wonderful neighborhood."

"Indeed," Lathyr agreed.

Kiri moved closer to him, so they brushed legs as they walked. Not as awkward as she'd thought. Though he was taller, Lathyr kept at her own steady pace. And he liked the Fanciful House, something that most regular American guys she knew would look askance at, with the round windows and a couple of turrets.

"Rafe owns it, but he's living with Amber in her house," Kiri said.

"Amber's house is bigger," Lathyr said, "and their yard is more extensive and they have large dogs."

Kiri shrugged and glanced back at the dark house. "And I heard that when Rafe bought it the house was painted peach. It's beige now." That was definitely a guy-change.

They'd reached the next house, the Spanish-influence one owned by Dan and Frank. The porch light was on, and bright light was shining out of a south window that showed a long, ornate desk with the couple sitting side by side. Frank was talking into his headphone mic, and Dan was grabbing the desk, he was laughing so hard.

"Looks like the Mystic Circle gang is having fun on Fairies

and Dragons tonight," Kiri said, a hint of envy in her tone, but only a hint. Her eyes still hurt and she didn't want to stare at a computer screen. In fact, she blinked and turned her head away to appreciate the darkness and the night.

Lathyr dropped her arm and she missed the connection and his warmth until his fingers found hers and intertwined.

She smiled as the buzz of attraction ran from her hand through her, also warming her.

"The next house is uninhabited? The Castle's southeast neighbor?" Lathyr asked as they walked on.

Kiri glanced at it, frowned and tried to recall what was said at the neighborhood party that seemed so long ago—a different world. She *had* changed. "I think the resident, an old lady, died and the estate has offers from both Eight Corp and Rafe Davail's company."

Lathyr grunted.

They passed the Castle. The gate at the bottom was shut, but there were lights on in both turrets and the main mansion block, making it look warm and welcoming. That had her smiling, too. "You left lights on even when you aren't home?"

"The brown—" He stopped and coughed, then answered simply, "Yes."

She gave him a sidelong glance but didn't comment and they walked farther around the Circle in a nice silence. The quiet didn't press on her, make her feel as if she should say anything, but she became more and more aware of Lathyr—his height, the easy grace of the man…his scent.

Tamara's house, the Tudor, showed only one light at the back behind a lace curtain and no shadow of the small woman. Kiri recalled that she played a tall, slender and blond avatar in Fairies and Dragons, but if she'd been in Transformation, Kiri would have cast her as a dwarf.

When they passed Amber and Rafe Davail's house, they heard yelling and cheering from an open window on the first floor. Kiri chuckled and Lathyr squeezed her fingers.

"The Mystic Circle residents enjoy playing that game together," he said.

"Yes."

"We haven't left the Circle yet. Would you like to return to your home and log on? Or go to the Castle?"

"You know, I haven't seen a computer set up in the Castle." Something she hadn't thought of until now.

"There's one in the east turret."

That was the opposite turret than where she'd bathed after the bus accident. She shivered.

"Are you cold? If you want we can go in," Lathyr asked. He gestured to Jenni and Aric Emberdrake's Denver Square house, lit up from roof to basement.

Kiri slowly let her breath release. "No offense, but I'm not up to speaking with Jenni right now."

Lathyr stopped, turned to her and grasped both her hands. His head tilted down toward hers, but when she looked up it was too dark to note the expression in his eyes. "Would you rather not see me, either?"

"No!" Kiri cleared her throat. "No. I'm liking our walk."

"Good." That was pure male satisfaction. He let go of her hand and they began to walk again, past the Emberdrakes, curving around to the last house, another empty one, the bungalow opposite her place.

They crossed the street and walked out of Mystic Circle and south. It was odd, but a half block down toward the business district, the atmosphere seemed to change—getting colder, darker…and not feeling quite right. She shivered and tripped over a crack in the walk, as if her equilibrium was a little off.

"You're safe with me," Lathyr said, but he began scanning the blocks as a fighter would for any trouble.

"I'm sure," she said. They continued down the few blocks to the business district, and Kiri got the impression that he wanted to talk to her specifically about something. She didn't know him well enough to lead the conversation around to what he might want to discuss.

The Sensitive New Age Bean coffeehouse was loud and cheerful and had live jazz, and she and Lathyr crowded in on folding chairs, sipping their cocoa. Lathyr seemed to ease, and from the half smile on his lips, enjoyed the music.

They stayed an hour, then walked back, and once more Kiri felt something like a demarcation of energy. If she'd been in the game, Transformation, she'd have believed that the flow of magic had changed. She'd explored enough of the edges of the Earth and Air Realms where they joined with the other zones to notice the difference in the type of magic.

When they reached the corner of the cul-de-sac, her corner, Lathyr stopped under the old-fashioned streetlight, turned to her and took her hands again. This time she could see the gleam of his deep indigo eyes. "Tomorrow you will be entering the Water Realm."

That he wanted to discuss the game surprised her. "Uh-huh."

"I am going to offer to team with you, and I hope you will accept."

Also surprising. "You haven't accompanied me before."

His lips flexed up in a smile, then down. "I am not much of a game player, but have followed your progress closely." His smile deepened. "I've practiced the water spells."

"Oh. Sounds good." She eyed him. "You won't leave me, like Jenni did."

"Never." He lifted her hands to his lips, kissed the back of one, then the other and she suppressed a girlie sigh at the sheer romance of it all.

"Jenni had just turned a corner," Kiri said, compelled to be fair. "I was only a few paces behind her." Enough for an ambush behind her that defeated her the first time and threw her totally off balance, which, of course, wasn't Jenni's fault but Kiri's own. She hadn't recovered well. Any of the times.

"We'll stay side by side, but I think you will do well in the Water Realm."

"Because I sucked in Fire?"

Lathyr laughed, full and nearly musical. "No, you might *suck* in the Water Realm, or even the Air Realm, but sucking isn't advised in the Fire or Earth Realms, seared or dusty lungs come from that."

Kiri laughed. "I'll take your word for that."

He drew her arm to link with his elbow again as he walked her up the path to her house and the steps and stopped at the front door. "But, yes, because you did poorly in the Fire Realm, the Water Realm may suit you better."

"As the Fire Realm suits Jenni Emberdrake." Emberdrake. Fire dragon. Duh!

"That is correct," Lathyr confirmed. So Averill had been right all around.

And for the third time that night, Lathyr took both her hands, gazed down at her. "Beautiful Kiri," he said.

Her heart thumped. He was going to kiss her. Oh, yeah! She tilted her head back, watched his face come closer as he bent down, wished she'd turned on the damn porch light so she could have seen him better, watched his eyes dilate or something.

Then his mouth was on hers, softer than she'd expected.

And she felt the shock of lip-to-lip contact zoom straight to her core, along with a wave of pure lust. He opened his mouth and their breaths mingled. He tasted of cocoa and whipped cream with the barest hint of salt that added a touch of deliciousness to the kiss.

His tongue rubbed along hers and her mind went blank… like the midnight-blue night befogged her brain and air rushed in her ears like waves…a tide that matched her heartbeat, fast and heavy. She grabbed his shoulders, sturdy muscle, and leaned into him, feeling the strength of his chest, the tenseness of his body, his arousal.

Then he lifted her, his tongue probed her mouth, withdrew, and he set her away at arm's length from him.

She gasped and blinked and actually put her hand over her chest because her heart thumped so hard it might beat right out. Major sexual attraction here. She hadn't been expecting that.

"Good night, Kiri." He reached out and brushed back some hair that edged her vision. "Sleep well. Sweet dreams."

His mouth looked darker. So did his skin. She'd definitely had an effect on him, too. But he could talk and words were still stuck in her mind, not flowing down to her tongue.

He bowed, then kissed his fingers at her.

Oh, man. Romance!

"Until tomorrow, Kiri."

He turned and swept down the stairs and strode up the curving sidewalk and was out of sight before her feet unstuck. She hurried to the side of her porch and yelled, "See you tomorrow! Thanks for the great night!" And did that sound lame.

She used her keys and opened the door, dropped her purse on the floor and followed it down to sit and pant. She'd never had a kiss like that. One that had completely turned off all thought. Wonderful.

Maybe too good. Especially with a guy she worked with, and one she'd only known for less than two weeks. Dangerous in so many ways.

She wanted to explore more than the Water Realm with him.

They swirled into the Water Realm by funnel, and hand in hand, hovered over sandy ground a few feet under the turquoise ocean's surface. Joy bubbled through Kiri and a wide grin spread over her face.

Her hip-long *green* hair moved around her when she craned to see—and her whole body turned—including a tail longer than her legs with a large end fin larger than her feet. She moved, flexed and looked at it.

Gorgeous, an iridescent greeny-blue, like teal sequins. Green hair, tealish tail, Kiri glanced at her hands, received a little shock as she noted they were a light blue. A low ridge of fins rose along her arms.

And she both felt bare and not, and didn't have any nipples. She put her hand on the minuscule scales of her abdomen.

"It's rather like a natural armor," Lathyr said, smiling. "Hardscale."

She stared at him, his upper body revealed, his lower also a tail, but with a bulge where his sex would be that looked like an athletic cup. She figured that portion of his body would be very well protected. His skin tone was lighter than hers, a silvery blue, nearly white; his hair a lighter shade of green than her own. He looked absolutely right, and pretty much like he'd been the first time she'd seen him that evening in the park, except for no pointy ears.

Her fingers brushed her stomach, as she tried to describe the texture. Cool, flexible, strong, and a few "nots." Not rubber or plastic or fiberglass. Now that she thought about it, she could feel a softer, inner skin under the tougher hide. She tapped her side with her knuckles. "Does it ever come off?"

He slanted her a look. "Ah. Portions can be thinned for sex or feeding young. As for the rest of the skin armor...only if you're dying."

She grimaced.

With a whirl of his tail that looked all too smooth and graceful, he turned and tugged her in the direction of...a pink glow? She tried to follow and flopped around, then thrashed and realized she was *breathing water* and went glug, glug, glug. Pushed with her fin on the bottom of the sea to shoot up and get air.

Lathyr stopped her. "Waterfolk have bilungs."

He sounded completely serious—and though he usually did, this *was* a game. "Lungs that process oxygen and other necessities in the water as you breathe water, and that process oxygen et cetera in the air. This is the Water Realm. We will not be going above the surface or on land." He squeezed her fingers. "Going above the surface could harm you if you haven't learned how to use your bilungs."

Her eyes got wide and probably bulged.

"The surface of the water is out of the zone, the realm," Jenni said through the visor that Kiri never felt in the game. "The game parameters would have stopped her."

Suddenly the Water Realm felt all too alien. She didn't have legs! Wasn't like the game Fairies and Dragons where most everyone had wings as appendages stuck to their back. Not that she could feel them. She froze.

"Watch and follow my movements," Lathyr said, ignoring Jenni.

He flexed his tail in front; Kiri mimicked him. They went through turns and flips, dives and whirls. At any moment

Kiri expected Jenni to scold them for fooling around, but the woman was silent.

In a few minutes, Kiri was laughing, sending bubbles of glee bouncing to the top of the ocean where they burst and sounded very odd to her ears.

Finally they faced the pink glow again. There was a click and her vision changed.

"Just your nictitating eyelid," Lathyr said, and took her hand again with his—his long, four-jointed fingers, with thick webbing between them and nails that appeared fearsome—like her own. They couldn't hold hands like humans, but the webbing was clingy, at least between them.

The water felt wonderful, sliding against her skin, and her nose actually twitched as more scents came to her than she'd noticed in other areas of the game. Maybe only because she was becoming accustomed to the virtual reality. The fragrance of water magic seemed to soak into skin and scalp, slide along the strands of her hair, gather on the webbing between her fingers, coat her arm and tail fins.

Soon colorful fish joined them, populating this realm. Once again she stopped and Lathyr hovered near, smiling. "Much more beautiful than the koi," he said.

She had to agree.

"What is that pretty light?" she asked.

"The great Pearl." Another slashing grin by Lathyr, showing teeth that weren't human. She vaguely thought that her dwarf teeth hadn't been, either. He shook his head and his shoulder-length hair floated. "The Merfolk—naiads and naiaders, mermen and merfems, swear by it…though I think it isn't so big in—"

"A great Dark one comes to attack and slay you," announced Jenni.

"WHAT!" DEMANDED LATHYR.

"A great Dark one, the most fearsome villains in Transformation, attacks," Jenni said.

Lathyr swore and grabbed Kiri by the arm, pulled her from the turquoise water and into a rough cave entrance she hadn't noticed since seaweed and stalactites obscured it. She scrabbled to find info on "a great Dark one" in her belt pouch. Deformed. Evil. Kills questors and sucks magic.

Didn't sound good.

Archvillains—that sounded even worse.

"Prepare to fight," Jenni said, "the great Dark one can sense you."

Lathyr handed Kiri a speargun with nasty barbs on the end, pulled a long and shining blade from an open treasure chest. "Does it have minions?" he asked.

"No minions at this time," Jenni intoned.

"Ready your spells," Lathyr said. "This Dark one is vulnerable to poison. You have a poison spell, right?"

For not knowing the game, the guy was moving ahead fine, right on top of events while Kiri struggled to keep up. Her spell info gave her the proper words and gestures to initiate the poison from an herbal mixture she had. When she touched her shell-belt bag a vial fell into her hand.

"Stay out of reach of your spears and my sword," Lathyr said grimly. "They're silver and can harm us."

She glanced at the hilt that looked wrapped in snakeskin or sharkskin or crocodile or something. "Why—"

"They'll hurt the great Dark one more."

That was good, but she eyed the weapons.

"He'll be within range in thirty seconds," Lathyr said, angling his body behind the cave wall so she could have a good shot. "Fade back—"

"I know!" She flipped open the shell top of the vial—good thing they didn't use a damn cork—and poured the oily mixture all along her spearhead, chanting what the spell instructions told her to. Her heart beat fast. Sure didn't feel like a game.

She tucked the empty vial back in her belt, sighted the gun. Gritted her teeth as she heard a high-pitched garbled sound and a grotesque *thing* came into view, vaguely humanoid but massive. Schools of fish scattered.

Head shot would be best, especially since he was leading with that as he swam toward her. Then his head tilted up and she saw glittering red eyes and a huge mouth with jagged teeth.

Don't choke. Too much at stake. Lathyr was beside her and if she missed the shot— No!

She sighted, pulled the trigger slowly.

Shhzzhht! Thunk.

The monster had been fast, dodged, but took the spear in his throat. A roar hit her ears. With long, bony fingers the thing pulled the spear from his throat, and the gaping wound began to heal like a zipper going up. He yelled again and his eyes glowed bloody as he saw her.

She backswam, fast. Luring him.

He shot into the cave.

Lathyr decapitated him.

Black ichor gushed from the severed neck, clouding the water and a huge suction swept her out of the cave, sending Kiri's heart racing into panic. She couldn't see. She wasn't on ground! Pressure—*stuff*—pushed on her. She was in some three-dimensional space; enemies could be under or above her. That was okay in Fairies and Dragons, but not here, not in virtual reality.

She wanted to scream but the ichor coated her tongue and she spat and spat and spat, *naasssty!* She tried to stay in the same place, forced herself to calm—and as her fear eased, she *felt* Lathyr near.

"Thing's dead and disintegrated. Great Dark ones do that fairly often," Lathyr stated calmly. He sang a lovely snatch of a strangely foreign song and the water cleared. Fish abounded, but she was within a large bubble with him. As she settled, she realized that she hadn't seen some of the fish before and a couple were large and gobbling at…the great Dark one?

"Scavengers," Lathyr said. "Lowering my shields now." The bubble vanished.

Lathyr pointed. A great peach-pink pearl, as large as a truck, was embedded halfway in a cliff wall.

"Well done!" Jenni said.

"What's with the pearl?" Kiri managed.

"That is your first goal, to find the great pink pearl, defend it from those who wish to take it and learn what you need from it."

"Learn what I need? What, like the next clue?"

"You might say that," Jenni said.

"I didn't know of this goal," Lathyr said. His body, nearly as fluid as the water around them, went stiff and tense.

"It was changed just as you departed. It's a later goal from the game that we decided to insert now."

"Along with an archvillain?" Kiri asked.

"I thought you might be getting bored," Jenni said guilelessly.

Snorting in the Water Realm wasn't wise, Kiri found out.

Lathyr nodded to the pearl. "Go take care of that."

Slowly she swam up to the large gem, held still. "Learn what you can from it," the mission info said. She reached out and brushed it with her fingers, satin under her touch. Her nostrils opened wide as she inhaled deeply. Yes, most excellent water magic! This close she saw tiny swirls of bubbles, the same pink-peach, lifting from its surface as if it were alive like a jellyfish, instead of a hard gem. She placed her hand on it.

And it popped.

Kiri gasped, heard Lathyr do the same. *Failed Goal*, scrolled across her vision in bright blue. Before they could take another breath, they were back in the computer room.

The rest of Friday passed quickly. Somehow the Water Realm simply *made sense* on an instinctive level to Kiri.

Since it was the end of the workweek, and now more than a full week since she'd started, a two-hour debriefing had been set for the afternoon. Though it was a time for Kiri to present her ideas on how to refine the game—and she was plenty nervous about that—she begrudged the time out. A good and bad sign that she was becoming invested in Transformation.

Jenni, Aric and Lathyr started the meeting by complimenting her on her progress, with only one line about her "difficulties" in the Fire Realm.

When it came to her turn, Kiri handed out suggestions she had for the program, ideas for story arcs, for new types of character aspects and costumes.

Those were well received, by Aric with a big grin, Jenni by interested humming. Lathyr only smiled at Kiri…and winked. He was changing, too, loosening up. Good to see.

At the end, as the others began to rise, Kiri stood and cleared her throat, lifted her chin and matched gazes with Jenni. "I'd like to take home the software again this weekend. And play in the Fire Realm."

The older woman sat and leaned back in her chair, tucking a strand of her hair behind her ear. "You don't think you're going overboard on this?"

"No."

"I do."

Kiri blinked. "Yeah?"

"Though I must admit that you might do better in the Fire Realm without the enhanced virtual reality gloves and the visor."

"Exactly! And if I can make my own character."

Jenni's fingers drummed on the desk. "Understood. But I still believe that you're pushing this too much."

Despite herself, Kiri felt her face go into sulk mode.

Leaning forward, Jenni said, "How long did you play Transformation last weekend?"

Kiri had to sit down and rack her memory for last weekend. Saturday she'd…pretty much hit the game in the morning and played all day. Her shoulders wiggled in stiff memory. "Sunday I only played—"

"Worked," Jenni corrected.

"Gamed a few hours."

"How many hours total?" Jenni's brows lifted.

"Um, four?" Kiri made her eyes big and innocent.

"On Sunday, right? How many hours on Saturday?"

Now Kiri's shoulders wanted to hunch. She kept them straight, but wet her lips. "I'm not sure."

"I didn't see you go out to look at the koi pond last Saturday," Jenni said.

Kiri jerked. "Of course I did. I do every day." She had, hadn't she? She honestly couldn't remember, and that *was* a warning. The days, the games, reality and realms were running together. She grimaced, flung up a hand like a fencer who'd taken a hit. "All right. I spent too much time on it last weekend—last Saturday." She leaned forward, too. "This job, this career is important to me."

Jenni's face softened. "It's very important to us, too, but we don't want you burning out."

Kiri longed to push a little, ask for the damn job. But she had three more days. "I can take it easier."

"You *will* take it easier. Not only did you play Transformation, you spent some hours writing up notes, making outlines of stories." Jenni tapped the thickish hard copy of the file before her.

Kiri said, "Yes."

Jenni swiveled in her chair, angled it toward Lathyr. "And your take on this, Lathyr?"

"Kiri is doing very well."

Always good to hear.

"But I think she should slow down and…savor…the realms, the experience."

Kiri's face went hot. She forced herself to meet his eyes.

He'd reverted to serious mode, didn't look like he was making a double entendre. What had their brief kiss meant to him—and why the hell was she thinking about that now! Absolutely the reason workplace affairs were bad.

"We don't want you to wash out of the program, Kiri," he said.

Now her insides went cold. Her face stiffened into what she hoped was impassivity.

"So I have an idea." Jenni raised her index finger and Kiri turned to listen to her with relief.

"Yes?" Kiri asked.

"We'll give you the regular program for the Fire and Water Realms this weekend. You may spend two hours in each realm. There will be a time limit on the software and it will lock after that."

"Only two hours each!"

"That's right. We are not looking for full immersion here, not this week," Lathyr said.

Thoughts buzzed in Kiri's brain.

"I will join you in playing in the Fire Realm," Jenni said. "I'd like to schedule that now." She pulled out her pocket computer, and Kiri did the same. Lathyr opened the protective cover of his tablet.

"Tomorrow morning from ten to noon would be good for me," Jenni said. "Come over to Aric's and my place then."

"Fine," Kiri said.

"And I have invited everyone in Mystic Circle to dinner Sunday evening at 5:00 p.m.," Lathyr said.

"We'll be there," Aric said.

"I'd love to," Kiri said.

"So why don't we schedule our session early Sunday afternoon, say 1:00 p.m.?" Lathyr said.

"Fine." Kiri wondered if Lathyr was having the meal catered. He didn't seem to be a guy who cooked.

"Your goal in the Fire Realm is to figure out how to cross the Lava River successfully," Jenni said. She slid a chip with the software down the polished wooden table to Kiri, who stuck it carefully in her wallet in her tote.

"Our goal in the Water Realm is to collect several jewels for a crown for the Water Queen. All of which are heavily guarded, of course," Lathyr said.

"Right," Kiri said.

"I guess that's it." Jenni rose and smiled and stretched.

Lathyr said, "We have no overall project meeting today?"

"Nope." Jenni linked fingers with her husband. "See you tomorrow, Jenni."

The couple left.

"Would you ride to Mystic Circle with me?" Lathyr asked, circling the desk and holding out his hand.

"This isn't a good idea," Kiri said, putting her fingers in his.

He smiled slowly. "I like the idea fine."

She shook her head. "Workplace…attractions shouldn't be acted upon. It becomes awkward."

Lathyr tucked her hand in his arm, picked up her tote. "All will be well, Kiri."

She didn't want to argue, and the workday—the workweek stress—began to roll off her shoulders. She liked being with him.

The car awaited on the street and Lathyr opened the door for her. They both greeted the driver by name and asked after his day. When the courtesies had passed, they let the quiet spread between them. She'd never been with anyone, let alone a man, who she was so easy with. That it was Lathyr was a mystery to her.

In the evening they walked around the Circle and watched the koi and went down to Clara's Creamery for ice cream.

And they kissed again and this time Kiri drew away.

The whole weekend went well, slid softly by with good food and good company and good fun.

By lunch break Tuesday, the second to the last day of her time at Eight Corp on the Transformation project, Kiri had become determined. She *wouldn't* lose this opportunity. She knew she was doing well in the games, though they gradually began to feel more and more real. Her files on the program grew to eight storylines—two that she thought would work in each realm. She remained unenthusiastic about Fire Realm, and had completely finished all the current goals in the Water Realm.

She'd sketched out some marketing bullets for the game, added more alternative character types, including various sorts of humans. She had lists of new spells, valuable items, weapons and rewards. She'd used the costume creator of Fairies and Dragons to give some idea of what she thought folks playing Transformation would like as garb. She'd shot all the files to Jenni, Aric, Lathyr and the CEO, Alex Akasha, who'd appeared on her company email list and requested to be updated.

Since it was a lovely autumn day, and Jenni and Aric and Lathyr were all stuck in a meeting and had told her to take a long lunch, she walked to the Downtown Mall and ate in an actual restaurant, even outside on a patio, sitting by herself in the sun. Good.

She was feeling confident, in charge and in control, sure she'd be fine, when clouds began rolling in and someone near her commented about the weather and how freaky it had been with the bus accident and all.

Kiri stood, caught the waiter's eye, stuck money under her plate and left. She walked around a long block, in the sun, keeping her mind blank. She'd had a feeling that this afternoon's game session would be like a final in class—and heavily weighted for her whole grade.

Still, muddy, cruddy streamers of thought slithered through her mind. She hadn't forgotten the bus accident, and when reminded her chest seized and she had to breathe through the fear. And she'd had bad dreams that she couldn't quite recall... but reality and the game, the changes and slight strangeness of her life, the advent of Lathyr and the lilting desire between them—all had dimmed the recollection of the tragedy.

People had died and there was a tight block in her gut that she should feel more, grieve for them, but she hadn't been able to. Except maybe that's what she was doing when she woke up with tears on her face and crying.

Too many things pressed in on her, and now the wind had picked up, too, and the day had turned cold.

She was glad to go back into the building, stuck a smile on her face as the elevator rose and was relieved when she walked into the computer room to see Jenni and Lathyr waiting for her.

Jenni shared a glance with Lathyr and grinned. "We've received approval for sending you into the portion of the prologue that removes the barriers between the realms. There are, of course, obstacles to overcome to pass between the realms that you should have already mastered."

The Lava River in the Fire Realm hadn't been too bad. Really. Especially since Kiri and Jenni had played it with regular computer keyboards and not the gloves and visors of virtual reality. Kiri had cleared the river with seconds to spare.

Kiri's mind zipped around, her heart picked up a beat—wonderful distraction from reality! Or the reality of lunch and outside and people as opposed to the reality of Eight Corp and the game and her career. Resolve swelled within her again. She would not fail.

"Lathyr will accompany you on the tour of the realms. Claim a marker in each realm and bring it to the Air Palace and you win the game." Jenni's grin widened. "With appropriate bonuses in game and out."

Excitement shivered through Kiri. Lathyr was already pulling on his gloves. He cocked a brow at her. "Which realm do you wish to start in?"

"May as well begin now where I originally began, Earth Realm."

Lathyr nodded and donned his visor. "The earth cave, then."

Kiri drew on her own gloves. "And perhaps my brownie."

Jenni scowled at her computer. The large monitor had flickered, gone dark and recovered. "No brownie or team. Just you and Lathyr, I think."

"Is everything okay?" Kiri asked as Jenni's fingers flew over the keyboard.

"Maybe," she grumbled. "Go."

Kiri put on the visor and in a few seconds felt like she was in the cave—but as a stronger character than before. She checked. Yes! Both magic user and melee fighter. She'd grown in the game. Cool.

Glancing at Lathyr, she found his avatar was much like herself. So they'd draw tough enemies and have to think and strategize more rather than rush out and bash.

"Ready?" he asked with a smile, as he did lately. He was finally becoming a gamer.

Kiri consulted her map, huffed a breath. "The goal is in the middle of that maze of twisty little passages all the same. Jenni probably did that on purpose."

"There's two of us—it will be easier."

"True."

After spending some time negotiating the little twisty passages all the same, they'd gotten the object—a golden nugget—and were headed toward the closest realm, Water—when the earthquake smacked them.

The earth shook and they fell to the ground. Lathyr hit hard, and felt every bit of it…the game had become even more real. He wasn't sure if the royals had manipulated it again, or the game itself was pulling reality and magic and power from the Meld Project housed in the same building, but Lathyr had a marrow-deep feeling that fighting and injuries were real—they could be hurt and die here.

LATHYR LEAPED TO HIS FEET, HELPED KIRI UP, scanned her chain mail. "Change into your earthen elemental armor," he ordered.

"What?" She rubbed her head, blood trickled from her hairline.

Would blood draw predators? Lathyr didn't know, but a heaviness and the stink of evil invaded the water molecules in the air—his nostrils widened to catch the scent, and he strained so much his nose frills unfurled.

Thunder came. Again. Motes of black dirt showed beyond the hill. *Crash!* and *Crash!* Footsteps, Lathyr realized with dread. Something huge. He sniffed. Something evil.

*Lathyr Tricurrent, to me! To fight!* the Air King shouted mentally, and Lathyr realized the building outside the game, in true reality, was under attack.

*Must stay!*

*Dark ones!* the king snapped, and began to *pull* on Lathyr through all the air in his body. He wouldn't be able to stay, and he had a terrible feeling that a Dark one had entered the game.

He grabbed Kiri's shoulders, gasped, "Being disconnected. You quit, too!"

Kiri fisted her hands, jerked—the motion to log out. She remained solid, her eyes widening, even as he felt himself fade. "Not working."

*CRASH!*

"Keep trying. Dark. One." He jerked his head at the horizon of hills and the thumping footfalls. "Coming. Real. This game is *real.* Look at your bleeding. *Run!*" Lathyr strove to stay with her, but the king was far more powerful than he, and he was yanked into the real world and the CEO's office.

To see a disheveled Air King with a fierce fighting grin, Cloudsylph. Sword in his hand, the elf ducked behind an upturned desk. *Fight!*

A clash came and Lathyr whirled—both guardians—the elf and the dwarf—fought also.

"Two great Dark ones!" shouted Cloudsylph, fighting sword against long and thorny claw-sword dripping venom of the monster. Huge black humanoid monster covered in black chitin, with seeping protuberances—when droplets hit, the rug burned. Nasty smell.

"Here!" yelled the dwarf, and threw a trident at Lathyr.

He caught it and it felt good in his hands. Adrenaline pumped through him. "The game's turned real. Kiri—"

The guardians stilled for an instant. The King of Air beside him grimaced. "Too bad, you're here now." He jerked his head at the side of the room and Lathyr's heart stopped as he saw a torn panel of meld-electrical conduits. The game server? How would that affect Kiri?

Then the wall to his left crashed down and the second Dark

one, horribly huge, lunged through. Lathyr snapped hardscale over his body, wishing for the armor he'd left in the game, angled his trident, yelled his war cry and charged. Praying with blood and breath that Kiri would be all right. She'd run. She'd find a place and hide. They'd pull the Dark one out of the game. And Lathyr would return to her.

Kiri watched Lathyr's face contort as he struggled to stay in the game, but he faded—and as he did, Kiri noticed that his skin turned the pretty pale blue. Good trick. But what fascinated her were delicate, transparent little ruffles seeming attached to the underside of the upper curve of his nostrils. Beautiful.

Another shudder of the earth under her feet jolted her alert. *Earth armor,* he'd said, and *Dark one,* and *run!* He hadn't been thinking, you couldn't run in earth armor, too heavy. Her head itched and she rubbed at it again. Hurt, too. Her fingers came away tacky with blood and her breath stopped. Looked *real.* She touched her fingertips to her mouth, tasted. Blood. Her blood.

The whole scene enlarged, brightened, as her eyes widened even more. She gulped. The game was real? WTF!

Her head really hurt. Her current armor weighed her down. What would happen if she *did* use earth armor, would she actually have stone sprout in plates along her body?

Crash! Crash! The thing's head, gigantic and round, with heavy brow ridge and features scrunched in the middle looking like nothing human, rose above the hill.

Time to get out of here. She motioned again. Nothing. Reached for her visor.

Touched nothing.

"Logging off," she said, voice quavering.

The monster advanced.

She remained in the game—in the game that had turned into reality? How could that have happened? Magic?

Magic. Maybe. Lotta stuff had been happening lately that was close to being inexplicable through logic.

Think later! She was stuck and didn't know the rules. Did she still have powers? Her breath came too fast, bringing dimness and tiny sparks—hyperventilating. Don't think! Don't analyze reality and game. Hell, not the time to *feel,* either. Tactics. Strategy. Whatever.

The thing thunked higher and higher against the horizon, like nothing she'd ever seen or imagined, bringing a hideous stench that flew at her in bits like wasps or flies or—yeah, she'd seen stuff like that in the game. She flung a shield around herself. They smacked into it with nasty buzzing and squashes. She *felt* the impacts against her force field. How could that be?

A bolt of lightning struck an inch from her feet, the blast rocked her, singed her toes.

Terror flooded her. She turned and ran into the forest, trying to recall what other game monsters inhabited it—though she and Lathyr had just fought through it—had they spawned again?

And now she felt far too squishy as a magic user instead of as the toughest warrior. Dammit!

*Crash! Zap!*

She wondered how many hit points she really had. How many the monster did.

How could she win?

Hell. How could she survive?

*How many of them are there?* Lathyr broadcast mentally.

*Two!* yelled the dwarf and elf guardians.

*Three!* shouted the Air King. *I saw three.*

Blood chilling, Lathyr's mind scattered. He whirled back to the Dark one he'd first seen, leaped over the desk, fought with the dwarf, slashing, backing the monster up, dipped his trident in a pool of steaming, smelly acidic green venom.

*Two Dark ones working together?* grunted the dwarf, slicing off a limb.

*Must really hate the Eight and the Meld, or want the Meld,* responded the elf, his face formed in a dreamy smile as he struck, slid aside from an attack.

*Where's the third?* demanded the Air King.

Lathyr's belly twisted. *In the game with Kiri.*

Curses came from the other men, and a wisp of feeling from the Air King brought on his breath near Lathyr's ear. Grief at losing a subject.

Lathyr couldn't think, could only thank the great Pearl that he'd been fighting in the game lately and his skills weren't as rusty as they had been.

He ducked under the tall elf guardian's arm, slid sideways, thrust his envenomed trident in the Dark one's belly, hard, hard, harder!

His weapon stuck.

Shrieking rage, thrashing limbs. Lathyr used all his skill, all his air power to leap back…but a huge hand with black and pointed nail-claws swiped at him, got his arm, sent him tumbling.

Immense pain surged through him, blood and water gushed from his wound—his arm drooped half-off at the shoulder! He went down as agony took his breath and sat crushing on his chest.

Stuff poured from his mouth, too, vomit and water and mucus and life force as his bilungs constricted. He was gone.

Worse, he couldn't return to Kiri.

He had failed.

"Greendepths!" Cloudsylph's voice whipped out like ice shards.

The King of Water wouldn't let his woman heal Lathyr this time.

Failure. Pain. Death.

Blackness swallowed his consciousness like a tsunami and threw him away.

Leaves and twigs crunched under Kiri's running feet as she sped through the forest. She heard a whole lot, more than she wanted to, like her own whooshing breath, all confirming this terrible game was real. If she ever got out, she'd never—effing Eight Corp could take their job and shove it up their butts till it stuck in their throats and strangled them.

Roaring. Not her. She whispered prayers.

Ripping wood, cracking. The forest wasn't safe, either. She strove to *think* through the terror. Map, remember the map! She was in Earth Realm. Forests. Caves.

*Crash! Crash!* The monster giant thing, *abomination,* came after her. From a horrified, compulsive glance or two back, she thought she saw wings. Spiny, bony, bat wings.

Kiri quivered. Trembled so much she fell and a log sailed over her head. Luck. Sheer luck had saved her.

Okay. Okay. Luck happened in a game, some good. Some bad. Your keyboard freezes up on you in a fight and you were down.

Your character was down.

*This* was real. She was pretty damn sure.

Map. Caves. Run to the caves. The monster couldn't squeeze

into the caves. Maybe the dwarves had made the caverns strong enough not to collapse on her. Real dwarves? Maybe.

She zigzagged through the forest, ducking under cover, repelling the insect clouds. She didn't know their powers but figured being stung wouldn't be good.

*Run.* In the Earth Realm she'd chosen the zip run travel power, feet on the ground, no flying or jumping. Run. Run. Run. Dodge through there. Roaring and thrashing and creaking and crashing and black thunderbolts snapping and sizzling, sensory overload. The smell of scorched earth and scorched electronics—oh, no!—and ripped-up plants and fresh wood, sawdust. Not good. The gag of putrification, of—evil? Vibration against her skin, her eyelids…her shields. She still had shields. She had zip run. What other powers? Earthworks. Battlements. She pivoted, flung her arms out in a circle, called the power. "Earthworks, there, and there and *there.*" Breath, breath. "Battlements, *there!*" She wouldn't think how little that would slow down a monster. Again she spun, and kept on spinning—rocks and broken wood shoved away from her, whirled away by her twister spell. That wasn't an earth spell. That was air! What was going on?

Shoot. She didn't *know* what spells she had or didn't and then there was that odor of fried wires, plastic, metal. How scrambled was everything? What kind of reality was this?

No time to figure it out. The caves were a short stretch to the northeast. She had zip run and *zoomed.*

And went straight off the cliff and into the ocean.

She hit hard, painfully, but this was the Water Realm, the easiest for her to maneuver in—and her character had changed once again with all the levels that she'd gained here. Much, much stronger. And she and Lathyr had fought a Dark one here in the Water Realm before.

A huge displacement of water sent her tumbling.

Gigantic, bat-winged Dark one.

She rolled with the percussion, scanned the bottom. She knew this place, the soft silt, the deceptive sand that hid huge eels ready to swallow an unwary mer. Where was the eel's fake-plant-frond trigger?

Moving fast, she zigged and zagged, got caught by an energy bolt. Real! Searing pain. Tears that mixed with water. Go. Go. Go. Lure again, like she and Lathyr had done before. No, don't think of him, what might be happening otherwhere.

Go!

There, dippy faltering swim, pretending even more hurt. Dark one following, immense presence behind. Walking instead of swimming. Stupid of him, good for her.

Something heavy weighed on her back. Quick glance. Speargun! Yay. Get it! Point it!

There's the eel-frond trigger. Zoom. Hit it hard. The quarrels move slow. Too slow. Push to surface. Is there a surface?

She popped up, gasped, bad hurt in lungs. Dammit.

Six pants and she was okay.

Thrashing below…eel and evil. But she'd put her money on the great Dark one, if she didn't go down and try to finish him off. Head toward the Water Palace—and what and who would she find there? The King and Queen she'd already met?

Fight!

Down she went again, sifting water/air through her teeth in an effort to avoid the lung pain. Yep, the eel had wrapped itself around the Dark one. Twice. Still looked like it was losing, with big chunks of it ripped off.

OTOH, Dark one didn't appear so hot. Kiri shot. Again and again and emptied her quiver-bag. Long tear in a wing. Coupla bolts in the head. Slowed it down a little.

The eel thrashed and died. Time to get outta here!

Blood, guts, ichor, *stuff* saturated the water. She turned and swam as fast as she could. Not as fast as zip run and it had nearly caught her when she used that. God. God. God.

Glance back. *Huge* ball of hard water crackling with black energy heading toward her. Cliff face ahead, surface!

She looked down, clenching her speargun tight. The Dark one was slower. One wing was gone. Didn't heal like the one she and Lathyr had fought in Water Realm before. Good.

Her gun weighted with another spear. She'd been all out. Magic.

Can't question. Pause. Sight. Shoot the thing in the eye.

A roar that banged her against the cliff. Huge pain. Grit teeth, raise the speargun, fire in the hellish open mouth!

This scream higher than she could hear, only feel the shock. More tears gushed from her eyes in pain.

Then the Dark one simply vanished.

And so did she.

She came back to the room with a thunk that had her knees crumpling her to the floor, only able to huff, "Uh, uh, uh." And with a serious case of the shudders. She still *hurt.*

What was all that about?

Too darn real.

She pulled off her visor and tossed it onto the counter. Then she peeled off her gloves—glad to have had them and the spells they projected, but wonderful to get rid of them. They stuck to her hands and turned inside out. Blinking, she saw that what she'd thought would be filaments were no more than lines. Huh. They'd left marks on her skin like henna.

A knock came on the door. "Kiri? Are you there? Are you *safe?*" Sounded like Jenni Emberdrake.

Kiri grunted, but apparently not loud enough. Turning completely paranoid, she scuttled on hands and knees away from the direct path from the door. “What happened?”

“Terrorist attack,” Jenni said crisply.

That froze Kiri’s brain. “In *Denver?*”

“Yes,” Jenni said, and her British accent was back.

There was a soft swiping sound of a key card and a click of a lock. Kiri had been locked in? Crap. The handle depressed and Kiri held her breath, looked wildly around for a weapon. Nothing.

But Jenni Emberdrake stood on the threshold, scanning the room and the computer equipment as if for damage. That felt right to Kiri, what the real woman would do. Then Jenni’s gaze lit on Kiri, crouched in the corner and a breath whooshed from her. The room seemed to get warmer.

Kiri stood, put a palm on the desk and leaned on it. Jenni looked the worse for wear. Kiri had never seen the woman’s hair so wild; usually it was smooth, or at the most, tied back and a little fuzzy.

Jenni put her hands on her hips, nodded once. “I guess it’s time to tell you what’s going on.”

Fear flowed through Kiri, up from her gut and down from her brain and meeting in her throat to close it. She didn’t want Jenni to tell her anything, didn’t want to confront all the little anomalies in the life of Kiri Palger.

Didn’t want to think the bus accident hadn’t really been an accident.

“Don’t look so shocked or horrified,” Jenni said. There was a hint of dancing blue color in her brown eyes, but her smile was warm and sympathetic and comforting and loosened the breath trapped in Kiri’s lungs. “I think you’ll be intrigued, and…pleased.”

"Huhnn," was all Kiri could manage.

Jenni turned. "Come along, we're meeting in the inner conference room, the outer offices are a bit of a mess. The broken windows are being repaired first."

Broken windows. On the thirty-second floor. Not good at all. The computer room looked downright friendly. Not one smashed thing.

Kiri sniffed. Still smelled fried electronics, just not here. Lucky.

"Come on," Jenni insisted and Kiri heard glass cracking under the woman's feet.

Stay or go? Jenni knew the situation. Kiri didn't. Yet she walked lightly to the door, saw the doors of the outer offices shut for the first time. There was glass underfoot, but the doors seemed unmarred as did the inner glass insets. The occasional sight she had of the offices showed much less devastation than what would have happened if the bow windows around her computer desk and home office had blown. Odd.

They entered the conference room and the first thing Kiri noticed was that the man sitting at the large table looked familiar. The guy at the bus accident with Lathyr. His skin was pale, his hair silver-white. His ears were pointed.

The door was closed behind them by Aric Emberdrake, who appeared even bigger in what looked like green leather armor and who had a sword at his hip. A sword. His long hair seemed a dark green.

Lathyr stood as they entered. He wore a sword on his right hip, a long dagger in a hilt strapped to his left thigh. He appeared very pale, with lines on his face and his mouth turned down as if in remembered pain. He held his left arm stiffly.

A sniff came from the bottom of the table where Mrs.

Daurfin sat, thick arms crossed over her sturdy body, glowering at Kiri.

"Please, sit," Aric said. He drew out a chair for Jenni, then Kiri.

She sat.

"I've ordered tea and cheeses. We need the protein and tea is civilized," Jenni said in firm tones. She glanced at her husband and away.

Now that Kiri thought of it, Aric wasn't exactly sending off civilized vibes. Neither was Lathyr. Or the head honcho at the head of the table. She'd bet her entire career that he carried weapons, too.

There'd been a fight, even outside here in the real world.

"Thank you, Jindesfarne," said the…man…in the power position in a melodious voice that had Kiri straining her ears to catch each nuance.

Lathyr sent Kiri a soft glance, as if he'd like to come over and sit with her. She wouldn't mind holding his hand under the table, and she was aware that he'd scanned her for any injury. Nothing major on the outside, but her insides quivered and her mind prepared for an incipient earthquake.

With a last nod, Lathyr sat. So did Aric, in a chair next to Jenni. He clasped his wife's hand, right there on the conference room table. Jenni twined fingers with him.

"I believe we are the only ones here," the one at the head of the table said.

"Except for the repair force," Aric said.

The man inclined his head.

"The Meld Project people left immediately," Aric said. "I checked on them, and none of their work was compromised."

"Of course not," said Mrs. Daurfin. "I guarded it."

"Casualties?" asked the man in charge, but as if he already knew.

"None among us." Aric's eyes gleamed. "We did a good job."

Lathyr gave a tiny cough. "So did Kiri. She was attacked in game."

"S'truth!" the silver-headed guy's exclamation wasn't loud, but intense enough to carry.

"Somehow a great Dark one reached the pocket dimension," Jenni murmured.

Power emanated from the end of the table. Everyone looked down, including Kiri; she couldn't help it. In fact, she couldn't move. Otherwise she'd have slid under the table.

"I will contact the guardians to understand how that might occur."

"Kiri defeated the Dark one," Jenni said with satisfaction.

And now the...person's full consideration weighed on Kiri. She met his gaze, glanced aside, stared at her hands on the table, wondered why they weren't trembling.

"A unique individual, indeed," the fabulous voice said.

There was a pop and a small man and woman each levitating a huge tray loaded with food stood by the door.

Kiri couldn't deny what was going on anymore.

They were brownies.

THE BROWNIES SET PLACES AND FOOD AROUND the table, poured tea and disappeared before Kiri got her slack-jawed, surprised hanging-open mouth shut.

And the whole room rippled and changed before her eyes and she smelled *magic* and everyone looked a little different. Jenni had a slightly reddish tint to her skin. Fire magic. Aric's hair was definitely green.

So was Lathyr's, around his pointed ears and pale white-blue skin. Merman. Kiri's heart beat hard, pulse throbbing inside her ears.

Mrs. Daurfin was a dwarf.

Slowly, slowly, Kiri slid her gaze to the end of the table. The tall thin guy was not a man. Or rather, not a human male. Most of the magical power in the room emanated from him. He definitely had pointed ears, was gorgeous. Her nose twitched in recognition at his fragrance that confirmed the notion spinning in her mind. Elf.

He caught her glance. Caught her, and the world stilled in the moment and so did her breath, then he looked aside. More memories, recollections, snapped together. Lathyr had bespelled her at the neighborhood party. She looked at him and his face remained impassive but he almost looked worse than when she'd come in. Was she seeing through illusion, now? Were they letting her, or had she changed beyond measure?

"First, we're sorry, Kiri. The people in the other project here at Eight Corp—the Meld Project—are all magical and have good transportation skills." Jenni shook her head. "But you, Kiri, are human, and more targeted by the Darkfolk than we'd anticipated." She hesitated. "Probably from the very beginning, the flyover of Dark evil minions at the neighborhood party. And since then, they were watching you."

Kiri recalled the nightmare she'd had, the bus accident, and shuddered.

"And, Kiri," Jenni said, leaning toward her.

"Yeah?" Kiri swallowed. "Yes?"

"Transformation isn't just a game."

Kiri teetered on the edge of logic.

"It's a tool to discover whether regular humans can be transformed into Lightfolk." Jenni's sweeping gesture indicated the whole table. "And Lathyr isn't from Eight Corp human resources. He is Lightfolk and can measure the potential of people who can become magical beings."

"All right," Kiri said, though it wasn't. She grappled with the sharp-edged idea. "The...gentleman at the end of the table—" her gaze slipped across his gorgeous face again "—is an elf."

"King Cloudsylph," Aric said.

Kiri caught herself bowing as low as she could over the table, muttered, "Honored." See, the game wasn't useless, had taught her manners for a royal.

It wasn't a game.

"Lathyr is mer, and you," Kiri stared at Jenni, "are djinn." Jindesfarne was Jenni's true name. Big clue Kiri had missed.

"Half-human, half-Lightfolk. That's what we call ourselves, Lightfolk. I'm a quarter-djinn and a quarter-elf."

Kiri felt her eyes rounding. "Wow."

"Princess Jindesfarne Weavers Emberdrake, adopted sister of the King and Queen of Fire, the Emberdrakes." Lathyr stood and bowed, too. Looked like it hurt.

"Are you okay?" Kiri asked him.

A corner of his mouth lifted in an unamused smile. "I will be."

"Uh-huh." She eyed him. "How hurt are you?" Worry pushed her to rudeness, and besides, she'd rather concentrate on Lathyr.

"I've been healed, and my body will continue to mend at a faster rate than humans."

She wet her lips. He'd been offended. "Okay." She inclined her head to the receptionist, Mrs. Daurfin, the dwarf, figured she should say something but had no clue. "Thank you for helping me." Kiri had no idea whether the woman had ever helped her or not, but the courtesy sounded good.

The dwarf eyed her suspiciously, then jerked a nod.

Kiri glanced at Jenni's husband, Aric, and away.

"I am a Treeman," Aric said, smiling. "The dryads and Treemen are native to earth's dimension. The Lightfolk are not."

Multiple dimensions. Uh-huh.

"I am also half-elf," Aric said. He took one of Jenni's restless hands in his own.

"Kiri, we would like to make you an offer," Jenni said.

Frissons of excitement and anxiety jittered up and down Kiri's spine.

Lathyr sat down again.

Jenni said, "Both Lathyr and the game's stats show that you have a great potential to become Lightfolk, transform into a purely magical being."

Wow. Just wow. Again she peeked at the elf. She could be an elf!

There was quiet and everyone looked at her as if she should say something. "My mind boggles."

"However," Jenni said, "if you wish to remain human, I want to tell you that you will always have a job on my team at Eight Corp."

She'd gotten the job! The career! Made the cut, the grade, her personal goal. Exactly what she'd wanted just that morning. Jenni Emberdrake had faith in her. Wow.

But all of that lost its shine in comparison to becoming magical. "This is for real? I could be a…merwoman?" She looked at Lathyr, who let his longer-than-human lashes shade his eyes.

"I will explain all the ins and outs later," Jenni said. "We need to know if you are interested."

"Right now?" Kiri's voice was high.

Lathyr said, "What you do need to know right now is that the transition is dangerous—you may lose your life and not become Lightfolk."

Kiri swung her gaze to Jenni, who nodded. "That's true."

Continuing, Lathyr said, "You could become a brownie or a naiad, not one of the major Lightfolk races. We do not determine your, ah, race, your inherent magic does that, as it did several times in the game. And if you do not accept our offer, you will have your memories removed of the magic you've learned to see."

Yup, mind dipping, spinning, boggling. "Gotta think about this," she squeaked.

Jenni looked at the king, who said, "If you wish to accept the human position as a game developer, I believe the proper sequence of events is for you to contact your current employer from whom you are on vacation and give your notice, effective immediately."

Kiri bobbed her head.

"If you wish to risk the transformation into a Lightfolk being, we can give you through the weekend to decide." He stood, then Cloudsylph, *King* Cloudsylph of Air, waved a languid hand. "You won't be able to communicate anything regarding our offer, or the Lightfolk, with anyone other than those in this room, and no humans at all."

Well, she hadn't really considered laying everything out to Shannon and Averill, but…her tongue stuck to the roof of her mouth. She scowled.

"Your Majesty." Lathyr stood again and made an elaborate bow, though his right arm moved a little stiffly. "This cannot be an easy decision. Perhaps you would loosen the bonds of the silence spell to include the humans Rafe and Amber Davail."

The King's brows rose infinitesimally. A flick of a finger. "Very well."

Kiri's tongue loosened but she didn't make the mistake of saying anything. Royal guy must be extremely powerful if he was at the top of the heap. She didn't want to alienate him. Would rather have not come to his notice at all.

But four days! She had to decide whether to become Lightfolk or have her memory wiped in *four* days. Crap.

"I think we can call this project meeting to an end, as well as the business day," the king said. He tilted his head. "The damage has been repaired, though I would like you to check out the electronics and the software, Jenni. Call whomever you need to help you. Good afternoon."

He disappeared into the faintest wisp of smoke.

Magic.

Guy gone instantly—like he and Lathyr had done at the bus accident site. Her gaze had been riveted toward the head of the table and her neck seemed to almost creak as she looked at Lathyr. Again she wet her lips. His glance went to her mouth, then rose to meet her eyes. He remained serious. No wonder. All this was…really…life-changing serious. Serious risks. Serious rewards.

"Did you get hurt much today?" she asked.

He nodded, touched his right shoulder with his opposite hand. "Nearly lost my arm."

"Uh." If there was Lightfolk, there would probably be Darkfolk—and real great Dark ones, just like she'd faced in the game. "A real great Dark one?"

"Couple," Aric said, shoving away from the table and standing. "We defeated but did not kill them. They fled." He tugged on Jenni's hand, but she remained sitting and pulled her fingers from his.

Nodding to Kiri, Aric said, "I should double-check on the damage and repairs." He left the room, this time regularly, by the door. She had no clue what a half-dryad, half-elf could do.

Kiri bobbed her head back at him, too late, but still stared at Lathyr. "Were you hurt during the bus accident?" She winced. "It wasn't an accident, was it?"

"No," he replied softly. "And I nearly lost my life. I absorbed the petrol spill into my body so neither the great Dark one nor its minions could set fire to it by lightning."

"So becoming a Lightfolk also comes with perils," Kiri said.

"Some, though usually only the royals are targeted." Lathyr

looked at Jenni. "Although we believe that some of our top projects may also be attracting attention. The game, Transformation, and the Meld Program—human technology has progressed to the point where we can combine it with magic."

Nope, not making sense. And she wasn't as interested in that as… "Archvillains?"

"There aren't many great Dark ones left, but they're nasty," Jenni said. Now she got up and came over to Kiri, put her djinn-fire-warm arms around Kiri and hugged. "You have a lot to think about. Call it a day and we can talk tonight."

"Uh-huh," Kiri said.

"Were *you* hurt in the game, the pocket dimension?" Lathyr pressed.

Kiri nodded. "Yeah." Her brows came down. "But not like you. I wonder why."

"We had safeguards on you," Jenni said matter-of-factly. "Apparently they continued to work." She actually kissed Kiri's cheek. "Good job defeating the great Dark one." Jenni grinned.

"Not sure I did. He just pulled out." At least she hadn't frozen. But she'd still been in the game landscape, used to fighting there. Sounded like she might be fighting here, too. With what, magic? More thrills.

"He looked like a pincushion," Mrs. Daurfin said as she stood, then smiled, showing red and pointy teeth.

Wow again. "Glad I amused you."

A chuckle rolled like pebbles hitting the sidewalk from the dwarfem. She squinted, eyes surrounded by hard brown flesh. "You might do, Kiri Palger." She walked away, heavily as always, surrounded by a golden aura of magic, and through the wall next to the door.

One last hug from Jenni. "See you later. Take one of the

magically armored cars home." She looked at Lathyr. "You'll see her home."

Another bow. "Of course, Princess Emberdrake."

Jenni's mouth quirked though her brows lowered in a mock scowl. "Call me Jenni, Lathyr, Jenni." She paused, hissed in a breath. "My friend, Lathyr." With a nod she left the room, too, opening and closing the door.

"Jenni is half-Lightfolk and half-human. Was she discriminated against?" asked Kiri. She moved and aches made themselves known all through her body. Her muscles had stiffened and she levered herself up with the table.

Lathyr was there, with his hand under her elbow. "You are perspicacious," he said. "Yes, full-blooded Lightfolk often ignore or discount those with human blood." He ran his finger over his pointed ear. "And those who are completely Water or Air or Earth or Fire didn't often look with kind eyes or treat kindly those of us who are mixed blood." He opened the door for her, though she got the idea that he could have somehow disappeared, too, had he wanted.

"You're part elf?" she asked.

"Yes, very minor, and a very minor Lightfolk."

"But a merman and an elf, major elementals."

He inclined his head. "Indeed."

"Just like Jenni set up in Transformation."

"Correct."

"Hmm. But Jenni is a princess and earlier you said the Lightfolk '*didn't* treat her kindly,' past tense."

"Yes, earlier this year a great bubble of magic rose from the earth's core..." Lathyr began. As they walked to the computer room, he told a story featuring Jenni and Aric.

Kiri noted that the King of Air was right. There was no damage to be seen, and once again Kiri understood something that she'd unconsciously noted had been "off." No one officed on the floor except Jenni and Aric and the staff of the other project. The offices she'd passed for nearly two weeks were dummies.

Lathyr continued to speak in a low tone and with circuitous words about the Lightfolk as he picked up her tote and they descended in the empty elevator. When they got out to mix with humans, she *saw* an illusion, the illusion she'd believed since they'd met at the neighborhood party, flick over him until his interesting skin became pale northern-European flesh tone, the tops of his ears rounded and his fingers turned from four jointed to three.

And it was Lathyr who explained everything about the real Transformation in the car behind a privacy screen, and a magical privacy shield, as they were stuck in mundane weekday traffic on the way back to Mystic Circle.

When they pulled up to her house, he dismissed the car with a wave, and walked her to her door, took her hands in his. "We had attraction between us," he said.

Past tense again, her heart sank. She turned her hands over to link fingers with his—he hadn't dropped his illusion here, but she could feel the difference. Then he disengaged and stepped back, his face in that damned polite mask. "I do not want to influence your decision."

Which meant that whatever attraction it was or had been, and if it had led to sex, he'd thought of only a passing affair, she supposed. And she'd been okay with that, had enjoyed the sexual tension, the affection. But now she was completely off balance. "Thank you," she said.

He hesitated, angled his head as if he might hear something she didn't. "I believe there will be a dinner tonight with some of the neighbors—the Davails, the Emberdrakes, me and you."

She made her mouth curve. "Sounds good."

He did a half bow and walked away. No matter that he was mer, he was still a guy, and hadn't understood that he didn't need to be around and kissing her to be in her thoughts.

She unlocked her door and stepped into her house, once again seeing it with a different mind behind her eyes. She'd loved this house—and would that truly be past tense if she transformed into a Lightfolk?

She didn't know.

Tears seemed to wash through her, mixing all sorts of strange emotions in her blood, her heart, behind her eyes. Tangled stuff she couldn't begin to sort out right now.

But one need was overwhelming. She had to talk to Shannon—as a touchstone to her old life, her present reality. Just general stuff, but she needed her friend.

She put a call through and got voice mail, and she had to fight the tears—reaction from truly fighting, the very real fear of the game?—to leave a calm message. "Hey, Shannon, can you please give me a call? Need to talk with you."

Limping to the bedroom, she stripped out of her clothes—which pretty much seemed all right despite whatever she'd gone through—and heard the peep of a text message. Thumbing to the cache she saw.

Sry, K. A & I got lst minute tics 4 expcting cpls getaway. WBB Mon. Talk then. Luv, S.

Kiri sat hard on her futon. They hadn't told her. She looked at her email. No, not one word there, either.

She *needed* them. Wanted them to just talk.

But Shannon was married and that change to their friendship had been weathered easily, expanding to include Averill.

This baby thing was different. Kiri would always be a distant third now. Very understandable.

And if she *really* wanted to intrude, Shannon would take the time to listen. But Kiri couldn't even talk to her about the major changes she was facing. Fuck.

She rolled over onto the futon and cried.

Whether she liked it or not, she'd have to make a decision to take one of two defined paths and each would exclude the other. She couldn't have it all.

The choice of the path was under her control; what followed after might not be.

Her computer timer clicked on and music filled the room, ready to welcome her home from work. The shuffle had picked screaming rock that she just couldn't handle. Enough screaming in the day—her own and the Dark one's and the eel's, and maybe she'd even heard stuff subconsciously in the offices as the others had been attacked.

She tromped toward her home office and saw the rat-thing outside her window again. Gasping, she stepped back. It hopped up onto the windowsill, four-jointed hands splayed, huge ears quivering, split pupils, stretching its mouth into a smile. "Hi, Kiri!"

SPIT WENT DOWN THE WRONG WAY AND SHE coughed.

The thing yelled at her. "You can see us fully now! I am one of the Emberdrake's brownies! I am called ROCK! Do you have some chocolate for me? I would be pleased to do any chores!"

"Uhn," she said.

"Can I come in?"

Did she want to see a real brownie up close and personal? The events in the conference room had been so odd that she hadn't paid much attention to the brownies. This wasn't one of the couple, though. The kitchen staff Jenni had once mentioned? Emberdrake brownies? "Sure."

Thankfully for her computer setup, he didn't come straight through the window but the living room wall next to it.

He was smaller than the others, was dressed in a little brown shirt and tiny leather vest and pants. His shoes turned up at the toes. Incredible.

She licked her lips, gestured to her chair and a half. Casually she turned away and walked to the kitchen cupboard where she kept some cooking chocolate. He didn't look like the brightest M&M'S in the bag. "What I'd really like is a little information about brownies and Lightfolk." She drew out a bar and thought she heard him swallow. Closing the cupboard, she crossed to him with a big smile. "You're right—I've just learned to see you, and about Lightfolk. Why don't you tell me about them?"

He was sitting on the round arm of her chair. He took the bar and broke off a corner. It disappeared fast. "I like you!"

"I like you, too," she replied automatically.

Then he began to tell stories…and it was the beginning of a night of immersion into all things Lightfolk.

Dinner was at the Emberdrakes and served by the brownies she'd met before. Rafe and Amber Davail, humans of Lightfolk descent and thus with a touch of magic, also brought their brownie and a firesprite.

Kiri liked the firesprite, too. It didn't act too much like the game's airsprite. She shuddered, though, when she thought of trying her own Transformation and dying if magic and her body didn't converge well and she tried to become a sprite.

She learned more about the major and minor elemental races. Apparently the weapons and the spells she'd used in Transformation for each realm were correct.

Once again she heard Jenni and Aric's story, and Rafe and Amber's, and when the brownies had retired to the basement to "play" in the tunnels beneath Mystic Circle, everyone except Lathyr had been brutally frank about the Lightfolk class system.

By the time Lathyr walked her home across the Circle—

again precious and serene quiet spinning between them—her head was crammed with the information the others thought she needed to make her decision.

She *had* taken Jenni up on the job, the career, in game development, whether human or Lightfolk.

As for becoming magical, most everyone thought that if she was going to be transformed, the dancing ritual should take place sooner rather than later. Decision on Monday, two days prep time, and becoming magical just as the new moon tipped into waxing early Thursday afternoon. One week from today.

Lathyr bent and kissed her cheek, saw her in, and Kiri moved to the shower, then bed, and lay staring into the dark, thinking. Feeling. Wondering.

The next morning, Thursday, Kiri called in and gave her notice, effective immediately, forfeiting her sick days. Her supervisor didn't say much since he was a good guy and knew she'd been trying out a new job. So she was off the hook there, a great relief. And the big corp was such that her supervisor's boss figured that most people in the department were eminently replaceable by the next IT applicant who hit their website.

The weather was great and she only needed a sweater when she walked around the Circle. She didn't see Jenni or Aric go to work, but thought they had, by some magical means. As had Lathyr.

Amber Davail and Tamara Thunderock—another magical-type name that she'd missed, thinking it was more Native American—both worked at home. Amber was a genealogist and Tamara ran her own bakery.

Kiri wasn't quite sure what Frank and Dan did, but they looked gone, too, probably not in a car sent for them. The gay couple might have some magic, but they didn't seem to be in the inner circle. Though an all-Circle dinner or neighborhood party was that—everyone was included.

The car Eight Corp had sent for Kiri had been for protection against great Dark ones, but evil couldn't get into the Circle because of the strength and the balance of elemental magic, and shields or whatnot. Another thing she was mushy on, but might be important. Later.

So she walked around the Circle as was her custom, then stood and looked at the koi pond. The fish were lethargic since the sun hadn't crept over their pond yet.

Decisions pressed upon her, great and life-changing, and as the sunlight warmed her shoulders, she turned and went back home.

Why would she want to risk the transformation, become a Lightfolk person?

That didn't seem to be the right question.

More like, why would she want to limit herself? A whole world of magic out there to see and explore and experience. One she hadn't even known existed.

But a new, expandable universe wasn't necessarily good. Change wasn't always better, and ending up a brownie with an inbuilt need to keep places tidy and serve others and dig and build underground areas sure didn't appeal—Rock, the brownie, had explained his race.

And despite the fun of playing in games, she didn't see herself as a fighter or a soldier. A healer would be good, she supposed.

She gave Jenni a call and talked a little more about what her life might be as a Lightfolk—and was assured she'd still have a job with Eight Corp developing story lines and working on the Transformation project. That resonated in Kiri's heart.

A game with a purpose. Entertaining people was important. Creativity was important, both using her own and sparking others. Transformation took it a step beyond.

Jenni and Aric also explained the Meld Project—where human tech was being melded with magic as a new power source and carrier. The Emberdrakes had shown her some computers—pocket and tablet and laptops that ran on Meld—and told Kiri that she might be able to make a contribution to that project, too.

So many wonders to contemplate!

Kiri had asked how her career might be different if she remained human and Jenni answered that Kiri might be moved to the Fairies and Dragons team instead, since Transformation was all about finding humans with Lightfolk potential and them becoming magical people. Jenni had paused delicately and reminded Kiri that her memory would be altered.

Kiri had thanked Jenni and hung up and paced her empty house.

A developer for Fairies and Dragons. Just what she'd yearned for, had been the pinnacle of her hopes and dreams a month ago. If she stayed human and her memory was altered, she'd be thrilled that she'd achieved what she'd wanted, be pleased and happy and work as hard as she'd intended. Right now that seemed hollow. Maybe, at the base of her nature, was the need to reach as far as she could. Doing magic didn't mean that she'd be richer, or independent, or have her life under control. But she'd be able to do magic. She'd be *more.*

The wonder of having magic. That was a huge plus. Being *more* than normal. Way cool.

Restless, she got in her car and drove around, and to her surprise, she found herself sitting before the house that had once belonged to her grandmother in the southwest part of town. The best home of her life before Mystic Circle—with her mother's mother. Where Kiri had spent most every summer, and had often visited when she'd gone to college here in Denver.

If she could tell anyone, and told her parents, they wouldn't believe her, couldn't believe in magic, were wrapped up in their own lives and not too interested in hers. They'd done their duty by her, chipped in to provide a nest egg, but sure didn't have the same values or ideas in their heads that she did.

And her grandmother...well, her mother's mother had been from Scotland and more than interested in fables and mythology, and dreaming large dreams and believing in what could not always be seen or proved.

Her grandmother—Kiri could see her grandmother risking all to become a Lightfolk being. Joyfully, even.

Another consideration was Shannon and Averill. Could she live as a magical creature and hide that from her friends? Lie to them on a long-term basis?

So far she was only silenced from talking about the offer. Someday she might be able to tell them. Then they would have the burden of a secret.

She wondered how long it took to cover herself with illusion. That probably was a nearly innate protective gift. But surely they'd notice something wrong. Not as if she could hide it if she became a brownie. And if she transformed into a naiad or merfem she reckoned that she'd have to live somewhere more humid and with more water than Colorado... not a lot of lakes and streams here. But maybe she'd get lucky.

If she lived. *Huge* downside. She'd risk death—and, right now, her life was good. If she stayed human, she'd be given a game development career at Eight Corp.

She'd be a human in a Lightfolk environment and would

never know—they'd keep those illusions solid around her, remove the memories of the past two weeks when she played in the "virtual reality" which was actually a pocket dimension.

God, she was glad she read science fiction and fantasy and played games, otherwise her mind would just freak out.

Her grandmother's old neighborhood had changed over the years and Kiri drove away, absently heading into the mountains, caught the gold of turning aspen and headed up her favorite hairpin road.

She knew the road, how to push the turns, go a little faster on the straightaways. She liked control of her life. And she liked independence. If she took the chance—a chance she might die—to become a Lightfolk, she might lose those two qualities, too.

She. Might. Die.

She'd already experienced the possibility twice and shivered at the thought of facing the Dark ones again.

She'd better be very clear and very committed to this action; she had no doubt that wavering intent could doom her.

All weekend long, notions and imaginings, prospects, possibilities and failure spun in her mind and wove through her actions—mostly her discussions. She spent one-on-one time with Amber and Jenni, Aric and Rafe, asking questions. Not only them, but Sargas the firesprite and Rock and Tiro and Hartha and Pred, the brownies, spoke with her, too.

She learned of the part magic played in Amber and Rafe's life and that they expected a distant cousin of Rafe's to move into The Fanciful House, and maybe accompany them on a quest.

Kiri even gamed a few missions in Fairies and Dragons and Transformation, scrutinizing the play, especially in the latter, since it was supposed to be based on reality.

When she went to visit Lathyr Sunday afternoon, she was admitted by a browniefem, then led to a pool where she saw him scaled and legged, lounging underwater, she knew.

She was going to do it. Sounded crazy, when all she'd ever wanted was already hers without becoming magic.

But she wanted to be more, wanted to be the best she could be. Bottom line, that was it.

And somehow, she had this bone-deep feeling that if she refused the transformation, she would always feel as if she were missing something—maybe something as major as a sense or a limb. That would probably drive her insane.

Or that particular reasoning could be a rationalization. She'd been coming up with a lot of them.

She really, really wanted this. Wanted wonder and magic in her life beyond what was already there.

But she said nothing. She'd texted Shannon that she wanted to meet with her for lunch on Monday, that she'd be at the Indian restaurant close to Shannon's work at eleven-thirty.

Then Kiri had told Jenni that Eight Corp would have her decision at 2:00 p.m. Monday afternoon.

Sunday evening Lathyr hosted another Mystic Circle dinner. Kiri watched two brownie couples—not including Rock—whisk around the place, preparing the food and setting the table.

The Lightfolk in the gathering wore simple illusions to alter their skin or hair color. Tamara Thunderock caught Kiri staring at her and dipped her head. Kiri speculated the small woman was full Lightfolk but an elf/dwarf mix, her hair was dark brown, but her eyes a brilliant blue. Tamara was of opposite elemental natures—air and earth. The standard stratified Lightfolk wouldn't like that. And the very idea of a mer/djinn mix messed with Kiri's mind.

She was the last to leave, mostly because she and Lathyr had been flirting, a lovely distraction, and she lagged out the door he held open and stopped on the porch. The other couples still walked the Circle—Dan and Frank, Amber and Rafe, Jenni and Aric.

Kiri swallowed, wanted to reach out and touch Lathyr.

"I do not wish to influence you unduly," he repeated, and she just nodded and went down the stairs and through the gate. Amber laughed and Kiri's insides squeezed. Mystic Circle had taught her magic, and fellowship, but she was wary of the place teaching her love.

Still, Tamara Thunderock hadn't lingered on the street. Maybe she was lonely.

Like Kiri.

Until she found Rock the brownie lurking in her bushes.

"Can I come in for chocolate? I told Hartha and Pred and Tiro I would."

Well, that was blunt—and she figured the brownies *were* trying to unduly influence her. "Do you brownies think I'll die?"

Rock's small and ugly features crumpled and he shivered. "Perhaps. Tiro is grumpy like that. But Hartha and Pred and I decided we must plan for the best."

Kiri unlocked the door and opened it and he marched in, went through her living room and paused at the kitchen door. She got down another hunk of chocolate for him. As he munched around it, his pupils enlarged and his ears rolled half-down. "We think magic likes you, muchly."

"Oh." That cheered her up a little.

"We have agreed that your Transformation ceremony can be the first ritual in the new main community room under the park in the center of the Circle."

"I didn't know there was a chamber under the park."

"Pred started the tunneling when he moved in, and Tiro and I have helped. It's a beautiful room and the right place for you to become Lightfolk."

"Oh." She wondered what size the room was.

Rock smiled. "It will hold all major elemental races, including tall elves and djinns."

"Ah."

"Anyway, I was to tell you that you may have the chamber to become Lightfolk in. Thank you for the chocolate."

He sank straight into her floor and was gone.

When Kiri entered the Indian restaurant, she found both Shannon and Averill waiting. She hadn't anticipated Averill, but supposed she should have. Hurrying over, she hugged them both, saying the first thing that came to mind. "You ever think that most of the time we're together it's when we're eating?"

"You wanted to talk today and it's lunchtime," Averill said, holding Shannon's chair, then Kiri's. They'd put her between them. "So we eat."

"Good company always demands good food," Shannon said. "We ordered the Chicken Tikka Masala for you."

Hard to complain, since Kiri always got Chicken Tikka Masala here and she'd already salivated when she opened the doors and smelled food.

Shannon leaned over and grabbed Kiri's hands. "So tell us the news. Did you hear already…did you get the job?"

Kiri swallowed hard and marshaled her words for misdirection or outright lying. At least she could start with the truth. "I got the job."

"Yay!" Shannon pumped her fist.

Averill smiled but his gaze was intent. "Did you accept the job?"

"Yes."

"But?" he pressed.

"But they want me to go away for some in-depth training." Kiri had decided this would be best if she had to spend time learning to be a different magical being, and if she didn't survive the transformation, she'd leave it to Aric to come up with an accident for her friends. She'd already paid her debts, made her will and left her meager savings and her house to Shannon.

"Oh." Shannon pouted, then poured the floral tea into each of their cups.

"Are you going to be able to stay in Denver?" Averill asked.

Kiri met his eyes. "I don't know. But I'll stay in touch with you."

"But you love your house and Mystic Circle!" Shannon objected.

"I do. And I love you." She leaned over to Shannon and kissed her, then did the same to Averill.

He smiled as the waiter came up with the food. "Life changes."

"Yes, it does." She relaxed her shoulders, grabbed an instant of calm serenity and lifted her handleless teacup, smiling at Shannon. "You're having a baby. That's a huge change. To life and to changes!"

They clinked their cups in a toast and Kiri thought she could feel the love. They ate and talked and were cheerful.

When they were ready to leave, Kiri knew she'd always remember the image of them as they stood together, the feel of them as they hugged her.

She'd returned to Mystic Circle by one-thirty, walked out to look at the koi—and saw Jenni and Lathyr and Aric sitting on the Emberdrakes' front porch.

Watching her. Waiting for her.

HER BREATH COMING SHORT AND CHOPPY IN her chest, Kiri crossed over to meet the people of Eight Corp. Ascending the steps to the Emberdrakes' enclosed porch kept her breathless and she struggled to look calm as she tapped on the door.

Aric and Lathyr rose. Jenni rocked in a bentwood rocker. Aric held the door open and gestured to a rattan chair. All the furniture was brand-new.

"Well?" Jenni asked.

Kiri rubbed her tongue on the roof of her mouth to give herself some spit to answer. Lathyr reached over to an unopened bottle of raspberry fizzy water on a glass-topped table, broke the top seal and handed it to her.

She could read nothing from his expression. Aric had propped himself against the wall, arms crossed, face mildly interested.

Jenni stopped and stared at Kiri, as if willing her to give Jenni the answer she wanted.

"Yes," Kiri said. "I wish to try the transformation."

Jenni leaped up, whooping, shot across the couple of yards and hugged Kiri. She didn't feel anything like Shannon, but Jenni was a friend, too, Kiri hoped. A friend and mentor who'd steer her through the whole scary process.

Then Lathyr had put his arm around Kiri's shoulders and smiled down at her, nodding. "I think you will do very well."

She nearly sagged with relief against him. "Thank you," she said.

No sound announced the appearance of the King of Air, Cloudsylph, as he materialized on the opposite end of the small porch.

"You have decided to become Lightfolk," he said matter-of-factly, looking at Kiri as both Lathyr and Aric bowed to him. Jenni rose and bowed, too.

"Yes," Kiri said. She bobbed her knees in a feeble curtsy.

The King nodded, not meeting her gaze, probably because he could ensnare her so easily. "Very good. I believe the ritual should take place as soon as possible. This evening."

Kiri stood frozen, but Jenni jerked. "We'd planned on it for Thursday afternoon, soon after the new moon."

"I understand," said Cloudsylph. "But I am available tonight, and I have a ritual myself on the new moon."

"I don't think—" Lathyr began smoothly.

"Is Ms. Palger not ready?" Cloudsylph's beautiful silver brows rose.

Lathyr stiffened beside Kiri. "Yes."

"It is always best to carry through immediately on an important decision. Doubts arise later. Don't you agree?" he asked Kiri.

She nodded. She'd had doubts, had them now, wouldn't voice them, figured she'd better damn well not feel them.

"Any doubts must be banished before you enter the ritual dance circle," Lathyr confirmed.

Kiri nodded again, said, "I know."

"King Cloudsylph, we would be honored for you to take part in the circle," Aric said, his voice slightly rough.

The Air King waved a hand. "I will return to Eight Corp until I am needed for the ritual." He glanced at the house and the Emberdrake brownies hurried out of the brick wall.

"We will begin the ceremony before moonset and end it before sunset," said Hartha, the female brownie.

Everyone nodded, but Kiri was clueless.

Cloudsylph vanished, and those who remained relaxed. Kiri swayed on her feet and Lathyr's arm came back around her. Nice.

"Most Lightfolk feel moon and sun phases," he said. "Moonset is 4:38 p.m. today and sunset is 6:38 p.m."

"We can start the ceremony at four," Jenni said with a questioning glance at Kiri.

A little more than two hours from now. Tension seized Kiri's muscles, then she forced herself to relax. "All right," Kiri said. She cleared her throat. "I've, uh, set all my affairs in order."

Without a word, the brownies whisked back inside.

Kiri met Jenni's eyes. "You've met—at least online—my friends Shannon and Averill Johnston. They are my heirs."

Jenni nodded.

"I think I'll go look at the koi," Kiri said blankly, and went back out the door. She crossed the street without looking and stared at the pond, not even seeing the fish. She stood in a daze for a couple of minutes, then headed home.

Half an hour later, a sharp, fast rat-a-tat-tat knock came

at her door. She went and looked out the peephole and saw nothing. Again. No evil in Mystic Circle…so she opened the door, to Rock, the brownie. She'd learned that the brownie-man didn't really serve Jenni and Aric Emberdrake, but Jenni's old cat, Chinook.

He strode in quickly, but with a swagger, hopped up onto the round arm of the chair and stared pointedly at the kitchen cupboards. While she was out, Kiri had bought some miniature chocolate candy bars. She put a variety in a bowl and took it to Rock.

He grinned, his eartips quivered, then his ears rolled up and down in delight. Plunging his small hands into the bowl, he stirred the candies around, then came out with one that was dark chocolate and nuts. He ate it, paper and all.

"The Princess and her Consort and the Sir spoke with us brownies," he said confidingly.

Jenni, Aric and Lathyr? Kiri raised her brows. "Oh?"

Rock inclined his head until his chin touched his chest, then took another miniature, crunched it down. "We checked the new community room hub and the wheel of tunnels, and all are ready." His little chest expanded. "We are very efficient beings. If you become one of us, you will be blessed—and welcomed, of course."

Kiri prayed she wouldn't become a brownie.

Rock hopped down and pulled out a paper and some small bottles from his flat pockets, a neat trick. "This is from Hartha, the Emberdrake browniefem. Instructions for your cleansing and preparation for the ritual. She will send over a robe for you a half hour before the ceremony begins."

"Thank you," Kiri said. Her stomach squeezed tightly. She assured herself she was committed and procedures had started.

Rock's eyes seemed to get bigger in his face. "You will love being Lightfolk."

"Uh-huh."

"You will see," he said, dropping all the chocolate candy into his pockets, which again remained flat, and trooped through the wall and outside.

Kiri sat down on the chair. Doubts were natural, so were the rationalizations, pros and cons that whirred in her mind like a hamster wheel—those that had plagued her all weekend.

Rock's head popped through the wall and she squeaked, shrank back in her chair at the sight of the disembodied head. "I forgot to tell you to look at the door to the tunnel and the chamber in your basement. It is visible now that you can see magic, and will open to your fingers." That said, he vanished again.

A door in her basement! A tunnel! And maybe she could get a good look at the space beforehand. Visualization was always a good tool before doing something important. It might even settle her. She glanced at the clock. Less than two hours.

She went to the basement door, turned on the lights and descended the stairs, that needed cleaning, especially if any visitors would be coming to her house from a hitherto unknown tunnel. Too late now.

And there, in the west brick wall, was a lovely door that matched the style of her house, and that neither she nor her Realtor had seen before. The frame was rectangular and wood of a light walnut color, wide with grooves and small squares with rosettes on each side at the top.

The door itself looked to be a darker wood, oak maybe. It, too, was rectangular, and the knob was one of those antique brass ones with a fussy pattern and polished so each curve and angle gleamed in the dull light.

When she touched the knob, a tingle of magic fizzed up her fingers, a feeling she was familiar with from the gloves in the game. Yes, magic, and from what she now knew, balanced elemental magic. She heard her own rapid breath, realized she had an inner trembling going on.

All the times she'd been in magical places—the executive floor of Eight Corp, the Castle at the top of Mystic Circle, even Jenni and Aric Emberdrake's house—she'd been unaware that they'd contained magic. Now she was about to walk through a door made by brownies, traverse a tunnel made by the small beings and find the place where she'd become a magical person herself…or die.

Gigantic deal.

Two good yoga breaths and she turned the handle and opened the door and blinked at the bright and cheerful pale yellow tiles that covered the corridor.

Wow. And they were pristine.

She stepped in, then decided to leave one of her shoes in the crack of the door just in case the thing might swing shut and lock her in. Taking both trainers off, she left them and padded down the hall stocking-footed. Again magic tingled, this time with every step she took.

As she proceeded, the tiles took on a deeper color, to gold, then golden brown, then brown by the time she came to the door at the end. Another deep breath and she depressed the iron latch and stepped into a large, circular chamber.

Rock was right—it was beautiful. The walls were set with panels of various stones: cream-colored marble with gold veins, brown granite; and semiprecious stones: rose quartz, malachite, turquoise, lapis lazuli. A rainbow of stones, and the largest panel was due north and made of gold.

There were nine doors, one for each house in Mystic Circle,

so the room she was in was like a large hub in the middle of a wheel, with the tunnels as spokes. She vaguely recalled some wheel images/symbols in Transformation.

Naturally the floor was mosaic. A few feet in, a pattern of rainbowed tiles began. They were set in a spiral that seemed to flow with magical energy, a path that was wide enough for one person to tread, and again the opening to that spiral path was in the north. Brownies and dwarves, earth elementals and the direction associated with earth was north.

Kiri couldn't imagine walking straight into the center of the room without following the path. So she stood, toes flexing under her, staring at the room.

The ceiling was arched and domelike and she marveled that this was all under the lovely park in the middle of Mystic Circle. That probably should have irritated her, because she liked the park so, and worried about tree roots and whatever, but instead this place augmented the feeling of serenity she got from the park. Comforting.

The door to the north opened and Lathyr walked through.

Their eyes met, and she thought she saw yearning in his, but he simply gave a half bow. He straightened but made no move to circle the room to her.

Power pulsed, and she became aware that magic cycled through her, affecting her. If she could feel it, so might every other human. If humanity on earth had no magic in and of themselves, she and others like her would transform and claim it now, and that seemed right. Making magic their own, on their own world, seemed right.

She stood straighter.

"A lovely chamber," Lathyr said. "Equal to any I've seen in the minor palaces."

Of course there'd really be Lightfolk palaces. "Where's—"

She stopped. Would he tell her, even before she became Lightfolk? As if she were a threat to them.

She shifted feet.

"Kiri," Lathyr said, in a deep rich voice she hadn't heard before. "You may decide against this action up to the very moment you step onto the path to dance to the center of the circle." He waved to the very middle of the room, a ruby heart inset into the final curl.

Dancing along the path? That hadn't been explained to her before. She swallowed and nodded.

"But once our circle closes around you, you *must* be dedicated with all your being to becoming a Lightfolk." His hand dropped, expression got even more intense. "I believe it will be an ordeal, Kiri, and one you must survive."

So she voiced her deepest hope. "Do you think I can become an elfem?"

Now he crossed to her, without illusion so she saw his gliding grace. He reached out as if to take her hands like he'd done so often before, but stopped.

She took his hands, enjoyed the connection between them, the magic, hoped she didn't show her pleasure, but kept her face properly serious. "Do you think I can become an elfem?"

He hesitated.

"Truth!" she demanded.

"In truth, then, no. I think becoming an elf is something your mind wants and not your heart."

"And my body will follow my heart."

His expression turned granite impassive. "I think you need to have no split in mind or heart." He cleared his throat. "I know you like control of your life."

"Who doesn't?" she shot back.

He inclined his head. "But I think you may need to surrender to this. Have faith in the magic in you, in the balanced power of this place, know who you are to your depths and surrender."

She let out a long and shaky breath. "Not a fight I should win?"

"Who would you be fighting, Kiri? The magic that will conform to your deepest wishes? If so, stop this now. Yourself? You should *not* fight yourself."

"All right. I understand." Breathe in and out. "Do you think I might become a sprite?" And die.

His clasp firmed around her fingers. "No. I think you have too much potential magic for that. I would not let you do this if I believed you would perish."

That was good news, and, like he said, she heard that in her ears, her brain accepted it, but she had doubts in her heart. "What kind of Lightfolk do you think my innermost me is?"

"Truly? I believe you will become mer or naiad. Water Realm called to you, Kiri."

"Uh-huh."

A last squeeze of her fingers and he let them go. "You have the ability to become a dwarfem, too."

"Not a brownie?"

"I do not believe so."

"And you're the best expert."

His lips twitched a grimace. "Yes. I do not have a great deal of experience with this, but I have more than anyone else."

"More sense of potential magic."

He kissed her cheek. "Kiri," he said in an American accent. "You're loaded with it. Later."

He moved faster than she could see and was gone, and she didn't quite know how he had vanished.

Oh, she wanted to know those secrets. How Aric and Jenni

and Lathyr appeared and disappeared. What travel powers they might have. She hadn't asked Rock, who had jabbered on about moving through the earth, a power both brownies and dwarves had, and she wasn't sure how fast that was. But with magic everything could be fast.

Absently she moved around the room, feeling the magic. All the elements were mixed and balanced. She *could* tell the difference in the atmosphere in here and the computer room at Eight Corp—which felt mostly of Jenni's fire and some of Lathyr's water. Closing her eyes in memory, she let her tongue curl to the top of her mouth. Eight Corp was mostly air. If the Air King was the most powerful dude who usually hung there, that would explain it.

And she'd made a circuit of the room, liked it. Definitely special.

She could do this. Being a naiad or a mer would be wonderful. Smiling, she went through her door and back up to her house and smelled luscious odors—brownies had left a rich stew on her stove along with a mouthwatering small loaf of bread that Kiri knew Tamara had made.

She dug in.

Then she followed the instructions, bathed and meditated to music and fixed her will to become Lightfolk, her intention in her mind, rooted in her heart.

She donned the raw silk robe, light but opaque, for which she was thankful. It felt odd, only wearing one long thing, but she figured so many other new and wonderful things were about to happen that she'd soon be distracted.

Kiri was ready when Amber Davail came to lead her to the circle—transformation or doom.

AMBER SPOKE TO KIRI ABOUT THE DAY, THE pretty sky, the warm weather, the small slice of waning crescent moon low in the sky, everyday matters, as they walked downstairs and through the tunnel to the new community ritual chamber.

When Kiri saw everyone there to dance the ritual for her transformation, her eyes stung. The Emberdrakes stood in the south of the circle, Jenni smiling at her. Rafe awaited Amber in the southwest and nodded at Kiri. Tamara Thunderock took the exact northeast compass point. All of the brownies were there. So was Jenni's old cat, sitting, tail around her feet, smiling smugly.

Kiri's breath hitched as she saw the King of Air, Cloudsylph, taking the power point of due east, and Mrs. Daurfin and a strange dwarf directly north.

Amber's firesprite, Sargas, wasn't the only sprite there, another firesprite hovered in the south, and a trio of airsprites in the southeast. The west point had Lathyr, of course, and a naiad and naiader on either side of him. There were even a couple of women Kiri stared at until she realized they were dryads. Fascinating.

"Who are these people?" Kiri asked Amber under her breath.

"Part of Eight Corp's technology-magic Meld team." Amber grinned. "We invited them to take part in the ritual and everyone came!"

"That's *so* nice of them. Thank you all for coming!" Kiri projected her voice.

"We are honored to be here," Cloudsylph said.

Huh. Wow. Excitement bubbled through Kiri.

Amber walked Kiri to the opening of the spiral path, then took her place next to her husband.

"Everyone join energies, please," Cloudsylph said.

One of the dryads bobbed up and down on her toes. "Oooh, such lovely *strong* and balanced magic." She aimed her comment at Lathyr with a fluttering of lashes. Kiri didn't like that.

Whoops. No negative energy. That could make things go wrong, she was sure.

The king nodded to her and smiled, and her feet stuck to the ground. "We will begin our dance as you dance the spiral path."

She didn't consider herself a good dancer, and it was unexpectedly hard to take that first step onto a path with her bare feet.

Of course, once she did that, she was committed to everything. Maybe her "dance" down the spiral would center her mind and her will. She told herself it would.

She felt the focus of everyone's eyes, but no one spoke. She thought that's what she was waiting for, some prompt. But as a minute stretched into two, she understood that they were all respecting her choice.

People, Lightfolk and human, respecting her. She liked that.

One last question to her heart. Did she really want to do this? Risk her life for the chance to become magic? No guarantees of what elemental being she might become. No guarantees of her skills or spells.

No guarantees of life.

Her gaze went to the Air King, the beautiful elf. His expression remained impassive, and it seemed as if he could await her forever. He had a preternatural patience.

Supernatural. Just like she wanted to be.

She looked in the opposite direction. Lathyr, too, was serious. Handsome in a different way than the king. And he, too, gave no prompting, no smile, no tiny nod of his head.

All up to her.

She closed her eyes. *Felt* the magic. The great and balanced elemental magic imbuing the chamber, just outside her grasp, for now. But if she believed in herself, she could have it, stand there in the outer circle and dance together with others who had magic.

Yes, she *yearned* for that.

So one last huge breath…one of the last breaths she hoped to take as a human, and she uncurled her toes from the tiny groove they'd found in between the mosaics and stepped onto the path. And felt a huge rushing of exultation from the others. Respect. Appreciation. *Belief.*

Dance! Dance on the path. She shuffled and swayed and music surrounded her, air rushed in her ears, her feet kept time with her pulse, then came a lapping tide, the roar of surf. Patter-patter-thump! Her dance. She raised her arms, swayed. Fire crackled and she could almost see it leap joyfully in a bonfire.

Yes!

Joy. Believe.

Now and then she heard low and earthy drumbeats from an instrument held by the dwarf, who circled, elbows linked, with others around the room in a blur of colors. They sang, magical elemental ancient songs with notes so sweet and pure Kiri wept.

And then she reached the center of the room and magic struck her.

*Who are you?* the magic whispered as it whirled. *Where do you belong? To whom do you belong?* Grammatical magic, who knew? But it shuddered and demanded the cells in her body answer.

The room disappeared and she hung in rainbow-glitter-streaked blackness. Awesome. The chamber was beautiful, but she hadn't liked it as much as the image she'd had in her head of a proper ritual room, a conservatory, like the one at the Castle, but without a pool. In the ritual room there were no living beings other than those in the dancing circle down here. No plants, not even an insect.

Then she thunked down.

*Who are you? Where do you belong? To whom do you belong?*

She stood in a…crib…bending and straightening her legs, whimpering, thin hands curved around the rail. People were shouting. People she loved. So she screamed. *Look at me! Look at me! Pay attention to ME!*

The man and the woman turned and yelled at her.

Black and rainbow glitter whirled her.

She stood on the shadowing staircase at seven. Her father opened the door and it was cold and he took a suitcase and left, slamming the door. The woman cried and cried and cried, and Kiri did, too, but nothing changed.

And she began to feel more than the wind that whisked the memories around her, yanking tears from her eyes, tangling her hair into painful snarls. Heat crisped the tiny hairs along her skin. Fire.

Searing her lungs as she gasped. Then a vision formed of her grandmother's living room, a modest ranch-style home in Denver. Peace. Rules, but no hysterical demands from her mother, no cold orders from her father.

Yes, this was a home.

*Who are you?*

*I am Kiri Palger and I am singular. I am special. I am unique.* She could scream that to the wind, that gut-heart-soul belief because she knew it to be true. Everyone was special and unique and so was she.

Her dorm room, with Shannon sitting in an institutional desk chair, went up in flames that licked Kiri. Love for friend. This one friend.

Memory flashed of her own green Mohawk hair, chains, a belly ring. Yeah, that had hurt.

She carved her own meaning of special into her soul. She had to, because she was creative…with games, with stories for games. Yeah, that got real respect in the outer world, sure.

*Who. Are. You?* The elemental powers mocked as she was torn apart, cell ripped from cell.

And she was screaming and crying from pain but nothing escaped her lost mouth, sounded on her lost ears, affected the rainbow sparkling night at all. But without sight or smell or hearing or touch, she yet knew who she was, yet kept the kernel of herself together, protected the seed of who she was and could become.

The searing fire stopped, the piercing wind, the tumbling earth that had smothered her, all washed away by a sea-green-white-frothed flood that threatened to send her molecules tumbling away and never to be gathered again, lost to the salt of the ocean and the four winds and the desert sands and motes of the universe.

*Who are you!* A demand she felt.

A demand she answered silently. She no longer had words, nor concepts, that she'd always thought were the basis of her being, a rational mind. No, the demand pulled something from her that she'd never imagined…a *shape.* Her heart, her blood, her marrow, her *being* fashioned it, threw it into the restless storm—a many-pointed star.

And with that burst of light, pain consumed her, and all she knew was enduring, surviving, *being.*

One last pummel and she lost herself, struggled all the way back for one last instant. She could not survive another. But the robe took on the water and the earth and twined around her and felt so heavy she fell.

She hurt. She lived.

A wild thing whimpered, desperate, but she couldn't help, could only hunch in the present.

"It's done!" some woman said-shouted, sounding happy.

Kiri wept—the woman was not her mother.

"We must immerse her in the Castle pool immediately," a man said, not her father, and she was glad and she liked the voice, the faint accent and should know it, should know him, but didn't and liked the feel of this man's arms under hers and his grip as she slipped and wiggled.

A light blue arm with four-jointed fingers, woman's arm, flopped before her milky vision, then away.

Air rushed by her, drying her lips and her skin and seemed

to be putting little cracks in her that dirt and dust caked around and hurt!

All of her hurt!

Blackness—without any rainbow sparkles. Had they all gone into her and turned into fizzy champagne? Sorta felt like it and she was smiling and her cheeks bunching and she cried and giggled—darkness swooped around her, then she was shoved into something warm and soft and liquid and she knew she was being born.

Lathyr and others watched through the window of the saltwater chamber as Kiri curled, then stretched, then curled again. She was in complete mer form, including tail, tail fin, fins along her arms and her legs and webbed feet and hands. Her skin was a slightly deeper blue than his own, but he had elven blood. Her hair was long and deep green. She lived.

His body wanted to sag against the tank wall, but he kept it straight. Naiad Kiri had nearly died in the pool, so they'd moved her to the saltwater tank.

A person nudged him and he forced his feet to shift aside so Amber Davail could look in. She smelled of perspiring human, not unpleasant, but not mer, and he wished to have mer around him. Wished to be with Kiri, but the Emberdrakes would not allow that. This last test she must pass alone, waking as a Lightfolk.

"Wow," Amber said. "That was incredible." She turned with wonder in her eyes and met his gaze. "Thank you for letting me participate."

He inclined his body. "You are quite welcome. We could not have done it without you."

Rafe Davail pushed close to his wife, looked in at the new water Lightfolk fem without a glance at Lathyr. "You think such a transformation will always take so many people of mixed races? And in a magically balanced chamber? Not sure it's cost effective."

"I—we—hope to refine the process," Lathyr said.

"Is she a merfem or a naiad?" Amber asked.

"A naiad," Lathyr and the other Waterfolk said.

"How can you tell?" Amber persisted.

Lathyr was in his two-legged, hardscaled form and gestured to his skin and the silver pattern of ridged scales. "Naiads and naiaders don't have these designs, and mers are born with them."

"Oh." Amber stared at his chest, and then gazed back at Kiri's unmarked blue torso.

The earnest young naiader said, "It's mostly a matter of power. Mers have more magic."

"Ah." Amber grimaced. Like the rest of them, she'd wanted Kiri to become one of the greater elemental beings…a merfem, dwarfem, djinnfem.

Rafe smiled and his lashes lowered over gleaming eyes. "Let's go home. All that magic was…energizing."

Sexual, he meant. Lathyr nearly begrudged the couple their happiness when Kiri remained in danger. Nearly. Now that he'd come to know them, he understood they'd fought battles in the past and would in the future.

Most of the others of the circle left, too.

"We did a great job. The project is a success." Jenni stuck out her chin.

"Yes," Lathyr said. Kiri still had to wake and accept her fate.

"Kiri will be fine," Aric said, wrapping his arm around his wife's waist. "Later, Lathyr."

"Yes," Lathyr repeated. The couple walked away, murmuring.

He stood by the window and brooded, watching Kiri. For

a moment or two he'd been terrified that he'd lost her, and sickness welled through him, poisoning his blood. He'd convinced her to take this chance. He'd wanted to prove his new powers were valuable. That *he* was valuable. He'd wanted to win his estate. Have a true home, a place of his own, forever. None of that was worth Kiri's life.

A small, wet cough attracted his attention and he saw the naiader who had helped in the circle, a member of the Meld team. The naiader was very young, under four decades.

Lathyr turned and bowed formally to the man, expressing gratitude with swirls of his hands. "Thank you for taking part in the circle."

The naiader shifted his weight, ducked his head. "It was great. Great circle, biggest—um—most important I've ever attended." He shoved a small note bubble at Lathyr.

Lathyr took it with a questioning look.

The young naiader said, "Jenni says that Ms. Palger might need to try out rivers and streams and whatnot."

"True," Lathyr said.

"I, uh..." The naiader shifted again. "My father lives in Maroon Lake. Anyway, he, Stoneg, is interested in this project, and if you need to show Ms. Palger options, like such a lake, Stoneg says she could visit."

There weren't that many lakes in Colorado, and Lathyr had memorized them all. Maroon Lake in the mountains was beautiful, but there was something—

The naiader continued. "I know, it's not a very deep lake, but with it being so shallow, not much harm could come to her. It's a mountain lake, not a city lake, stocked with trout, and natural enough. Twenty-five acres for her to roam and feel right in. Good exercise for her bilungs in a natural setting, and for learning to mask her appearance."

Only a naiader would want to live in so shallow a lake. This Stoneg must cloak himself in illusion all the time. Lathyr repressed a shudder. "I will consider that. I thank you for your offer." Again Lathyr bowed.

With a casual wave, the naiader dissipated into the air and moved his molecules from the Castle to wherever he called home.

Lathyr waited by the window all night, watching as Kiri curled and stretched, curled again, woke and half dozed and swam. After a while she reverted from a tailed mer to the legged form with hardscale, and a couple of hours after that her skin turned back to its original color and texture and she became human.

Amber dropped by early the next morning. She gazed at the human Kiri. "Can you get her out of the water?"

"Why?" he asked, feeling sluggish from lack of sleep.

"She'll be frightened if she wakes up surrounded by water. She'll think she's drowning. You should take her out now."

"Her bilungs—"

"Won't they automatically change?"

They should. Lathyr could only hope.

"I really think you should get her out of there," Amber insisted.

Lathyr should run the idea by Jenni, but now he was more certain of his contribution to the project, of himself and his worth. "Very well." Slowly he drained most of the water and when the chamber contained only a meter, he went into the tank, held Kiri close, then rose with her into the air.

Her breath caught. Stopped.

He waited, counting off the seconds. No more than twelve before he'd decide whether to return her to the water or try to force the air-breathing part of her bilungs to work.

She coughed, coughed again, sucked in loud and noisy breaths. Something a mer would not do. Were her bilungs good?

She clung to him and he prayed she would not drown in air.

One more cough, then her eyes opened and she blinked and the nictitating lids went away and her befuddled gaze was the same sea-green he'd always admired.

"Lathyr? I had a dream—"

"You are naiad, Waterfolk, Lightfolk," he said.

"YAY!" A MUFFLED WOMAN'S SHOUT HIT KIRI'S ears and she blinked again. Her eyes…felt funny, and sounds to her ears had a funny tone, too. She'd thought she'd heard other noises and voices and conversations, but couldn't recall them.

She coughed again, throat raw and burning, felt wobbly. Lathyr steadied her and she realized she was plastered against him. He didn't seem to mind.

Lathyr, ritual.

"You okay, Kiri?" Amber shouted.

Lathyr, ritual, Amber.

"You breathing?" Amber insisted.

Lathyr, ritual, Amber and breathing. Kiri drew in a deep breath, the pain in her throat easing. She looked up at Lathyr, his pale blue face, his slightly pointed ears, his green hair. His chest was harder than muscle and skin against hers.

Lathyr, ritual, Amber, breathing. *Lathyr Lightfolk merman!*

Knowledge slammed down on her, even as water lapped

around her legs. Holding on to his biceps, she looked down at herself.

She was naked, her body the same.

"Whew," Amber said, in a loud voice. She waved at Kiri through a round window. "Good to see you're doing good after spending most of yesterday afternoon and all night in the water."

A day and a half in the water? Kiri's toes weren't even wrinkly. "I made it." She gripped Lathyr harder. "Say it again, what you did before, when I just woke up!" She had to hear the words, had to have them thrum against her ears.

"You are naiad, Waterfolk, Lightfolk," he repeated.

"I made it."

"Yes," Lathyr said.

"I don't feel any different."

"You are," Amber said.

"You are in your human form," Lathyr said. He bent so his mouth was close to her ear. "Are you pleased?"

"Hell, yes." Kiri slid her feet in a small boogie. She didn't slip.

"We are in the saltwater tank in the Castle," Lathyr said precisely, as he helped her through a large porthole.

"I didn't even know there was a saltwater tank in the Castle," she said.

Amber grabbed Kiri and hugged her hard—differently than Shannon, but Kiri's eyes stung all the same.

"Thank God," Amber said. She stepped back and grabbed a lush terry robe from a browniefem and helped Kiri into it while Lathyr closed the door.

"Do you recall the Water Realm banishing spell from Transformation?" asked Lathyr.

It took a minute to call up the gesture and the words. "Uh, yeah."

"Send the water into the air or the earth."

Magic. Her first real magic. Pressing her lips together, Kiri turned to face the tank and visualized the finger-flexing and hand-waving a couple of times before she tried.

It worked! The remaining water vanished.

Kiri gasped.

"Excellent!" Amber said.

"I guess." Kiri felt a little dizzy.

Lathyr pulled her arm through his elbow. "You need food and water."

"I'll have breakfast with you," Amber said.

"Great," Kiri said faintly. She felt the magic around her, inside her, had used it, and that had tingled, but she wasn't as changed as she'd expected. And she was a naiad, not a mer or an elf.

Lathyr guided her up the wide stairs, and a brownieman ushered them into the breakfast nook on the ground floor in one of the turrets, with a view of the gardens.

Well, at least she wasn't a brownie—that had been a fear. And she wasn't a dwarf.

Kiri was eating scrambled eggs Florentine when Jenni bustled in, a wide grin on her face. She bent down and kissed Kiri on the cheek. "Welcome to the Lightfolk."

"Thanks."

"We believe that you should stay here at the Castle where Lathyr can keep an eye on you," Jenni went on. "If you'd turned djinn or dwarf, you would have stayed with me."

"Oh." A twinge went through Kiri at the thought of not being in her own little house, her own bed. She tried to think logically. "So I'm a naiad. Do you, like, measure my magic or what, first?"

But Jenni was shaking her head. "I think your magic is still, um, flickering into a flame inside you. We'll wait. Isn't like we've done this before."

"All right." Kiri looked at Lathyr. "What first?"

He put down his napkin. "Forms," he said.

"Forms?"

"A Waterfolk has various forms. Full mer with tail."

She'd missed having her tail! Dammit. "Forms like in the game."

"That's right. You need to practice your forms and your breathing."

Kiri sighed. What had she expected, zooming through the ocean and playing with dolphins? Despite all the time she'd taken to make her decision, she hadn't quite imagined the immediate afterward of her transformation.

"Okay."

"Eventually you will be presented to the Lightfolk royals," Jenni said. "The four elemental couples, the Eight."

Eight Corp. Now it all made sense.

"Okay."

"You'll do great," Jenni said in those cheerleader tones she'd used all through the project.

And Kiri felt better for eating. Magic really did wash through her. She managed a big grin back. "Yeah, I will."

Later she stood in human form, naked with Lathyr in the shallow end of the pool. The water only came up to her knees and she was all too aware of her nudity, but Lathyr seemed to be all right with having no clothes on. At least he wasn't reacting to her as if she were attractive to him, and she shouldn't be thinking of sex.

She kept her eyes on his face...well, no lower than his chest...after she'd given him a quick check-out to see that he was human despite the pale blue skin and the pointy ears. She'd been right about the ears all along.

"Listen to me, Kiri," Lathyr said patiently and she met his eyes as her gaze traveled back up. She thought his lips held a satisfied curve.

She swallowed. "Listening."

"We have four forms."

"Whoa."

He chuckled.

"Human form, as I am."

"Your skin is blue."

"That it is," he replied austerely. "An outer manifestation of my elemental magic nature. Just as Jenni's skin is reddish and Aric's has a tint of green."

Words escaped Kiri as she understood that she'd been blind to so much around the Circle. She wondered about the other inhabitants, but wouldn't ask.

"Kiri?"

She wet her lips, more from nerves than need. She seemed to have more spit in her mouth. If she thought about it, she could sense water from the pool penetrating her skin and going... somewhere. Plumping her tissues?

"Our form that you will feel most comfortable with is human," Lathyr said, as if he knew her mind wandered. "Our second form is legged-mer with hardscale."

Before she could ask anything, he'd turned *different*. She'd felt the spike of magic that made him *other*. His skin became more like tiny scales, and there was a raised pattern on his scales on both torso and legs, most beautiful. And that part of him that she'd been distracted by and was *not* looking at, was gone behind a bulge, nicely protected?

"Do you have an anatomy book of mer forms?" she asked.

He appeared surprised, but grinned, tilted his head toward the front of the house. "There may be one in the library."

"Okay."

"Now you try."

"Wait, I want to see the differences." She stared at him. His fingers were longer, with an extra joint, there were fins along his arms and the backs of his legs. He spread his fingers and she saw they were webbed and as she watched, hard nails extruded into claws. Looking down at his feet through the clear and still water, she saw they were also longer, webbed and clawed.

"Awesome," she said doubtfully.

He shook his head, still smiling, and turned.

His back and butt and legs looked the same except for the fins on his legs and spine.

He swam a few strokes, his shoulder-length green—hair? plant fronds?—floating around his head. His facial structure had stayed the same.

Just like the game.

With just his head above water, not doing any paddling or anything to stay afloat despite his muscular mass, he said, "And there is full mer." He ducked underwater and became a merman, complete with long fishtail ending in a double fin with more webbing between it. A beautiful blue-green-silver glittery tail. Sexy.

He had the same pattern on his tail as he'd had on his legs, only more complete. And when he flipped and zoomed around the pool, he was breathtakingly beautiful in his grace. He seemed longer as a full mer than he was tall as a man. Looking at the tail, it was obvious there were no legs in there, pure fish structure.

Kiri swallowed again. Fish hadn't been her favorite thing.

But she loved the koi.

Lathyr stopped just beyond her, bobbing chest high in the water. She'd been wrong about his face. It had subtly altered, and there was tiny, delicate webbing around his nostrils. Inside?

So many questions—that she could find answers for herself if she tried to change. She *knew* she'd been legged-mer, and full-mer earlier, just after the transformation.

And why was she delaying? She was a *magical* being! She'd wanted this.

Despite all logic, she'd wanted to be an elf.

Instead she was a naiad. And that was really cool. Really.

"Think of your magical power," Lathyr said, his voice lilting more, with undertones she could hear that humans—or even other elemental beings—might not be able to distinguish.

Lovely tones. She could be a beautiful mermaid—naiad, she corrected.

And she couldn't go back.

She closed her eyes and *felt* her magic, huge and liquid and wonderful. She had this, more senses, the ability to do wondrous things, experience fabulous adventures unknown to humankind.

Smiling, she let the sense of her own magical power infuse her, *felt* it all along her skin, in her tissue, blood, bones. She *was* magical. She'd fought to become magic, to have such power, to be able to *use* it.

Whether she'd anticipated it or not, she was Waterfolk, mer, a naiad. Her smile widened as water lapped around her legs, as she sensed each droplet in the air around her, some even lying on wide-leafed plants, and being sucked up.

The heat of fire, the rich scent of earth, the soft press of air magic, all balanced, enveloped her. To be magical, to be naiad, was a very good thing.

"You have changed to your legged-mer form," Lathyr said softly.

She opened her eyes and looked down. She hadn't truly *experienced* the change, but now that she thought back, she recalled the fizz along her skin. And she felt different. Like his sex, hers was protected behind a fold of skin. Her nipples, too, were covered, as if she'd grown another skin-with-scales over her body. She felt slightly heavier. Sucking in her breath, she caught a fluttering around her nose. Those little curtains of web!

Slowly she touched the pad of her light-blue-skinned, longer finger to them.

"Nostril frills," Lathyr said.

"Pretty."

"You are exquisitely beautiful," he whispered.

Kiri blinked, and another lid came over her eyes, one she could see through. She squealed, lost her balance and fell into the water.

Lathyr was there, taking her hand and drawing her into the deep section of the pool. Her hair had extended again, and caressed her all the way down to her waist, emerald fronds.

She angled up to take a breath, and he shook his head.

*Can you hear me, Kiri?* His voice came into her mind.

Startled, she backpaddled, then nodded strongly.

*That is good. Now you must become accustomed to your bilungs.*

Once again Kiri thought of an anatomy book. *Bilungs?* She thought the question at Lathyr, in what she hoped was a normal tone of "voice."

*Lungs that will take what you need from the air…or the water. Bifunctional.*

"Uh-huh," she said, and the sounds warped and escaped on bubbles and she got water in her mouth and went quiet with incipient panic.

*Don't think about breathing, just do it. Your lungs will adjust.*

She didn't see how. Almost couldn't believe him, but had those murky recollections of being in the tank—and she couldn't afford to *disbelieve* or panic.

*Should I, should I open my mouth?* she asked.

*Swim with me, lovely Kiri.* He took her hand and drew her down to the bottom of the pool. She gasped, shuddered. Trembled.

Breathed.

She kept her mouth slightly open. Probably looked odd, but it seemed to feel better…for right now. They swam slowly, then to the middle of the pool, Kiri looked down and colors there were no names for exploded into view. The pool bottom wasn't white, like she'd thought. There was neon-purple-silver, red-violet-shining-blue, and as she stared, the pattern became a mural.

*This is wonderful!* She dropped his hand and sank closer… and curled her tail under her.

At the sight, she gobbled water, spewed, her lungs—bi-lungs—compressed, trapping water, air, *stuff.*

Lathyr swam close, drew her into his arms, turning her head against his chest. *Breathe. Yes, you are full mer with tail. Breathe with me. One-two-three.*

She did, and felt his tail brush hers…not quite sensual, or sexual, but made her very aware of her own, wide and muscular at the hips and strong all the way down, but so flexible.

She felt powerful. Her beautifully curved and delicate fin at the end of her tail wiggled. She had a tail! Eeek!

*You are exquisitely Kiri. Breathe with me. One-two-three.*

Exquisitely Kiri. She liked that, smiled wide and water went in and out of her mouth, necessary air went in and out of her lungs. Impossible? Or only possible with magic? Probably, but she *was* magic. She angled her tail to see it. Darker green than Lathyr's, as her hair was darker.

*Breathe with me. One-two-three.*

She hadn't needed the last reminder from him, breathed on her own fine, now, but bent her tail up close. *I don't have a pattern,* she projected her thoughts.

*Naiads and naiaders don't,* he said calmly as if it didn't matter, though disappointment pinched at her.

*I want to see YOUR pattern.* She let go of his hands, backed up, and hummed with pleasure. His pattern of raised scales was nearly silver, curves and angles with white dots as punctuation above the topmost straight line. She wanted to touch but didn't quite dare be so intimate.

She had no clue of the sexual mores of Lightfolk, or of Waterfolk, though Jenni and Aric were married, and the royals were royal *couples.* So much to learn.

Glancing at him, his expression now hard for her to read, she sent mentally, *Do patterns matter to Merfolk? Do they indicate status?*

He nodded. *Very intelligent. Yes, you must have noticed my white circles, they show that I have elven blood.*

*Really! How cool.*

He continued on, *My blood is considered tainted by many mers since I am only ninety-two percent mer.*

She snorted and it didn't go right and she sucked in water or air and thrashed around until Lathyr came and grasped her, swam them to shallow water and lifted her head from the water, where she really seized.

"Breathe with me. One-two-three. Air, now, one-two-three."

It took several minutes for her to calm and get the hang of air breathing again. "That's, that's..." she sputtered spit—so uncool!

"I'm sorry if I presumed."

She grabbed his shoulders and her hands slid off the slickness, so she went for his hair. "That's so stupid, to judge a person by their skin, their pattern...their elemental purity."

Now his expression appeared remote. So she took a hard grip on his hair and tilted her head and kissed him.

His lips were damp with tastes of the water he'd been in... the slight floral-jasmine hint of the pool they swam in now, a trace of salt from the chamber in the basement that her tongue swept from his lips, and a tang of fish....

She pulled back. "Koi? Really? You've been in the koi pond?"

"It is more natural and always better balanced magically than the pools here. The koi pond is easier to transport to and from in our droplet form. Which I also need to show you." He stepped back and away from her, and her arms dropped. She didn't know if she'd offended him, if he was as attracted to her as she was to him. His skin seemed paler, and had a pearly sheen that she hadn't noticed before, exciting. His features appeared sharper.

Best to be blunt. "Did you like the kiss? I did. Would you like to kiss again, or have sex?"

LOUD TITTERING AND SMALL GUFFAWS CAME from the edge of the pool. Kiri looked over and saw the brownies—the couple who lived with Jenni and Aric and the ones who took care of the Castle. The two males bowed and the females curtsied.

"Now you are formally living in Castle, we formally introduce ourself," said the browniefem. "I am Melody. My new mate, Dade. We assigned here at Castle. You stay here so should know us."

"We are assigned here to the Castle, and you are staying here because you are now naiad and Waterfolk, so you should know us, and that we are here to care for you," corrected the brownieman. "We would like to know which room or suite we should prepare for Kiri Palger…or whether she will share your rooms."

Kiri's heart thumped behind her hardscale.

"Kiri must always have rooms of her own for sanctuary,

here," Lathyr said austerely. "Prepare the secondary Merfolk suite."

"Yes, noble Sir."

"Meanwhile, I need to demonstrate the droplet-form to Kiri and help her practice it," Lathyr said.

The brownies bowed and curtsied again. The Emberdrakes' couple vanished with little pops, but Kiri thought they'd actually dematerialized themselves and sped through the walls.

Melody stared at them, her eyes protuberant. "Lathyr not... *do* not belong in chamber on *this* floor. We move you to water elemental room."

Another chuckle and a wink from the brownieman. "We'll make the water suite nice for you both." Then they sped from the pool area into the hallway. And Kiri became aware that Lathyr was stroking her long hair and her back in a soothing matter.

She smiled up at him and he leaned down and brushed his mouth across hers, nibbled at her lips and said, "Yes, I like kissing you. Yes, I'd like to have sex with you. Yes, we should practice your droplet form." Again he separated himself from her. "And once you are good in each form, we will find what kind of naiad you are."

She blinked in confusion, still wanting his lips on hers, and her second set of eyelids came down and went up, distracting. "What do you mean?"

"You might be more comfortable living in a stream, or a pond, a spring or a lake, a river. Whether you live better in fresh or salt water. We must determine that."

"Oh." She looked around the beautiful room, felt the flow of water against her legs. "Not a swimming pool naiad."

"I hope not. That would be a failure of the transformation,

and I'm sure that isn't true. You are a fully magical water elemental."

Her mouth turned down. "And I won't be able to live in Mystic Circle."

"Not in your house without a pool."

"And not here, not for long," she said mournfully.

"No."

"So, I will have to find my own spot."

"That is so. We will all help you."

"Oh, all right."

He transformed from legged-mer to full human, keeping his paler, sparkly skin.

"Do I sparkle, too?"

"What?"

"Your skin. It has a sparkle. No, more like a sheen."

He glanced down at himself, frowned. "I don't see that."

"One of the first things I noticed about you," she insisted.

"Hmm." His muscles flexed in his chest and upper arms. "Highly magical water elementals have more of a sheen to their skin and scales than others. That I sparkle..." He shrugged. "I gained new powers with the magic in the spring, but not enough for a permanent sheen, due to my elven blood, probably more like an occasional flicker."

She didn't think so, but didn't contradict him.

"Also, we met in the evening, so it may be better seen in the twilight."

"I suppose so."

He walked up the ramp to the poolside and as he did, he dried off. Must be a neat water elemental trick.

"How do you do that?"

"What?"

"Dry off?"

"One absorbs all the water on one's body into one's skin. Were Jenni here, she'd sizzle it off with fire."

"Oh." Again she kept her gaze on his face, well, no lower than his nipples. As a human he had them, but as legged or full-mer they were behind that other skin, hardscale.

"It is best to practice droplet form out of the water with young mers. In the water, you might disperse too much. In the air, you hold together more." He grimaced. "Especially air as dry as this."

The conservatory and pool—the whole Castle—was a whole lot more humid than outside.

"Become human, Kiri," he prompted.

It took but a thought and the fins on her arms, legs and spine disappeared as well as that other, harder, almost armor-like flesh encasing her own. Though when she studied herself, she remained blue.

He faced her and offered her his hands. When she put one of hers in his, he linked fingers. *We will mind-speak in droplet form also.*

*All right.* Nervous, she shifted her feet.

*First, feel me dissipate. I am separating my molecules into the water droplets in the air around me.*

*Uh-huh.* Her brain hurt if she tried to think about how that worked. Like everything else in her life, it could be answered in one word, *magic.* And if it worked, she didn't need an explanation, right? Or she could learn one later.

She looked into Lathyr's focused face, saw him begin to vanish, or turn invisible, disturbing. And her fingers began to lose his grip. Then he, as human, was gone. For a moment a colorful mist remained near, then it, too, was lost to sight.

*I can move in this fashion, slowly through the air, faster if I find water, streams and rivers above or underground. Faster still with a storm.*

"And the more humid the area, the faster you can go."

*That is correct.* He faded in right before her as if he'd never moved, in his legged-mer form.

"Um, you just spread your molecules out, and put air molecules between them?"

*That is correct.* His hands were holding hers again and he lifted each of hers to his lips and kissed them. A nice little erotic shiver went through her. Romance and sex. Later. Concentrate on the now.

"What happens if something comes in between your molecules?"

*Usually we are moving in this form, and keep together by magical bonds. If something threatens, we can contract or expand, or move around the other body.*

"Uh-huh."

*Mental communication, please. It is better that you learn.*

*Very well,* Kiri projected stiltedly.

*Yes, you DO very well, Kiri, never think you do not. You are fully naiad, fully magic, lacking nothing. You must not doubt that.*

*If I do?*

His body rippled in a Waterfolk shrug. *You will be…a crippled mer, not reach your full potential.* He paused. *What is your goal as a mer?*

*The same as when I was a person,* she replied automatically. *To be the best I can be.*

He smiled, kissed her lightly again, as if he'd known that all along. *Perhaps you need a more solid goal, like visiting the Pacific Water Palace. It is the most beautiful of them all.*

*A naiad could do that? A Colorado mountain stream naiad? A Denver crick naiad?*

*Yes. Freshwater Waterfolk are Waterfolk all the same, though the oceans hold many dangers for the unwary, so they might wish an escort.* He squeezed her hands again.

She didn't say she'd follow him anywhere. Right now she felt like that, but mostly because he was her lifeline and she was afraid.

*It is difficult for two mers to disperse together, but it can be done. Again, breathe with me.*

She stared at him with wide eyes. *How can we breathe if we disperse?*

*Our breaths slow, you do NOT think of organs such as lungs or heart, but beingness.*

*BEINGNESS!*

*Think of your essential you, your soul.*

*What of my body?*

*It will follow your soul, your magical essence.*

*And magic will hold me—all of me, physical and…whatever… together.*

*Absolutely. Breathe with me.*

She did and her breaths were loud.

*Perhaps it would be easier for you if you close your eyes. Ah.* He paused. *Do you meditate? A human once told me that dispersal sounded like meditation.*

"You talked about this to a human?"

He gave her a half smile. *He was much evolved spiritually.*

"Uh-huh," she said uncertainly, then bit her lip. *Sorry for speaking aloud. Yes, I've meditated.* Since he was holding her hands, she couldn't cross her fingers with the fib. She had. Well, she'd given meditation a shot—several times.

*We just want you to learn, Kiri, not to be troubled by success or failure. We all have failures.* Then his brows came down as if he might even be listening to himself and applying the knowledge.

Kiri closed her eyes. Again the warmth and humidity of the room pressed on her, as well as the green and growing smells of the plants, the rich humus of earth, the tiny whiff of smoke that indicated the brownies had lit a fire in another room. The tiles under her feet were warm, too, and she sensed the thickness of the floor, the basement space below.

Deep breathing. Right. She could do this. Shannon's instructions echoed in her mind from college and made her smile. Shannon had been better at meditation than she, and Shannon meditated a lot. She'd continue to do so while pregnant and it would be good for the baby.

The thought of Shannon, of her words, of her image in Kiri's mind's eye, sitting cross-legged opposite her, relaxed Kiri. Relaxation, letting go, was key. Pretty much the antithesis of gaming, of work, where she had to be on her toes every minute. She wished they were doing this lying down on a mat. No, she didn't. If they were lying on a mat, she'd roll over and touch the merman.

Stop. Thinking. Wound too tight. She'd heard that before. *Relaxing every muscle,* she said to Lathyr.

*Also good.* His voice held humor, amusement at them both, trying hard to relax? He wouldn't laugh at her. She'd noted that before and it was an important quality for her in a man. In anyone. But especially in a man she wanted to be intimate with.

Lathyr didn't laugh enough at all, she didn't think.

She breathed with him. Very slowly. Maybe too slowly for a human. Don't question that, let…that…notion…go. Thoughts drifted through her mind and she didn't follow them to logical conclusions, but allowed them to fade.

*Come with me,* Lathyr said.

He wasn't holding her hands. Don't panic!

*Can you feel the air around you?*

She did. She blinked. Did she blink? No. She had no eyes. Don't panic! But the air sparkled, or fizzed and popped. Or just sat there, pretty little globes of…air stuff.

*Move with me,* Lathyr said. She could "hear" him in her mind. She had a mind.

Wow, this was strange, experiencing the world with no eyes or ears or nose or…

She panicked. And fell straight into the pool, slapping it hard for instant sunburn. Well, she was all the way back in her body.

"Are you all right?" Lathyr asked, pulling her close, obviously using words because her mind had shut down to telepathy. Damn.

She whimpered with pain.

"Dunk in the water and change into legged-mer," he ordered, brows coming down.

Grumbling, she did, and the sting dissipated. The water soothed, the water cradled…water was her friend.

When she bobbed up again, Lathyr was smiling. He framed her face with his lovely, long-fingered hands. "You did it! You became droplet form on your first try and you *moved*."

"That's good, right?"

"Absolutely. Now we will try again." He slid his hands down her neck, shoulders, arms until he linked fingers.

"Right now?"

"Yes, right now." He bent a frown on her that was belied by his gleaming eyes. "Breathe with me."

So she did, and got into the right rhythm, and her mind slowed and her eyes blurred and sight became some other sense, and she dispersed.

*Come with me,* Lathyr said.

And she did. She followed him through the house. Melody glanced up sharply at their passing. What did Kiri look like to brownie eyes? Was it different to other eyes? Could humans see her? Maybe not see Lathyr since he was expert, but her? She nearly lost it and decanted into human form, but Lathyr soothed and they moved on. Slowly. Slower than walking. Geeze. And it was taking a lot out of her, too; she could feel the energy drain. She hovered just inside the door when he passed through.

She'd felt safe inside the Castle, the place where she'd transformed. Just like she always felt safe in her house. Somehow she'd felt as if nothing terrible could happen in the Castle... but *outside* in the scary world... She could lose herself.

LATHYR GAVE HER A TUG, AND SHE WENT WITH him. She sensed echoes of old water in the wood door, what had been in the living oak, but that was all.

Then she was outside in the high-altitude, dry and sunny air and she shrank and struggled a bit, *sensing* the next set of water droplets she could move to, reaching, striving and moving. Less than a walking pace, now.

Outside was dazzling. With the odd other-sight, the sun gleamed in the air around them, bright and yellow. The water droplets looked like half-filled bubbles, not full and turquoise like in the pool area, but gray or sky blue.

*Feel Jenni's balanced magic. It is RICH. Draw on it!* Lathyr reminded.

So she did. Yes! Great streams of magic—earth and air from Tamara's house, a rainbow of colors and essentially human-descended-from-Lightfolk from Amber and Rafe Davail's, hot fire and cool green from the Emberdrakes. Other types lingered from the houses. Dan and Frank's Spanish-style home also showed human-descended-from-Lightfolk, but she couldn't figure it out.

Kiri's tissues plumped…or *she* plumped, full of perfumed magic. She even thought she tasted chocolate.

Before she obediently condensed after Lathyr. In the koi pond.

Which was fine until Dan and Frank showed up to feed the fish and caught them naked. Despite everything, making illusion clothes was beyond Kiri. So cutoffs and shirt appeared on Lathyr and she looked bare.

He doubled over with laughter and she dashed away to the Castle, muttering curses as her feet met pebbles. Magic or not, Mystic Circle had loose rock and gravel on the street.

She was back in the pool, soaking up water and magic, when Lathyr returned.

"You did very well. Now, I think, you should try it on your own." His mouth still twitched.

"All right."

"But not in the pool. We will practice dispersing in the pool later. Perhaps tomorrow."

"Okay."

She tromped out of the pool, then dispersed into droplet form, condensed and spoke to Lathyr mentally all the while, for a good hour, until her cell phone rang and she became human. Fingers dripping, she eyed it, drew in a big breath, and with the inhalation tried to absorb all the water on her skin. It worked! And the puddle around her feet was gone, too.

She went to the table and picked up her phone. Jenni was calling. "Hey, Jenni."

"Was that you I saw streaking from the park to the Castle a little while back?" Jenni asked, amusement lacing her voice.

"Yeah. It was me," Kiri admitted. "I'm doing pretty well with the droplet form of Waterfolk, but I still haven't mastered how to make an illusion of clothes."

Lathyr joined her. "It should be easy," he said.

"Yes," Jenni agreed.

Kiri fiddled with the phone. "The thing is, I can't decide."

"What?" Jenni asked.

"I can never decide on the clothes."

"Really?" Jenni asked as Lathyr stared at Kiri.

"Whether the clothes I imagine should be my own clothes, and if they are, are they really illusion or will I find them in my closet? And if they aren't my own clothes, how can I manifest them? I hardly pay attention to how my clothes feel on my body, let alone imagining how something else might."

"Hmm." Jenni sounded thoughtful. "I think Eight Corp should give you a clothes budget and we should go shopping. I'll be right over and we'll head out to a mall."

"Okay."

Lathyr sent her an appalled glance, and left.

Jenni and Tamara and Amber all went shopping with Kiri. Jenni informed her that she could become lightning and zap from one place to another, but that was it since she was only half-human. The idea still was enough to have Kiri's mouth drop open. Tamara, being fully magical, though half-Earth and half-Air, could vanish completely, like Kiri in her droplet state. But Tamara had learned that skill on her own, since the technique wasn't quite what Airfolk or Earthfolk did. She demonstrated, but didn't talk about it much.

Amber took charge of the shopping expedition, and they got clothes that had definite texture or weight to them, so Kiri would *feel* them on her body.

The women dropped her off at her own home, and as she opened the door and smelled the familiar scents of favorite candles, Kiri nearly cried. Yes, her home was bare and sterile compared to the Castle, but each and every bit of furniture was what *she'd* picked out and wanted to have around her. Exactly to her taste. She hauled the shopping bags to her bedroom, took off all the tags and folded them on a chair so she'd move them to the Castle later, then lay down on the bed and stared at the ceiling.

This becoming a magical being—and the lack of a structured workplace schedule as she learned her new self and magical powers—was wearing. Not to mention she'd be lying to Shannon. She didn't like that, but Shannon would never believe the truth. Hard to believe. So hard, Kiri wondered how many people, humans, would actually make the change. A lot would be more tied down with family and friends than she…but the twenty-somethings…yeah, the development team might want to market the game, the transformation, to them.

Yet the echoing in her heart made her think that they'd need some professional counselors. Jenni and Tamara and Lathyr were good, but they also had their own backgrounds, not someone who'd made the transformation, like she had.

Is that something she'd want to do? Maybe stay near, like Lathyr?

As long as she could work on the game. That would be helpful in the first place, and to her surprise, she still wanted to entertain as well as educate. Just in her makeup, probably. Though how she was going to work with the game when water and electronics didn't exactly go together… Maybe she needed to understand more of this Meld business, get something going with magic constructs…she wasn't sure.

Everything was so very different. Her body needed frequent submersion, and Lathyr was talking circumspectly about streams or lakes, and she was smart enough to do some deductions. The Lightfolk had been around for a long time, and there wasn't much water in Colorado, probably all the choice places for naiads were already taken, so she'd have to move somewhere else. Just how many Waterfolk were there? And how many homes underwater, or whatever. In the ocean, you'd need more than caves, wouldn't you?

More stuff she didn't know, hardly knew where to begin to question. Maybe her brain was catching up with the fretting that she'd set aside to meditate and become droplet form. It would have been helpful in the game, Transformation, if she'd known becoming nonphysical was a possibility.

And she drifted off to sleep, only to wake a couple of hours later when Lathyr politely knocked at the door. She moved and her skin cracked, leaving bleeding scratches. Owie!

Damn. Trudging to the front door, she accepted her fate. She wouldn't be staying in Colorado unless it was in a body of water.

When she opened the door, he stood impassive, once again in his tailored gray suit. Narrowing her eyes, she noted that he was *not* clad in illusion, the silk was real. He frowned. "We must get you into a tank as soon as possible."

"Yes." She got the new clothes and her purse.

"The day is more humid than usual for Colorado," he said. "Perhaps you can draw some water from the air to soothe your sores and refresh your skin."

"Yeah." She grimaced and regretted it as her lips cracked and bled.

He offered his arm in an old and formal manner and she linked elbows with him. His expression lightened.

"I just needed a little time alone," she said.

"Of course."

"Not used to living with someone, or brownies to clean up after me."

"It didn't appear as if you had much to clean."

She stared at him. "Did you just make a joke?"

"A statement."

"No, it wasn't. You were teasing me."

The corner of his mouth that she could see, lifted. "Perhaps."

She studied him, still a guy with a lilting accent and European sophistication, old-worldly manner. And a merman. "Hey, is Cherry Creek claimed?" That's where he belonged, in upscale waters.

"Yes, there are strict boundaries for the naiads and naiaders who live in the creek, so they each have their own stretch."

"Ah, and how does that work? The creek doesn't seem deep enough to me." She frowned. "Come to think of it, neither does the Platte River."

"If absolutely necessary, we can adjust our size."

"Huh." Kiri thought of naiads being no larger than a trout, or a finger, for that matter. She shook her head. "I don't think I'd like that."

"I'm not sure that it is an option for you this century," he said.

"Oh."

And they were at the Castle, the brownieman swinging the door open for them and frowning disapprovingly at Kiri. As soon as they stepped on the porch, Melody popped out and took Kiri's new clothes, tsking. "Put you in water elemental suite, too," she said before she vanished again.

"Water suite?" Kiri asked.

"We checked out the elemental suites when you were gone. The royals occasionally stayed here, you know."

"Nope, didn't." She stared at his handsome profile. "No wonder you didn't want to stay there."

"I do not overstep," Lathyr said. "And the Water King is not a power one trifles with."

"Oh."

"He expanded the water suite at the expense of the air rooms. So there are two bedrooms and a small sitting room. The Water King wanted the second bedroom for staff."

"Oh. Well, I don't mind a small bedroom."

With an inclination of his head, as he led her upstairs, Lathyr said, "The earth suite also has two bedrooms and a sitting room, the fire chambers are one bedroom and sitting room and the air has one very large room with screen dividers."

"Royals." The notion had penetrated her mind. "The best of the best Lightfolk? The most powerful?"

Lathyr chuckled. "Your meritocracy again." He dropped his arm and slid his fingers down until he held her hand. "But, in general, yes. The royals are the most powerful of the Lightfolk."

"The Eight."

"Yes."

"The Eight of Eight Corp," Kiri persisted.

Lathyr nodded. "That is true."

"Can I see those rooms?" Her curiosity itched.

"Yes." Melody appeared a pace in front of Kiri and she stopped and squeaked. "But only after you soak." The browniefem glanced up at Lathyr, and Kiri was glad to see that she was less formal with him than before. The man—the merman—was nice.

"I have prepared the large tub in the water suite for her," she informed Lathyr, hands on her skinny hips.

"Sounds fine," Kiri said, but the browniefem kept her gaze on the guy.

"I will take care of her." Lathyr's voice was soft, but his words sounded like a promise.

Melody nodded decisively and vanished.

"I'm not used to that," Kiri grumbled. "People appearing and disappearing so often."

"You're hurting and cranky."

She couldn't deny that, nor that when she entered the water suite, her mood improved at the sound and scent of water. She nearly ached to get into the tub. He led her through the suite that was furnished in deep blues and greens, and to the large bathroom, which neither he nor Melody had mentioned.

Even as Kiri just stood in openmouthed wonder at the gold-veined white marble sunken pool, Lathyr stripped her, then set his hands on places where her skin was good, and lifted her into the water…the healing water with jasmine petals and smelling of aloe.

She whimpered when she went in, and sank to the bottom of the marble pool and shifted to tailed form, her bilungs filling with cool water. Which let her know that Melody, and maybe her new mate, too, had worked with Waterfolk before.

Then Lathyr got into the white marble tub with her, curled up around her in his legged-mer form, and whispered mind-to-mind, *Go back to sleep.*

He'd known, of course, that she'd remained tired, and was also afraid of sleeping in the water in case she drowned. He was there for her, and she could depend on him. Reliable and trustworthy. Like Shannon and Averill. Not like her parents.

Lathyr was with her. So she let go and slept.

She awoke alone in the large sunken tub. She panicked and writhed and sucked in water and *breathed*, in and out. No problem. When would her unconscious figure out that she could breathe underwater? Soon, she hoped.

*You are fine,* Lathyr said telepathically. He sat in a large chair where she could see him from the tub, if she'd bothered to look instead of reacting.

Well, hell, she'd gone twenty-six years without being able to breathe underwater, what did everyone, *she,* expect? She arched her tail under her and found that the bottom fins were more powerful than she'd imagined. Not as useful as feet, but strong. She surged out of the water, actually rising above it, and as she did, she turned into legged-mer, used the water magic in the air to move her a few feet and land on her webbed feet in front of Lathyr, surprising herself.

He raised his blue-white eyebrows. "Well done," he said mildly.

She didn't feel naked. She wasn't, the armor-flesh-skin panels encased all of her but her face. Turning in place, she noted the whole room was dry, though water should have sprayed everywhere. "Wow."

"You are progressing extremely well," he said.

She tilted her head to listen whether there'd been a patronizing note in his voice, stared at him with narrowed eyes. No. He looked and sounded sincere. Then she tromped flat-footed—her feet were larger in this form, that was so not fair!—to the towel rack, automatically reaching for it until she remembered she didn't need it. Pivoting, she looked hard at Lathyr. No smirk. That was really good.

Crossing her arms over her chest, she said gruffly, "Well, it takes time to break twenty-six years of habits. What were *you* doing at twenty-six?"

He smiled at her first words, then his gaze went distant, considering, then blank as if he faced pain.

And she suddenly understood that she knew very little about this man…a merman she planned on having sex with later. She respected him, had affection for him, and so did the other residents, the more knowledgeable Lightfolk residents, of Mystic Circle.

So she went and drew up another chair, set it beside his, under the warming yellow lights situated around the skylight. An odd setup, but for some reason, it comforted, as if it would always warm whatever gray light might come through the glass. She reached for his hand, then paused, staring at her blue skin and four-jointed webbed fingers.

Then he took her hand with his own even lighter blue and more delicately webbed hand—the color and fineness from that tiny bit of air elemental nature he had.

"What?" he asked.

She glanced at his face and caught the smile that had returned. She reckoned her next words would banish it. Cradling his larger hand in her own, she stroked the backs of his fingers with her thumb. "Tell me about yourself."

His expression shuttered, his muscles tensed—not a lot, but enough that she could sense it when a human, maybe even a mer who didn't know him, might not.

"Come on," she persuaded, then shook her head ruefully. "You know a lot about me, both good and bad."

"There is very little bad in you," he said, and she wondered if he contradicted her automatically or really believed it. In any event, she snorted.

"I have my share of faults." She was deceiving her best friend, and that chafed like sand under her new skin. Keeping her eyes on his and her voice the same soft tone as his, she said, "I don't know enough to…be intimate with you, Lathyr."

Pain spasmed across his face; his hand tightened around hers. "I am no one."

Irritation flashed through her and she squeezed his hand right back. "That's not true. You're a full Lightfolk magic being, a merman...of the ocean?"

His nose frills were out and rigid, but he nodded. When he turned his head to look at her, his eyes were covered by the protective nictitating lid.

"What I know of you, I like." She kept stroking his hand. "You've been kind to me, and treated me with respect." She took a stab in the dark, lowered her tone even more. "It doesn't matter to me that you are part air elemental." She shrugged and the fins along her arms fluttered. Huh, she didn't know they were that sensitive to emotion, or that flexible. Don't be distracted, this is important! "I think that bothers you?"

"Waterfolk believe I have tainted blood," he said emotionlessly.

"Because you're eight percent elf?"

His head inclined.

"Then the Lightfolk must dislike Tamara, who is half-elf and half-dwarf, and really hate Jenni, who is half-human." Kiri laughed. "Now me, human-become-Lightfolk. Mystic Circle should be called Misfit Circle."

That tugged a wary smile from him. "You don't mind."

She rolled her eyes. "Lathyr, anyone with a bit of magic awes me." That was still true. Bottom line, she'd wanted desperately to have magic, and she'd paid the price for it, and here she was. She should count her blessings.

"And my blessings in being magic include having a very sexy merman interested in me," she murmured.

His shoulders relaxed and his fins along his arm did a tiny quiver, a good sign, she supposed.

He lifted her fingers and brought them to his mouth and laved the backs of them with his tongue, sending shocking desire straight to her core. Whoo!

Chuckling, he did it again, then separated her fingers and touched his tongue to the webbing. Zowie, a little more of that and she'd be as hot as Jenni.

She yanked her hand away. "Stop that," she said as he grinned. "I really do want to know more about you."

But his mouth stayed straight. "I have no home."

"What?"

He looked down at his hand in hers, but didn't withdraw, then met her gaze again. "I have no home. My mother gave me to a high noble for a servant soon after I was born. I did my duty, but when I was of an age to leave that noble, I did. But I do not, did not, have the blood or the power to earn my own place, my own estate as a grant from the royals." His mouth flattened.

And that mattered to him. He needed a home, as she had needed one. She swallowed down appalled anger on his behalf, kept her nose frills rigid inside her nostrils so they wouldn't give her emotions away. Reacting would have him shutting up.

His gaze cut to her, then away. "So I made myself a charming guest, and lived on the sufferance of others for…centuries. I am a professional guest, a reluctant drifter." Again his fins rippled as he shrugged. "Most of my time is spent in small, dark estates in the deep oceans. Occasionally the water royals found me useful for a decade or two at a palace here or there." He lifted her hand, and this time his kiss on her fingers was chaste, and his smile seemed more easy. "For a while, I even lived as a human in a French coastal town, though most of my compatriots were Lightfolk."

Kiri nodded. "All good experience for when your new talent appeared," she said stoutly. She thought that a home, to him, would show he'd been accepted, worthy of not being abandoned ever again. Also sort of like her. They had those feelings in common.

"Perhaps." He stared into her eyes, and she kept her own gaze steady. "I may be essential for this new experimental project of Jenni's. If all goes well…"

"You'll get your estate." Kiri nodded decisively.

"Perhaps," he repeated, then he stood and stretched, and Kiri admired the view. He scooped her up, she felt air pass through her as her body followed his lead in changing to droplet form, then they were legged-mer again and in the large swimming pool in the conservatory and Lathyr grinned, eyes with a certain gleam. "Let's play. I'll teach you some Waterfolk games."

Kiri figured that "play" really meant "foreplay," but that was all right with her.

THEY PLAYED, AND SHE LEARNED MORE ABOUT Lathyr as he taught and she interacted with him. Well, she confirmed more. He was generous, he was competitive, but not so that he *had* to win, and as they played, they shifted form and she practiced, practiced, practiced until she was almost waterlogged.

Then they ate and twilight came and they walked around the Circle. Lathyr seemed to have caught her habit. When they stood at the koi pond, he just shook his head at the colorful fish. "They are so ugly."

"You think so?"

"Yes." He bent and kissed her cheek. "Someday I will show you the true beauty of the seas."

"Um-hmm." She rolled her shoulders. "I'd like that, I suppose." Once back at the Castle, she stripped and soaked and swam, expecting Lathyr to come to her, but in the end, she dressed again and found him sitting in the living room, drinking brandy on the couch the farthest from the hearth and watching the fire pop with elemental magic colors.

Since she'd turned mer, even a contained fire discomfited her. Something else that had changed that she'd never anticipated when she'd made the decision to become Lightfolk.

Lathyr saw her at the threshold and set his glass down on a table and stood. The low-level sexual tension that had spiraled between them all evening ratcheted up. With slow steps, he walked toward her and when she raised her gaze, his own was intent, and his pupils were dilated, the blue of his irises so deep they looked black.

"Tonight I will sleep in the Waterfolk chamber, in the bed. Will you come and dance the dance of ages with me?"

Her mouth dried. "That's a lovely way to ask."

His lips turned up at the corners, but his gaze stayed steady. "Waterfolk usually…show affection in legged-mer form and underwater. It has been a very long time since I shared sex as a human, with a human woman, but I think you would prefer it?"

Her thoughts scattered. How long was a long time? Did he have something against human women as lovers? Would they ever have had sex if she'd remained human? *Underwater!*

But she held out her hand. "Thank you. I would like to dance the dance of ages with you in a bed in human form very much." She kept the same gentle, formal tone, and gestures, as if they were opening steps in some ancient pattern dance.

He drew her arm under his, and they walked from the library to the large staircase. Each movement attuned her to him. Their breaths began to hitch in, sigh out in the same quick rhythm, and she thought she could actually hear the thud of their hearts' matching beat. They took each stair and it *was* like a dance, first her body would sway toward his, then he'd step away, hesitate and wait for her. Advancing, retreating, to the third floor and down the wide corridor.

Then they were in the dim room and the waterbed was turned down, showing smooth sheets, inviting. With a whisper, Lathyr's clothes were gone and hers were, too, and his hands were stroking her and she touched him and they fell on the bed and tangled and danced and took each other.

Afterward, as they spooned together, he whispered, "You are a very special woman. Stay with me."

"For now," she mumbled, and fell asleep.

In the middle of the night, she noticed vaguely the waterbed rippling as he left. Her heart squeezed with pain, rejection, but that eased when she realized that he didn't go far, just into the huge bathroom. She strained her ears and all noise sharpened around her—another benefit of the transformation? Maybe, and, if so, most excellent. Anyway, she heard him slip into the water. He'd be sleeping as merman, then. The thought was enough that she awoke fully and rolled onto her back, the bed moving gently under her. She stared at the ceiling, deep blue and painted with constellations she didn't know. How long would it be before she slept a full night as mer?

What would losing her humanity do to her? She hadn't thought it would be different; she would be the same person as before. But she wouldn't. She perceived things differently now and she'd change.

She could only hope that she would continue to be the best she could be—human or mer.

The next morning she and Lathyr were finishing up a good breakfast of omelets and croissants and cocoa in the circular breakfast nook when Melody came and stood in the doorway.

Kiri jerked, still not used to the small creatures—beings—outside of the game.

"Princess Jindesfarne requests you come after food," the browniefem said.

Lathyr dabbed at his lips with a cream-colored linen cloth and, leaving food on his plate and coffee in his china cup, rose. "Let us go."

"When the royals call, you go immediately?" she asked.

"That is correct."

"Because they have your future in their hands."

He inclined his head. "And I am accustomed to the Water King, who must not be flouted."

She shoved a last bite of rich melty-cheese-and-egg into her mouth and savored, then poured out a few swallows of cocoa from the carafe and swigged them down. They were too hot and burned the roof of her mouth. Dammit! She ran her tongue over her teeth. "I need to brush my teeth."

Lathyr opened his mouth to show her his clean and gleaming teeth and puffed a breath of real mint at her. She frowned and hustled from the room. "I want to do it the old-fashioned way."

Once they were outside, they walked hand in hand to Jenni and Aric's place. The browniefem Hartha opened the door and showed them to the living room, where Kiri and Lathyr took a love seat opposite Jenni and Aric.

Neither of the Emberdrakes appeared happy.

"I'll get to the point," Jenni said. "We've been monitoring Kiri's vitals."

Not in the game but *now* they were doing that, and hadn't told her.

"And though she is doing extraordinarily well with being Waterfolk mentally and emotionally, and learning her forms at an amazing rate, her physical body is not adjusting as well as it should be."

Kiri stared at a scowling Lathyr. He said stiffly, "I have not seen that."

"You are accustomed to Merfolk more than naiads and naiaders." Jenni switched her gaze to meet Kiri's angry stare. "We were told that your physical deterioration is minute, but ongoing. It must be stopped before it becomes a problem. We were also informed that the probable reason this was happening was that you are spending most of your water time in artificial pools."

"By the great Pearl!" Lathyr put his arm around Kiri. "How do you know this?"

Jenni's gaze shifted.

"I thought you were our friends?" Kiri said.

Jenni winced, glanced away, then back. "Ah, I believe the King of Water was in town last night and, ah, made a very discreet examination of you. As a royal, he has the magic to see what others might miss."

Lathyr stiffened beside Kiri.

"He did a flyby of us when in droplet form," Kiri stated flatly. She didn't like being spied on, especially when she'd thought she was safe and private.

"He is a rude man and I have attempted not to make an enemy of him—" Lathyr began.

"Silence, Lathyr," Aric ordered.

Jenni sighed, waved a hand. "The upshot of this is that we need to find Kiri a place to live sooner rather than later."

Lathyr exhaled slowly, then held out his hand with a bubble on it.

"What's that?" asked Kiri.

"It's a Waterfolk memo. You have been invited to tour Maroon Lake near Aspen."

"Really!"

"Yes."

"Sounds like a good first step," Jenni said. "Can you arrange something for today?"

"I will contact the naiader who lives in the lake," Lathyr said.

Kiri hesitated, then blurted out. "I'd like you to go with us, too, Jenni. Please?" She gave Jenni a big-eyed look. Waterfolk *had* big eyes.

"For sure," Jenni said. "If we go together, we'll probably need a limo."

"Driving," Lathyr said sourly.

Aric said, "I haven't been in that area. I can't use trees and greenspace for transportation."

"Not enough clouds here for lightning, might be different in the mountains, but lightning wipes me out. It's about a four-hour drive."

Lathyr said, "The naiader might give me enough information to *snap* to the lake with Kiri."

She put her hand on his thigh. "I need the others, too." She wasn't afraid to admit that.

Aric looked at Lathyr. "We'll go armed. The Dark ones have retreated…we hurt them last Thursday."

Lathyr nodded. "We must not take any chances."

Aric frowned. "We can hope that their unusual alliance fell apart."

"And that they are blaming each other for defeat. They do not play well with others," Jenni said.

Kiri barely heard the byplay. She'd collapsed against the soft back of the couch. Less than a week ago she'd been human, had no idea of the Lightfolk. So short a time for such a complete change in her life.

Jenni said, "I'll call the limo service and set up hotel rooms for us in Aspen or Snowmass." She looked at Aric. "Or does the Eight have any properties in the area?"

He'd already started checking his handheld computer. "Yes, there's a mansion in Aspen."

"Of course there is." Jenni sighed. She raised her voice and Kiri felt the magic in it when Jenni spoke. "Do any of the Mystic Circle brownies know of the mansion in Aspen?"

To everyone's surprise, Rock popped into the room, with an outthrust chest and a wide smile. "I do. I have moved things from the Earth Palace to the Aspen place. It is on a nice big mountain. Very pretty." The tips of his lips quivered. "What will we be doing?"

"You will be taking care of the mansion for us overnight."

"Are you going, too, Kiri?" asked Rock.

"Yes." She smiled at him. "I'll bring you chocolate."

"Of course you will," Jenni said.

And several hours later, in the bright noon light that Lathyr was becoming accustomed to, Maroon Lake appeared ahead of them. They drove as far as they could, then walked to the lake, where the hoary and tough-looking naiader Lathyr had spoken with earlier, Stoneg, rose from the water and changed from legged to human. The naiader clothed himself in falling-apart jeans and a flannel shirt.

He turned to Lathyr and Aric and Jenni and said, "Go, walk around my lake or something." The naiader scowled and got even uglier. "I don't like Firefolk and I don't like mers." He smiled widely at Kiri. "I like humans just fine. And I like very new naiads who come from humans."

Kiri tilted her head. Lathyr didn't know what she might be sensing from the guy, but he remained wary. She stepped close and kissed Lathyr on his jaw. He liked that—the affection rolling from her warmed him.

He stared grimly at the naiader. "Why are you doing this?"

The naiader snorted, and that told Lathyr the older one had spent some time in his legged form or even human.

"I pay my tithe to the royals." He waved a webbed hand, his nail claws looked dark and gnarly and sharp. "Pink crystals. Fresh mountain trout—Rainbow and Cutthroat." Finally a smile, showing Waterfolk teeth. "And when the Water Queen asks for a favor, like showing a brand-new, full-grown naiad around my lake—" he reached out and tugged a long strand of Kiri's hair "—I do that, too."

The Water Queen. Very interesting.

Kiri laughed, patted Lathyr on his shoulder. "Go on, enjoy the day and the view. Stoneg reminds me of my late grandpa. Crusty."

Stoneg appeared pleased.

Lathyr bowed. "Thank you for helping us."

Again the naiader snorted, but put an easy arm around Kiri's shoulder and said in an almost-gentle tone. "We'll practice your changes and breathing and illusion, huh?"

"Sounds good."

Walking around the lake, Lathyr kept an eye on Kiri and her new mentor that he shouldn't resent, but did. She'd turned two-legged and hardscaled. She'd ducked in and out of the water—sometimes visible to his human eyes and sometimes not. Grudgingly he accepted that the naiader was a good teacher and didn't seem to have any sexual interest in Kiri, two things that he related to Jenni and Aric when he returned to where they were waiting.

As they strolled in the sunshine, he said, "I did not know before this morning that the Water Queen had arranged this."

"And the Water King checked on you both last night," Jenni said softly. "Perhaps you should speak with the elf scholar, Etesian, about this, at the Earth Palace in Yellowstone."

"I will think on it."

Jenny handed him a small crystal ball. "This has his crystal image programmed into it so you can set up a meeting."

"Thank you," Lathyr said. He'd use it.

Kiri longed to just jump into the lake and zip through it. She'd already seen that it wasn't very deep. But Stoneg was as meticulous as Lathyr in making her use her bilungs—and better at explaining how to bend minute water droplets around her to make an illusion that she was human, or even reflect stuff around her so it didn't seem as if she were even there. Close to invisibility. Cool.

When he spoke, it wasn't exactly like telepathy, it was more like Kiri understood the vibration of water against her skin and her temples and her ears from the sounds and vocalizations he made.

Eventually she made it fully underwater and into her completely tailed shape. With a flick of his fingers in easy sign language and a big smile that creased his face, Stoneg let her zoom around the lake.

It wasn't deep, but it was fabulous—real plants and fish and silt and mud. The water so much more energizing than that in the Castle's pools and tanks and tubs.

And she went *fast*. As fast as a motorboat, which wasn't allowed here. There was a shadow on the water from a rowboat—humans!—and she swam back and grinned with glee at Stoneg, paddling in place.

"Well, lookit that," the old naiader said as fish began to gather around her. "Huh. Swim a little distance." He flapped a hand.

She did, slower this time. Still exhilarating. And returned to the naiader.

"The fish followed you."

Kiri was delighted.

Stoneg's nictitating lids clicked over his eyes; his expression sharpened. With a flip of his tail, muscles bunching, he lunged toward a *huge* fish. *I've been wanting to catch that canny old lake trout for decades.*

He snatched. He missed. Even thick water didn't hide his grumbling. As he swam back he grabbed a smaller fish, bit off its head and crunched the rest down. *One thing's for sure,* Stoneg said. *You'll never go hungry.*

Most of the other fish hadn't reacted to the death and remained near her. Kiri sank to the bottom of the lake, stunned and horrified.

*What?* Stoneg's thick green brows twisted down. *You think you'll always eat as a human?* A contemptuous stream of bubbles rose from his lips to the surface. Then his expression turned sly. *Or would you prefer to eat them live?* He opened his mouth, slurped in a couple of small fish caught in the suction of his magic. Munched.

If she'd been human and on land, she'd have lost her lunch. Her nice, well-done hamburger lunch. Her stomach didn't feel the queasiness of her mind.

*Naiad-girl, you gonna have to learn to eat.*

She was afraid of that. And from her physical reaction, knew she'd have to turn off her mind and imagination…and empathy.

He gestured to the fish around them, but made no move to eat more. *These trout are predators, Kiri.*

Now that he'd mentioned it, she'd noticed that. There was a trace of newly-dead-fish in the water that quivered her nose frills and made her salivate. Her hand moved fast, grabbed a fish as big as her hand, hit its head against a rock hard, killing it, and stuffed it in her mouth.

Chomp. Chomp. Her formerly human mind shrank into a ball in the back of her naiad brain, and her full Waterfolk body hummed in satisfaction at the delicious taste of fresh fish, the pleasure of eating.

Stoneg shook his head at her. *If you must do it that way, you must. Go explore, little girl, I have my lake's health to survey.*

She wasn't sure what that meant, but knew a dismissal when she heard one.

Stoneg glanced back over his shoulder. *It's a beautiful day, and there's a good rock I put out in the lake to sit and sun on. Go. Enjoy yourself.*

*Shouldn't I be doing something?*

Again bubbles rose from his lips. *Girlie, sometimes doing ain't necessary. Sometimes just BEING—who you are, what you are—is what's important.*

That was something to think about, for sure. Kiri swam around the lake at various speeds, noting how silt and mud moved, and practiced her illusion spells, and using her nictitating eye membranes, and her bilungs. Then she found the rock and simply *was.*

Female and magic and Lightfolk.

Awesome.

But as wonderful as the whole experience was, when she

was scanned again that night at the Aspen mansion, she was still deteriorating.

Slowly dying.

LATHYR AND SHE HAD SWEET AND TENDER SEX in the bed that night, then slept in a huge tub, but they didn't talk.

The next morning the four of them had another meeting, standing out on the deck of the mansion and breathing in the sharp air and drinking wonderful coffee Rock had provided. Even in human form, Kiri didn't feel the cold, and she noticed the others didn't, either.

Jenni had sent the limo home without them since they'd all be returning to Mystic Circle by magical means.

Lathyr said, "It might be good to try Kiri in a large river."

Jenni clapped her hands. "That's a great idea."

Aric's brows rose. "The Mississippi?"

"Yes!" Jenni enthused. "What we knew before Kiri's transformation, and what we've learned with her scans, is that she has very good potential for water magic, but must develop it."

"I'm right here," said Kiri.

"You should be given a challenge, flex your elemental muscles as it were, so you should go to the Mississippi!"

Dread mixed with excitement in Kiri. Her mouth and lips were dry so she pulled water from the air…even from high clouds that might bring the first snow. Not that she thought she'd be around to see it.

"I had decided upon the Colorado River," Lathyr said, "but you have a point." He shook his head. "I'd also thought of traveling in our droplet form to the river. The Mississippi will take us a while to transport there, either through the air or in streams, or underground waterways." He frowned. "Faster with a storm, but I don't want to chance a storm. I will have to stay near Kiri, probably 'herd' her molecules together."

"Huh," said Jenni.

"Sounds like you should be human and fly," Aric said. "I'll get first-class tickets for you to St. Louis, and have a car ready to take you to a hotel. A place that is for all Lightfolk." His fingers flew, tapping, over his handheld. "Wait, St. Louis. Might have pure Waterfolk lodgings."

"I'm sure," Lathyr said politely.

"That's settled," Jenni said. "Today to prepare and leave tomorrow."

"First good flight's midday," Aric said. "I'm booking them on it."

"Good." Jenni smiled at Lathyr with a hint of wickedness. "You are going to hate flying."

Jenni was right. Lathyr hated the flying—the air was far too dry for his skin, and Kiri's, despite the carry-on bags that they'd filled with water after passing through security, which he'd also hated.

But once they landed, he let out a sigh of relief, and Kiri

caught her breath and smiled at him as he took her elbow. "The humidity!" She lowered her voice, vibrating the water droplets with her breath. "A human can feel it, of course, but not like this." She stretched, nearly hitting a man with her flat canvas carry-on.

He scowled, but she turned her smile on him and her pure goodwill imbued her with glamour. The man blinked, leaned forward as if he might actually kiss her.

Lathyr set Kiri aside, stepped into the space. "We're delaying others."

"Oh, of course. Sorry." Another dazzling smile, even Lathyr could feel it.

"Kiri—" he vibrated droplets, too "—watch your glamour. It's strong, especially effective on the opposite sex."

Her eyes went huge. "I have glamour now?"

"That's right." He touched the small of her back with his fingertips, liking the simple contact. She moved a little faster, and he kept up.

Outside of St. Louis security, there were several people holding signs with names…and a dwarf.

Kiri stared, murmured, "A dwarf? How does he drive?"

The dwarfman threw her a look over his shoulder as he led them away. Kiri stopped in her tracks, bowed. "Forgive my rudeness."

Eyes narrowing to slits showing only an obsidian gleam of black, the dwarf jerked a nod, rumbled an answer, "I don't know what you are. You smell odd." He smiled with red pointed teeth in an approving way.

Kiri flushed, her human temperature still warmer than Waterfolk. She opened her mouth. Lathyr touched his forefinger to her lips. "Dwarves view rudeness differently than other peoples," he said quietly.

"Oh." She kept quiet as they followed the dwarf driver out to the curb, stretched again, then looked around, startled. "What about our luggage?"

Laughter flaked like sharp shards from the dwarfman as he opened the door for them. "The brownies have it."

She stared. At the dwarfman, at the trunk of the car, at the interior, until Lathyr prodded her to get in. "Well, thank you. And thank the brownies." Fumbling in her jacket pocket, she handed the dwarf some chocolate drops. His eyes widened and lit, and he bowed. "Thank you!" Then *he* stared. "Denver. You're from Denver." His glance was sly. "I've heard of a certain Fire Princess."

"Jenni Emberdrake, she's my friend." Kiri nodded, then frowned at him. "Make sure you share that chocolate."

His fingers began to curl, but high titters came along with blurring motion and his stash diminished. The dwarf slammed the door as soon as Lathyr was in and didn't say another word until they were at an outwardly shabby hotel.

"What is that really *wet* feeling?" Kiri asked as they exited the car.

"The river," Lathyr said. "We're within a couple of miles of it."

"Wow." She turned innately toward the river, spread her arms. "Wow, I can *feel* it." She grinned at Lathyr. "And see it and hear it." She ran her tongue over her lips. "And *taste* it and smell it! Wow."

The driver grunted, and held the hotel door open for them. This time Lathyr had his own chocolate tip ready for the driver and brownies—who dropped their illusion of invisibility once they were in the lobby. Both brownies and driver bobbed bows as they stuffed the chocolate in their mouths.

"Ahem," a half-breed naiader-human coughed, shaking his

head and saying with a strong accent that Lathyr didn't know the origin of, "I don' think you should be givin' them brownies chocolate."

Kiri shrugged, smiled again. "It's done."

"We cater mostly to Merfolk, though we have sittin' rooms for each of the other elementals," the man said. "You're on the second floor, have a balcony facing the river, but can't see it." He dipped his head. "Feeling it is usually comforting enough."

"Uh-huh," Kiri said.

"The brownies took your bags up," the guy said.

This time Lathyr tipped the man with paper currency.

"Thanks," he smiled, pocketing the bills.

"I want to see the river!" Kiri nearly bounced.

"Fine." Lathyr nodded to the man and linked fingers with Kiri. Sweet attraction slipped along his nerves.

"Easy to find," the half-human said. "If you want human food, the restaurant on the way and back has good barbecue. Hob's BBQ."

Lathyr stared at the huge and calm river, brown under the cloudy sky.

"I can sense the ripples and the currents beneath the surface, ever changing, ever moving. Fascinating." Kiri's voice trembled with excitement. "Just wonderful."

"It is an imposing river. Full of mer, we are just two more." Lathyr found a bench and they sat. His arm came around her and her head fell against his shoulder as if heavy—perhaps from dizzying sensory input.

"I think I can *hear* fish swimming in the water. Can we just sit here for a while?" she asked.

"Of course."

"Have you been in big rivers?"

"There are many layered habitats in a river. I do not know this one." He'd have to be careful of her when they entered it, keep a wary eye on her. He was armed again, and would remain so.

They remained until the day got even grayer and rain began to spit. Lathyr stood and pulled her up. Again she stretched and smiled widely. "My muscles aren't stiff."

"You're Lightfolk now. You have a better body, and magic also."

Once they were back in the hotel, she didn't settle. She paced back and forth, her forehead creased, the pale blue skin on her arms a contrast to her wide human gestures that appeared odd when she was in two-legged mer form. "I need more."

His stomach sank. "More what?" He'd give her anything.

"More *data*."

"Data," he said blankly. He was afraid she'd been asking for more emotional commitment from him, or his heart…which he suspected was already hers. But with all in flux, he could not expect her to feel the same, or the attraction…passion…love…to last.

Her hands threaded through her long hair, separating the frond-strands. "The problem is that I don't feel like I know enough. What I learned was only from the game and what I've heard from you and the others at Mystic Circle. I have great gaps in my knowledge."

"I will answer whatever you need me to," he offered.

"But I don't even know some of the questions to ask, and you know so much—you can't imagine what I might need to learn."

He wasn't quite sure what she was saying, but he captured her hands for a moment. "I will do whatever I can to help."

"I know that, but it isn't enough."

When was he ever enough for someone? Never. He took the stab to the heart, felt his confidence shrivel.

She paced again. He'd rather see her expending her energy playing in the pool.

"Surely your people must have primers or readers or something that explains the other elemental magic races to your children?" She stopped and her expression held appeal. "Stories of dwarves and brownies, mers and naiads and naiaders, elves and airsprites, djinns and firesprites."

"Children's tales?" His second eyelid blinked down.

She pumped her arms. "Yes! You know stories."

"I've forgotten them." He swallowed. No one had cared to tell him stories. "I can get such for you from the Earth Palace in Yellowstone." He glanced at her. "I have a matter I would also like to take care of there. I know that palace fairly well and should be able to *snap* to the pool they keep there. I could be there and back by this evening."

"Most excellent."

He paused and stared at her. "But I don't want to leave you alone."

She pouted, then said. "Jenni gave us some contacts here, right?" Kiri heaved air from her bilungs. "Call one of them to babysit me."

"Get into the tub," he said, noticing her skin was drying even in this humid air.

She did, and the naiad, Stargrass, arrived.

He kissed Kiri's pretty, wide blue forehead before she submerged, playing splash with her tail, curling and uncurling… something a water baby would do.

Then she began quizzing the amused Stargrass about being naiad and the Mississippi River and St. Louis.

Lathyr visualized the huge pool in the Earth Palace, *felt* its texture, inhaled its composition, turned into droplet form and sent a tiny thread to connect with the place, then *snapped* to it.

The elf scholar, Etesian, was lonely.

Lathyr had the volumes for Kiri and after the second cup of tea, brought up the subject that had been plaguing him. "I didn't know that the Water Queen had a strain of elf in her background."

The scholar looked at him sharply. Lathyr swallowed, but continued, "It was my understanding that all royals must be pure in that element, one hundred percent water."

"From the first time Marin saw Alika, he fell in lust and love." Etesian's gaze went distant, as if he recalled the very moment. "The prince wanted her for his mate."

Sitting tall, Etesian continued, "It isn't often that one who holds less than a full complement of elemental magic can become a royal, but she is very strong, and she is a prized healer. She passed the tests," the elf ended simply.

"Tests?"

Etesian shrugged. "Each royal house has challenges and quests one must survive and master to be considered royal."

"Ah."

"And Alika Greendepths is only two percent air." Etesian smiled. "The genetic disposition for pointed ears," he ran his finger over his own left ear, "is very dominant."

Lathyr smiled back.

"And you are eight percent air elemental?" the elf asked.

"That's right." Lathyr waited as long as a beat of a drip of water. "My merman father was the last of his line. I was told his and my elven, air magic heritage is of the Squall family."

Etesian nodded, but stood and walked to the wide window of the room, a little too far up the mountain for Lathyr's comfort. The elf whistled an exhalation through his nose. "There are not many of the Squall family left."

Lathyr jerked upright from a casual slouch. "I was told that there was no one." His mother had been shamed that she'd had a child from one who wasn't fully mer. Later, he'd learned that his father, the last of that tainted-blood family, had died in an underwater carouse party.

"There is one other," the scholar said, softly enough under his breath that Lathyr would not have heard him had he not been that small portion of air.

"Yes?" he whispered his question.

"Alika Greendepths also carries Squall blood."

Lathyr was stunned as facts rushed like a torrent inside his mind. His breath caught so he couldn't speak. His nictitating lids slid over his eyes.

Etesian had continued, "I believe that only three of us know of your Squall blood now." The scholar turned, a sober expression on his face.

"You, me..." Lathyr hesitated, but could guess. "And the Water King?"

Etesian inclined his head. "That is correct. I believe you have a slight broken line in your pattern of scales that would show this when you are mer."

"Oh."

"So you understand that you are distant relations with the Water Queen, but on her elven side, that part of her family that she thought she'd lost forever."

"Yes."

"And that she would be thrilled to find another relative."

Emotions churned inside Lathyr, delight, hope, despair. "Yes."

"Marin Greendepths, the Water King, is a very jealous man."

Sipping a fragrant but too-flowery tea, and keeping his gaze on the view of mountaintops out the windows, Lathyr said, "Understandable, since his lady is beautiful and compassionate and generous." Wonderful qualities, much like Kiri.

"Yes. Marin loves his queen and wishes to keep her to himself. One has speculated that they have no children due to the King's possessiveness, and their current heirs are presumed to be the Seamont couple who live in what the United States humans call the Puerto Rico Trench."

That explained a few things.

Etesian gave a little cough, also seeming to study his view. "Have you ever seen the Water Queen?"

"Only vaguely, once and recently, as she healed me. I was not in any shape to speak to her." Lathyr kept his tone idle.

"I believe the percentage of Air elemental magic in her blood is even less than that which you have."

"No doubt. She is royal."

"And beloved of the Water King," Etesian said.

"And beloved of the Water King. Naturally I would not care to irritate the Water King in the slightest."

"Naturally not."

"Yet..." Lathyr let the word hang in the silence, turned to meet Etesian's eyes, knowing that his own gaze had gone very elf-blue. "The Water King did make a point of warning me against being near his lady."

The elf flicked his fingers, activating a strong privacy spell, and stared directly at Lathyr. "The Water King has been successful in ensuring you remained unknown to Alika all your life, from the moment your mother abandoned you. Shuffling you here and there at his whim. Most of his court know this."

Lathyr's breath came a little faster. He hadn't known that, either. A major effect on his life had been hidden from him all these years. But he would make no move to come to Marin Greendepths's awareness again. Lathyr's chest had expanded with…pride. Though he wouldn't claim the relationship, he wasn't as alone in the world as he'd thought since his mother had committed suicide by orca.

He put down his cup and stood, bowed formally as a child to an esteemed elder scholar, dropping his gaze. "Knowledge is always treasured," he said, then looked the old elf in the eyes. "Even if one will never act upon it. I thank you for the very delicious tea." He wanted to be back with Kiri and all the potential of the future, not dwell on the past.

"You are quite welcome. Anytime." The elf paused as if he might say something more, shook his head. "You'd best return to your fledgling."

On impulse, Lathyr asked, "What do you think of that matter?"

A gleam lit the elf's eyes. "I think it is a very interesting venture." He made a shooing gesture with his hands. "Be off with you."

Another nod from Lathyr. "I'll try to keep these volumes safe."

Etesian chuckled. "They are old and meant as punishment to bore fledglings. We have all the information on other media."

"Oh."

"We'll see what your new one makes of them, whether she is a curious one who follows through on her curiosity, whether her perusing such old volumes is an indicator of how well a human might make the transformation."

"I hadn't thought of that."

"Good to know I can still be useful," Etesian's eyes twinkled. "Thank you again." One last bow.

There was a scent…it colored Kiri's dreams with an iridescent sparkling trail and woke her…to the dimness of a giant, quiet and cool tub in the hotel room. No sound but the beating of her heart…in a different rhythm than she was accustomed to, she noted for the first time since her change. Because she had a different heart? She knew she had different lungs, and different skin, and, wow, cool—tail!—in her naiad form, but heart? She wished she could see an anatomical chart of the Merfolk. Maybe one of the books Lathyr brought her would include that.

If Kiri had anything to say about Things To Be, there would be info—maybe 3-D graphics—for humans who were transformed.

And the fragrance still tempted. She rose from the pool, her tail turning to finned legs without thought this time, and relief washed through her, even as she sloshed up, then out of the tub, becoming fully human again.

"Lathyr?" she called, but knew before the tiles echoed her words that he hadn't returned. Stargrass wasn't near, either, but who could blame her? Watching someone else sleep would be boring, and Kiri had succumbed to weariness pretty soon after Lathyr had left.

Kiri walked from the bathroom, and the air didn't dry her skin as quickly as back home. Stopping before a full-length mirror in the short hallway, she studied herself. Her features were pretty much the same, as was her height, but she'd lost weight.

She recalled the first time she'd logged into Transformation, how hungry she'd been after the game, and how she'd thought burning calories would be a great deal…the true transformation had nearly killed her, but had made her thinner. For the first time in years, her stomach was flat. She frowned. Hadn't Lathyr disapproved of that?

Well, a nice layer of fat would insulate you from the cold of mountain lakes, she guessed, not that she'd seen any fat on Lathyr or Stoneg or Stargrass.

What *was* that smell? She went into the bedroom, very dark since there was no skylight like there had been above the pool. No light and no Lathyr.

Slipping into clothes—big, but at least comfortingly her own—and shoes, she opened the door to the balcony.

Oh, *yeah!* She wasn't sure what the fragrance was, but it was wonderful, astringent and herbal and beckoning. Even better than what she recalled magic smelling like when she first whiffed it in the game. She drew in a large breath. Really, not much magic here, and what there was, was Merfolk because they owned and used the hotel.

But with the breath came the *tang* on her tongue. Spicy, vibrant. Lifting her face, she turned in a circle until she caught the scent again, and temptation, and promise. If she followed her nose, she'd come to a fabulous land of delights.

It came from the direction of the river, as if it were one tiny component of the great flow of waters.

A wind kicked up and she fell under glamour again, this time of scent and not any magical being stronger than she. Putting her hands on the railing, she leaped over it. In the second before she lit a story below, her mind cleared with a *what the hell am I doing* instant, then her mass thinned to air-water-droplets and her knees flexed and she landed softly.

The wonderful smell was much stronger here and she was

lost in the fragrance of it and she began to run in the direction of the river.

Then she was there and it was big and muddy and smelling of itself—biggest river in the United States, rich with odors from ten states and peoples and cultures and food and fish and a little magic and that teasing, luring smell and in she went, and swam out of her clothes, kicked off her shoes, turning into legged-mer, then tailed-mer, coughing once as her bilungs changed from breathing air to air in water and swimming, swimming, swimming.

Her nose frills unfurled and quivered, bringing more of the scent in a lilting vibration smell-taste, coating *need* along her scaled skin and she went to the fast deep current and let the river whisk her downstream where the scent throbbed in rich lushness.

LATHYR COALESCED FROM THE AIR ONTO THE balcony, nose twitching at Kiri's fragrance. She'd been practicing her forms, good. Hands full of ancient volumes, he shoved the slider open farther with his shoulder, calling, "Kiri!"

No answer.

"Stargrass!" he snapped as he raced through the empty rooms. The pool in the bathroom showed a lower level of water, no drips of water on the floor.

More silence.

*Stargrass!*

The naiad coalesced on the bed, naked and languorous, smiling with lowered lashes. "Here, Lathyr."

"Where's Kiri?"

Stargrass rolled a shoulder, yawned. "In the pool."

"No." He dropped the books on the floor, went again to the balcony, stared hard at the faint molecules where Kiri must have stood. "Did you practice forms with her?"

"Bo-ring. She's in the pool."

"No. She isn't. She isn't in these rooms. Can't you sense that?"

Stargrass's thin green brows dipped a little, her lower lip thrust out in a pout. "Seems like the same energy as always."

He stared. "I didn't know your power was so low."

Sitting up angrily, she tossed her hair, strode past him to the bathroom. He followed, crossing his arms. Stargrass looked in the pool. Mouth set in a frown, she thrust her arm in the water, as if Kiri had dispersed into the water and only a touch would solidify her. "She's not here." She looked around in confusion.

"Where is she? When was the last time you saw her?"

"I…uh…" The naiad turned, dropping the illusion of clothes over herself. A strained smile flicked on and off her face. "She must be in one of the hotel pools. I'll check." She dashed from the room.

Dread squeezing his tissues, Lathyr stepped back onto the balcony, strained to sense Kiri, opened his mouth to try and taste her essential magical flavor. A hint, nothing more, not even a tiny droplet of Kiri.

Humid air near a river—not the best atmosphere for him to trace her—he who usually lived in or by oceans. Below him, a blur caught his attention, Stargrass moving fast in her own native air, checking the entire hotel. Closing his eyes, he leaned against the jamb of the sliding door, pushed his senses out in waves, hoping to touch Kiri. Nothing.

"Stargrass!"

She was back in the room, hunched, diminished. "She is not in the hotel," Stargrass whispered.

Lathyr's gut contracted. "Follow her essence."

Panic came to her gaze. She wet her lips. "I don't know it."

He would not let her fear infuse him. "You. Do. Not. Know.

Kiri's. Essence." He could feel the hair on his neck lifting. "You were assigned to watch her. You have been in her company for several hours and you don't know the feel of her essence? You didn't touch her, scan her, *sense* her?"

Her shoulders hunched.

Lathyr crossed to the far end of the balcony, pointed to the faint residue of Kiri's change to air-water droplets. "There, that's her trace. Learn it, follow it, and I will follow you."

"Now?"

"We don't have much time. If we lose her, I will have to report to Eight Corp."

Stargrass sniffed in dismissal.

"Do you not know that Eight Corp is the royals?"

The naiad's eyes rounded, her chest heaved with bellowlike breaths. "No. No."

"That's who I work for. That's who I report to." His smile sliced at her. "But first I might tell Fire Princess Jindesfarne Emberdrake of this fiasco."

Stargrass screamed, too high for any mortal to hear. Lathyr pointed to the spot again and she fell upon it, sank *into* the wood of the balcony floor, then misted away. Lathyr stripped and followed.

Kiri's path wandered…like she'd been mortal human, that gave more sensation—the lovely feeling of her warmth, still warmer than most mers, the unique fizz of energy on his skin. The fear clogging his throat, tightening his muscles, eased.

Soon they were at the sloping riverbank, and Stargrass cowered in legged-mer form, her long toes buried in soft mud. "She went into the river. *Deep* into the fast current."

"How long ago?"

"I dunno." Stargrass trembled.

"Lead on."

"I can't. I'm a shallow water naiad. There are *things* in the deep and fast."

Fury boiled within him and all the fins on his body stiffened to knifelike sharpness. The river overwhelmed his senses; he'd not be able to track her. Not know if or when she'd leave the current or the river...might not even sense her blood or death if he cruised in the mighty waters. His skin hardened to battle armor with his ire.

Stargrass flung herself facedown into the mud.

"What is going on?" roared the Water King, rising from the river.

"I have lost the new naiad," Lathyr said.

The king backhanded him into the river and Lathyr tumbled, face hurting, bones shattered. He could use his anger and fear and guilt to mend the bones, but figured the Water King would prefer seeing the damage on him. Lathyr shook his head, oriented himself, swam upstream to where the king remained. As he lifted himself from the river to stand, air stinging, he saw the Water King had become legged, with his foot on the back of the crying and whimpering naiad. The royal glanced over at Lathyr.

"You were at the Earth Palace today."

Lathyr bowed, swirling his arms in the air as if he stood before the king in the depths of the ocean. He kept his head low, but his gaze on the temperamental merman. "That is so. I lingered too long speaking with the scholar."

"Scholar." Water snorted in muddy streams from the king's nostrils.

"My mistake."

"But, not, I think, as bad a mistake as the failure of this miserable, foolish naiad. She did not listen, *did she?*" The final words thundered in Lathyr's mind and he had to sink his own feet into the riverbank.

*No,* the naiad mewled in a tiny mind-voice.

"She did not pay attention to our instructions, did she?"

*No,* Stargrass whimpered.

*She lost the human-turned-Lightfolk, the experimental transformation, did she not?*

*Yes.* Stargrass shuddered now.

The king stepped aside, flung his arm out toward the river. Lips curling at Lathyr's and Stargrass's failure, at the whole project, too, no doubt, the merman said, "Find her."

Stargrass flung herself into the river. *I search!*

*Wait!* Lathyr shouted telepathically. Stargrass hovered in the water near the fast and deep current. He inclined his torso even lower. *Please let me and Jenni Emberdrake handle this.*

The king's teeth showed sharply in a grin. *Very well, but there will be...repercussions...if the new one is not recovered.*

No help for it, Lathyr dipped his head, gaze on the water rushing around his feet. His neck vulnerable to a mortal strike from the king.

With a whoosh, the merman was gone.

The pale green face of Stargrass bobbed a few yards away, wet from more than the river, fear had water from her tissues beading on her face.

*Jenni is compassionate,* Lathyr said.

Stargrass shook her head.

He gestured her to join him and she swam, then trudged up the bank, again appearing much diminished. He didn't touch her, didn't want to, his anger still deep. "We will see if Jenni has any ideas for tracing Kiri. Meet me in the lobby fireroom lounge."

Weeping, Stargrass disappeared.

* * *

Kiri submerged herself in the current, in the river, becoming one with it…flowing fast downstream, only paying attention when she had to *stretch* to feel the smell-song-taste of what she yearned to find.

Stargrass was fully human with light green skin and dressed in a flowing gown that covered most of her body when Lathyr went down to the fireroom lounge. He had dressed in one of his silk suits of deep blue with a pale blue silk shirt after telephoning Jenni and relaying the information that Kiri was lost.

Jenni had sworn and promised to be there shortly.

"You'll be all right," he said to Stargrass.

She shook her head and took a plush red velvet chair far from the fireplace. "I am doomed."

"I doubt you'll ever be called upon again by the royals for any duty, but we should save your skin."

He was fairly sure his skin would be all right, too. His face was mending. But his own potential estate might be lost. That hurt, a deep ache pulsing with every heartbeat, but not as wrenching as his continuing fear for Kiri.

Could she survive the huge river? What *were* the monsters in it deadly to Waterfolk?

With a crack, the fire flamed high in the hearth, then Jenni stepped from it onto the flagstoned floor before it.

Her face was redder than usual, her complexion all fire, eyes blue-flamed, and hair springy and crackling.

"What happened?"

Stargrass shrieked then prostrated herself on the floor. "Please don't eat me. Please, please. It was all my fault. I was bad, bad, bad. Foolish naiad. Please don't flame me!"

As Lathyr watched, Jenni settled down. She sighed, looked at him.

"Stargrass was...inattentive...while I was at the Earth Palace today and Kiri slipped away, into the Mississippi River."

Now Jenni paled. That river could be the death of her and she knew it. Her lips formed, "Why?" but her voice didn't come out.

"Why?" Lathyr frowned. "What do you mean?"

Jenni swallowed. "Kiri isn't stupid. Why would she do something like that?"

Lathyr shrugged. "I don't know." He spread his hands and fluttered his fingers. "The call of a huge and moving body of water? She'd only experienced the pools in the Castle, a mountain lake. Nothing of the magnitude of this river."

Jenni looked at Stargrass. "Did she say anything to you?"

"No, Your Highness."

"Do you have any insights why Kiri might do this?"

Stargrass's gaze rolled in mute appeal in Lathyr's direction. He didn't think she'd done anything but absently answer Kiri's questions, might not even be able to describe Kiri. He kept his own gaze hard. Stargrass hunched further in front of Jenni. "No, I have no insights, your fieriness."

"Are you of any use to us whatsoever in this matter?" Jenni asked.

"No, Your Highness."

"Then go."

"Go where?"

"Go home."

Stargrass didn't wait for another word. She vanished. Lathyr was glad.

"Do you have any way to track Kiri?" Lathyr asked, chest tight with trapped hope.

Jenni crossed her arms. "What, mysterious *fire* royal ways, in the *Mississippi River?*"

He stood straight. "What of mysterious human ways?" He continued to breathe shallowly, still hoping.

"I'm sorry." Her direct gaze met his. "You're lovers—you should be able to trace her."

Lathyr was unsure whether the woman approved or not, but wouldn't deny it. "Her essence is still new to me and would be lost in all the multitudinous sensations of the river."

"You're a strong mer!"

"I am new to this land, and never saw that river before earlier today. I don't know its standard essences." His jaw flexed. "And Kiri's magical signature is yet evolving. I left her talking to Stargrass in the pool." He gestured to the bathroom and Jenni strode in there, held her arms out over the water, her forehead furrowing as she sensed the magical energies as no other person on the planet would. Humming, she nodded, and brought the elemental magic to full water in the room…Lathyr felt it, and it was good, but not as lovely as when everything balanced. If he hadn't lost his chance at a home of his own, he'd—no, Jenni was primarily fire elemental, she wouldn't guest in an underwater residence. His traitorous mind built a home with dry areas for friends who were human or other, the people from Mystic Circle. That abode would never be, too expensive for anyone but royals.

Jenni was done, and strode once more out to the balcony and the mighty river she could no doubt feel as opposite to her power. She leaned against the rail. "Kiri's lost in that."

"I'll go after her," Lathyr said.

Turning toward him with a hip on the rail, Jenni said, "Like you told me, you're ocean mer, and more on the eastern side of the world." Her mouth flexed down. "And I'd forgotten you have that bit of air in you." Sweeping a hand down herself, she said, "Like me."

"I'd forgotten that about you, also."

Her eyes warmed slightly. "Something we have in common."

"I thought that all those of Mystic Circle had qualities common to my own." He lifted his shoulders, where a great burden lay...he *had* to find Kiri, couldn't leave her alone in such a river. "I'll go after her." He folded his clothes in his suitcase and packed Kiri's. Inclining his head to Jenni, he asked, "Will you take care of these, please?"

"I'll do that, and I'll contact the royals."

"I've spoken to the Water King. He wants Kiri found, but I doubt he will help, or tell his wife to help." He paused. "I believe if we bring the Water Queen into this matter at this time, against the King's wishes, we will make a bad and longtime enemy."

Jenni's mouth tightened, but he saw her considering how the Water King could block her in this situation and future endeavors. Her mouth turned down before she answered, "I understand, though the Water Queen's innate magical power is stronger than the King's."

"Is it?"

"Yes, second only to the Earth King's, the royal dwarfman."

Interesting but nothing to think about right now. Lathyr stretched, preparing to enter a massive waterway new to him. He'd need all his senses sharp. All his defenses, too, physical and magical. He strapped what would have appeared like a toy sword and dagger to humans at each hip.

"The other Water royals are distant relations to the king, and smaller in power. I don't know them well enough to call on them at this time," Jenni said. "We need to coordinate… plan on meeting places so we can exchange information."

"No." Now his voice was harsh. "The longer I wait, the less clue of her I will find." He let his fear show on his face. "And the more things can happen to Kiri. There are many, many mer in that river, but none of great stature, royal stature." He frowned, tested the air again. "I do not believe the denizens would allow a very noble mer to claim a large stretch of river."

Jenni grimaced. "This is the United States."

Lathyr shrugged again, began changing to his water droplet form feet up, keeping his weapons close. "I will find you in six hours, near the shore of the Mississippi."

"How fast will you be going?"

"I don't know. I don't know the current, my magic here, what I will face. I don't know how quickly Kiri progresses, either."

Surely he'd be able to find her. Please the great Pearl. "I'll meet with you in six hours." That would be full dark, but after the evening activity settled and before the night hours truly began.

"Right," she said. "Later."

He gave in to fear for Kiri, need for her, moved quickly to the river, plunged in. His form shifted to full mer with tail, and he sensed others around, naiads and naiaders, even some with power—not as strong as he, and none who would challenge him.

Not him, but what of Kiri?

NOW AND AGAIN KIRI'S FORM SHIFTED…AND when it did, and her mind came back online, she understood that something was happening with her scales, like being etched. With new experiences? Because she was using her new magic all the time?

She didn't know, and logic and thought faded as she followed the growing lively-song-smell-energizing-touch-LIFE-taste component of the river that continued to draw her.

A naiader got in her face.

*You trespass.*

She could barely understand him mentally, his water accent was so strong, and she didn't like the arrogance in his tone.

*Pay fee,* he said, swimming close to her and his long and grubby nostril frills fluttered as he sniffed her. *Smell good magic. Nice. FRESH.* He smacked his lips. *Tasty.* Then he circled her, sniffing!

She didn't know if it was an offense, but she chose to be offended. She dove deeper, down to the muddy bottom of the river that concealed interesting shapes and smells and sensations of ancient times and peoples—humans.

*Pay!* He grabbed her arm.

Reflexively her sharp fins deployed, cutting his fingers, dark gobbets of blood joined the water. She swam fast.

The naiader looked surprised, then his face contorted into anger. *You. Will. Pay.* Flicking out a hand, he caught her on her tail fin and the pain was nothing like she'd felt before, nothing she could describe as a human—searing, stinging—as if delicate tissues were beaten with a bat, sliced. She gasped in water and river bottom and doubled up. He laughed and swam closer, sliding a palm down her hip around to curve her tail. No! She shot away in a spurt that left churning water and nasty man behind. Fast, fast, faster!

Until she got tangled in tree branches and came to an abrupt stop, thumping against a thick trunk that took all her air.

Lathyr had cruised rivers in his time…even partied in some when he was young—the Nile, the Yangtze, the Danube. All had different tastes, but unless his memory was wrong, this American one had more present-human textures than he'd experienced. Perhaps it was only the fact that he was closer to humans, or partial-humans than he'd been before, or paid more attention to human cultural essences than previously.

Because Kiri had been human and that was and would always be a portion of her essence, and he stretched to find the scent-sensation-signature that he occasionally caught a wisp of. He swam deep, with the fastest current, but still very aware that he seemed far behind her.

If she turned out to be a river naiad, she would of course move faster than he, who was essentially an oceanic merman.

And this was her native land, so she would feel comfortable here. Though she was so damn *new* as Merfolk, appearing adult, yet without any of the experiences in growing up as Waterfolk...hardly able to change from form to form without thought. She didn't know common Waterfolk speech—either telepathically or the hand signing, or the esoteric writing in water.

She didn't know manners.

There! There, wasn't that her essence? Just a slither of a molecule of new-mer-Kiri-human-DENVER. Denver?

But Denver was dry, and now the greatest river in the land enveloped her.

Lathyr went faster, speeding by shallows' naiads and naiaders in backwaters, in joinings of tributaries, not wanting to stop to ask of Kiri, not wanting to notify the more predatory of this river society that a prized one was lost.

He had to believe he'd find her before anything dreadful happened to her; to think otherwise would break his heart.

His heart. How had he come to love Kiri?

Her scent! With anger and pain and trailing fear. The trace older than he'd hoped. He spurred himself onward.

Kiri gasped and thrashed, turned legged and still fought the branches that trapped her, caught in her now-long hair, tangling it. Twigs and branchlets poked her, scraped her face with rough ends she'd broken. Air!

And she heard Lathyr's voice, from her first memories as a mer.

*Do not THINK of breathing, just do it.*

But she couldn't. Her lungs seized.

Not lungs, bilungs. Visualize them. Water in, siphon the air. Siphon oxygen from water!

*Here, you, what are you doing there!* Unkind laughter followed the thought from a portly naiad. She was coming near, though Kiri couldn't see her swimming. Something seemed wrong with Kiri's eyes, too.

There was a tug and a branch ripped away, along with her hair. Louder laughter now, mocking. *By the Pearl, the shallows' naiads get stupider every day.*

A cold, too-long-fingered hand curved over Kiri's shoulder, squeezed hard. And the smell! She didn't like the odor of the naiad—merfem?—oily, fishy. Eeew. Completely masked the strange and wonderful fragrance-sensation Kiri'd been following, that had lured her.

She couldn't lose it! And she couldn't bear the waterfem's clawlike fingernails piercing her skin.

*What a finling.* The waterfem chuffed laughter and the breath she expelled hit Kiri in the face and it was too much and she let go…just let go of her form. Let herself intermingle with the water—stagnant water, here—and *pushed* toward the fast, free-flowing clean current that had swept her here and now would sweep her away.

*By the Pearl. You SPRAT, you will DIE.*

But she didn't think so, didn't care now that she discovered the wondrous scent again.

*Too stupid to live,* were the last words she heard as she let herself subsume into the current, keeping only the lightest awareness of herself.

Finally her energy drained, and though she wanted to continue to follow the lure of the song, the scent, she knew she must stop. The water began to feel cold, and she'd learned that was a bad sign in Maroon Lake. She didn't have the magic and energy to keep warm. Not good.

The first time she tried to solidify, she couldn't and panic spurted through her. *Breathe.* She wouldn't die, she *wouldn't.* Wouldn't waste all the time and energy Lathyr and Jenni and others had given to this project. Wouldn't prove that humans were too fragile or stupid to transform into Lightfolk.

But it hurt to gather herself back together, as if instead of being all spread out in a zillion molecules, she had hunched into the smallest fetal ball she could make of herself, had stayed that way until her muscles had stiffened, and tiny movement stretched each cramped thread of her, shooting pain.

After long moments she became legged-mer—easier for her to visualize and she flailed in the water, bilungs pumping. Had to allow the current to drift her toward another, equally smelly, stagnant backwater. And she had to stay legged-mer, she had no energy or magic to become human or tailed or even construct a protective bubble around her with a magical spell.

And she found that the water was dark with night and she couldn't see the sky.

And that she could still cry, tasting salty tears on her lips from sheer fatigue.

The river rolled on and took Lathyr with it. No time to appreciate its beauty. Every moment he strained his senses to find Kiri. He had to accept as usual that he would only find a minuscule vestige of her. After six hours, he surfaced and sent his magic questing up and down the riverbanks. He didn't find Jenni, but did sense her husband, Aric. That one could travel faster and with less expenditure of energy since he was totally magic.

Aric was several hours behind Lathyr as the river flowed. With a lightly bubbled sigh, Lathyr *flicked* to the location.

He strode from the river as human. Instead of clothing himself with illusion, Lathyr took the boxers, jeans and soft cotton sweatshirt Aric offered and donned them before he chilled from being in his human skin. He'd expended too much energy to keep him warm in such thin skin.

"Any news?" He croaked the English words, neither his throat nor his mind used to the language.

"Jenni's talking with the minor royals, hoping a Princess or Prince of Water will help."

The royal couple had had no children, but a few cousins of the king were scattered in their smaller palaces in the oceans of earth.

"Where?" Lathyr asked blankly.

Aric smiled with satisfaction. "The great Water Palace in the Pacific."

Lathyr raised his brows and Aric laughed. "She's been wanting to go there for a while, and now she is."

"Must be a little uncomfortable for a Fire Princess."

Aric shrugged a shoulder, angled his chin at Lathyr's pointed ears. "Though Jenni's fire nature is most evident, she's a quarter-elf and half-human."

"She acts like a Fire Princess," Lathyr said.

"She has to, and she was adopted by the royal Emberdrakes, since they were distant relations." That reminded Lathyr that he shared blood with the Water Queen, which yet felt odd. Strange enough that he wouldn't talk to the Treeman about it. Didn't know anyone he could share the news with except Kiri, and that felt lonely.

He strode up the riverbank and followed Aric to a place where the Treeman had parked a luxury car.

"Let's talk about this over dinner. Jenni will be meeting us." Aric scanned him. "You need more fuel…you're too pale."

Lathyr shrugged, but when he thought of Kiri, his stomach squeezed. He'd eaten absently as he'd searched for her. "I didn't teach her how to hunt fish and eat."

Driving, Aric slid him a glance. "That's all right, the Maroon Lake naiader did, or did you forget?"

He had, since he hadn't been allowed in the lake. "Doesn't mean she will be good at it," he muttered.

"Hunger is a good teacher." But Aric's jaw had firmed.

Aric and he hadn't been in the restaurant long before Jenni turned up with a merfem, as tall as Jenni and voluptuous in the manner of Waterfolk women. Talk stopped in the place when they appeared. Lathyr, who had been drilled in formal European manners, stood and bowed to each, which broke the silence and caused the room to buzz with talk.

The merfem ignored him, and he thought it better for their cause, for Kiri, to remove his plate and flatware to a table close to the royals' booth, which caused raised brows from the staff, but little comment. Lathyr figured it was because of the wealth they displayed with rich clothes, and both women wore jewels.

He was close enough to hear Jenni's summary to Aric. He hadn't often met Princess Whitefroth, but knew of her. She was the princess of the North American continent and lived in one of the great lakes, was magically powerful, and was estranged from the Water King, all to the good. The North American Waterfolk should follow her orders, even those of the huge Mississippi. He wondered what Jenni was paying her.

Whitefroth would send out a call for those who had seen or interacted with Kiri, offering a reward of gold nuggets, and punishment for failure to report. Without sparing a glance toward Lathyr, the merfem stated that "the tainted-blood merman would interface for her." She sounded smug at that, as if she'd been put out to think of interacting with the riverfolk herself.

"So you will only send out the call?" Jenni asked, as soon as the waitress took her order for blackened catfish.

The merfem's nostrils pinched; her frills would have deployed had she been underwater. "I will enter the river and lay a *compulsion* that all must follow or sicken."

Jenni's mouth dropped open. "Sicken?"

Whitefroth rolled her hand. "You want results, don't you?"

"Yes." Jenni stared penetratingly at Lathyr, as if trying to speak mentally.

He looked down at his plate and said, "One would only be sick." But a sick naiad in such a predatory place as the main river…even he wouldn't care to chance it, though a native merfem or merman might—if they resisted the offer of gold. "However, to remove the binding that caused the sickness, one would have to request that in the presence of the great lady who set the compulsion."

Jenni hissed between her teeth. Firefolk hissed very well. The Water Princess drew back against the cushions of the leather booth, but snapped, "Do not threaten me!"

Jenni lifted cinnamon-colored brows. "I don't. But do not think me, *us,* weak."

*Half-breed,* Princess Whitefroth sneered mentally to Lathyr. He did not reply, but popped another piece of steak into his mouth. He'd developed a taste for beef in Colorado.

The Water Princess didn't speak directly to him again until they stood on the bank of the river. Like most major rivers of the world, it was awesome. Her gaze swung to him. "There will not only be naiads and naiaders in this river, but some true merfems and mermen."

He nodded. "Yes, Your Highness." Keeping his head low but his eyes on hers, he said, "The new naiad went into the river some miles upstream, so your compulsion need only be sent down the river." The length was significant.

Her lips tightened at the effort it would take to roll out a compulsion, but she nodded and dropped the illusion of clothes, though she still wore her diamond jewelry. Jenni's gems sparkled in the moonlight, too.

Slipping into the river, she changed into tailed shape, her skin a pale blue-green, her long hair the same color, and the pattern of her scales curves and whorls, ridges pure green.

Not more than one or two angles on her pattern, not as powerful as he'd thought, which surprised him.

Because he didn't wish to be subject to her compulsion, Lathyr stayed well out of the water. Whitefroth glittered and gleamed as she swam to the strongest current, then held herself there.

She opened her mouth, formed an image and essence shape of Kiri and sang the compulsion. "See this naiad, come to me, reward or punishment will reveal thee." Lathyr saw the force of the spell ripple the large breadth of the river and continue downstream. He was impressed.

So he shucked his clothes and converted to full tailed merman and swam to the merfem. Whitefroth struggled to stay in place in the current that gave him no trouble, surprising him, but he knew she wouldn't accept physical help. He formed a bubble around her, steadying her, and did the same for himself so she wouldn't see that a despised one had more power.

He shouldn't have…but perhaps more had changed with his magic when the great orb from the earth had broken in the spring.

*I will need to hear-feel the responses,* she snapped.

He flicked his nictitating lids up and down in apparent surprise. *The bubble is permeable to sensation.*

She turned to him, frowning. Before she could answer, two voice projections came.

*Claim gold reward,* boomed the voice of a naiader.

*Ah wan' some gold,* said a softer, mellower female tone. *Ah saw your missin' naiad. Plumb stupid, she is.*

Lathyr winced, and fear crawled along his nerves once more.

A spurt of water hit him midchest. *What did they say?* asked Whitefroth.

*One naiader and naiad have seen her. They wish the reward.*

*Get it from the half-breed princess,* the Water Princess said.

Lathyr nodded and returned to Jenni and Aric in his legged-mer form, glad to be away from the arrogant merfem. "We've received two responses."

Jenni's face lit with hope. "She's alive?"

He had to swallow before he could answer. "So far as we know."

*Get the gold and come back here,* ordered Whitefroth. *The naiad and naiader need a tow to us to report,* she added and Lathyr reckoned that he would be the one expending energy in bringing the two to them.

*How far away are they?* he asked.

*How should I know? They garble their communications.*

He gave Jenni a half smile. "I must return."

She tilted her head. "I didn't realize that the Merfolk treated you so poorly."

The fins along his spine ruffled in embarrassment. He shrugged.

She took his webbed hand and turned it over, pressed a couple of good-sized nuggets in his hand and curled his fingers over the gold. "You are much more tolerant than I."

His lips twisted. "If I want to live the way I do, I must endure whatever slights my hosts mete out."

Jenni frowned, studied him more intently than she ever had. "What do you want, Lathyr?"

"KIRI SAFE," HE SAID.

Aric put his arm around Jenni's waist. "So do we all," he murmured. "But what do you hope for as a reward for your service?"

Lathyr received the impression that Aric was asking as the royals' man. None of the others had requested that information, and he had been waiting for the right moment to let his needs be known. "An estate of my own in the ocean."

"Any ocean?" Jenni smiled, curiosity peeking from her eyes.

"Any I can get," Lathyr said.

"We will do our best to award one to you," Jenni promised.

He stared. "Even now, when I lost her?" Lost Kiri. His gut twisted again. He'd been trying to stay positive.

*WHERE ARE YOU, MIXED BLOOD!* shouted Whitefroth.

"Mixed blood." He repeated the words that coated his tongue with a bad taste.

Jenni canted an arrogant hip, lifted her chin. "I am a Fire Princess. I have my sources for rewards and help."

He dared to hope so. "First we must ensure Kiri's safety."

"Why would she leave?" Jenni worried her lip.

"I don't know," he repeated, then sent to Whitefroth, *I come.* He dived back into the river and joined the merfem. She sent a stream of large, irritated bubbles at him, whisked a gesture. *The naiader is closer.* Mentally she gave Lathyr the visualization the naiader had given her.

*Gold, gold, gold,* he chanted, *I want me some go-old!*

He was about an hour farther down the river than Lathyr had gone. Flexing his shoulder muscles, he flung a line of magic to the guy. *I need to drop the stay-in-place bubbles surrounding us to pull the naiader to us,* he lied to Whitefroth.

*Very well*, she pouted.

*If you please you could stay on land with Princess Jindesfarne Emberdrake. Or the shallows,* he offered.

She looked at him sharply to see if he'd insulted her with his mild tone, which, of course, he had. Evidently, she didn't think him so bold. *I will remain.*

With a nod, he began reeling the naiader in fast. Yes, Lathyr's power had definitely improved. More than a born-princess's. The knowledge was heady, even as he wondered how that could happen, how he might have gained power and Whitefroth…others…had not.

The naiader arrived, grinning and snorting. The man was as large as he, and rough-looking, hair and beard unkempt, his tail fin ragged, his trunk scarred.

Lathyr questioned him, and as the man wove in the water, knew that the naiader had threatened Kiri. Lathyr kept his nostril frills folded so as not to show contempt and wrung every minuscule detail of Kiri from the naiader. He handed off the gold, and sent the guy away with a hard shove of water that spun him into the deep and fast current of the river, watched the mer flail as he strove to remove himself from the stream.

The only other person to answer the call was a plump and cheerful naiad. She'd told them all about the slight incident with the "stupid as mud" shallows naiad. After being given her reward, she'd just shaken her head with regard to Kiri and stated she didn't think she'd make it much longer in the river and swam off.

As Kiri slept, a merfem haunted her dreams, shouting at her, insistent, making Kiri's head ache. The woman wanted something. Kiri wasn't sure what, and *she* wanted to sleep. Not deal with some arrogant and demanding woman. Still the demand itched at her, *felt* scratchy more than echoed in her ears, pulled at her. She shifted a little, woke to half doze. Gathered her thoughts and sent back, *I am here and tired and sleeping. Nag, nag, nag. Go away now.* And she dropped back into her sleep.

While they awaited results, Lathyr and Whitefroth had moved to shallower water, both taking legged forms.

*The new naiad has contacted me!* Whitefroth beamed at Lathyr.

He wanted to grab her, shake the information from her. She'd knock him out of the water and onto the bank. *Where is she? Tell me!*

*You made me lose her!* Whitefroth's nose frills fluttered. *She did not have much power to answer, said she was sleeping. And she was...far distant...she must have spent much time pushing along the greatest current, most likely in droplet-form.* Whitefroth shook her head. *Chancy for a naiad.*

Frustration seethed through him. *You can't give me a location?*

A shrug of green shoulders. "No. But she lives. You'll be able to find her."

*You got a solid signature for me to follow, then. I've been having trouble with that, since she's been changing, as all young do, growing into their powers.*

Whitefroth froze. Her nictitating lids rapidly clicked up and down, the first sign of nerves Lathyr had seen.

*You will have to parse Kiri's trace for me in all senses.*

The princess drew herself up haughtily. *I don't have time for that.*

Why was he plagued with inefficient mers? Because they didn't take him or the project seriously.

"It's vital we find her."

Another shrug along with lip curl. "Not to me."

"That's unfortunate," Aric said. He'd come up behind them, and stood upright and solid in the water. He held Jenni, who didn't appear to be bothered by the great river as much as Lathyr would have expected.

"We might have to renegotiate your price."

"I have given you all I've gotten!"

Jenni raised her brows. "Well, we obviously expected too much of you, then, and you promised what you couldn't deliver."

Opposing magic hissed around the women. Lathyr stepped back; Aric stood stoically.

Whitefroth's face dewed with anger droplets. She glided forward and took Lathyr's right hand in both of hers and *sent* the impression of the communication she'd received from Kiri.

The strength of her power should have pushed him to his knees, his head underwater, forcing his bilungs to change from air to water breathing, a rude punishment. It didn't. He dug his feet into the mud and stood, drew *more,* every iota of information from her, the scent…warmer, farther downriver, human scents-sounds-tastes different from where they stood. And, yes, there was the inherent feeling of distance, Kiri was a lot farther away than he'd anticipated. He wasn't sure if he, himself, could have gone so far in such a time period. He certainly wouldn't have tried in a strange river. He shuddered, then suppressed fear.

Focus! Focus on all the myriad details Whitefroth had sensed. Light—the light was poor, the scent stagnant. Whitefroth had said Kiri was sleeping. Closing his eyes, Lathyr steeped himself in the merfem's brief experience.

Night dark, so little or no time had passed since Kiri had answered. Feel of the water around her was soft and lapping-calm, no current. Since an unpleasant smell came with that, he deduced that Kiri had found a small backwater…there was a caged feeling…of branches. Water overhead, so she rested in legged-mer or full-mer form, probably legged since that was the closest to human. Wise, he didn't like the idea of what might happen to a naked woman on the bank of the river in the lands of the humans.

Resting. Sleeping. Weariness and the taste of hunger on her tongue. She hadn't eaten? Damn.

"Ha! I will set a compulsion on the naiad to come!" Whitefroth announced.

Lathyr opened his eyes to see a fierce smile on her face, her eyes damp with gleaming recklessness as she raised both hands and began to dance in place. He knew that look—no one had contradicted her for many decades in her own home, and she cared not for any consequences of using her anger, she was so offended.

He caught her wrists, pulled her from her feet that she would lose connection with her magical pull of earth as well as water to fuel her spell. Easier to distract her than he'd anticipated. She made her arm scales sharp and they cut into his fingers, but he held on, met her furious gaze. "No. A person under compulsion cares for little else, would not take care of herself on the way to you, would ignore danger. No."

"You dare, tainted-mer. I will have your fins and tail."

"Kiri is more important than anything you might do."

"My cousin will hear about this!"

"So will all the royals, the Eight," Aric said.

"I'll love telling my brother and sister-in-law, the Fire King and Queen, of a Water Princess's bad behavior." Jenni chuckled like fire cracking.

Whitefroth spit poison in Lathyr's eyes. Luckily he'd been expecting as much and had his nictitating lids down, but the spew burned his face. Still holding her, he dunked under the river's surface, taking Whitefroth with him. *You curb yourself now, or all will hear of your lack of control. The royals cannot have a princess in power who lacks control.* And that was the truth.

She yanked at his grip and he let her loose—a misjudgment since she made a sweeping motion with her hand, sending the incomplete compulsion-spell downriver.

Then she shrieked and clapped hands on her head, plunging deeper into the river. Lathyr saw black and curled fronds on her scalp, scented burning. The top of her head must have been above water, and Jenni had called fire to burn it. He backswam away from the shrieking virago, only rose from the river when Whitefroth did, to spew curses at Jenni, who was smiling smugly.

"You can go now." Jenni waved a hand in dismissal.

Choking, shaking with fury, Whitefroth vanished, taking droplet form. Narrowing his eyes, Lathyr watched her race upriver, using the humidity the great river afforded her to move huge distances quickly.

"Wow," he said, a human sound, Kiri's word, something he'd never said before.

Aric had doubled over with laughter. "Not good to anger my beloved," Aric said.

Jenni gave a human punctuation-sniff. "Can't deliver on her promises. I'll make a notation in Eight Corp's books not to ever use her as a consultant again." Then Jenni huffed a breath. "But she was the best we could get at short notice." Her forehead lined as she stared downriver. "Half-assed half-cast compulsion spell." She turned her worried face to Lathyr. "How much trouble are we in?"

"I don't know, but I'd better head after Kiri." Good thing he'd eaten well. He took the few strides to Jenni, grasped her hand, turned the palm up and shook a few droplets of his blood onto her skin and met her eyes. "This should allow you to track me."

"We can meet up—" she started, stopping when he shook his head.

"No. Nothing that will slow me down." His mouth flattened. "I don't know this river, the length or its outflow, but I must reach her before she gets lost in the ocean."

"We still don't know why she's doing this," Jenni said.

"That we must wait to learn until later. It's a pity we weren't able to speak with her." He went closer to Aric, grabbed the Treeman and tossed him toward the bank with Jenni. "My blood in the water is drawing creatures you don't want to have biting you." Lathyr drew a protection bubble around him—a small one because he would need all his magic, all his guile, to find Kiri and keep her safe. He raised a hand. "Later." He paused, saw Jenni and Aric lean together, wrap arms around each other's waist. Envy twinged inside him. "Later, my friends."

Aric inclined his head. "Later, my friend."

The man's acknowledgment glowed in Lathyr's heart.

"Bye, Lathyr, my friend and colleague. See you later," Jenni said softly.

He dived under the river, letting the image of their affectionate expressions linger in his mind as he searched for and found the fastest current and propelled himself downriver, trailing Whitefroth's compulsion spell, watching as it affected creatures.

It drew predators.

Kiri slept and shivered and finally woke, cold and still legged-mer. Still cold. Still not a good sign. Her energy and magic were depleted.

She was hungry, had no money, no clothes if she became human, so she'd have to hunt and eat fish or other stuff. She'd nibbled on some weedy plants that were safe and filling, but she needed protein.

*Hungry.* And she had no idea what she could eat in the Mississippi River. Crap. No, carp. There were a lot of carp, but they reminded her of the koi in the pond she cherished.

A small school of minnows swam by and without thought, her webbed hands swept out and shoved them into her mouth, crunch, crunch.

Yum.

She'd eaten *live* food. Ewww. Ewww. But the bits had already slithered down her gullet and her stomach was happy to receive them.

She opened her mouth to wash it out and narrowed her

eyes at the smell of something like food. Easy food to keep and catch and eat. Mussels!

Diving down, she found them, against the bank and at the bottom of the river—a plethora of kinds. Oh, wow. Stomach grumbling, she forced her hands *not* to grab a few more minnows. No. Ewww. No. Even centuries wouldn't change that reflex, she didn't think. But killing things wasn't much better, like bashing a trout to death in Maroon Lake—up close and personal, life and death in the raw.

But she had to eat, and mussels were better than fish, easier for her to kill—though she said a little prayer for them—and tastier, too. She drifted down the river, looking for food. Not many Waterfolk seemed to be awake.

Still night—what time, she didn't know and didn't seem to care. Hypothermia? Maybe. But maybe as she stayed more as a naiad, the more her mind became that. Who knew?

And the scent, song, feeling yet beckoned. An enchantment on her? She hadn't even considered becoming human. As she chewed another mussel, she pondered that.

Tough if she became human. No clothes. Unsure of where she was—even what state she might be in. Heaven knew what might happen to her, even if she had magic and glamour. She didn't know how to use glamour to help herself and wouldn't feel right doing that, either.

Here in the river, she could continue to travel safely. She should call Lathyr or even Jenni.

But they would probably haul her ass out of the river and bundle her…where? She had no home, now. Time to accept that. She couldn't live in her beautiful house on Mystic Circle—it had no pool. Even the Castle might be beyond her. She ached for her friends, for Shannon and Averill. Their lives had changed and now hers had transformed beyond belief.

She might be able to stay in touch, but she didn't think she'd be living in Colorado unless it was in a tank. She shuddered.

The smell-dance-song swirled around her, making her nostril frills strain to feel it…leading away downstream. Making her scales quiver instinctively. And that was it!

Instinct. Pure instinct told her to follow the smell. Something in her subconscious alerting her that she wouldn't reach her full potential as a naiad, as Waterfolk, unless she found that smell and sucked it into her bilungs, and sang the song and danced the dance.

She had to do this to be Kiri the Naiad. That was the goal of this quest.

A fish newly dead and not eaten drifted down from above her. She dived in and scooped it up, ate greedily, even licked her fingers of its juices, her ewww barometer had changed so much.

Feeling more chipper at her revelation and the food in her belly she drifted upward, and saw light flickering across the water. Dawn had come and she hadn't noticed.

Moving faster, stretching her toes, she zoomed upward, and bumped a log. It flipped in the water and snapped. She plunged back and down, but remained nose to snout with the alligator.

HELL!

Panic whipped through Kiri and she found the low and fast current, flung herself into it at too steep of an angle and bounced right out. At least on the other side.

She *pulled* on her magic. Water formed a tough bubble around her—oh, she'd pay for this sooner rather than later—and let the river bob her way too slowly to another backwater. Her antics had stirred up the mud, and that also hid her. She curled up in the bubble and it shrank around her and she went a little faster, then got swept into the mouth of a tributary. The bubble popped with the rougher water since she'd depleted her energy. And when she found another downed tree in the mouth of that other river, she scouted it for inhabitants, then hid, gulping water and crying *again*.

The food she'd eaten had replenished her, but now she was tired once more and the song-smell echoed in her ears and blood and teased her nose frills and she couldn't turn back but wasn't sure she could go on, and as she watched, a black-webby film of *something* magic and nasty floated down the main river in front of her and so did the now-lively alligator, and…and…a shark.

What had she gotten herself into? Should she give up? Turn back? Yell mentally and see if she could find Lathyr? Could Lathyr handle an alligator and a shark?

Of course he could. Kiri herself might have been able to use magic to fight them, but had let panic and tears and weariness rule her actions. She considered. Humans, alligators, sharks… other Waterfolk. Who were the most predatory?

She found, dug and ate more mussels, then headed back out, following the song-smell that had her firmly in its grasp.

No choice and no turning back.

Lathyr hadn't caught Kiri by the time he sensed the ocean, and then, of course, he understood everything. Because the call of it danced in his blood, skimmed through his nerves, caressed his skin. Even as far as St. Louis he had felt it, the tide ebbing and flowing, but it was so familiar, he only noted that he could feel distant salt water.

Kiri had felt it, too, but it would have been new and fabulous to her, wouldn't it have been? The pull on marrow and molecule? She probably didn't even know what she was feeling.

Despair trickled through him. She'd been absolutely right when she'd said that he could overlook something basic. He hadn't believed her, but it was true.

But if she reacted to the ocean the way he thought she would now, that meant she was a sea naiad, and they were few. And he and the other Lightfolk had already underestimated her, so she could actually be a *merfem,* one with power and a taste for the brine of the ocean, one who belonged in the depths. Like he did.

Her lack of scale design had marked her as naiad, but the pattern of scales showed the heritage of the mer—the family lines strong in magic. Kiri had no mer family.

In any case, he doubted he'd reach the ocean before she did, and there were so many more dangers—oceans and multitudes of dangers—that could maim or kill her.

And he couldn't stop, take the time to find Jenni or Aric, who might be the only ones who would believe his new theory. He didn't know this particular river, but he knew great rivers and how the waters acted when a storm arose, and one was coming, a big storm that might affect both the river and the area of the ocean it flowed into.

Even he knew that hurricane season in this area peaked in late September and it wasn't that far past the end of the month.

So he began to pray, for Kiri, for himself because he was going into the teeth of whatever storm that raged to find and keep her, and he prayed for them both.

Kiri floated, half-conscious, not altogether solid. She knew that wasn't smart, but every time she'd donned her two-legged or tailed mer form, she'd gotten into trouble—chased by mers or other predators, pulled by some stupid lingering spell in the water to struggle upstream to the north, even had her tail caught in a fishing net! She still wasn't sure how that had happened.

And she knew, in the back of her mind that yet had an occasional thought, that she was in danger of losing herself to the river, of losing track of the molecules that comprised her body, period. Of dying.

It didn't seem so bad...just dissipating.

That *was* the extreme danger.

What saved her was the very thing that had lured her. The smell. The scent of magic…and something else. She *had* figured out that part of the fragrance was magic, but it was magic wrapped around something else, or some other thing embedded in the magic.

And she reacted to the presence of it in the water. As a discombobulated, scattered being she couldn't *really* smell it—the thing she longed for. So she began gathering herself together. It hurt, the water seemed cold, and it took energy she didn't think she had to spare. She'd have to eat again.

But with nose frills, she could smell it, she could catch the scent and bring it close, draw it into her lungs.

Nearly taste it.

Her tongue came out and swiped her lips, and an explosion ran down the synapses of her brain.

*Salt water!* That's what it was. Sea salt. In the water. That's what she *needed*. Her tail flicked faster, and she moved with speed and grace, following the scent-taste, much stronger and richer here. Must be far south in the river, closer to the ocean—and she didn't know where.

But the magic-sea-salt invigorated her, caressed the ridges of her scales with sweet energy, power.

Something that she knew innately was necessary for her being. She was an ocean naiad. Who knew?

Who could have known?

She only dimly recalled her transformation, but knew they'd put her in the saltwater tank. That liquid didn't have the rare spice she felt here. Why, she didn't know. Because there wasn't any other living things in it? No plants, no hint of living fish and mussels…and the decay of that which had died?

But the salt-ocean-magic called to her, and even now that

she knew what had her in its grip, she couldn't turn aside. She *did* spend a spare thought to reach for Lathyr, but he was too far away. She could vaguely sense his mind, his worry, but could not stop to reassure him. Could not go back.

Not ever return to the human Kiri Palger had been. She was Waterfolk.

Oh, love for Shannon and Averill yet remained in her heart, but the currents washing through her had carried much of human Kiri away—both good and bad.

She wouldn't be able to stay in Denver, no matter how much she wanted, and tears dribbled from her eyes and gave the water her own salt at the thought of her once-beloved house in Mystic Circle, the community she'd just begun to discover and the loss of it.

As for Lathyr…confusion seeped into her. He was an ocean mer, one of the major water elementals, a merman. Yet he'd been able to stay in Denver, appreciated Mystic Circle and the Castle. She didn't understand. Maybe it was just the fact that he'd been around so long that allowed him to live away from sea salt magic. She didn't know and would have to ask.

Soon, when she was able to go back to her human form, after…after…

After she reached the ocean?

Hopefully.

In a moment of clarity, after swallowing a few mussels, she understood that she didn't dare forget her humanity or her human form, all the knowledge she'd gained. To have believed so earlier was wrong. She had to stay herself, reclaim herself. Somehow.

As for now, she didn't know if she still swam in the main river of the Mississippi, the current wasn't as strong, and the banks were closer—but she'd followed the strongest fragrance of the magic. The ocean was near, a thrill to a woman—a *naiad*—who'd lived most of her life landlocked.

She'd experience exciting tall waves of many colors, colors she'd see differently under the water, sounds that would resonate differently in her ears. The taste that was like nothing she'd ever known.

Now she was in her full naiad form—tailed and with her hardscale skin, the first transformed human woman to Waterfolk.

Definitely needed to reclaim her human self and identity.

Later, after the wonderful and exciting ocean.

Several hours had passed and Jenni had ordered Lathyr from the water, and Aric had brought his wife to where Lathyr had left the river. Jenni had also insisted he eat. He had used much of his strength and felt thinner.

They sat around a table in Natchez, Mississippi. Lathyr didn't drop his eyes, didn't feel out of place with Jenni and Aric now. And the others' faces showed pale with lines of strain.

"The weather report is bad," Aric said baldly. "A hurricane is coming."

Lathyr didn't bother to hide his shudder. He'd weathered a hurricane. Two. Two only and had never wanted to do those, let alone another. "If I knew where she was, I'd get her."

Jenni slanted him a sympathetic look, placed her warm fingers over his fisted—and webbed—ones. He'd lost a little control. Drawing a breath—at least the air was humid with a salty tang—he made his hands human again.

"We know," Jenni said.

His jaw flexed and he made his teeth more human, too, minded the color of his skin, the shape of his ears as their waitress came by and he ordered absently. He couldn't shut away the worry. Kiri had made a place in the chambers of his heart, in the tide of his blood. He'd never be free of her, didn't want to be. But that connection wasn't wise to display to anyone before he could make plans, *find Kiri.*

He forced his jaw to unlock long enough to say, "I do know that she's beyond New Orleans, close to the ocean."

The couple exchanged a glance, and Jenni actually looked haggard. "Right into the hurricane's path," she said. "No one will allow us into the area."

Humans and their human rules, but a hurricane was no place for a half-human, quarter-fire princess.

"Yes, you must stay here." Glancing around to make sure they were unobserved, Lathyr used his knife to slice his palm again, deeper. He'd ordered a huge dinner and would eat it all. Again he took Jenni's hand, then Aric's, murmured a small binding chant—something he hadn't done for centuries, and the last had been with a good human friend, now long dead. But both Jenni and Aric had a softness for him that the binding would stick to; both were friends.

The princess watched with wide eyes, flexed her fingers and smiled. "Feels a little odd, but not unpleasant."

Aric grunted. "Feels good."

Lathyr nodded, Jenni's fire magic had brought a brief sting, Aric's woodman and elven nature had been…nice. "Now you will sense if I die." His face tightened. "And I will be able to use the bond to push an urgent message to you when I find Kiri."

Jenni sighed. "Also good. We'll do what we can when we can."

"Of course." It felt good connecting to friends. He should not have stayed so solitary—but no one had offered him friendship in any of the places where he'd stayed.

That was the past.

The food came and Lathyr gobbled it down, went to a stall in the men's restroom and took his droplet form and moved back to the river. Now he used storm weather and magic to skip down the river until he got to where he'd sensed Kiri.

She wasn't there, and he had to go deep into the current to find her.

She was in her full, tailed form, reveling in the scent and feel of salt water on her skin, when water churning with wind and wave picked her up and grabbed her. She panicked, fought, to no avail. She was caught, trapped by the current and the weather, being battered.

Ducking into the main water stream, she concentrated on working her bilungs, getting enough air in the frothy water, but debris shot at her and she deflected it with a tight field she formed around herself, and her skin that she'd hardened as much as she could into armor.

Scary. Out of control. Keep her head.

This wasn't a man-made situation, didn't feel like anything an evil Dark one would do, either.

What?

And it struck her landlocked brain—the South, New Orleans, autumn. Hurricane weather. Oh, *shit.*

She curled into a ball, flipped until her head pointed upstream, tried again with all her magic, all her augmented physical strength, to push against the current that carried her down the river, would dump her out…somewhere. Gulf of Mexico? She thought so. Dammit. She didn't know much about the Mississippi River Delta, not even the configuration of lower Louisiana.

Only that it was no safe haven in a hurricane.

Once she broke the surface, but was dragged under too quickly to see more than night black, no stars, bad clouds. She wasn't sure how long it had been night, how soon it would be morning, or even if she could hang on that long.

Fighting only tired and weakened her, so she gave up and tucked tight and saw the banks of the river blur by, the occasional naiad or naiader huddled safe in a nest they'd made. *They'd* been wise.

She'd been ignorant and foolish and soon she might be dead. She mind-yelled, trying to reach Lathyr, Jenni, anyone.

Nothing.

So she endured, and the rushing weather and waters surged into the ocean, taking her with them.

It was colder and darker than she'd imagined, but the turbulence lessened as she sank deep.

Among the dim and muddy waters, a group of tough-looking mers approached her, radiating anger in every fin at her invading their territory. She'd learned that look on her trip down the river.

And the pure truth was that she had no clue how to deal with them, except that she couldn't look vulnerable.

*Smells of mer, river, salt, magic.* The words came to Kiri's ears in an odd cadence, reverberated into her mind at the same time.

One sniffed, his nose frills were long, outrageously beautiful, as was his body, his pattern, and his powerful tail. And he knew it.

He added sign language that she didn't understand. She was culturally blind, and that was a problem. Her heart pulsed hard in the fringes of her tail fin, so hard she had to control the tremble of the beat. Deadly to show weakness.

*Look what the winds and waves have brought us,* a merfem bubbled in such a way that it sounded like a cruel purr to Kiri. *A lost river mer. Let's play twist her tail.* The merfem smiled with awesomely jagged teeth. *Off. Twist her tail off.*

Kiri knew that was literal. The merfem had noted the merman's long study of Kiri, of scales on her body that had raised and begun to take on a tint in ragged spots, splotchy bits. They didn't look anything like a pattern. Naiads didn't have patterns. She scanned the beautiful designs these mers showed. Nope, they were mers and she was a naiad.

She didn't know how to fight, but she'd do her best. How she wished she'd spent more time in the Water Realm. But she hadn't known magic was a reality.

Her mind skittered. Was there any way she could call for magical help and not alert those before her…send her mind out on a different frequency maybe? Low or high?

She didn't know, but in her fear she *reached* for magic, sent a yell for help in as high a tone as she could make it, then as low.

The mers laughed and the merman rolled his shoulders. She wasn't sure whether they'd heard her or not. *Hardly worth bothering about.* His lip curled and when he tossed his head his long hair caressed the cheek of the merfem. *She's yours to play with, Flawn.* He backswam, then watched with amusement as the others of his band closed around her.

*Slowly, then. She will give us much sport,* the merfem said.

They circled, poked, threatened, teasing and playing with Kiri before the kill. And she knew they'd kill her. She was too strange and different. She smelled of naiad, and the river, and salt and magic. She was sure that the fragrance of her magic was foreign and from their wrinkled noses, not an odor they cared for.

A long, cylindrical shape sticking out of the side of an ocean wall caught her eye. She grabbed it, tugged. More laughter.

*It's too stuck to use,* Flawn mocked.

But Kiri put her power into it, her panic, her magic and yanked. The thing came free and she tumbled head over tail.

More laughter, but edgy now.

She had a weapon, even though it turned in her hand, flaky with rust.

*Let's finish this,* Flawn said.

KIRI'S MIND SPARKED WITH THOUGHTS FAST with fear. Remember fighting in the Water Realm. Think of this as a game. Calculate the drag on the pipe, the power to put behind the swing. Angle *there.* Swim so back is against that shelf wall. Aim for Flawn and the other two most aggressive, leave those hanging back alone. Don't aggro—aggravate—them. Don't make them enemies. Leader guy might not follow up if not too much damage is done. Hit, make a hole in their defenses, run through them when disorganized.

She held her staff like a bat, a metal rod of about five feet, just the right thickness for her to grab well. Clenching her jaw, she formed a bubble around herself…and Flawn hesitated. Why? No matter.

Kiri watched the merfem's eyes, her body language, to gauge when to swing.

Then a keening alarm came from the rear and the group scattered.

A great swarm of stingrays, swimming in formation—blacker than anything she'd seen—black with *evil* against the surface of the water zoomed into view ahead of her

*Ha!* gloated a shapeless form of pure darkness riding the largest stingray. *I have found you. You escaped me in that hideous building in that horrible inland city, but now my great power discovered your trace and I have found you where I can take you.*

The snapping of teeth. *And eat you.*

Worse than the alligator. Worse than the mers—who watched from nearby folds in the earth but would not intervene. Fear froze Kiri.

Her rod wobbled in her hands.

She'd go down fighting.

A sweet, sweet sound struck her. Music whispering through her ears, twining down into her very heart, bucking her up. Someone came in response to her call.

Some *ones*. More than the group of stingrays. More than the band of mers—who she heard whispering among themselves, their thoughts impinging and bouncing away from her mind.

*Tis Twilight Hope's pod,* a merman said.

*Why would they come? Here? Now? For that THING?* Contempt from Flawn.

*She is different than we,* said the alpha male.

An almost human snort with words Kiri translated as the sarcastic, *You think?*

The music became so unbearably lovely that Kiri shuddered. It drew her, demanded that she respond.

She raised her arms and *sang* with her naiad's voice, tones and musical scales.

And she moved, tail swirling, torso dipping, whisking figures in the water, gathered magic around her, fisted in her hands. Yelling with triumph she released it—straight at the dark ugliness.

Stingrays flapped and keened as if they hurt.

*No! Stop! No!* ordered the evil Dark one.

The singing increased and she was surrounded by dolphins.

And the stingrays blew apart as if they'd been only illusion or formed of evil thoughts or nothing of this earth or dimension.

But the chill of the evil one yelling and cursing shoved thought and fear back into Kiri's mind until he disappeared, too. Yet he left a threat against her that smeared her like spilled oil. *I will EAT you, you mutation. Soon.*

Joy at the dolphins, fear at the threat mixed, emotions overwhelming her.

And her scales itched and stung all along her torso, front and back, and edging her spine and tail, as if using her magic had marked her.

Lathyr *appeared,* displacing a volume of water, just in front of her. The local mers converged on them. And Kiri tasted salt again, from the ocean around her and the tears that had started to her eyes and mixed with the sea.

Her lover held out his arms—an offering, but no demand. She swam into them and they hugged her tight against a body she knew that gave her bone-deep comfort.

*Dear Kiri,* he whispered next to her ear. *You are safe.*

*A near thing, the dolphins saved me,* she said.

*Part of your magic, I think,* Lathyr said. He looked at them swimming around her. *They sense emotions, so project your gratitude.*

She did, mixed it with awe at their beauty, appreciation for their singing. And she received a wash of affection back as they danced and leaped, then swam away.

*Luckily we only caught the edge of the hurricane,* Lathyr said, then slid his hands down her arms, folding her fins flat. That gave her pleasurable shivers. *You're developing a scale pattern, Kiri, look at yourself.*

She could see the angles on the top of her breasts, brushed the raised scales with her fingers, shivered again. The design was barely tinted differently than her skin. Everyone else had a distinctively colored pattern. She wondered if hers would change.

*None of us knew,* Lathyr said. *None of us imagined you held enough magic to ally with a dolphin pod. That you were not naiad.*

*Not naiad,* Kiri repeated.

*Not naiad but full merfem. You were just born without a pattern, and full mers are born with designs on their scales. But you had no mer blood family background to show in your scales—you had to develop the pattern with your magic yourself.*

*Wow,* she said, blinking both lids to comprehend.

Lathyr smiled, met her gaze with his dark and serious one. *You are a greater elemental being, and one who needs the ocean. Your physical deterioration would have stopped once you, an oceanic merfem, reached the sea.*

As Kiri struggled with the fact that she was an oceanic merfem, he turned to the other mers and executed one of his fancy bows. Flawn eyed him with approval.

Yeah, he sure was a beautiful merman. Not as chunky as the local leader, more refined. Classier.

Lathyr stood—somehow, okay he was upright not angled—projecting a confidence that bordered on noble arrogance. With hand signs and mental telepathy, he said, *The only good thing you did here was help distract the great Dark one.*

*A Dark one!* a merfem squealed and vanished with a flick of the tail, along with the rest of the band except the leader and Flawn. Even they paled and trembled.

*I am authorized by the royals to award gold for services rendered to Kiri and myself.* Lathyr shrugged. *You, however, did not show a modicum of hospitality or generosity to Kiri.* Another shruglike gesture that rippled his whole body. *A pity you lost a fortune and the goodwill of the royals by threatening Kiri.* He smiled a shark-sharp smile. *In fact, I'm tempted to report your behavior to the Water King himself.*

Now the two seemed to pant with distress.

The guy flourished a bow, not nearly as good at it as Lathyr. *Our deepest apologies to you and her.* He didn't look at Kiri, but did shoot a glance at Flawn. *You're on your own.* He dissipated into the water.

Lathyr's nostril frills closed as if he smelled something bad and he raised his brows at Flawn, who hunched over in terror. Kiri got the impression he was holding her there.

*As for you. One should not assume strangers have no friends that will call you to account for torment.*

Hands moving in a blur he compressed water into a tight, hard ball about the size of two fists and shot it at Flawn, hitting the sensitive webbing of her tail. She screamed and disappeared.

*Lathyr?* Kiri questioned. His face had set and showed little but he emanated fury.

An aura of light flared from him, then he turned and his eyes showed guilt.

*They scared you…they should be frightened themselves. They were going to kill you.*

She didn't know good mer body language so she just lifted her chin. *They were going to try.*

She got a faint smile.

*I was too late. I lost you. I didn't protect you.*

*I didn't stay for you. Didn't talk to you. I was stupid.*

*Shhh.* He pulled her close again, and their tails bumped.

Kiri recalled how much hers had hurt when injured. *What about Flawn's tail?*

*It will heal, not even scar. Her community should take care of her.*

Kiri wasn't sure of that, but let it go.

They floated for a few minutes, before he said, *We have been summoned by the Eight and the closest palace is in what you call the Puerto Rican Trench.*

She hadn't even known there was a sea trench near Puerto Rico. She was still sorting out what and who she was when he moved fast through the water in a way she hadn't learned—too fast for Maroon Lake. They seemed to teleport, and as she caught her breath, they hovered outside a gorgeous palace that looked like it was built of glass or clear crystal.

In the ocean. And deep, if she read the pressure around her well.

A few glass spires rose above them, though the wings of the palace made it look more horizontal than vertical, reminding Kiri of several glass conservatories mixed together. Oddly charming.

Lathyr twirled her so he was behind her, his arms wrapped around her, in legged-mer form. So she turned legged-mer, too, easily.

Other mers swam near in various forms; she even sensed some dispersed in the water. The palace seemed a busy place. In a mental tone that Kiri believed only she could hear, he said, *I will take you to the door outside the royal audience chamber.*

She clutched at him. *Stay with me!*

*Of course.* His telepathic voice became tender. *I will not leave you, Kiri.*

No, because he'd been abandoned himself. And, deep inside, had she felt that way, too? She'd been older when her parents had established their second families and seemed to squeeze her out, but had she thought they'd abandoned her? Maybe.

*I won't leave you, either,* she said.

And she sensed his emotions, clearer and more intimate than the dolphins, a huge rush of delight and tenderness.

Then they were inside the palace and it was dry and her bi-lungs pumped hard as she gasped for air.

Lathyr eased his hold on her. "Don't think about it, just—"

"Breathe," Kiri said at the same time he did.

"I should have told you we were going to the air atmosphere portion of the palace."

Another wet and sucking breath, a couple of pants, and she could answer. "I should have figured that out. Royal audience chamber and summoned by the Eight means all the royals and that includes all the other elemental royals, none of whom live underwater. Right?"

"Right."

Breathing easily now, she noticed the opaque crystal glass door in front of her. Tall naiader guards in two-legged form stood on each side. They wore additional armor and held long tridents.

"Wait!" someone called in a high-pitched voice and Kiri blinked at the sight of Mystic Circle Castle's browniefem Melody hustling toward them with a bundle of material in her arms.

Before Kiri could ask the woman what she was doing here, Melody had flipped a long green cut-velvet scarf thing around Kiri, handed a blue one to Lathyr.

The browniefem's ears flexed. "Good I brought a ruana. You have mer pattern skin. This good garment for you. Mers prideful of their designs. Like to show."

Melody sniffed and twitched at the garment that had fringe

sticking to Kiri's damp scales. With a deep breath, she drew all water from the surface of her skin, puddled around her and Lathyr, and the cloth.

Little browniefem fingers adjusted as the woman exclaimed in satisfaction. "You look good now. Ready for the audience."

Melody stepped back, and back...and into the wall of the corridor.

Kiri gaped.

Trident butts thumped against the floor, drawing her attention back to the guards. They moved toward the two leaves of the door and opened it.

Lathyr slipped her hand onto his arm.

A naiad's high voice called out. "Attention, the transformed human, Kiri Palger of Denver, United States, and Lathyr Tricurrent of Trobriand Trough."

The buzz from the voices of about thirty people in the large room faded abruptly and everyone stared at her. Kiri felt like a freak.

Lathyr put his other hand on hers, squeezed her fingers, then removed that hand. *You are beautiful and magical and merfem. Know that.*

Kiri straightened her spine and used every smidgen of grace she had to look like she glided across the marble floor.

The chamber was deep in the side of the trench, not close to any of the glass windows, and Kiri got the idea that it wasn't used much. On each side of the door were huge fireplaces crackling with fire-eating great logs.

A mural on the far wall appeared to look out on an airy view...a cliff showing an ocean beneath...with storm clouds and lightning in the far corner. She narrowed her eyes since it reminded her of scenery in the game, Transformation.

No one stood within ten feet of the eight thrones.

*This is not one of the major Water Palaces*, Lathyr reminded her. *So this room is kept for the royals only. It is the most secure room in the place, but less comfortable for us Waterfolk than the rest of the residence.*

*The rest of the palace is gorgeous,* Kiri admitted.

Lathyr nodded, his expression becoming more immobile with every step he took toward the thrones.

The closest royal couple were djinns, and Kiri kept cutting her gaze toward them since she'd never seen djinns, not even in the game. Their skin was ruddy, maybe even red, their hair was mostly black, though the woman had auburn highlights. Flames seemed to dance in their eyes, flickering with yellow and red and orange. Like all of the Lightfolk, they were exotic and beautiful.

*The Fire royals have only been king and queen for a few months. As a couple, they are fairly equal in power and they are the least in magic of the Eight. Of the others, the greatest in magic is the Earth King, then the Water Queen, the Water King, the Earth Queen, the Air King and then the Air Queen.* Lathyr stopped and made a flourishing bow.

Kiri snatched glances at the royals, did not meet their eyes. Even though she was Lightfolk now, they might be able to glamour her. The Earth King looked old and stern, his wife grumpier and lumpier of feature than Mrs. Daurfin at Eight Corp. She knew the Air King, and his queen was so exquisite that Kiri caught her breath.

Time to curtsy. She touched the sides of her ruana, bent her head and did a deep dip, hoping she looked all right.

"Let's see her pattern." The words came sharp as teeth from the large merman in two-legged form, handsome in a sensual way, with green-blond hair. His gaze fastened on Lathyr, glittering with animosity.

Lathyr stepped behind her and drew off her ruana as if revealing a prize, draping it over his arm and bowing. "As you can see, Kiri's pattern is angular with significant power."

She glanced down at herself and saw straight-lined ridges, a couple of diamond shapes. They *had* changed color, gleaming deep emerald against her green skin.

The Water Queen leaned forward, her gown of water droplets on threads of fresh seaweed moving with her. She hummed in approval and smiled at Kiri. "Our new merfem could possibly become royal."

"Unexpected," rumbled the Earth King as people in the room gasped. He turned dark eyes that looked as gentle as granite on Lathyr. "Tell me, Sir Tricurrent, is this usual, that a human might be transformed into one who might be as powerful as we?"

"No, Your Highness," Lathyr said. "Kiri is quite unusual, and the person with the most powerful potential to become Lightfolk that I have sensed."

A sigh rippled through the room.

"We'll see if she can become royal," the Water King murmured. He lifted a hand and shot a bolt of glowing lightning to hit Kiri in the chest. "I hereby accept you as a prospective royal and send you on the test of the great Pearl. You are subject to this geas."

She rocked, but managed to stay upright. Lathyr hadn't reached out to help her, and she'd known that would have been bad. Just as she knew that the king had no belief that Kiri could manage the quest, more like he expected her to fail, maybe even die.

The Water Queen made a quiet sound of disbelief, hurt in her eyes, and she looked at Kiri with pity, as if Kiri were a kitten about to be drowned.

Kiri wanted to rub the stinging on her chest to relieve it.

Instead she bowed, smoothly straight down and up, keeping her stare on the Water King. "I thank you for this opportunity, Your Highness, and your belief in the Transformation project."

"I will go with her," Lathyr said.

"Of course you will, Tricurrent fry." The Water King grinned in triumph and smashed a power stream of energy at Lathyr. "I hereby accept you as a prospective royal and send you on the test of the great Pearl. You are subject to this geas."

Lathyr had hunkered down into his balance and the magic coruscated along the pattern on his entire body, sizzling and leaving a smell of burning fish and human. He spasmed but didn't fall.

Kiri strove not to gag. "You shouldn't—"

*Stop now,* Lathyr snapped at her mentally. Moving jerkily, he draped her scarf jacket around her shoulders.

But the words burst from her. "This smell reminds me of what the great Dark one did to humans in Denver last month."

There was shocked silence as everyone stared at the Water King.

Tension, danger buzzed in the air from the merman. His eyes went wild. Kiri groped for something to defuse. "I am honored to receive the geas."

The Water King bared his shark teeth at her, and she wished she hadn't seen them, but he seemed to ease away from viciousness. Give the man a bone, remind him of his status, and he reacted in a positive manner. Good to know.

"Thank you again." Kiri slid her gaze along the royals, feeling a hint of support from the Water Queen, the Air and Fire couple, and, oddly enough, a deep and waiting sort of curiosity and patience from the Earth King.

Lathyr bowed, and without another word they backed to the door. Wise not to take your eyes off volatile royals. There,

Lathyr paused and looked back. "I have decided to use my merman father's family name, also, so I am Lord Lathyr Squall-Tricurrent."

The Water Queen straightened, hopped from her throne and stood staring at him. Lathyr inclined his head. "A pleasure meeting you, my distant cuz."

Whirling, the Water Queen demanded, "What have you done, Marin?"

Inner guards opened the door and they escaped, leaving loud gossiping voices behind them.

Now-smirking hall guards closed the doors behind them, muttering something nasty in a mer language Kiri didn't understand. Lathyr whirled and set his hand on the hilt of his sword, sneered something back.

"Easy, lad." A dwarf appeared and put his hand on Lathyr's arm.

"They must apologize," Lathyr insisted. "Or we will fight."

"I WILL JOIN YOU IN THAT FIGHT," SAID A SMOOTH voice, an elf, who stepped from behind Kiri to confront the guards, too.

She hadn't heard either the dwarf or elf arrive and could have sworn they weren't in the hall when she and Lathyr had exited.

Droplets appeared on the guards' faces and scales that weren't hidden by armor.

"As you wish, great guardian elf, Pavan. I apologize to you, woman," the slightly shorter one said to Kiri, bowing…and keeping his eyes down.

"I, uh, I, too, apologize, Tricurrent."

"Lord Squall-Tricurrent and Lady Palger," Pavan corrected silkily.

"Lord Squall-Tricurrent and…Lady—?" The merman stopped.

"The Water King has marked Sir Squall-Tricurrent and

Lady Palger as royal questors. According to all our traditions, she is now royal."

"Until she fails," the first guard muttered.

"The girl won't fail," the dwarf said, a little too heartily. "She'll—they'll—succeed at the quest and earn their status and rewards."

"Apologize to the *Lady,*" Lathyr insisted.

"I apologize, Lady," the second guard said, with the shortest bow she'd ever seen, but he kept his face and eyes expressionless.

"Come on, you two," the dwarf said, shooing them down the hall before him. "You're guesting in our wing."

The guards behind them tensed into statues.

Lathyr said, "Salutations, and many thanks, Guardians." He looked down at her. "These are the two great guardians of the Lightfolk—they...observe...the royals."

"This was not well-done of Marin," the dwarf snapped, like shards chiseled from rock. He touched Kiri's elbow, directing her into a branching, still-dry, hallway. "But it is done...the quest geas lodged within you, and cannot be undone."

Kiri swallowed. "What does it mean?"

"You will be compelled to search for the great Pearl and complete the quest to prove your magical power is strong enough for you to become royalty," the elf guardian said.

"And what does *that* mean?" Kiri asked flatly.

"You'll be in the line of succession. Currently the female couple who hold this palace are the heirs to the Greendepths. Whether you replace them or fall after them in the hierarchy list will be determined by your quest," the elf continued, then they headed toward a perfectly circular iron doorway at the end of the hall.

"What happens if I fail?"

"If you refuse the quest compulsion you will wither and die." The elf bent a stern look on her.

She shook her head. "Not going to do that. This is interesting."

Both the guardian's expressions warmed.

"Good you got curiosity," the dwarf said.

"What if I fail the quest? I don't become royal, I guess, but what else?"

The guardians shared a look, then the elf said, "We will ensure any consequences of the geas are not fatal."

The strength of her sigh surprised Kiri, but she hadn't been able to hold it back. "But I'll be a failure for the Transformation project." She lifted her chin. "I want to show them what humans-now-Lightfolk can do."

"Kiri, we're not sure what you *can* do," Lathyr reminded.

"We'll find out, and best if I complete the quest. I. Will. Do. My. Best."

"That's all anyone can ask," the elf said as they stopped at the door.

"This is our wing," the dwarf said gruffly. "It's dry, three stories and composed of glass and iron and magic."

"Um-hmm." Kiri cleared her throat. "Thank you for putting us up."

The elf smiled at her and she noted he had more lines in his face than any other Airfolk she'd seen, but stronger charisma. "You are welcome to always stay here with us." He bowed. So did the dwarf and Lathyr in response. So Kiri dipped her knees, too.

"Our apartments are heavily shielded." His eyes gleamed. "And we have Meld and a state-of-the-art office, including a number of electronics that run on Meld." He rubbed his hands.

Kiri sighed. "Sounds good."

"Kiri needs water chambers."

"We have that," the dwarf mumbled. He set his palm on the door and it opened. "We have areas for all elementals." He laughed like the sound of cheery pebbles slipping down a hill. "And unlike the rest of the place, Jenni Emberdrake keeps our wing balanced with elemental magic."

"We prefer it that way," the elf agreed. He, too, put his hand on the door and sang a few spell rhymes. "We have keyed the portal to you and Kiri, Lathyr."

"Our thanks," Lathyr said, at the same time Kiri said, "Thank you."

The door opened and she walked into a room that reminded her of the Castle. A room that could be in any inland human's home and tears gushed down her cheeks.

Lathyr was there, his arm coming around her waist.

"What is it?"

"I haven't talked to my friends, Shannon and Averill in..." She'd completely lost track of time.

"Only five days, and I think you told them you were going on a trip?"

"Yes, but still..." She counted days. "I missed the Mystic Circle Fairies and Dragons they joined, whatever emails they might have sent. That would have concerned them."

"Jenni would have tried to soothe them." Lathyr stroked Kiri's long hair down her back.

"It's not the same."

"No," the elf said.

The dwarf grunted loudly and they looked at him. He pulled at his beard. "Summons from the Earth King. Gotta go."

He pointed a thick forefinger at Kiri. "You remember, girl, that you can do this."

She met his intense dark brown eyes. "You think so."

A nod. "I do. Later." He tromped back out, apparently not in a hurry to answer the king's summons. Must be nice to be more powerful than the royals.

The elf said, "Come with me. We have video conferencing in our office."

They walked through the entrance room that looked like a living room, into a hallway.

The elf waved to a staircase curving up to the left, watery green light filtered down from the stairwell. "The third-floor apartments on the left are my rooms." He gestured to the right. "These are my fellow guardian's, the dwarf Vikos."

Didn't sound like they were lovers, but they hadn't acted like it. More like business or soldierly partners—army buddies. Not that she knew much about army buddies.

They reached a round-arched door and it swung open, revealing a small, round and domed chamber. Like the gaming room at Eight Corp, a wooden counter-desk curved along most of the wall. Kiri's eyes widened as she saw a stack of unique-looking tablet computers, and another set of handhelds. Four large monitors were hooked up to desktops and there were game pads, gloves and visors, game sticks, keyboards, microphones and speakers.

"Wow," she breathed, and tension left some of her muscles.

"Do whatever you need to do to reassure your friends, explore the wing."

Lathyr had gone to one of the stations and turned on a computer.

Kiri stepped to follow, then looked down. Grass grew thickly on the floor. She trod on it, loving the feel on her soles.

"By the way, Lathyr," the elf said, standing at the doorway just as Lathyr had in giving his parting shot to the royals.

Lathyr turned from the computer counter and straightened, his shoulders in a taut line. “Yes.”

The elfman smiled, amused. “Good job on finishing the Water King off.” The guardian tilted his head toward Kiri. “Your lady set him up and you finished him off.” The elf paused a beat. “Which means we will not have to intervene. His wife and the other royals will discuss his behavior with him. Finally. A good option for Vikos and me.” He winked at Kiri, “Call me Pavan.”

She’d figured out being gifted with the guardians’ names was an honor. Once again she did a bow, which was getting really tiresome.

“The Waterfolk suite is a two-story circular area off the living room as we came in,” Pavan said. “Part of it is dry, the rest water.”

“Thank you.” Lathyr bowed.

Pavan waved his hand and left.

Application icons appeared on the huge monitor’s screen. One was for a video conferencing program she had an account with. Another little sigh. She put her hand around Lathyr’s arm. “Thank you for standing with me.”

He glanced up at her with a smile. “Always.”

“Do you have any idea what the time might be in Colorado?”

“After work, I believe.”

Kiri nodded. “And I’ll have to tell my friends that I’ll be going away again. Does anyone know where the great Pearl is?”

Lathyr blinked in surprise. “Of course. It is in the deepest part of the ocean.” He touched the tip of one ear. “I doubt I can swim that far down.”

Biting her lip, Kiri scoured her internal database.

"What humans call Challenger Deep," Lathyr said, "In the Mariana Trench."

"The Mariana Trench, near the Mariana Islands? What ocean is that?"

"Tell your friends you are going to the Philippines. That should sound fine to them."

"Yes. It might."

He held out a chair for her and she slipped into it, logged on to the program.

And got an immediate ding from Shannon. She was sitting on the old love seat she and Kiri and Averill had shopped for when they'd first married.

"Kiri, it's so good to see you! What's been going on?" Shannon's eyes narrowed. "You look a little rough."

Kiri licked her lips. She didn't want to lie any more than necessary to her friends. "It's been a very intense few days."

"You're okay?" Shannon asked sharply.

"Yes, I'm fine."

Shannon's lips compressed and her face moved closer to the screen as if she examined Kiri. Squinting, she said, "Who's that in the background?"

Lathyr came up and put his hand on Kiri's shoulder.

Suddenly it was easier. "My new guy."

Shannon's expression lit with happiness. "You have a new guy!" She moved over a little on the love seat and Averill joined her.

Now Averill narrowed his eyes. "Who is he?" he asked, at the same time that Shannon said, "Is it serious?"

Lathyr kissed her hair.

"Maybe." She found herself flushing…she could still do that. "I've been busy," she added weakly.

"I completely understand," Shannon said, with one of those explosively relieved breaths she had.

"Who's the dude?" Averill said louder.

Lathyr lowered until the camera caught most of his face. Shannon made a yummy noise. Averill nudged her. She glanced at her husband. "Not my type, you know that, but very nice to look at."

"Thank you," Lathyr said politely.

"Hey, good to see you," Shannon said.

"Hello," Lathyr replied. He nodded to Averill. "My name is Lathyr Squall-Tricurrent and I work for Eight Corp."

"Human resources," Shannon said promptly.

Kiri choked. That had a whole different meaning to her now.

"That is correct," Lathyr said.

"So you're Lathyr, and you're Kiri's new guy."

"I am her lover."

Shannon laughed and Averill scowled. Kiri felt fluttering in her middle, glanced at Lathyr's face. Intent, as always. Surely the quest would begin tomorrow, so tonight… Yes, she wanted to have sex love with him, again.

"Mind if I do some checking on you, Lathyr?" Averill asked. It wasn't truly a question, just something to say while that sharp brain of his calculated angles.

"You are welcome to," Lathyr said. "Though I doubt I am much on the internet." He hesitated. "If you wish to confirm my character, you may speak with Alex Akasha, the CEO of Eight Corp."

"CEO," Averill said neutrally.

"We are—acquaintances. I believe he will vouch for me."

"Where do you come from?" Shannon asked.

"Currently I am living in Mystic Circle."

"Yeah, we knew that. Kiri spoke of you. Hey, Kiri, can we ask Jenni Emberdrake about him?"

"Yeah, sure," Kiri said. Her eyes slid in Lathyr's direction.

"We'll ask Jenni," Averill said. "We know her a little now from playing Fairies and Dragons."

"You're good, Kiri?" Shannon asked.

"Yes, I'm very good," Kiri said steadily.

Shannon's expression turned sly. "But you're going to be busy some more and probably out of reach?"

One way to put questing under the sea. "That's right."

"Okay." Shannon took Averill's hand. "We'll try not to worry."

"You take care of her," Averill said to Lathyr.

"I promise," Lathyr said.

"I suppose you can't stay and talk." Shannon sighed.

"Not right now," Kiri answered.

"We have a plane to catch," Lathyr lied.

"Where?" Shannon asked, again leaning forward.

"We are going to the Philippines."

"The Philippines!" Shannon said.

"Eight Corp is considering an Asian office and wants me there," Lathyr said. "I have permission to take Kiri."

"Nice." Shannon grinned, then wiggled her brows at Kiri. "Have fun."

"I'm sure it will be interesting," Kiri said primly, also fibbing with her tone.

Averill grunted. "This gonna be a permanent office that you or Kiri or you both might man?"

"Unknown," Lathyr said. "I reiterate my promise to you to take care of her."

"I can take care of myself," Kiri grumbled, even though she doubted. She had a lot to learn.

But Averill and Shannon smiled, then blew kisses at her. Though Kiri just wanted to look at her happy friends more, Lathyr signed her off. She sagged in the chair.

Lathyr swiveled the chair and lifted her from it. "You need food and rest…."

"And loving." She stroked his cheek. "That, too."

LATHYR'S EYES DARKENED, THE IRIS BECOMING blue-black, gaze intent. With a single sweet note he had the door opening and slamming behind them.

Then he just stood, cradling her, and it felt good and right… for now.

Slowly he walked back the way they'd come to the entrance room. The atmosphere charged around her, as if every molecule that held a bit of water slid against her skin, leaving a tingle.

He said, "There will be a warm, natural pool in our suite. Will you let me take you there and make love with me beneath the water?" His voice lilted, his mer accent noticeable.

She stared up at him, matching his gaze, her mouth drying. "I…I'm not sure how that is done."

His head tilted back as he laughed, then bent and kissed her temple. His pace picked up. "Much as humans mate. We use our legged form. But…in the water, it is a true dance, our coming together."

She thought of the glass walls of the palace, was sure that the Waterfolk area would be surrounded by ocean, and wondered how the pool would look, what kind of light might be there. What other mers might be outside watching.

"Um, we'll be private, won't we?"

"Yes, lovely Kiri. All the panes in the palace can be tinted to various shades that will shield our loving. Don't worry and don't plan. I promise you will think of nothing. You will only follow me into blissful sensation."

He couldn't enthrall her again with glamour, but she didn't want to deny him or herself. Just thinking of the sensual excitement ahead had her nipples beading, her breasts feeling heavy, her sex aching. She stared once more into his indigo eyes. "I would like that very much." Her own voice whispered from her lips.

As they left the warm living room behind them and stepped into a glassy area, anticipation wound tight within her. This was special, a loving in the night, in the water.

Soon they were in a dry chamber with a pool inset into the floor. The glass walls on three sides of them appeared clear but Kiri sensed a magical coating. There *were* mers swimming beyond the windows, though those outside paid no attention to her and Lathyr.

A slight whisk of air brought the scent of night-blooming jasmine. She could almost believe this was the conservatory at the Castle in Mystic Circle…then schools of colorful fish swam by.

Lathyr put her down, and keeping his eyes on hers, he took off his robe and her own, then led her into the pool. It was warm, and large and…deep enough.

And as they circled, danced, swam, sliding hands, teasing with light feather touches, and magic enveloped them as much as the water—hers matching his—she understood that in this matter, it would be harder for a male to force a female. And that she was being wooed and seduced by a master.

Kiri panted as they came together, then rocked with her lover until waves of sensation crashed over her and she swirled away in pleasure.

Early the next morning they stood in the top dome of one of the glass towers that was designated as a transportation room.

Though they'd spent the night in submerged chambers, this one was dry. It even had a huge tree growing in the center. Nice magical trick.

Kiri was getting very good at changing from form to form, breathing with her bilungs, and using her nictitating eyelids. She was sure she'd learned more in the past couple of days than she would have in weeks if she hadn't gone into the Mississippi River. And time was so relative! Those hours did feel like weeks ago, her job at Eight Corp months ago...and it had been at least a year since she'd been human.

And Lathyr had been with her for most of it, supporting her. Would have been with her for all her lessons if she hadn't been tempted by the ocean salt smell. He stuck with her like most people hadn't.

Maybe her lessons wouldn't have been hard, wouldn't have forced her to grow as a mer...but she thought the time with him, as the time with him now, had helped her become a better person.

Caring for another, considering their wants and needs as well as your own did that to you.

Lathyr gestured to a portal opening into a stationary water

funnel outside the palace. "Hold my hand. We'll go through and I will take us to Agat Bay, Guam, the closest water I know personally to Challenger Deep."

"Know personally?"

He whirled his hands. "The *feel* of the water, the pressure and scent of it, the temperature, the emanations of humans and mer and fish."

"Oh."

His brows knit. "Guam is about two hundred miles from Challenger Deep and the great Pearl. I am vaguely familiar with the waters and we will be able to move quickly through the ocean. We will be at the trench in under an hour."

Yoga breaths...she'd learned how to do those, even underwater. "Oh-kay," she said, stood a little taller. "Better sooner than later."

He took her hands and smiled down at her, at least his lips curved and she felt tenderness, maybe even more from him, though his eyes were dark and held secrets.

The door of the elevator opened and the Water Queen strode in.

Lathyr bowed. Kiri did the same, even managed a modified hand swirl, while studying the voluptuous merfem. Her heart-shaped face held a determined expression that hardened her soft features. Her hair was dark green and her pale green skin had the faintest tint of blue that Kiri hadn't noticed before.

"Salutations, my Queen," Lathyr said.

"Your distant cousin," she corrected in a slightly husky voice.

"As you wish, Highness."

She strolled toward them. "Or perhaps a distant auntie." Her gaze was fixed on him, and Kiri stood still, since a thread of yearning ran between the two.

"My last relative," the queen said softly, stopping near them. She was about the same height as Kiri.

"My last relative," Lathyr echoed, then blinked and bowed his head. "If you please."

"I do please to acknowledge you."

"And your king?" asked Lathyr.

Her voice hardened. "He knows not to thwart me in this any longer." She put her hands around his face. "Tadling." She smiled and was so sensual and beautiful that Kiri wanted to be her.

"I acknowledge you and we will speak after this quest is done. Come back to me, Lathyr Squall-Tricurrent."

Before he could answer, the queen turned to Kiri. "You will bring him back to me healthy and whole," she ordered.

Kiri raised her brows. "I hope to. I hope we both come back healthy and whole."

"Good," the queen said, then stared at Kiri. "A new merfem from a human, powerful in magic." She shook her head. "Astonishing, though I knew of the experiment, of course." She narrowed her eyes, and Kiri *felt* the woman's magic trace her angular scale pattern. The queen had very few curves in her design. She nodded, but didn't comment. She glanced at Lathyr again. "You are lovers?"

"Yes."

Her smile curved as she studied them. "It is well."

The door opened and two merfems hurried through, hand in hand, also obviously lovers and a couple.

"There you are, Highness," the taller, thinner one said.

"I have come to see my nephew off to his quest for the great Pearl," the queen said calmly. "Lathyr, I make you known to Frond Seamont, the Water King's heir." Then the queen gestured to the smaller merfem, who had totally different features and skin tone from the first, "and my heir, Urchin Seamont."

Kiri kept her sigh between her teeth as she used her bow again. "Honored," she said.

"As are we," said Frond. The two new merfems did some fancy curtsy dips and Kiri decided she'd stick with bows.

Urchin's full mouth thinned. "The Water King is…annoyed."

The queen lifted and dropped a shoulder. "He will grow out of it." She flashed an apologetic smile at Lathyr. "I should have broken him of some of his bad habits long ago, but the truth is—" she sighed "—I love him madly."

"I never doubted that," Lathyr said. Everyone looked at everyone else, and finally he said, "And I do not expect to garner a tenth of that love you feel for him as affection to myself."

"I suppose you think those pretty words will make me like you more." The king simply appeared in the room, and Kiri's mind went off in speculation about how he could do that, until she gave up.

"You are too high above me for me to understand," Lathyr said with such simple sincerity it had to be believed.

One side of the king's mouth kicked up in a half smile. "I suppose I might regret placing such an onerous geas on you," the merman said, offering his wife his arm. "Come, we Eight are discussing our primary project."

"Very well." The queen took his arm, but moved to angle them both to face Lathyr and Kiri. Then she lifted her hands and chanted and a soft web engulfed Kiri. Lathyr made a quiet noise beside her. "You have my blessing."

"Thank you," Kiri said.

The queen nudged the king sharply in the ribs. He turned his large and handsome head toward Kiri and met her eyes.

She felt the pull of him, and his anger, but dug her webbed feet into the tile floor. "You can do it, girl."

"Th-thank you."

The king turned and strode back to the door.

"And she will bring him back safe to me," the queen said.

Grunting, the king waved and Kiri felt another touch of magic smack her, energizing her. Huh.

"My thanks," Lathyr gasped, just as the royal Water couple entered the elevator and the doors closed behind them.

"He can be quite annoying himself," Urchin said.

"True," Frond said. She smiled at them. "We wish you well."

Kiri blinked. "You went on this quest."

Both merfems nodded and wrapped arms around each other's waist. "Indeed we did," Urchin said.

They looked at each other, and like the queen, Kiri sensed they were keeping themselves from talking about the quest.

"Thank you for your hospitality." Another swept bow from Lathyr.

"You are quite welcome," Frond said, paused, then continued delicately. "You have the guardians on your side, too."

"They informed us that you are to be considered occupants of their wing."

"They're very kind," Kiri murmured.

"They aren't," Urchin said. "But they take fancies to people and apparently you are a couple of them."

"It's the Mystic Circle connection," Kiri said decidedly.

The women appeared clueless.

"Mystic Circle, the balanced area where Princess Jindesfarne Emberdrake lives," Lathyr explained.

"Balanced magic does boost power," Frond said.

Urchin angled her head. "We're being called to the meeting. Good luck. Hopefully, more changes will be coming, like Marin Greendepths mellowing."

"That would be fine with me," Frond said, then called out, "Good luck!"

"Thanks!" Kiri said before they entered the elevator. Then she looked up at Lathyr. "Did you get the idea that we'd need luck?"

He nodded. "Oh, yes."

No more than two hours later, they hovered before the dark crevice in the earth. Lathyr turned her in his arms and kissed her and she shuddered at the sensuality of his tongue and his taste.

He drew away first. "We will do this together."

"Of course," she said.

He formed a shield around himself and she followed suit. Linking hands, they started down.

Dark. Cold. Strangeness and hideous pressure. Ghosts of her human origin haunted her.

They stopped some way down, Kiri didn't know where—either in relation to the ocean floor or the surface, or the bottom.

Lathyr let go of her hand. *I can descend no farther with you—the pressure and the water demands only one who is pure water elemental proceed. I have too much air elemental.*

He had barely any air elemental in his blood, and his face was impassive so she couldn't see whether he was disappointed. He twined tails with her, put his hands on her face and brushed her lips with his; she felt the pressure of them even through her shield that lay like a second skin around her. His tail squeezed hers, then released and he backswam and now he was smiling. *Go on!*

She stared at him, let the gentle current sweep her long hair in front of her face and mask her expression.

She wanted this. Wanted to fulfill every last bit of her potential. She hesitated, but her inner self yearned too much for the experience. So she nodded, and blew him a kiss and swam down.

She knew the water was odd, very different than most of the ocean. There were creatures she couldn't see. Those she sensed were nearly pure magic and glided in the shadows around her, themselves hardly more than a quick blur in her vision.

Strangeness enveloped her, the acidity of the water, the quiet of the deep, the knowledge she was completely alone.

That was more frightening than she'd anticipated, and had a lonely note echoing dull and low in her heart. Lathyr waited on a ledge in the trench, as far as he could go, and she descended alone.

Down and down and down and with every flick of fin, the dark became more oppressive.

Then she saw the glow. A coral-pink-peach glow that wasn't at all how it appeared in the game—and wasn't a true glow of light, but of magic. She stilled in momentary surprise that the game of Transformation had resembled reality once more, then resumed swimming.

She swam toward the glow that lured her.

Finally, she saw it.

Unlike the great Pearl in the game, this was not huge, nor was it partially embedded in the side of the trench. But it emanated more magic.

Tiny worm things and magical creatures circled around it in a graceful pattern, dancing in their way as other beings did in other atmospheres. She watched them and loneliness seeped even more into her blood. This sight would mean more if shared. Who could she talk with about this, the Water Queen who thought of her as a child? The king, who found her uninteresting?

In the stillness she became aware of a pulsing, the innate sound of the planet itself. With a bubbling breath she let herself sink to the great Pearl, holding pure magic from the earth, and balanced magic. Jenni would like to see this, but Kiri would never be able to bring her here.

The pearl was the size of a large crystal ball, and set on an intricately carved stand that reminded Kiri of those supporting fake ivory balls in Chinatown shops. Very fancy and no doubt dwarven made.

She reached out to brush her fingers on the surface of the pearl, touch it and finish this test the royals had set her.

And vividly recalled how, in Transformation, she had failed that mission.

THEN SHE KNEW. THIS SPECIAL PEARL WASN'T hers alone to touch. This test wasn't a quest for an individual, no matter how smart, how independent, how talented or in control that individual was.

This was a team effort—more, it was an *intimate* effort. And if she wanted to place her palm on this pearl, and, oh, she did!—she would have to accept and acknowledge an intimate bond.

*Acknowledge* was the right word. She had an intimate bond with a lover, a bond that could grow if she allowed it. Into what—she didn't know. But if she didn't admit it, she would forever be empty in a part of her that should be filled.

There was really nothing wrong with not wanting to share your life, she assured herself—not if that was how your heart truly wanted to live. But avoiding love because you were afraid of pain was a totally different matter.

The Mystic Circle people were the closest friends she'd allowed herself in years, outside of Shannon and Averill.

And wasn't it time for her to stop being hurt by her parents? And time she grew out of her childhood fear of being abandoned emotionally?

Well, maybe she'd always carry a hurt from her parents, but she didn't have to make that the central factor of all her heart-decisions in her life. Get over it. Move on.

Grow.

She knew Lathyr loved her—perhaps deeply. Deeply enough to put her wants and needs before his own. Deeply enough to let her come here to touch the great Pearl that he also wanted to see, to experience, but was unable to reach.

By himself.

Time to accept the feelings of her own heart. She loved Lathyr, too. He didn't abandon her. He stuck with her. He offered love without demanding it in return—and she'd been wary. Time for that to stop. He deserved her love. She'd be wrong in withholding her own feelings, when all she'd have to do is open up and let the love flow both ways.

She wanted him in her life for now and the foreseeable future of always. She didn't want a life without him.

She wanted to share the great Pearl with him.

So she backed away and rose gently through the sea, letting love, letting hope, carry her upward.

Somehow they should be able to touch the pearl together. She'd provide the pure water magic, he the finesse of experience.

But if not, if they couldn't do this together, then she wouldn't do it at all.

Being loved was more important than any outward trappings of respect or fame or status. All this time she'd thought those things had mattered, more than they did.

And she'd been afraid.

She returned to the ledge where Lathyr waited and when he saw her, his serious face glowed with love and he smiled, his gaze searching her face. *You are not as changed as I expected you to be.*

*But I am changed,* Kiri replied, taking his outstretched hands and pulling them together. *I did not touch the pearl.*

She felt the jolt of his surprise.

*What! Why not?*

*Because I learned from the game. This is not a pearl that should be touched by one. Only two.*

His eyes looked even bluer to her vision, elven eyes more than mer. Wonderful, cherished eyes in her lover's face.

*Let's see if we can do this together. You have the experience with shields, and I can feed you water magic and power and maybe get us both down there.*

*What if we can't?*

She shrugged. *Then we can't. Being with you, loving and being loved, is more important than status.*

*Then you love me.*

*Yes, but you knew,* she said.

*Yes, but I didn't know if you would stay with me.*

He, too, had had abandonment issues. And he had had faith, more faith and grace than she.

*I'm older,* he said, as if following her thoughts, then a line formed between his brows as he considered the logistics. *If we layer shields, and the innermost links us together with your water magic encasing the two of us, this might work.*

*All right.* She fed him raw power, her own and a tiny draw on the huge oceans of the earth.

He grinned, shaped the power, slowly, so she could see what he was doing. Then she understood she couldn't form the shields as he did, perhaps she could never form shields as good as his. He used a little air magic, and she told him so.

He looked surprised, frowned, then nodded and kept on layering the spells around them, cocooning them safely.

And when they were enveloped, she took his hand, smiled at the attraction and the connection between them. His slow smile back at her closed her throat. She hadn't been a very wise person lately, but accepting love—and *giving* it—had been the best decision she'd made in her life, including becoming Lightfolk.

So they swam slowly down and he exclaimed at the beauty, and the odd creatures, and the landscape and the texture of the water that flowed against the shields in a different manner than usual.

He paused, chest rising and falling hard. Kiri sent elemental water power through their link, saw it bead on his skin, then they dropped another few yards and Lathyr remained all right and the tension in her shoulders lightened.

Together they followed the glow of the pearl, then hovered near it.

She lifted her free hand, fingers spread.

Smiling at her, he did the same, and they curved their palms on opposite sides of the precious gem.

And as she did, the shield over her palm thinned to nothing. Magic. She shot a glance to Lathyr; he grinned and nodded. He felt the pearl, too.

She wasn't sure what she'd been expecting—a huge flow of power, some electrical shock, a wave of magic, but all that happened was that it gently glowed brighter, dazzling her senses.

*Listen,* Lathyr said.

So she did, frowning, because she'd adjusted to the magical glow and saw Lathyr's head tilted, his body rippling. She closed her own eyes and paid attention. Magic. Vibration. Humming. From the planet itself. Like the dolphin and whale songs, something more sensed than heard, and in a different range than human.

Felt more than heard.

Love.

Love for all its beings. For life from the single cell to those as complex as she and Lathyr.

And with that realization, Kiri also felt the minute pulse of the pearl, and magic seeping through her palm, her own blood falling into the same rhythm of mother Earth.

She was connected with the planet, and always would be, had the magic from the Earth inside her.

She wept.

After long moments, Lathyr said, *Enough. We must go. We must not be greedy and soak up more magic than we need.*

With a sigh, she nodded and drew away from the pearl. Her hand tingled and she flexed her fingers, saw Lathyr do the same. A slight pull from him had her spinning into his arms and she let him swirl her around in pleasure.

*Thank you, my lady, my love, for bringing me with you.*

*It would have meant less without you.*

*I do not know if the royals will accept you, or that you took me with you.*

She laughed, and it was free and easy, and she was free of her own ambitions, living in the moment, accepting what life had for her, not struggling. *Failed Goal? Like in the game?* She laughed again. *I don't care.*

*Good.*

*Besides, if this is THE test to become a Water royal, and no one but a complete water elemental could do this, the king must have helped his lady, right?*

Lathyr grinned. *Right.*

Peace lasted until they were a few yards away from the trench.

*Hello, human baby merfem.* It was a rough purr from a huge shadow separating itself from the gray landscape.

The great Dark one.

*I've come to eat you and your little magic.* Large rubbery lips smacked. The huge head turned, a wide eye staring at Lathyr. *And I get another snack, too.*

Kiri shuddered.

*We go*—yelled Lathyr.

But a white-fireball-energy pulse hit her—hit them—scrambled her mind. Hurt!

*You STAY,* the great Dark one gloated.

Lathyr's jaw flexed. *We can't go. My location sense is seared for the moment.*

She didn't ask for how long. She knew. Too long.

He separated from her, and most of the protection bubble snapped around her.

*No!* she protested.

But he pulled a long sword and a short wavy dagger and prepared.

Another ball of energy. Yellow. They dodged.

Kiri scrambled to comprehend the fight. She had no weapons.

Then Lathyr closed with the monster. Lathyr was fast and agile and clever. He turned and struck the Dark one's head, zoomed away, flipped and came back, ducking and weaving, for the thing's throat. Hit, but did not cut a major artery.

Dashed away and went *through* a leathery-looking wing, slashing it into more shreds.

The Dark one shrieked, sending a sound wave through the water that had Kiri tumbling, losing her bearings. This time she didn't move quickly enough and a green forceball hit her tail. She heard bones snap.

Lathyr shouted at the same time she did. A swipe of the giant's clawed hand raked his side.

Using magic, Kiri grabbed him to her. He lost his dagger as he slapped a hand against his wound. His hardscale had ripped open, blood looking black in the water. Bringing more predators.

Her tail was damaged. She couldn't take him away, feared for them both if she convinced him to take droplet form. They wouldn't survive.

The great Dark one was circling back.

They couldn't survive him, either. They were going to die. Lathyr was too wounded to fight and she too inexperienced to win against the Dark one.

There was only one thing she could do.

*Help! Great Dark one. Mariana Trench. HELP!*

The Dark one's laugh rolled to her, hit her like a nasty, sticky web, flipped her broken-tail-over-head. Lathyr passed out.

Yeah, the Dark one was powerful.

Kiri grabbed Lathyr and hauled him down into the trench, using arms and magic to propel them. Where was that shelf? Where, where? She found it, frowned and with a thought summoned a rope to her hand. She settled it around him, tied him loosely to the ledge so he wouldn't sink and perish while unconscious, and wouldn't rise and be prey for others. She hoped.

She hoped she'd have the chance to learn of the oceans from him.

*You think to hide from Me in there?* Pure contempt in the mental blast that sent her head hitting the side of the trench. Ow!

She didn't know the thing's capabilities.

*Maybe,* she sent a whisper and a tiny trail of bubbles. He would follow her. He wouldn't look for Lathyr. Perhaps she'd saved her love.

And the pearl. She understood the Darkfolk weren't like the Light. The Dark gobbled up power from anywhere, anyone, anything. They were not elemental beings.

Could it descend to the great Pearl? Besmirch it? Break the threads between the pearl and all life?

She couldn't risk that, either. She sensed something really bad would happen if he got his claws on it.

She sobbed. Quieted. Saw the skim of his body as a black shadow in the water. He leaked blood, ichor, stuff. That was good at least.

Forcing herself to relax, she formed an image in her head of the speargun and spear-quarrels she'd used before. In the game she could bring weapons to her. Maybe in reality she could, too. A small chance to fight and put off her death as long as possible.

Perhaps take the thing with her when she died.

How the gun felt in her hands. The sting of silver as it brushed her fingers.

Silver, yes! And with that need, the gun slipped into her grip, just there.

She blinked and blinked again. Couldn't see down here even with her second eyelids. How fast was the monster healing? She'd better get up there and give the battle her all.

Fight to the death.

She'd done it in the game, seen her avatar motionless on floors, in caves, in forests.

This was real and she *hated* it.

Must save Lathyr. Warn the others again.

Go out fighting.

She angled up out of the trench. The monster saw her sooner than she'd wished, laughed again, but she used her draining energy and magic to stay in place, masking the speargun. It didn't seem to sense the silver or the gun.

She filled her bilungs, and with oxygen came power from the ocean, a trace even from the pearl. Enough to steady her nerves, set aside the fear making her hands tremble.

Closer, closer. There! Huge nasty eye. Creepy zombie hair. Shoot!

Hit!

Horrible scream. Move, move, move, *fast*.

Maybe could blind it. Maybe.

Thrashing stopped and gigantic anger whipped toward her, hitting like stinging blows. Should she be that sensitive? Losing magical shields.

*HELP!* she screamed again. *HELP, Dark one, MARIANA TRENCH. TO ME!*

White waterspouts churned around her, bubbling, then *people* were there. Mers. The King and Queen of Water. The Seamonts.

The guardians.

Others.

The Dark one roared—backswam a bit, then began to circle in his attack path again.

A merfem sent Kiri a filthy look and vanished.

*Formation!* snapped the Water King, a huge and threatening trident in his hand. *Net!*

*I HATE fighting underwater,* Vikos, the dwarf guardian said.

He scowled at Kiri. *Good use of your magic, though. Good summons, not binding. Only requesting. Good.*

Silver weapons gleamed as mermen and merfems took position behind the Water King. Kiri strove to swim to the battle triangle. The Water Queen stopped her. *Where is your mate! Where is my nephew! He lives?*

*Yes!* Kiri gestured to the trench. *Down there, on a ledge. His side.* She gibbered even in her mind.

*I FEEL him. His essence. His life!* The queen's face lit with joy. She plunged downward. Kiri recalled she was a healer.

Long, firm fingers clasped around her forearm and she found the elf guardian floating beside her. He didn't look much pleased to be here, either. *Hang back, you're hurt.*

*I can still shoot him in the eye,* she said.

One white eyebrow arched. *You have a broken tail.*

*I can still shoot him in the eye!* She paused. *The OTHER eye.*

*Bloodthirsty, I like that,* the dwarf sent mentally. *Need help here.*

She looked around. The dwarf was marching across the bottom of the ocean and the trench was coming up.

*He sinks,* the elf said. *Go get him.*

Kiri let herself descend to the dwarf.

He sent water from his nostrils. *You can't carry me. You're nearly all out of magic and energy. And your tail is broken.*

She put her arms around his waist and tried to lift the dwarf, cried out in pain as her tail moved. The dwarf didn't move. He thumped her shoulder, sending her backward. *Go on up and shoot the fucking Dark one in the other eye. The Water Queen comes. She has the power to help me.*

Kiri nodded and rose.

Fighters hovered behind the Water King as the great Dark one came near, forming another of his energy balls in his hand, sneering. *One minor king and other very minor royals. I can take you all. Eat you all and be full of magic.*

Didn't he see the guardians?

Kiri looked for the elf and couldn't see him, glanced down at the dwarf and he seemed to be part of the rough rock landscape.

*POW!* A searing blue energy ball shook the water with a hideous explosion.

Screams, blood. Someone bulleted into her. Merman with half his head gone. Hit her right in the tail. She screamed, even as she saw the mers blur fast toward the great Dark one, a net thrown by the elf guardian capture him, the Water King thrust his trident into a massive chest and clouds of blood filled the water.

She couldn't hold on. Pain took her breath and her balance and her speargun fell from her hand and she fell downward, too. Right into Challenger Deep.

"KIRI, WAKE UP. PEOPLE TO SEE YOU," LATHYR ordered.

She groaned and stretched her tail.

Her tail!

She had a tail!

She was merfem!

Her eyes opened and her nictitating lids slapped down.

Lathyr cradled her against his body and that was good.... because he was alive, and so was she. She swallowed hard.

"Hey, Kiri," Jenni Emberdrake said in a choked voice.

Kiri spun in Lathyr's arms and found she was in a tank chamber. Again. But this one was furnished and had plants and mussels growing in it. "Where—"

"The minor palace in Puerto Rico Trench," Lathyr said.

"I see your tail is fixed," Jenni said. She was leaning against her husband and her eyes were too bright.

Duh. Fire Lightfolk, of course her eyes were bright.

Kiri arched her tail under her. An angular pattern spiraled up it, matching some of the dark blue diamond lines on her chest.

"Lovely pattern," Lathyr said, steadying her.

"Thanks." She met Jenni's eyes. "Hey, Jenni, can you hear me?"

"Yes. We have a mic and speaker set up."

"Oh. Good."

"I want to talk to you about staying with the Transformation game."

"I'll be wanting to work with humans before and after their transitions," Kiri said.

"Done," Jenni answered promptly, came up close to the tank wall and stared in. "Please say you still want to work on the game."

"I *must* work on the game. It's just not good enough, Jenni."

The Fire Princess grinned. She breathed on her nails and buffed them on her shirt. "Even my work, very rough, was good enough to snare you."

"I guess so." Kiri looked around the place. This was a tank in the water suite. She wished she was in the underwater bedroom with Lathyr instead.

A banging came at the door and a naiad who appeared to be a servant opened it. The King and Queen of Water entered.

They nodded to Jenni and Aric, who left with a nod and a "Later."

The naiad brought poufy pink chairs for the royal couple to sit on then went out the door when a wave from the king dismissed them.

The royals stared at them and Kiri stared back, glad Lathyr loosely held her with an arm around her waist.

"You took Lathyr with you to the great Pearl," the Water

King said. As always, his fingers were linked with his queen's, but his whole manner seemed to have changed.

"Yes," Kiri said. She blinked. He even seemed less crude, more thoughtful, and that she wouldn't have anticipated. She'd judged him and stuck him in a little cubbyhole and he was defying her expectations.

"I remember the pearl," the queen said softly, her eyes going dreamy as she looked at her husband. "You took me."

He met his wife's eyes and stared into them. "Yes, I did, and I never regretted it."

She lifted his fingers to her lips and kissed them, a gleam came to her eyes. "Though I don't think you remember the Pearl as often as you should, or the lesson it teaches," she chided.

Boundless love for all creatures? Live in the moment? Or lessons that would be revealed later, too? "Lesson?" Kiri whispered.

The queen looked at her. "I think one lesson might be the same, but others are unique to the individual."

Kiri tried an underwater courteous tail swirl. It went well. She smiled.

The Water King grumbled. To Kiri's ears it sounded as if he'd started the punctuation as a belch, then decided to change it. "We are pleased you met the great Pearl," he said. "Demonstrating your magical power and your acceptability as nobles and being included in the royal line. It pleases me that a relative of my lady's has proven to be as strong as she and as clever." He looked straight at Lathyr.

Who, of course, bowed. "Thank you."

"And in succeeding with the royal water quest, you will be awarded lands commensurate with your new status. That doesn't mean, however, that you are our heirs." He glared at them, but Kiri didn't feel any inimical intimidation from the man. "We fully intend to leave Earth for a more magically rich dimension when the gate is opened."

The queen smiled and hummed with pleasure.

"What?" Kiri asked.

"We have garnered all the magic we can here on Earth and deserve a richer magical realm," Marin Greendepths said. "The Eight's current primary project is to create a permanent gate to other dimensions—richer magical dimensions where we—"

"Both we Lightfolk and we humans," the queen interrupted.

The king grumped, then continued, "Can interact with others. Where magic can flow through."

"A permanent dimensional gate," Lathyr breathed. He squeezed Kiri, and she sensed, like her, that he was curious, but loved this planet more than power.

The king smiled with satisfaction. "With the bubbles of magic that were released earlier this year, we Eight have enough magic to build a temporary gate so a true gate creator can come through and establish a permanent one here on Earth."

Kiri could only think "Wow" and decided it might be too human to say.

Continuing, the Water King said, "The Seamonts remain our heirs. They showed well during the fight with the great Dark one and its execution," the king said matter-of-factly. He glanced at Lathyr. "Unlike Whitefroth of the North American Great Lakes, who deserted us. She has been removed from her rank, though she has been allowed to remain in the lakes."

"A wise decision," Lathyr said.

Marin Greendepths turned his gaze back on Kiri and Lathyr,

waved a hand. "It is time for the Seamonts to stay with us and learn our rules and traditions. You Squall-Tricurrents are hereby confirmed as our heirs *after* the Seamonts. Every quest has a reward. For succeeding with that of the Pearl, and becoming royal, you receive a major estate. We hereby convey to you this minor Water Palace here in the Puerto Rico Trench." He clicked his tongue. "As the humans call it."

Even without physical contact, Kiri sensed the quick leap of Lathyr's heart. "Very gracious, Your Majesty," Lathyr said.

"Thank you," Kiri managed, her own voice sounding breathless as visions of the gorgeous glass palace flashed through her mind. And fairly close to the States, if not Denver. "Thank you, thank you." She did the three times thing that Lightfolk preferred.

The Water Queen beamed. "You are most welcome."

They stood and Kiri did the bow-thing again and it was a lot easier and more graceful in water.

A naiader showed up and opened the door for them, then departed after the couple.

"Wow," said Kiri.

Lathyr said, "According to Waterfolk traditions, you took me with you on a quest. We fought together, we bled together, we loved together. We are mates."

Kiri grabbed a strand of his floating hair and tugged his face down to kiss him. "Fine with me."

She reached out and traced his pattern, the angles and curves, the small dots that showed his special air nature mixed with mer. He shuddered under her hands and returned the gesture until her mind blew apart and they joined in rapture.

Later, she swam to the door of the tank, recalled the spell to drain it. She changed to two-legged form, then human as the water level lowered, all the while holding Lathyr's hand. Then they stepped through the opening as human. Breathing deeply of the pleasingly fragrant air, she said, "Just think, all of this is ours."

"We do not need to make haste to claim the royal apartments."

She chuckled. "No, I don't think either of us will become as arrogant as the Greendepths. Though I haven't noticed you being as…obedient…as you were."

"I am not. We can make our own way, should we care to, in the sea or on land or in between."

Sighing, she said, "You're right."

"Humans have special parties for declaring a mate."

Kiri blinked. "Weddings?"

"Yes. I would like a wedding. In Mystic Circle. Before Winter."

"All right." They discussed the date as they walked to one of the dry rooms in their suite, something she thought the guardians might have furnished especially for them. When they claimed their official chambers, there'd have to be dry portions. She glanced at Lathyr, relaxed her shoulders, knew her expression showed vulnerability. Bracing herself, she said, "Weddings usually include families. Both sides of my family don't talk to each other."

He just looked at her, then took her hand and led her to a room she hadn't been in yet. "Jenni and Aric gifted us with a computer room."

"Nice." Under her breath she muttered, "Get notifying my family over with. Fast."

"And we have a piece of furniture like your friends sat on." He gestured to a love seat, then fiddled with a mobile computer desk and the laptop on it. He booted up the video conferencing program and pulled Kiri down next to him.

To her astonishment, she easily reached her father and he agreed to give her away and her half siblings were excited to come.

Her mother agreed to attend, too. Probably to show off her new, rich husband, but that was okay. Her half sister wanted to be a bridesmaid, so Kiri said yes.

She turned to Lathyr, stunned. "You didn't use magic, did you?"

He kissed her hand. "No."

"I didn't use magic?"

"No. But you are royal. You carry that in you. People will want to please you."

"Huh. That was just weird." She leaned into him. "I want to call Shannon and Averill."

"Of course." Once again Shannon and Averill answered quickly. Kiri's friend laughed when she saw them. "You two look cozy."

"We're getting married! The invitations will be going out in a couple of weeks for a ceremony in Mystic Circle."

Averill toyed with Shannon's fingers. "In the park?"

"I'd have liked that, but it isn't big enough for all the people who are coming. The ceremony will take place on the Castle grounds. Dad will be giving me away and he and my stepmom and my half brothers will be there. So will Mom and my stepdad and my half sister."

Shannon's brows went up in nearly comical surprise. "I don't think I've ever seen them all together."

"I don't think they ever have been," Kiri said. She glanced at her love. "Lathyr insists."

"They should act like civilized people," Shannon said.

Averill laughed, then winked at Kiri. "I always thought I'd give you away."

"We'd talked about it," Kiri agreed. "Shannon, you have to be matron of honor."

"Oh, yeah!" Shannon jumped up and Kiri only saw her swaying torso for a bit.

"On other news, we're going to stay in Puerto Rico." Kiri was still too new a merfem to live in the middle of a continent, even if she and Lathyr didn't have duties. They'd stay in the oceanic trench, but that wasn't something Kiri could tell her friends. "Enough about us. We can catch up later. Do you have any news?"

Shannon nodded. "We've decided on a water birth."

Kiri's eyes gleamed. "I bet I can help with that."

Averill gusted out a breath. "Good. We were always a little wary of asking you to be with us in the birthing room. Didn't know if you really wanted to help."

Kiri nodded. "I can do this." She squeezed Lathyr's fingers. He hadn't so much as twitched.

"I've been at several births," he murmured. "You can do this."

"I know," Kiri said. "I can't wait to see you and tell you everything." She would, someday. She might even talk about *everything*—after all, what else were friends for?

Subjects like the fact that change was scary, but she'd wanted to be more.

And she was. More than human.

More than one, part of a couple.

She'd learned so much, all the way to her cells. Change was scary and inevitable and could be embraced. Respect of others was important but confidence in yourself even more. Life without loving friends was not worth living.

Becoming magical didn't mean she was allowed to leave her human faults and fears behind, it meant dealing with them.

But she had love now to help her with that, and with becoming magical for the rest of her life.

★ ★ ★ ★ ★

# Acknowledgments

For helping me on a daily basis: the global Word Warriors, a chatroom established by C.E. Murphy.

For research: Leonard Leonard & Associates for Denver Architectural Styles, www.leonardleonard.com/neighborhoods/styles.shtml; *Denver, The City Beautiful* by Thomas J. Noel and Barbara S. Norgren, published by Historic Denver, Inc., Denver, Colorado, 1987; Denver Public Library;

WWF—Lower Mississippi River
wwf.panda.org/about_our_earth/ecoregions/lower_mississippi_river.cfm
Experience Mississippi River
www.experiencemississippiriver.com/
America's Wetland Resources
www.americaswetlandresources.com/background_facts/detailedstory/MississippiRiverAnatomy.html
Google Maps for the Mississippi River Delta, offshore Louisiana, the Gulf of Mexico, and the Pacific Ocean particularly;

My Beta readers, whom I haven't received permission to name, THANK YOU SO MUCH;

and Final Eyes copyediting service, i.e. Rose Beetem.